A Mother's Secret

A Mother's Secret

The Battersea Tavern Series: Book 1

Kitty Neale

ORION

First published in Great Britain in 2021 by Orion Books,
an imprint of The Orion Publishing Group Ltd
Carmelite House, 50 Victoria Embankment
London EC4Y 0DZ

An Hachette UK Company

3 5 7 9 10 8 6 4 2

A CIP catalogue record for this book is
available from the British Library.

ISBN (Hardback) 978 1 4091 9733 1
ISBN (eBook) 978 1 4091 9735 5

Typeset at The Spartan Press Ltd,
Lymington, Hants

Printed and bound in Great Britain by Clays Ltd,
Elcograf S.p.A.

www.orionbooks.co.uk

To my lovely mother-in-law, Susan Webb, and my
fabulous father-in-law, Graham Webb.

We miss you very much and we are really looking
forward to seeing you soon! Lots of love from us xxx

I

3 September 1939
Battersea, London

'Well, that's it, then,' Winnie Berry said, sighing heavily as she reached across from her armchair to turn off the wireless. 'You heard the man, we're at war with Germany. I'd best get downstairs and make sure everything's shipshape.'

Her husband, Brian, was sitting in the wingback armchair opposite her with yesterday's newspaper across his lap. As he tapped out the tobacco from his pipe, he looked over his black-rimmed glasses and Winnie could tell from his scowl that his mood was dark.

'Did I say you could turn the wireless off?' he asked ominously.

'No, but...' Winnie answered, searching for something to say that wouldn't rile him again.

'Then turn it back on, woman!' Brian barked.

His loud and abrupt tone caused Winnie to flinch, even though she knew she should be used to his aggression by now. After all, he rarely spoke to her unless it was to shout his orders or to complain about something that, apparently, she'd done wrong. But at least he didn't raise his hands to her so much these days.

Winnie pushed her plump body out of the chair and quickly turned the wireless on again. She'd learned years ago that it was easier to do Brian's bidding rather than to argue with him. She much preferred to have a quiet and peaceful life.

'I ... erm, I'd better open up or I'll have the customers banging down the doors. Shall I pour you another cuppa before I go?' she asked meekly, looking at Brian for a response.

He sucked on his pipe with his eyes closed and his head resting on the back of the green armchair. It grated on Winnie. She knew there'd be a large grease mark left there from the pomade he used on his thick, brown hair. She thought he was lucky not to have gone bald like his father had. At sixty-three, eighteen years older than she was, Brian had aged well with just a little light greying around his temples. But his brow was deeply lined and she thought it was because he was always frowning.

Smoke curled around his face but Brian didn't even so much as offer her a grunt.

'Suit yourself,' she muttered under her breath as she slipped from the front room above their pub.

As she went downstairs, Winnie smoothed her navy-blue dress over her ample body and patted her mid-brown, waved hair. The smell of stale beer and cigarettes wafted up the stairs but she was used to the aroma from the pub and quite liked it. She'd been the landlady of the Battersea Tavern for nearly a quarter of a century and the familiar smell of the place brought her comfort. It was home. The walls had seen her tears and heard her laughter – the customers had become like family. And it was the place where she'd raised her beloved son, David.

As she reached the bottom of the stairs, Winnie heard someone hammering on the door.

'Here we go,' she said to herself. 'Hang on, I'm coming!' she shouted. Her customers were early today but, no doubt, the announcement of war had brought them out.

She assumed it would be Leonard Garwood, one of her regulars. A quiet old boy who always sat in the same spot at the end of the bar. Or maybe it would be Hilda Duff, a loud-mouthed, peroxide blonde who was, unfortunately, the much older sister of Winnie's barmaid, Rachel Robb. Whoever was knocking, it wasn't Rachel. The girl would never bang so loudly.

Winnie unbolted the door and her heart sank when she saw it was indeed the notorious Hilda Duff. The young woman's grey, calf-length coat with a small velvet collar had once looked smart, but now it was grubby, and her greasy hair poked out from a green cloche hat.

'Have you heard, Win?' Hilda asked. 'That Chamberlain bloke has only gawn and declared war on Germany! Quick, let me in. I need a large whisky to calm me nerves.'

Winnie rolled her eyes and stood to one side for Hilda to pass. The woman could find any excuse for having a large whisky but the strong spirit fuelled her vicious tongue and Winnie hoped she wouldn't have to throw her out of her pub again.

'Where's my sister?' Hilda asked as her sunken blue eyes scanned the room.

'She'll be here any minute.'

'Give us a large whisky, then,' Hilda said and leaned her forearms on the bar.

'Let me see your money first.'

'Oh, come off it, Winnie. You know I'm good for it,' Hilda said, but their conversation was interrupted suddenly by the unmistakable wailing noise of the air-raid sirens. 'Christ almighty, the bleedin' Jerries are coming! We've got to take cover!'

Winnie could see that Hilda was visibly shaking and her eyes were wide with fear. 'It's all right, love, it's probably a false alarm. They'll just be testing them, that's all,' she offered reassuringly.

'Do you reckon? Oh, Winnie, I don't mind telling you, I'm scared out of me wits. The thought of a bomb landing on me head ...'

'I won't have talk like that in here, thank you very much. You'll put me customers off their ale. 'Ere, get this down your neck,' Winnie said firmly and she poured Hilda a drink.

The woman downed it and it seemed to settle her nerves. 'Thanks, Win, I needed that. Cor, don't they make a bleedin' racket? It's enough to scare the rats out of the sewers.'

Winnie felt a gush of fresh, crisp air as the door opened and Rachel bustled in wearing a burgundy wool coat which matched her fashionable felt hat. Rachel was dainty with light blonde hair, and she thought the girl looked a picture – unlike her sister, Hilda, whose clothes needed to go in the boiling pot. Hilda, at thirty-nine, was seventeen years older than Rachel and it showed.

'Sorry I'm late, Winnie. There's mayhem going on out there,' Rachel said as she hurried towards the dark brown-painted counter. 'Everyone's running around like headless chickens. It ain't for real, is it? The siren.'

'No, love, I shouldn't think so. But if you're worried, get

4

yourself down to the cellar. It could do with a good sweep through.'

'No, I'm not worried. The Germans would be stupid if they wasted any of their bombs on Battersea,' Rachel answered. She went through to the back where Winnie knew she'd be slinging her coat over the newel post at the bottom of the stairs.

'See that?' Hilda asked, her mouth set in a grim line.

'What?'

'She walked straight past me. Didn't even say hello.'

'Well, she's probably still smarting over what you said to her last night.'

'What? She's got the hump cos I told her she oughta find herself a decent bloke to look after her?'

'Hilda, that's not exactly how you said it,' Winnie remarked.

Rachel reappeared and stood behind the bar with her hands on her hips. 'No, that's not what you said at all. As usual, you were drunk, so you probably don't remember telling me that I'll end up an old spinster because no bloke would put up with me. According to you, I'm spoilt, selfish, stuck-up and haughty. Thanks. It's nice to know you think so highly of me.'

'You silly cow. You know you shouldn't take any notice of what I say when I've had a drink.'

'But you've *always* had a drink,' Rachel snapped.

'Oh, don't start again. We can't all be Miss Goody-Two-Shoes like you. Maybe there was some truth in what I said last night – you need to get down off your high horse and take your hoity-toity nose out of the air.'

Winnie interrupted, saying firmly, 'All right, ladies, that'll do. It's bad enough with that wailing siren outside. I won't have cat fights across my bar.'

'Yeah, sorry, Win. I'll go and fetch the mixers up,' Rachel replied and threw her sister a dirty look before heading towards the cellar.

Once they were alone, Winnie leaned over the bar and whispered to Hilda, 'You could try being kinder to Rachel. She's a good girl, you know.'

'That girl has always been the bane of my life. You don't know the 'alf of it, so keep your bleedin' nose out,' Hilda answered, snarling, before turning on her heel and stamping out.

'Thank goodness for that!' Winnie muttered as the door closed behind Hilda and the air-raid sirens fell silent. At last she had two minutes to think clearly – Britain was at war! Her mind raced with fears of David being conscripted. She'd seen the state of many soldiers who'd returned from fighting in the Great War. They had been broken in body and mind, and could never be fixed. Thousands hadn't come home at all. She couldn't abide the thought of that fate for her son and a shudder ran down her spine.

'You all right?' Rachel asked as she plonked a crate of bottles on the bar.

'Yes, love, I'm fine,' Winnie lied.

'Hilda's buggered off, then?'

'Yes, but she'll probably be back before we close to have another whisky. She can be the nicest of people, but it's such a shame to see a woman in the state she gets herself into.'

'She's always been the same, nice as pie one minute and then, well, you know. Yet the cheeky cow has got the nerve to slate me. I'm not stuck-up, am I?'

'No, love, you're just selective,' Winnie answered diplomatically, hiding a smile. She thought Rachel could be aloof at times, though she was always polite and friendly to the customers. Rachel had no real girlfriends and Winnie had never known her to court a man. It wasn't as if she was short of offers – being a good-looking barmaid, she attracted plenty of attention, albeit mostly unwanted on Rachel's part. Though from what Rachel had said about her past, she couldn't blame the girl for being guarded.

'Do you know, Win, I'm sure the worry of Hilda sent my dear old mum to an early grave. But then she had fourteen kids, so she was always worried about one or other of us.'

'I'm sure she was. You all may have grown up, but you'd still have been her babies. I feel the same about my David.'

Rachel giggled as she stacked the mixers on a shelf behind the bar.

'What's so funny?' Winnie asked.

'I just can't see David as a baby,' Rachel answered.

Indeed, David was far from being a baby. He was a grown man of twenty-three but Winnie still mollycoddled him, much to her husband's disapproval. He thought she should cut the apron strings and that David should fly the nest. But she was happy to have their son at home where she knew he was safe and cared for. After the casualties she'd seen from the Great War, the thought of David having to join up with the British army and fight the Germans terrified her.

David Berry sat astride his motorbike and threw a half-smoked cigarette to the ground. 'Yeah, all right, Ted, I'll go to the dance on Saturday night and hopefully one of the girls will put out this time.'

'You wanna try your luck with Maureen. She fancies you,' Ted answered from under the car bonnet where his head was buried in the engine he was working on. 'So do most of the girls around here, you lucky sod,' he mumbled.

'Maureen! I wouldn't go near her if my life depended on it. Her nose would get in the way. Ain't you noticed the size of her hooter?'

'Yeah, but she's got a nice pair of tits,' Ted said and he emerged from under the bonnet to wipe his greasy spanner with an oily cloth.

'Maybe, but I still wouldn't touch her.'

'Who've you got your eye on, then?'

David smiled wryly. 'That would be telling, mate,' he answered, thinking of Rachel Robb, his mother's pretty barmaid.

'You're a sly bugger, you. Anyway, shouldn't you be at work?'

'I jacked it in. I couldn't stand the old bastard breathing down me neck and getting on at me all the time to pull me weight. So I told him where he could stick his job.'

'Bloody hell, Dave, that's the fourth job in as many months. What you gonna do now? Cadge some money off your old girl again?'

'Yeah, probably. She's a soft touch.'

'Long as your old man don't find out.'

'He won't. The lazy git hardly gets up from his chair.'

'But if he did, he'd give you a good clout round the ear.'

'He'd have to catch me first,' David answered.

'Talking of a clip round the ears, did you hear about Mickey?'

'No, what about him?'

'He got a right pasting from Errol Hampton. I bumped

into his sister yesterday. She said Mickey's face looks like a smashed-up tomato. He's got teeth missing and everything.'

David's blood ran cold. He'd seen Errol three days earlier and the man had asked after Mickey's whereabouts. David had known that Errol wasn't asking because he wanted to pay Mickey a friendly visit. Hoping to keep in favour with Errol, he'd revealed Mickey's whereabouts. After all, Errol wasn't the sort of bloke you'd want to fall out with! 'Bloody hell. How did Errol find out that Mickey was hiding out at his sister's place?' he asked, hoping that Ted didn't suspect him of telling on Mickey.

'Dunno. I wouldn't be surprised if Errol put pressure on someone to grass him up. Plenty of people knew where Mickey was hiding and not many of them would have stood up to Errol.'

'I suppose not, but you'd like to think you could rely on your mates.'

'Maybe, Dave, but would you take a beating from Errol to protect Mickey?'

'Yeah, course I would, and so would you. That's what mates are for; we watch each other's backs. Anyway, I'd best get off,' he said and revved his engine. 'I'll see you Saturday, Ted. And send me best to Mickey,' he called before he sped off.

Twenty minutes later, David walked through the door of the Battersea Tavern. He made his way through the hazy smoke-filled pub, spotting the familiar customers supping their half-pints. His mother was serving and, as usual, Len was at the end of the bar. Then his eyes fell on Rachel.

'Hello, sweetheart,' he said with a cheeky wink as he approached her.

At just over six feet tall and broad-shouldered, he towered over Rachel's petite frame.

'What are you doing here at this time of the day?' she asked.

'I've come to see the best-looking barmaid in Battersea.'

'Don't give me that crap, David. You've lost your job again, haven't you?'

'Yep,' he replied shortly. 'What you doing Saturday night? Fancy coming to the dance with me?'

'And how are you gonna afford to buy me a drink, if you ain't got a job? You needn't think I'm letting you take me out on your mother's hard-earned money.'

'Your loss,' he said with a shrug of his shoulders as he sauntered off. Bloody condescending cow, he thought. He'd been trying it on for years with Rachel but she'd rejected all his advances. That made her more of a challenge and, truth be known, he enjoyed the chase. Most girls fell quickly for his swarthy good looks and easy charm but Rachel was different. They were almost the same age but she treated him like a boy and it got right up his nose. One day in the not-too-distant future, he intended to show her that he was a *real* man.

'Hello, Son,' his mum said cheerily as she almost waddled along the bar towards him. 'You on your lunch break? I can do you a nice corned-beef sandwich, if you like?'

'Yeah, thanks, Mum, that would be smashing,' he answered and followed her through to a small back kitchen.

'I suppose you've heard about the war?' she asked as she sliced the bread.

'It was only a matter of time. I've just been to see Ted. He's dug an Anderson shelter in his backyard and the silly beggar only got inside it when that siren sounded earlier.'

'Better safe than sorry, I suppose,' his mum told him. 'I mean, it could've been genuine. One minute the Prime Minister is on the wireless, telling us we're at war, the next thing you know, the sirens are wailing. From what Rachel told me, there was a lot of panic on the streets.'

'I weren't bothered, was you?'

'Course not, Son, you know me. It would take a darn sight more than an air-raid siren to get me out of this pub.'

'Yeah, I bet the Jerries haven't come across someone like you before.'

'Did you ask after Ted's mother? I heard her gout has flared up again.'

'No, Mum, he never said anything. But he was on at me to go to the dance on Saturday.'

'Aw, that's nice. Are you going?'

'I'd like to, but the thing is,' he said, quickly glancing from left to right to check he wasn't being overheard, 'I'm a bit strapped for cash...'

'Oh, David, you've been given your cards again, haven't you?'

'No, I walked. And if you'd heard the way Atkinson spoke to me, you would have told me to jack it in. I won't tell you the language he used because you'd be round there like a hare out of a trap and pulling him over the coals,' he said, elaborating on the truth. In fact, Mr Atkinson had been very patient with him, but he wasn't going to tell his mother that – he wanted her sympathy and the contents of her purse.

'The cheeky sod!' she said heatedly. 'I'll give him a piece of my mind the next time he shows his face in here.'

'Leave it, Mum, it ain't worth losing customers over.'

'Yeah, all right, if you say so. I must admit, he spends a fair bit over the bar. Anyway, there's a couple of quid in my purse, so help yourself. Just don't tell your father.'

'Thanks, Mum, you're a gem.'

David wasted no time in emptying the contents of his mother's purse and tucked into the sandwich she'd made him. 'Any chance of a cuppa to wash this down?' he asked, knowing she'd readily jump to his request.

As his mother made his drink, David smiled inwardly. She was a doormat. He'd grown up watching her pander to his father's every whim, and he'd seen her get many a back-hander when she was slow to obey him. David tried to blot out the memories of his mother crying and her using make-up to conceal a black eye. He hated the way his father treated her but David had soon discovered that he could get what he wanted from her by being nice. He didn't see the need for violence and wasn't a fighter. His father had once called him a coward but David didn't care what the man thought of him. His dad had never shown any respect for his mother and not once did she stand up for herself. As far as he was concerned, they were the cowards, not him. He had worked out exactly how to get the attention he felt he deserved from his mother, and she fell for it every time.

'I'll be out front, if you want anything,' she said and ruffled his hair as she passed.

Bloody hell, thought David. He'd already told her enough times about mucking up his hairstyle. Still, it was a small price to pay in exchange for a full stomach and a pocket full of cash. And now he knew exactly where he'd be heading to spend his money.

2

Winnie threw her legs over the edge of the bed and rubbed her tired eyes. The morning sun was shining through a crack in the curtains and when she turned to look at Brian, the rays were illuminating his sleeping face. She sighed and shook her head. His features looked soft when he slept, but she knew that the moment his eyes opened, his frown would return. She'd once loved the man, but, over the years, he'd worn her down and now that love had been replaced with contempt. She didn't entirely blame him for his cold ways and felt sure that she'd been a part of him becoming a miserable bugger. However, before her thoughts went any further, Brian's eyes slowly opened. The instant he saw her, he grimaced.

'What are you doing sitting there? Put the kettle on, woman,' he growled.

'Good morning to you too,' Winnie answered sarcastically and she heaved her weary body up.

She made her way through to the larger, upstairs kitchen and yawned as she filled the kettle. The previous day had been a busy one with all the locals coming in to talk about the declaration of war. By the time she'd called last orders,

Winnie had been sick to the back teeth of hearing about it. After cleaning up, she'd waited for David to come home but had eventually nodded off in the armchair. When she'd woken in the early hours, she'd been relieved to find David in his bed and so, finally, she'd gone to her own.

'Morning, Mum,' David said as he came into the kitchen.

Winnie was surprised to see her son up and about so early. When he was out of work, he'd normally stay in his bed until midday.

'Morning, love. You were late home last night.'

'Yeah, me and the boys went to the pictures and then over to Ted's place. I didn't realise how late it was. It's the last time we'll be able to see a film for a while. Ted said he heard on the wireless that they're closing the Granada and all cinemas today.'

'Yeah, I heard about that an' all. I reckon there's worry that if a bomb drops a load of people will get hurt at the same time. I suppose there'll be lots of changes now. There's already kids being evacuated to safer places outside of London.'

'They reckon all our cities will be targets, especially the docks.'

'I'd rather not think about that, so that's enough talk of war. What did you see at the flicks? Anything good?'

'That George Formby film. It was really funny.'

'Oh, I love him. Mind you, I ain't been to the cinema in yonks. Your father's hardly likely to take me and I can't leave Rachel by herself downstairs.'

There had been a time when Winnie had asked David to work behind the bar but he'd done nothing but moan about it so she hadn't asked again. She could do with a break, but as much as she loved her boy, she was fully aware that he had a lazy streak, just like his father. There was no chance of Brian helping out either. He used to pull pints with her but nowadays her husband only balanced the books for the pub, and as far as he was concerned, it was her job to do the rest of the work involved.

'Mum, could you lend me a few bob?'

'I gave you a couple of quid yesterday. You ain't gone through that already, have you?'

'Yeah, sorry.'

'Blimey, David, money goes through your hands like water,' Winnie said and tutted. She went to a tin on a shelf next to the larder and emptied out several coins onto the kitchen table. 'There, that's all I've got, so make it last.'

'Thanks, Mum,' he said and kissed her cheek before scooping up the coins.

'You'd better not be scrounging money off your mother again,' Brian said, his voice low and rumbling.

Winnie jumped and turned to see him standing in the kitchen doorway, his large frame almost filling it. 'No, Brian. I – erm ...'

'I thought as bloody much,' he interrupted, glaring at his son. 'Give it back to her, every bleedin' penny. You're good for nothing, David. What must people think of you, eh? You'll never amount to anything and I won't have a son of mine sponging off his mother!'

'But it's all right for *you* to sponge off her?' David retorted as he slapped the money down onto the table.

Winnie gasped and her hand flew over her mouth. David's boldness was sure to enrage his father.

'I do not! This is my pub, I pay the bills, and I ain't standing

15

for any backchat from you,' Brian snarled as he marched across the kitchen towards his son.

Winnie reacted instinctively and quickly leapt in front of her husband. 'No, Brian, please,' she pleaded, blocking his path.

He pushed her roughly to one side. She stumbled but managed to stay on her feet. She saw Brian with his fists clenched ready to punch David.

'No!' she screamed, the sound long and harrowing.

Her plea fell on deaf ears and with horror she saw Brian swing his arm forward. David dodged the blow, a smirk on his face.

'I'll have you,' Brian ground out through gritted teeth, and he threw another punch.

Again, David managed to move away in time. 'Come on then, old man, but you'll have to be quicker than that.'

'Stop it! Stop it, the pair of you!' Winnie screeched and ran in between them. She was used to breaking up the odd scuffle or two in her pub but never between her son and husband.

'He's asking for it,' Brian barked.

'Enough! David, apologise to your father, this instant.'

'What? Say sorry to him? Never,' he answered defiantly.

'You bloody well will! You live under his roof, so you show him some respect.'

A look of shock passed over her son's face. There was a long, silent pause, and then, to Winnie's relief, he said a half-hearted, 'Sorry.'

'Good. Now, Brian, go and sit down in the front room and I'll bring you a cup of tea. David, go to your room and get dressed. And we'll say no more about it.'

Both men walked off and Winnie drew in a deep breath.

She'd never spoken so firmly to either of them and had been taken aback when they'd done as they were told. Her heart was still pounding but she was pleased she'd managed to diffuse the fraught situation. She'd have words with David later. She had to discourage him from giving his father backchat because, at the end of the day, it was more than likely that she'd be the one to feel Brian's wrath, probably with a smack across her face, or worse.

David had been happy to retreat to his room. Despite his bravado, his father's attempted assault had left him shaken. He ran his hands through his coarse, brown hair and stared at his pale reflection in the mirror. Thankfully, his dad wasn't as quick as he used to be and David had been spared a hard whack. But his pockets were empty again and he desperately needed to lay his hands on some cash.

He heard a light tap on the door and his mother popped her head round.

'You all right, Son?'

'Yeah, I suppose so.'

She crept in quietly and closed the door behind her. 'You shouldn't talk to your father like that. You know what he's like.'

'Yes, I do. I've seen you get enough lumps off him. He's a bully, Mum. I can't stand him.'

'Please don't talk about your dad like that. Whatever his faults, he's still your father.'

'Huh, some dad, eh! All he cares about is what people think of him and money.'

'He ain't all bad. We've got somewhere nice to live and we don't go short, do we?'

'That's got nothing to do with him! It's you who runs this place. His name might be over the door but apart from looking after the takings like some old miser, he doesn't lift a finger to help you,' he blurted angrily.

His mother didn't say anything but just looked at him. Feeling a pang of guilt, David lowered his eyes to the floor. He did nothing to help his mother either, but he soon reasoned that it wasn't his responsibility to do so – it was his father's.

'When he was younger, your dad did more,' she said finally, 'so just hold your tongue around him in future, please. And stay out of his way.'

'Yeah, all right,' he answered reluctantly.

As his mother went to leave his room, he added quickly, 'About that money, Mum ...'

'I'll slip you a few bob downstairs. And do your best to find another job today, eh, love?'

'Don't worry, I will. Thanks, Mum.'

Once she'd closed the door, David threw himself down on his bed and stared up at the ceiling. He'd cocked up, and the few bob she'd promised him wouldn't be enough to bail him out. He'd need more than that if he intended on keeping his face from being rearranged like Mickey's had been. He knew of only one place where the sort of sum he required would be readily available – the cash register behind the bar. But getting to it without his mother or Rachel spotting him would be tricky. He didn't want to be caught with his hands in the till because that would be the end of his mother bank-rolling him. If he was going to get away with daylight robbery, he'd have to be canny. And with no other option available to him, he sat up and thought about how to pull it off.

★

18

An hour later, spruced up and with a plan in place, David was feeling confident. The pub wouldn't be open for a while yet and the till wouldn't be full until nearer lunchtime closing. He'd wait. After all, he couldn't go outside and run the risk of bumping into Errol Hampton. The local hard man had made it clear that if David didn't cough up the money that was owed, Errol would rip his face off. The thought filled him with dread as he knew Errol wasn't one for offering idle threats. Mickey was proof of that. If Errol said he was going to give David a beating, then he meant it!

He could have kicked himself. He felt stupid for having been sucked in by Errol. It had started with a few friendly card games but had soon progressed to playing for money. The stakes had steadily increased and when he'd gambled away all his cash, Errol persuaded him to keep playing and offered him a loan. David had been desperate to win back the money he'd lost so he'd readily accepted the offer. He'd lost that money too and then Errol informed him of the added interest on the loan. He could see now it had all been a ploy to fleece him and he wouldn't be surprised if the cards had been rigged. He realised that Mickey must have been fooled by Errol too and shuddered at the thought of what had happened to him. Mickey had got off lightly with just a smashed-up face. Some hadn't been so lucky and had been left with broken bones. In fact, the bloke who lived down the end of the street and walked with a limp had been one of Errol's victims. He hadn't limped until his run-in with Errol.

There was only one good thing to come out of it, he thought; it had taught him a lesson, and once he'd taken the money from the till to clear the debt, he'd never make the mistake of getting involved with Errol Hampton again.

★

'Hello, Winnie, it's raining cats and dogs,' Rachel said when she arrived at the Battersea Tavern for her morning shift behind the bar. 'I'll just put this dripping umbrella into the sink,' she added, heading out the back.

'Put the kettle on while you're out there,' Winnie called from the bar.

Rachel happily obliged. She enjoyed their morning cup of tea and chat before the customers arrived, unless Hilda turned up the moment the doors opened, which she frequently did. As the water heated on the gas stove, she crossed her fingers and hoped the wet weather would keep her older sister away. The shocking news of war yesterday was drama enough and she couldn't face any more today.

'Penny for 'em?' Winnie asked when she came into the kitchen.

'Oh, nothing really. I was just thinking it would be nice to have a day without Hilda turning up. I know she's my sister an' all, but she drives me crazy.'

'I know, love. They say you can pick your friends but you can't choose your family so I'm afraid you're stuck with her.'

'Hilda's always been the black sheep. I remember my mum and dad, God rest their souls, they used to go hammer and tongs at it with her. God knows what they were arguing about but she'd scream at my mum and then Dad would get involved. I know we're at war now but the neighbours must have thought there was one going on next door to them for years.'

'Hilda can be a bit punchy,' Winnie commented.

'A bit! That's an understatement. We wouldn't see her for weeks on end and then when she did show up, all hell would

20

break lose. Hilda is the oldest of the fourteen of us, and me, the youngest. Talk about chalk and cheese.'

'You can say that again. But there's not fourteen of you now, love,' Winnie gently reminded her.

'No, but I still count us all. Mum lost three to diphtheria and two to measles. Broke her heart, it did. Then after Mum died, my oldest brother was killed falling off a ladder, Frank, well, Gawd knows what happened to him and Beth died of lung cancer.' Rachel paused, then added sadly, 'You know what happened to my other sister and least said soonest mended on that subject. It's a shame there's only the six of us now and I hardly ever see them, except for Hilda.'

'No one can blame you for not wanting to go back there. Anyhow, they live on the other side of London and it's quite a trek.'

'I thought I'd got away from Hilda but she followed me here. Trust my luck to get lumbered with her,' Rachel said, smiling wanly. As much as Hilda infuriated her and often showed her up, she still thought the world of her. She just wished she could encourage her to cut down on the booze.

Winnie chuckled, then said, 'It could be worse. At least Hilda's got her own place and isn't living with you.'

'Good job an' all. There's hardly room to swing a cat in my room. Not to mention the fact that I'm sharing the privy in the backyard with them upstairs and now next door too.'

'How come next door are using your lavatory?'

'Their one's broken. I don't mind as long as I'm not following Pa Roberts. I don't know what his wife gives him to eat, but whatever it is must be rotting his stomach,' Rachel said and wrinkled her nose in disgust at the memory of the foul smell.

'Oh, you poor love. I thought you went to look at a place up near York Road?'

'I did, but it was infested with bugs and vermin. That's the problem. I can't afford much.'

Winnie frowned in thought and then said, 'Maybe it's about time we looked at giving you a bit of a pay rise. I'd hate to lose you and you're worth every penny.'

'Oh, I wasn't suggesting...'

'I know, love,' Winnie cut in, 'but you've been on the same rate since you started here and that was four years ago now. It's no more than you deserve.'

Rachel impulsively threw her arms around the kind, portly woman. 'Thanks, Win. Thank you so much. A bit extra would come in ever so handy.'

'All right, you daft mare, get off me,' Winnie said warmly as she unpeeled Rachel's arms from around her.

Rachel sat at the table again and sipped her hot tea, looking over her chipped china cup at Winnie's wide hips swinging from side to side as she walked across the kitchen to fetch the biscuit tin.

'Let's celebrate, shall we?' Winnie said and placed the full tin on the table between them.

'Yes, let's,' Rachel said, feeling chipper as her hand pulled out a ginger biscuit. As it crumbled in her mouth, she looked fondly across at Winnie. Her boss had become a friend and even if she hadn't been offered a pay rise, Rachel knew she'd never leave her job. She would miss Winnie too much. Rachel's childhood had been tough. Her family had lived hand to mouth in a cramped and damp house. And with so many children to care for, she hadn't received much attention from her mother. Now Winnie had filled that void in Rachel's life and she'd grown to love the woman. It was just a shame that Winnie's husband wasn't as nice as his wife. And their son, well, he was attractive enough, but Rachel didn't like the way he sponged off his mum. She thought it was about time David grew up and started behaving like a man instead of a spoilt brat. To make matters worse, there was something about him that reminded her of Jim, the man she had been going to marry. She couldn't put her finger on it; maybe it was the way David looked at her or the way his cheeks dimpled when he smiled. But whatever it was, she didn't like it. Though she tried hard to forget Jim, he'd often invade her thoughts and it didn't help that David put her in mind of him. Jim was a big part of her past that she'd tried to leave behind when she'd moved to Battersea. But, just like Hilda, he'd followed her. Not physically in person, but in her head.

Winnie's voice broke into her thoughts. 'Come on, then. We'd better open up. Poor old Len will be waiting for his drink. A bit of rain won't keep him away.'

They went through to the bar and Winnie unbolted the doors. Like clockwork, Len ambled in with rainwater dripping off the front of his flat cap.

'Your usual?' Rachel asked as Len took his seat at the end of the bar.

'Yes, pet.'

She reached for his own pewter tanker and a bottle of stout. As she set it down in front of him, she smiled and said, 'Nice weather for ducks.'

Len simply gave one nod of his head. The elderly gentleman never said much and would sit quietly for a few hours making two bottles last the duration. He'd never make Winnie a profit but he'd become like part of the furniture.

Terence Card breezed in next and Rachel moved along the bar to serve him. Winnie had once tried playing Cupid between them, but Rachel hadn't been interested. She liked the bloke well enough and with his blond hair and commanding height, she thought he was good-looking. But she didn't want to be involved with anyone. She preferred to keep herself to herself – and for good reason too. Jim had almost destroyed her but now she'd built up her defences and no man was going to break them.

'Hello, Rachel, I'll have a quick half-pint of beer.'

'You not working today, Terry?' she asked as she poured his drink from the pump.

'Yeah, but I'm on an errand, hence just a swift half.'

'A little dickie bird told me that you've got yourself a new girlfriend.'

'Ha, that news didn't take long to travel.'

'It's true, then? What's her name? Do I know her?' Rachel asked, fishing for more information.

'Yes, it's true, and, no, you don't know her. Her name is Jan. Janet Board.'

Rachel couldn't help herself and spluttered with laughter.

Terry appeared perplexed and asked, 'What's so funny?'

'You two. Can't you see it? Your names – Card and Board. You go well together.'

'Oh, yeah, right. Very funny,' Terry answered but clearly he didn't find it quite as amusing as Rachel did.

'In all seriousness, I'm happy for you. So, when are we gonna meet Jan?'

'I dunno. She's never been in a public house before and is a bit nervous about coming here. She reckons pubs are for blokes.'

24

'Did you tell her it's different here? I mean, there's me and Winnie for a start.'

'Yeah, I told her, but she's still not sure. She's a quiet little thing and a bit shy. Given time, I'm sure I'll be able to talk her round.'

'Make sure you do, Terence Card. You know she'll get a warm welcome here.'

'Oi,' Winnie called from the other end of the bar, 'stop gassing and serve some customers, Rachel.'

Rachel smiled at Terry. Winnie sounded tough but everyone knew she had a heart of gold. 'Duty calls. Don't forget, work on Jan. I'd love to meet her,' she said before going to pour a pint for another customer.

Jan Board closed the book she was reading aloud to Mrs Savage and rested it on her lap. The elderly lady and fallen asleep in her chair and was quietly snoring. But over the noise of the gentle snuffling, Jan's stomach rumbled and she thought about the cold chicken in Mrs Savage's larder.

Carefully, she placed the book on a side table, tucked a strand of her long brown hair behind her ear and pushed herself to her feet, keeping her eyes fixed on the old lady. Mrs Savage would most likely snooze for at least half an hour, and though Jan knew it was wrong to steal, her hunger drove her to the kitchen.

She'd been working as a companion to Mrs Savage for over ten years. Her mother had thought it was a suitable position and had arranged the job for her. It didn't pay much, not that it mattered, as Jan had to give her wages to her mother. But the job was easy, a welcome relief from being at home, and Mrs Savage was a kind lady.

In the kitchen, Jan's heart thumped and she sneaked a look over her shoulder before opening the larder door. A pot sat on the middle shelf. She lifted the lid covering the chicken and instantly her mouth salivated. She could have asked for some chicken and Mrs Savage would have told her to help herself. But that would mean she'd have to confess to her mother's harsh punishment which Jan found too humiliating. As she pulled off some breast meat and quickly put it in her mouth, guilt consumed her and she could hear her mother's voice in her head warning her she'd go to hell. But she'd gone without supper and breakfast. Penance laid down by her mother.

As she swallowed the delicious meat and reached for another piece, she heard Mrs Savage cough. She turned around, horrified to see the woman standing in the kitchen.

'I – erm, I...' she stuttered, regretting giving in to her hunger.

'Go ahead, Jan. I couldn't possibly eat a whole chicken by myself. It's far too much for one person, but you know how generous my son is and he will insist I eat well. In fact, I'm quite peckish myself. You can make us both a nice chicken sandwich.'

Jan could feel her cheeks burning with embarrassment but she was grateful for Mrs Savage's generosity. After all, most other employers would have fired her for stealing food. And there would have been severe consequences if she had to go home and tell her mother that she'd lost her job. She made a sandwich and carried it through to the sitting room.

'Where's yours?' the frail lady asked as Jan handed her a plate.

'I'm fine, thank you, Mrs Savage.'

'You're obviously hungry. Don't be so silly and go and make yourself one or I shan't eat mine.'

Jan smiled warmly and dashed back to the kitchen. She was careful not to slice the bread too thickly or slather on too much butter. Gluttony was a sin. Her mother had drilled it into her often enough.

Sitting opposite Mrs Savage, she ate slowly, enjoying each delicious mouthful. It had been a long time since she'd had fresh meat. The meals at home with her mother were always basic. Bread, cheese and eggs mostly. But the previous evening, after not reciting Psalm 3 correctly, her mother had denied her even these basics.

'I didn't get a chance to speak to your mother at church. How is she?' Mrs Savage asked.

'Very well, thank you,' Jan answered, reluctant to admit that she'd been in trouble with her.

'I know you prefer not to talk about it, and pardon me for prying, but has she been withholding food from you again?'

Jan looked down at her plate and half-eaten sandwich. She felt it was ridiculous that she was twenty-six years old, and yet her mother treated her like a child and ruled over her life with an iron fist.

'What was it this time? She hasn't found out about your young man, has she?'

'No,' Jan exclaimed, her brown eyes wide.

'Don't panic, dear, she won't discover anything from me. I'm not quite as batty as I look.'

'Thank you, Mrs Savage. And I'm very grateful to you for helping me to see Terry.'

'There's no need for gratitude. I find the whole clandestine thing very romantic. Just like Romeo and Juliet. Actually, let's give up on that dreary book,' she said, pointing to the side table, 'and after your sandwich, you can fetch *Romeo and Juliet* from the library.'

Jan nodded and resumed her sandwich. She must have read the Shakespeare work to Mrs Savage at least a dozen times but it was a tale they both enjoyed. It made a refreshing change from the Bible, which her mother made her read for three hours every night.

Ten minutes later, as she sat with the familiar book in her hands, Mrs Savage sighed and rested her head back, a warm smile on her face. Jan knew the sweet lady was reminiscing about Benjamin. She'd heard the story from Mrs Savage many times and knew she was about to be told it again.

As expected, Mrs Savage began. 'I've missed romance in my life because, like you with your mother, I had a strict father who wouldn't allow me to court. But I'll tell you a secret.' She lifted her head and looked at Jan. Her rhuemy blue eyes twinkled in delight as she recounted her secret affair with Benjamin, the vicar's son. 'Of course, it came to an end when my father caught us in a tryst in the woods and then he moved us to Battersea. But I'll never forget Benjamin. I haven't seen him in over sixty years but I can still picture him as clear as day.'

Though she'd heard the tale several times, with each retelling of her memories, Mrs Savage would add more details.

'Tell me again about how you met Terry. It reminds me of when I first met Benjamin,' she said excitedly.

Jan grinned and could feel her cheeks reddening. 'I met him a few weeks ago when mother had sent me on an errand to a shop. It had been a nice day, warm for the time of year, so I didn't take a coat. A sudden thunderstorm caught me unawares, so I made a dash for cover under the railway bridge. But I wasn't alone. A young man was also sheltering there.'

'You've missed a bit,' Mrs Savage interrupted and corrected her. 'An *attractive* young man,' she added.

'Yes, very attractive,' Jan said, beaming. 'He made a comment about the awful weather and introduced himself as Terence Card. After ten minutes or so, the rain eased and I said farewell. Terry asked if we could meet again, maybe for a walk in the park or an ice cream at Notarianni's. I declined his offer. Mother would go berserk if she thought I was meeting a man! But then, the next day, Mother sent me back to the shop and I ran into Terry again, under the railway bridge. He said he'd been there for over an hour hoping to bump into me. This time when he asked, I agreed to secretly meet him. And, thanks to you, I've managed to see him on several occasions.'

Mrs Savage let out a small squeal and clapped her hands together. 'Delightful! You see, it was meant to be. Fate, my dear. When are you meeting Terry next?'

'I – erm ... I'm not sure.'

'Why the hesitation?'

'I – I don't like to ask you to cover for me. I feel I'm taking advantage of your kindness.'

'Poppycock,' Mrs Savage exclaimed. 'You must take full advantage or I shall be most upset.'

'Thank you. Thank you so much,' Jan replied gratefully.

Without Mrs Savage's discretion, she'd have little opportunity for the romance with Terry to develop. But then she was struck by a sobering thought – her mother. If she discovered that Jan was seeing Terry, there'd be severe consequences.

Nonetheless, she was willing to take the risk. Terry was worth it and though she'd been wary at first, she realised she was falling in love with him and even if she wanted to, she couldn't stop seeing him now.

The rest of the morning passed quickly, custom brisk, and Rachel was pleased when she saw it was half past one. Her feet ached and she was looking forward to closing time in half an hour. Best of all, Hilda hadn't been in, though her good mood was marred when she saw David appear behind the bar. No doubt he'd be after a favour or something from Winnie.

'Is my mum about?'

'I think she's out the back making a cuppa,' Rachel answered and looked him up and down. 'You're looking a bit dapper. Off somewhere nice?'

'No. I thought I'd make the effort for you. Like what you see, do ya?'

'You scrub up all right ... if you like that sort of thing.'

'Thanks, I think. You look nice too,' David drawled as his eyes brazenly ran over her.

Rachel was wearing a green, softly fitted, calf-length rayon dress. It was home-made from a pattern she'd found in Woolworths and which she'd asked Hilda to run up for her. Hilda's old sewing machine was a godsend. It was cheaper to make a dress, especially one like this. She'd seen a similar one in her Littlewoods mail-order catalogue which was priced at ten shillings.

'Thanks,' she said shortly.

'Pour me a half of Red Barrel, Rachel, I'm parched.'

She walked to the pump but had to pass David, and as he deliberately didn't move out of her way, she was forced to edge past him. With a frown, she was sure she felt him blow gently down her neck, though she chose to ignore it. 'Oh, Christ, the barrel's gone,' she said as the pump spluttered and the glass filled with froth. 'I'll nip downstairs and change it. Keep an eye on the bar, I'll only be a few minutes.'

She dashed down the stairs to the cellar and straight to the empty keg, but when she went to change the pipes to the new one, she noticed that the seal had been removed. Thinking it odd, she shook the new barrel and discovered it felt about half full. It must have been used already. Maybe Winnie had accidently assumed it was empty and had prematurely swapped the kegs? Rachel soon changed the pipes around and hurried back upstairs.

After pulling the beer through and pouring a drink for David, she looked around for him but he'd gone. Then Winnie came from the kitchen.

'Sorry about that. I was making David some lunch and he insisted I toasted his bread. You know how long it takes on that silly cooker. He's a pain in the bum.'

'Yes, he is. He asked me to pour him a beer, but I had to go and change the barrel first. Now he's disappeared.'

'I shouldn't worry. Len will drink it.'

Len curled his lip. 'No I won't,' he said. 'I ain't drinking that pasteurised muck. I'll stick to me stout.'

'Oh, well, pour it down the sink,' Winnie told her, glancing out of the window. 'It looks like it's clouding over again. You get off, I'll finish up here.'

'Are you sure?'

'Yes. Go on or you'll get soaked through. I'll sling this lot out soon, make my Brian his lunch and then I think I'll give the brass a polish.'

'I'll do that tomorrow,' Rachel offered.

'No, it's all right, love. I enjoy it. I find it relaxing. Get on your way and I'll see you later.'

Rachel only had to dash along four streets of narrow terraced houses before she arrived home, and thankfully she got there before it started to rain again. She kicked off her shoes, slung her coat and hat on a chair in the corner of her room at the front of the house, then flopped onto her single bed. Though a couple of the springs poked through, Rachel loved her bed. As a child she'd had to share with four of her sisters, so having her own felt like a luxury. Her stomach grumbled but she was comfortable and couldn't be bothered to get up and prepare herself some food. Hunger pains were nothing new to Rachel. She was used to the feeling and had known it for most of her life. Instead, she tried to dismiss fearful thoughts of a German invasion and drifted off to sleep. But soon she was disturbed by someone tapping on her window and slowly she opened her eyes. Still dazed from sleep, she wasn't sure what the time was but she noticed that the sun was still up. When the tapping became more urgent, she went to the window and pulled back the net curtain, expecting to see Hilda. She was surprised to see it was Winnie and was immediately alarmed when she saw the woman's worried expression.

She ran to the front door and ushered Winnie in, asking, 'What's wrong?'

'Do you mind if I sit down?'

Winnie was shaking like a leaf, from head to toe, and Rachel quickly removed her coat and hat from the chair. As

Winnie sat down she said, 'You're scaring me now. Please tell me what's wrong.'

'It's the till. When I opened it to remove the lunchtime takings, it was empty. All of it, gone. Did you put the money somewhere safe before you left and just forgot to mention it?'

Rachel staggered backwards to sit on the bed. She could feel the blood draining from her face. 'No, Win, I didn't.'

'Just as I feared. I've been robbed.'

Rachel hoped Winnie didn't think she had anything to do with it and blurted, 'It wasn't me, Win, I swear.'

'You daft moo, I know that. But who? And when? What cheeky bugger has dipped his rotten, filthy hand into my till, eh? When I find out who it was, I'll skin 'em alive.'

Rachel's mind raced. She'd only left the bar for a short time when she'd gone to the cellar. With Winnie busy in the kitchen she'd asked David to keep an eye on things. Her heart sank as she realised it must have been David who had stolen the money. It was a despicable act, the lowest of the low, especially as Rachel knew that David only had to ask his mother for money and she happily gave it to him.

'Can you think of anyone who'd have nicked it, Rachel?' Winnie asked.

Too shocked to speak, she shook her head. She couldn't tell Winnie that she strongly suspected David. The woman was blinded by her maternal love and could see no wrong in her son. If she dared to accuse him, Winnie would likely snap her head off – or worse, sack her.

'Did any strangers come in today? Anyone who looked suspicious?'

Again, Rachel slowly shook her head. But the more she thought about it, the more certain she became that David was the culprit. The confusion with the kegs downstairs – had he orchestrated everything so that she would be in the cellar at the same time that he'd asked his mother to toast him some bread? None of the customers would think it strange to see Winnie's son at the till. It was clever. Sly and wicked, yet still clever. She fumed inwardly. David had underestimated her in assuming she wouldn't have the savvy to work out what he'd done. The scheming, thieving toe-rag, she thought, angry that he would stoop to stealing from his mother. Rachel had no intention of turning a blind eye. She didn't know how yet, but David Berry was not going to get away with this, she'd make sure of that.

3

The next morning, Winnie trudged through to the front room and placed a fresh cup of tea on the side table next to Brian's chair.

'What you looking so miserable about?' he asked.

'Nothing. I'm just tired. I didn't sleep much last night,' she answered, reluctant to tell him about the stolen takings as he'd probably blame her for being incompetent.

'I noticed. Your bleedin' fidgeting kept me awake too. It's about time we got rid of that bed and bought two singles.'

'Suits me,' she replied. She wouldn't put up an argument. In fact, she thought it was the best suggestion Brian had put forward in years. He often elbowed her in his sleep and she couldn't stand it when he broke wind.

'Where's David? Has he got himself a job yet?'

'He's looking for one,' she said, though she hadn't actually seen any evidence of that.

'You tell the idle layabout he's got until the end of next week to get back into work or he's out of here. What's he going to put down on his National Registration card? Unemployed? It's a disgrace.'

Winnie sighed. She'd heard talk about the introduction of the National Registration card being implemented at the end of the month, but why on earth Brian would worry about their son's listed occupation was beyond her. Mind you, appearances meant everything to Brian. She was about to walk away, but his booming voice stopped her in her tracks.

'Did you hear me, woman?'

Slowly, she turned round to glare at her husband. Her patience was wearing thin and she could feel fury bubbling just below the surface, yet she was too afraid of Brian to speak her mind. Instead, in a sickly sweet tone and with a false smile, she said, 'Yes, dear, I heard you. I should think they heard you over at Clapham Junction railway station.'

Brian slammed his fist down on the arm of his chair. 'Don't get funny with me. You just tell that lazy bastard to get his slovenly arse out of bed and down to the labour exchange.'

She wanted to tell Brian that their son was obviously following in *his* footsteps when it came to idleness and that David was most certainly not a bastard, but, instead, she bit her tongue.

'Don't just stand there, woman, go and drag him out of his bed – now!'

She rushed from the room and tapped lightly on David's bedroom door. There was no response. She knocked a little harder but still there was nothing so she pushed the door open and peeped inside. His bed was empty and she could see that it hadn't been slept in. She'd been so preoccupied with thoughts of yesterday's theft that she hadn't noticed David's absence. 'Oh no,' she muttered, 'this is all I need.'

Quietly walking through to their kitchen, Winnie sat at the table and propped her head up with her hands. First the stolen money and now her son hadn't come home. What next? she wondered, thinking that she had enough to be worrying about already.

'Is he up?' Brian shouted from the front room.

Winnie didn't feel she had the energy to call back and slowly pushed herself up from the seat to join her husband in the front room. She flopped into the armchair opposite. 'He didn't come home last night.'

'Well, if he doesn't find himself a job soon, he needn't bother coming home at all.'

She stifled a yawn. She was too tired to argue with Brian and whether David found a job or not was the least of her worries. She was more concerned about him not coming home last night.

'Get the takings from yesterday. I want to see if there's enough to buy the beds. If there is, you can go to Earl's Emporium and order a couple of second-hand ones. He'll have some in the basement.'

This made Winnie feel instantly awake and very much alert as panic coursed through her veins. Brian didn't normally balance the books until the end of the week. She'd been hoping to cover the loss by then with some sort of excuse.

'Don't just sit there,' he barked, 'bring me the money.'

She swallowed hard and bit on her bottom lip as her mind raced. Could she give him just last night's takings and say they'd had a quiet day? At least it would buy her some time. But he wasn't stupid and would know the money was short. She couldn't think of a feasible lie quickly enough, so she resigned herself to owning up and telling him the truth. She knew he'd be furious and said nervously, 'There was a bit of a problem yesterday lunchtime. The till got robbed. Someone pinched all the money.'

She could feel herself cringing inwards and Brian's eyes widened until they looked as if they'd pop out of his head.

'And you're only telling me now?' he said, surprisingly quietly.

'I – erm, didn't want to worry you.'

'I ain't worried, I'm bloody fuming! You useless woman, how did you let it happen? Too busy chatting up the punters, were you?'

'No, Brian, it wasn't like that, I swear,' she protested, her heart racing and her stomach in knots.

'All you have to do is stand at the bar and pour drinks. If you was doing what you were supposed to be doing, explain to me how some robbing git got his hands on my money?'

The veins in Brian's neck were bulging and his face had turned purple with fury. Winnie was surprised that he wasn't foaming at the mouth. 'I – erm ...' she stuttered, frantically trying to think of an explanation.

'Spit it out, then, woman!'

'Rachel was in the cellar and I got caught short,' she said, desperate to hide the fact that she was in the kitchen making toast for David instead of tending the bar. 'I couldn't help it, Brian, I'm sorry, but I couldn't hold it. I had to go to the loo or I'd have had an accident right there in the pub in front of everyone.'

She ducked as Brian swiped the cup of tea and saucer from the table, venting his obvious anger. The china smashed against the tiled hearth and tea splattered over her winceyette dressing gown.

'Get out of my sight,' he yelled, 'before I knock you through to next door!'

Winnie didn't need telling twice and she ran from the room in floods of tears. She'd known Brian would react this way, but at least he'd spared her his fists. She fled to their bedroom where she sat on the edge of the bed and drew in several long, juddering breaths until, finally, she calmed down. What a mess, she thought, what a right bloody mess! The war, the robbery, David was goodness only knows where and now her husband was spitting feathers too. She wished she'd been up front and had told Brian about the missing money straight away. Yes, he'd have been annoyed, but she'd made it worse by trying to keep it from him. 'You stupid woman,' she told herself. 'He's right, you are useless.'

The moment David's eyes flickered open, pain set in. His head throbbed so much he could hardly move it from the pillow. But as the room began to come into focus, he realised he wasn't in his own bed. Wracking his brain, he tried to recall the events of the previous evening to work out where he was. He remembered paying Errol his dues and then getting talked into another card game. He'd lost, but had won the next two. Quit while you're ahead. That's what he'd told himself, but he hadn't listened to his own advice. And Errol hadn't been happy with him leaving the table, so he'd stupidly stayed until he'd lost every penny he'd stolen from the pub. Yet still he'd continued, and now he was in debt to Errol again. David could have kicked himself. He knew he should have stayed off the brandy. The alcohol had given him a sense of euphoria and had muddled his judgement. And now he had a stinker of a hangover.

He felt an arm drape over his side and looked at the delicate hand with long, crimson nails. The penny dropped. Stephanie Reynolds was lying behind him and he was in her bed. Bile rose in David's throat and his body tensed as he realised he was in big trouble. Not only was he in debt to Errol, the hardest bloke in Battersea, but he'd made it so much worse by sleeping with the man's girlfriend.

'You awake?' Stephanie whispered.

David gulped.

'I need water,' she croaked.

David gently threw her arm off and sat up. He glanced to the side of the bed where he saw his clothes on the floor. He got up and dressed quickly, keeping his back to Stephanie.

'What's the matter?' she asked.

David turned to see her sitting up against the oak head-board, her auburn hair tousled and her nakedness on display. She hadn't even pulled a sheet over herself and he felt embarrassed, unsure of where to look.

'You look like you've seen a ghost,' she said.

'This ain't on, Steph. Errol will bleedin' kill me if he finds out about this.'

'Huh, so you're scared of him too. Well, you weren't bothered last night when you promised to save me from Errol. You said you'd look after me and I wouldn't have to worry about him anymore.'

David scratched his head, unsure of why he'd made such outlandish promises. Errol was a thug, treated his woman like a possession, and he couldn't imagine why he'd offered to be the hero. Probably to get her into bed, he surmised, another alcohol-fuelled mistake.

'I'm sorry, Stephanie, I ... erm –'

'Don't bother,' she snapped. 'You're just like all the rest of them. You ain't the first to make empty threats about Errol and you won't be the last.'

'You'll keep this quiet, won't you?'

Stephanie reached over to the bedside table and took a cigarette from a packet. She lit it and drew a long breath before blowing smoke rings into the air. 'I dunno. I might,' she answered, watching the rings disappear.

'Please, Steph, you know my life won't be worth living if Errol finds out.'

'How much is your life worth, then, Dave?'

'What do you mean?'

'Is it worth enough to pay me for my silence?'

So this was her game. She was intent on blackmailing him. But as David already owed a substantial amount of money to Errol, he had none to give to Stephanie and felt sick to his stomach.

'Two quid a week will do,' she said, her face steely.

David sighed heavily. He couldn't even manage two pennies let alone two quid. But then a thought occurred to him. 'If you tell Errol we slept together, you'll be dropping yourself in it too.'

'Not if I tell him you forced yourself on me.'

David's stomach clenched as he glowered at Stephanie and thought what a hard, ruthless bitch the woman was. A right tart too. He knew of several blokes who'd had her before Errol. In fact, a lot of people had been surprised when Errol had got together with her, but no one had dared to mention her reputation. Only one fella had and he'd had his front teeth knocked out. 'Look, Steph, I'll be honest with you. I already owe Errol a small fortune and I ain't got the money to pay to you an' all.'

'You'd better find it, then. You had plenty to throw around last night. Get me the money or I'll definitely drop you in it. And you needn't think about denying what I tell him. Errol adores me and would never believe *you* over me.'

David walked round to the bedside table and lit himself a cigarette. He couldn't see a way to get out of this and reluctantly agreed to Stephanie's demands. 'Can you give me until next week?' he asked hopefully.

'I suppose so. But then I want two quid a week – or else.'

He carefully sneaked out of Stephanie's flat, relieved to see his motorbike outside. As he headed back to the Battersea Tavern, his mind crowded with worrying thoughts. He could rob the pub again but it would only be a matter of time before he got caught. He could ask his mother for money but he doubted she'd cough up two quid a week. He could get a job but at least half his salary would go to pay Stephanie – and no, that wouldn't do.

The ten-minute ride home helped to clear his headache but by the time he arrived outside the back door, David had worked himself into a state. He just couldn't see how he'd avoid receiving a hefty beating from Errol. There was no way he could pay the man back, along with stumping up money for Stephanie to keep her quiet. Yet he knew he couldn't face being physically hurt either.

In the kitchen, his mum was at the stove, probably making porridge.

'Morning,' he said sheepishly.

She spun round and looked relieved to see him but he could tell from her red and puffy eyes that she'd been crying.

No doubt his father had given her a hard time about the till being robbed. David thought that maybe he should feel guilty about it but he didn't. He was too consumed with fear about the punishment he might soon be getting from Errol.

'Oh, there you are, love,' his mother gushed. 'I've been worried sick about you. Where've you been?'

'Out, Mum. I'm twenty-three years old, not three, and I don't need your permission to go out to play,' he answered shortly, pleased that it appeared she didn't suspect him of the robbery.

'All right, calm down. There's no need to jump down my throat. I was only asking.'

'Sorry, Mum, I'm just a bit knackered. Me and the boys had a bit of a late one and I stayed over at Ted's.'

'How's Ted's mum? Did she make you some breakfast?'

'I didn't see her. I left before she got up.'

'I'm doing some porridge for your father. Would you like some?'

The thought of it made him want to throw up and he shook his head.

'Did you have a nice night?'

'It was all right.'

'I don't suppose you noticed anything dodgy downstairs yesterday, did you?'

David could feel his pulse quicken but he tried to remain calm. 'No. Why?'

His mother turned off the gas and pulled out a seat at the table before slowly lowering herself onto it. 'We were robbed. Someone helped themselves to the lunchtime takings. We were pretty busy so I reckon there was a fair bit of cash in the till.'

'The thieving gits,' he said, feigning disgust.

'I know. Your father was none too happy about it. I can't think who would have done it. I thought I knew all my customers and could trust them. Honestly, David, this has shocked me to the core.'

'I bet it has, Mum. I was only in the bar for about five minutes and I can't say I noticed anything out of the ordinary. What about Rachel, has she got any idea who nicked it?'

'No, love, she's as stumped as me. I'll have a word with Len later. He might have seen something.'

David could feel himself breaking out into a sweat and he made an excuse to leave, saying he was knackered and needed to lie down. He closed his bedroom door and plonked onto the edge of his bed. Leonard bloody Garwood – he'd forgotten about the quiet old man who always sat at the end of the bar. He must have seen him opening the till and though the man probably never thought anything of it at the time, when asked, he was bound to tell his mother what he'd seen. That would be it, curtains.

It had just gone nine. He had two and a half hours before the pub opened to think of how he was going to worm his way out of his mother discovering he was the thief.

Rachel felt slightly perturbed at being interrupted. She'd been reading on her freshly made bed and was at a particularly good point in her book when someone tapped on her window. When she looked out and saw David, she panicked, assuming something awful must have happened to Winnie. Rushing to the front door, she pulled it open but no words would come from her mouth.

'Sorry, Rachel, I know it's early, but can I come in?'

'Is – is your mum all right?' she managed to ask but she dreaded David's answer.

'Yes, she's fine.'

Relief washed over her but her legs felt quite shaky. 'Come in,' she said and led David through to her room. 'What's this all about?' she asked curtly as she pulled herself together, not forgetting that she knew it was David who had stolen the pub takings.

'It's a bit delicate.'

'Just spit it out,' she said, feeling nothing but disdain for the man.

'I feel terrible about bringing you into this, but I don't know who else to turn to. It's about the robbery in the pub yesterday.'

Rachel pursed her lips and tried to keep her mouth shut. She wanted to scream at David and tell that him that he was despicable. She'd have liked to have thumped him one, right on the nose, but she stood quietly and allowed him to continue.

'See, the thing is, I was stupid and got myself into a really bad situation. I needed money or else I would have had my head kicked in. I was desperate. Really desperate, and I didn't know what else to do.'

Rachel glared at him, hardly believing that he'd freely confessed. 'So you're saying you nicked the money?'

'Yeah, but I know what I did was wrong. I'm really sorry.'

'Why are you apologising to me? Surely it's your mother you should be talking to.'

'She can't find out it was me, Rachel. It would break her heart.'

'Yeah, well, you should have thought about her feelings before you stole from her!'

'Like I said, I was desperate and wasn't thinking clearly.'

Rachel sat down on her only chair, seething inside. 'Let's hear it, then, this fabrication about getting your head kicked in.'

David paced the small room, clearly distressed, not that Rachel cared about his feelings of woe. Good, let him suffer, she thought.

'I got conned by Errol Hampton. He roped me into a few card games and stung me for a fair few bob. Then, when I couldn't pay him the money I owed, he threatened me. Before you say anything, I know I should have gone to my mum, told her the truth, but I was too ashamed, so I took money from the till to pay off Errol.'

Rachel shook her head in utter abhorrence. 'You stole from your mother to pay off gambling debts. And now you want my sympathy?'

'No, Rachel, not your sympathy, but I need your help.'

'Go on, this I've got to hear.'

'My mum is going to ask Len if he saw anything. You've got to help me cover this up.'

'Oh, have I, indeed! I don't think so, David. It's about time your mother found out what you're really like.'

'Please, Rachel. I'm not asking for my sake. I don't want to see her upset.'

'Don't give me that. Of course you're asking for your sake. No, David, I won't be a part of your lies and deception and, quite frankly, I'm really annoyed that you've asked me to be.'

'But, Rachel, don't you see what this will do to her?'

'Yes, I know exactly how devastated she'll be. But this is *your* fault. Don't try and put it on me!'

David turned and looked out of the window as he lit a cigarette. When he spun back to face her, Rachel could see his eyes had welled up with tears. Still, she felt no sympathy for him.

'I hate to ask you, Rachel, but if you refuse to help me I'll have no choice but to do a runner. I can't face my mum if she finds out.'

'Good. Do a runner. Bugger off and don't come back. Your mother will be better off without you bleeding her dry.'

'What, and leave her to deal with my dad alone? You know what he's like. She's got no one, only me.'

'She's got me,' Rachel was quick to remind him.

'But you ain't family.'

That remark hurt Rachel. No, she wasn't, but Winnie was like a mother to her. 'Maybe not, but you *are* and family don't steal off each other,' she said furiously.

'I know, and I'll never do it again. My mum needs me, Rachel. I don't want to abandon her, but I will if I have to. You'll have to pick up the pieces. She'll be in bits.'

She drew in a long, slow breath. Yes, Winnie would be inconsolable if David suddenly disappeared, or if she knew her only son had robbed her. It went against the grain to help David to conceal the truth but if it spared Winnie's feelings, then maybe she'd have to consider it. 'What have you got in mind?' she asked.

'You'll help?'

'I might, but only because I think the world of your mum and can't stand the thought of her being hurt.'

'Thanks, Rachel. I promise I'll never let her down again.'

47

'You'd better not. She deserves better.'

'I know,' he said and hung his head in shame but Rachel doubted it was with any real sincerity.

'Come on, then, let's hear it,' she said, annoyed that David would probably get away with what he'd done, and that she was going to help cover for him. She just couldn't see any other way of protecting Winnie.

'If Len says he saw me at the till, you could say you'd asked me to put the money in for the beer I'd ordered. When you came back after changing the barrel, I'd gone, but you served a customer and didn't notice any missing money.'

Now it was Rachel who hung her head in shame. She couldn't believe that she was going to blatantly lie to Winnie.

'So you'll go along with it?' David pushed.

She nodded but couldn't bring herself to speak or even look at him.

'Thanks, Rachel. You're a lifesaver.'

'I hate you for this, David,' she hissed, her jaw clenched. 'Now get out!'

David stubbed out his cigarette and was gone, leaving her feeling sick inside. He'd put her in an impossible position – either stand by and watch her dearest friend fall apart in despair, or go against her morals and principles to deceive the dear woman. She'd opted for the latter but didn't feel comfortable with her decision. Surely Winnie had a right to know the truth about her son? But could Winnie handle the truth? Rachel wasn't willing to take that chance.

4

Three weeks had passed and Winnie was none the wiser about who had stolen the lunchtime takings. She'd resigned herself to the fact that she'd probably never know but would be more vigilant in future. And Rachel had vowed to keep a more watchful eye out too.

It was a normal morning. Len was halfway through his first bottle of stout. Terry had called in briefly to drop off a bag of washing that Winnie did for him for a bit of extra money. Several other customers were sitting around, some reading newspapers, two playing crib and one rolling tobacco. This was how Winnie liked things – orderly, peaceful and calm. And, so far, David had avoided his father, so things were pretty harmonious upstairs too. Though she guessed that if David didn't find himself a job soon, her husband would undoubtedly kick off again. But at least they now had separate beds, so she didn't have to lie next to the miserable so-and-so every night.

Winnie sighed, her thoughts drifting. Brian handled the takings and gave her housekeeping money. She was thrifty and managed to have a bob over every week, which, along with the money she earned from doing Terry's washing, gave her a small measure of financial independence. But for all her hard work, she didn't have much to show for it.

Her thoughts were interrupted when the door flew open and several high-spirited young men piled in, laughing and almost tumbling over each other as they came to the bar. Winnie recognised three of them, sons of her regulars, and wondered why they weren't at work.

'Drinks all round, please, Mrs Berry,' one said.

'Are you celebrating something?' she asked.

'Yeah, we are. Me and the boys have just signed up. What do you think about that, eh?' he answered and they all cheered.

Winnie tried to smile. She didn't want to dampen their elated mood, but inside, her heart cried for what was coming to them and for their mothers. She'd seen it all before during the Great War. Men young and old had rushed to sign up, excited to offer their services to the country. But so many had paid the ultimate sacrifice and been killed in action. And those who had come home had returned damaged men. Solemnly, she remembered Alex, the boy she'd lived next door to when she was growing up. He'd been a few years younger than her and had only been fourteen when he'd joined the army. She recalled the first time he visited his mum, having been away at war for over a year. He'd looked so proud of himself as he'd walked down the street in his uniform, head high, whistling a tune. A year later, the next time Winnie saw him, he was sitting in a chair in the front garden, misery etched on his face. And then she'd realised his legs were missing. She'd gasped in shock and had dashed indoors, feeling sick. Her mother told her that Alex's mum would often stuff a pair of trousers with newspaper and he'd sit with a blanket over his lap, pretending he still had his legs. The thought of something so tragic happening to David made her stomach knot.

The young men drank up and left to go on to the next pub. Winnie said a silent prayer, hoping their blood wouldn't be spilt on foreign soil.

'Good on 'em,' Len said. Unusually, he was smiling.

'I've got to be honest; it saddens me, Len.'

'They'll go to war as boys but will come back as men.'

If they come back, she thought, upset at the idea that she might never see them again.

'Oh, no,' Rachel groaned quietly.

Winnie looked towards the door to see Hilda staggering in. Her hair was dishevelled and her coat was even dirtier than the last time she'd seen it.

'Quick, shoot out the back,' she told Rachel.

But Rachel didn't move fast enough and Hilda spotted her. 'There she is,' the drunken woman slurred scathingly, 'my bitch of a so-called sister.'

'Don't start,' Winnie warned Hilda.

'I ain't. I'm only speaking as I find. She is a bitch and as for being me sister, well ...'

'I won't have you speaking about my staff like that. If you can't hold your tongue, Hilda, I shall ask you to leave.'

'I ain't going nowhere. My money's as good as the next person's. I'll hold my tongue but I don't see why I should. Rachel ruined my life, but now she's looking down her nose at me like butter wouldn't melt in her mouth. Fuck her, that's what I say.'

'Right, that's it! I ain't having language like that in my pub.

Sling your hook,' Winnie said forcibly as she came out from behind the bar and ushered Hilda towards the door.

'Get your bleedin' hands off me,' Hilda shouted as she tried to shrug Winnie off her.

An elderly gentleman pulled the door open and Winnie shoved Hilda out in an unceremonious manner. 'You'll be welcome back when you're sober and have washed your mouth out with soap,' she told her and turned back towards the bar, brushing her hands together as if she'd just dumped a bag of rubbish in the dustbin.

'I'm so sorry about her,' Rachel said quietly, her cheeks flame red.

'No need for you to apologise. It isn't your fault.'

'I feel responsible for her.'

'Well you're not. Hilda is a grown woman and needs to sort herself out. Fancy being plastered at this time of the day. She's a disgrace.'

'I bet she's split up from her latest bloke again. They never last more than two minutes. She must have got her hands on a bottle of whisky, no doubt to drown her sorrows again. I don't know where she gets the money and, to be honest, I don't think I want to know.'

'Yes, there's some things you're better off being in the dark about,' Winnie said, though she'd heard gossip that Hilda offered men favours in return for money. She'd hoped it was nothing but a nasty rumour and had tried to nip the talk in the bud before it had reached Rachel's ears.

'I don't know why she's so horrid to me when she's drunk. She's as nice as pie when she's sober, which is less and less these days.'

'Try not to let her get to you, love. She won't remember any of this tomorrow.'

'I know, but I will.'

Len interrupted their conversation when he asked for another bottle of stout. Rachel went to wipe down some tables and as Winnie handed Len his drink, she saw her second disappointment of the morning when Errol Hampton walked in. She was grateful that he rarely visited her premises because where Errol went, trouble normally followed. The man was well dressed, his three-piece brown suit obviously tailor-made. But Winnie knew that his clean-cut appearance masked a vicious and unscrupulous monster. A bully who thought nothing of kicking a man near to death.

'I'll have half a bitter,' Errol said to her, but his eyes were following Rachel in a way that made Winnie feel uncomfortable.

She poured his drink and watched him suspiciously.

'Is Dave here?' he asked.

Immediately, her hackles rose and she wondered what Errol would want with her son.

'No, he's not,' she lied.

'He's not upstairs, then?'

'I said so, didn't I?' she answered without her usual smile that she offered to customers.

Errol downed his drink in just a few large mouthfuls. He wiped his mouth on the back of his hand before saying, 'Right you are. Pass on my regards to Dave. Tell him I was looking for him.'

With that, Errol sauntered out, leaving Winnie concerned. She was sure there was a veiled threat in his words and wondered what David had got himself involved in. She didn't believe Errol was the sort of bloke who her son would be friends with.

'Errol Hampton, Battersea's answer to Al Capone, or so he thinks. I'm glad he doesn't show his face too often. He frightens the life out of me,' Rachel said when she came back behind the bar.

'Yeah, me an' all.'

'What did he want?'

'I dunno, love. He asked after David. Keep an eye on things, I'm popping upstairs,' she answered, and she headed up to David's room.

She found him still in his bed.

'Oh, Mum, give it a rest,' he moaned as she shook him awake.

'What have you been up to with Errol Hampton?' she asked, ignoring his moaning.

'Nothing. Why?'

'Because he's just been in here looking for you. Are you in trouble, David?'

'No, course I ain't.'

'Are you sure?'

'Yes, I'm sure. Just leave me be.'

'No, I won't. If you're mixed up with that Errol, I want to know about it.'

David huffed and pushed himself up on his haunches.

'Tell me the truth, Son.'

'All right. I owe him a few quid and haven't paid him. He's probably come after his money.'

'What on earth do you owe him money for?' Winnie asked in despair. She couldn't believe her son would be stupid enough to get into debt with Errol Hampton. The man had a violent reputation and she'd thought her son had more sense.

'I got myself sucked into a few card games with him and he wiped me out. But it weren't my fault. He plied me with brandy and you know what Errol's like. He ain't the sort of bloke you say "no" to.'

'Oh, David, you idiot! You know what he'll do to you if you don't pay him back!'

'Yes, Mum, of course I know. That's why I ain't been out looking for a job. I've been lying low, trying to avoid him.'

'How much do you owe?' Winnie asked gravely.

'Twenty quid.'

'Twenty quid!' she squealed, shocked. 'Blimey, David, that's a lot more than a few quid. How the hell are you going to pay him?'

David didn't answer but she knew what he was thinking. 'No, Son, I don't have that sort of money. And since the robbery, your father has been checking the takings after every shift. For Christ's sake, what are we gonna do?'

'I really don't know, but I can't hide in here forever.'

Winnie went to the window and pulled open the curtains. She looked down to the street below. Then her heartbeat quickened when she saw Errol leaning against a lamp post opposite. He was smoking a cigarette and gazing threateningly up at the window. She quickly pulled the curtains back together and turned to her son.

'He's not going away. He's outside. We'll have to pay him,' she said, her mouth dry with nerves.

'I'm sorry, Mum. I never meant to bring trouble to your doorstep.'

'I know, but we've got to get rid of him before your

father gets wind of it. He'll go berserk if he finds out you've racked up debts you can't pay, especially to the likes of Errol Hampton.'

'How, Mum? How are we gonna pay him?'

'I don't know. I'll have to take the money out of the till, I suppose, and think of something to tell your dad. There won't be twenty pounds in there but something will be better than nothing. You take the money to Errol and tell him there'll be more in a couple of days.'

'I don't know if I can face him. What if he gives me a hiding?'

'He won't. I know his sort. Give him some of the money and it'll keep him happy for now.'

'All right, but I hope you're right.'

'I am. Now get up and get dressed. I want that man gone from outside my pub,' she insisted, then she turned and went back downstairs.

'You look as white as a sheet. Everything all right, Win?' Rachel asked.

'Erm, yes,' she answered, her mind turning as she went to the till and opened it. How was she going to explain to Brian a shortfall in the takings? Her lips pursed. She'd worry about that later. Right now, her priority was David.

It had been a quiet morning so there wasn't much available cash, but Winnie took out several coins and hoped it would be enough to keep Errol off David's back for now.

Her son came downstairs and she discreetly handed him the money. 'Come straight back,' she told him.

David nodded and slipped outside while Winnie's heart raced. She felt clammy, fearing for the safety of her son.

'What's going on?' Rachel asked. 'I can see you're upset about something.'

'Trust me, you don't want to know.'

'It's David, isn't it? And something to do with Errol Hampton?'

'Please, Rachel, you're best out of it,' Winnie answered brusquely.

Thankfully, Rachel didn't push any further and, a short while later, David returned to the pub.

'Well?' Winnie asked, searching his face for clues and pulling him through to the back.

'He wasn't happy, but I explained it was all I could get. He's putting interest on for every day the debt is outstanding.'

'Then the sooner it's paid back, the better. No more running away from it, David. Get yourself a job. I can't afford to clear it by myself, but I'll help as much as I can.'

David nodded but she wasn't convinced he'd bother to find work. But whether he did or didn't, Errol Hampton still needed paying and Winnie would have to think of a way to do it behind her husband's back.

Rachel could see that Winnie's nerves were jangled and had worked out that it had something to do with David and Errol. She'd noticed the woman take money from the till and though Winnie had tried to be discreet, Rachel had seen her give the cash to David. It had riled her. She knew that David had stolen from his mother to pay his debts to Errol, so what was he up to now? She wished that she hadn't covered for him in the first place! However, it was too late to say anything. She'd have to keep the secret. And just like

Jim, David had shown himself to be deceitful and a liar. She wondered if any men could be trusted.

At two o'clock, Rachel cleared away the empty glasses and grabbed her coat from the newel post. She had wanted to coax Winnie to open up and tell her what was going on, but the woman had remained unusually quiet all morning. She'd made it clear that she didn't want to talk, so reluctantly Rachel left for home. She didn't like to leave Winnie upset and would rather have stayed.

As she turned the corner onto her street, her heart sank further when she saw her sister sitting, legs sprawled on the pavement, leaning up against the front door. She was in no mood for another confrontation with Hilda and was about to turn and walk in the opposite direction when Hilda saw her and shouted her name.

Rachel walked towards her sister and braced herself. Hilda looked bleary-eyed and struggled to climb to her feet. She reached out and offered a steadying hand for Hilda but had to turn her face away from her body odour and vile breath.

'I've been waiting for you,' Hilda said, stumbling to the side.

'I'm tired. It's been a long morning, so I'm gonna put me feet up for a while and relax until my shift tonight,' she said, hoping that Hilda would get the hint and leave her in peace.

'That's all right. I'll keep you company for a bit. I ain't got nuffink better to do.'

'What's the matter? Did you break up with Fred?' Rachel asked, but already guessed that she had.

'Yeah. He was seeing that woman who works in the big furniture shop on Falcon Road. Ugly old cow, she is. I dunno what he sees in her but she's welcome to him.'

The news came as no surprise to Rachel. Hilda's boyfriends came and went as frequently as the waning of the moon. They either discovered Hilda's drinking problem, or they were drunks themselves and dumped her after using her for what they could get. Either way it never had a happy ending and her sister would turn to the bottle to console herself. Rachel thought it was very sad. Her sister craved love but looked for it in the wrong places. Since Hilda's husband had left, Rachel had always hoped that a good man would see the kindness in Hilda and keep her sister off the booze. But, so far, it hadn't happened.

She opened the front door and Hilda followed her in. Once in Rachel's room, Hilda threw herself across the bed. 'Got anything to drink?'

'No, and I think you've had enough,' she answered.

This was the wrong thing to say. Hilda glared at her and Rachel knew her sister was about to become aggressive.

'How dare you tell me when I've had enough to drink… what gives you the right? What do you know, eh? I'll tell you – you know nothing. Nothing at all. But I do. Oh, I know plenty. I could tell you stuff that'd change your perfect and clean little world into something putrid. Would you like that? Do you wanna know what I know?'

Rachel had no idea what her sister was talking about and assumed this was her usual drunken ramblings. 'No, Hilda, I don't,' she replied, exasperated.

'Nah, course not. We wouldn't want to spoil your life. It wouldn't do to wipe the smile off your pretty face. Perfect Rachel. Huh, after what your bloke did, you still think you're so much better than me, don't you?'

'No, I've never thought that.'

'Yes you have. It's written all over your face, but you ain't got a clue. You're just as tainted as me, except you don't know it. If I told you the truth, it'd break your precious heart. Maybe if you knew everything, you wouldn't be so stuck-up.'

'Please, Hilda, I've no idea what you're talking about and I don't really care. Like I said, I'm tired and I'd like to rest. I don't want to be rude, but I'd like you to leave now, please.'

Hilda rolled over on the bed so she was on her side and facing the wall. 'I'll be as quiet as a mouse,' she whispered and giggled.

Rachel heaved a sigh, shook her head and took her shoes off before sitting on the chair. She knew it would be pointless to try to get her sister to leave. When under the influence of whisky, Hilda's moods were quick to change and at least now she was placid. She did her best to ignore the smell emanating from her sister's body that filled her small room as she picked up her book and began reading, trying not to think of her ex-fiancé. God, she hated it when Hilda mentioned Jim. As she turned the pages of her book she could hear Hilda snoring loudly. Her sister had passed out and Rachel hoped that when she woke, she would be back to being her *nice* sister again.

David was still shaking as he paced his bedroom floor. Lucky for him, Errol had accepted the small pay-off but had made it quite clear that he'd be back for more. Thankfully, the man hadn't mentioned Stephanie, so David could only assume that she hadn't yet told Errol about her encounter with him. However, unless he paid her off too, it would only be a matter of time before she opened her mouth. When that happened his life wouldn't be worth living. Errol would see to that.

At least now that Errol was off his back for a while, David could confidently venture outside again. He sucked in a deep breath, then lit a cigarette and sat on his bed to smoke it as he tried to calm his nerves. It had been terrifying facing Errol but it was done, thanks to his mum. And now his mother knew about the debt he felt sure she'd find a way to stump up the money.

Feeling better, David jumped up, ran a comb through his hair and looked in the mirror. Not bad, he told himself, even if he did look a bit pasty. A ride on his motorbike over to Ted's would soon put a bit of colour back in his cheeks, he thought, grabbing his flat cap and shoving it in his pocket before dashing downstairs. Hoping to avoid his mother, David sneaked out of the back door. Just as he threw his leg over his bike, he looked up to see her standing beside him.

'Where do you think you're going?' she asked.

'Out.'

'Out where?'

'To see Ted.'

'And what about looking for a job?'

'I will, Mum. Give it a rest, will you.'

'No, David, I won't. Errol Hampton needs paying back and I can't afford to do it alone.'

'I'll find work soon, I promise.'

'You should be going down the labour exchange, not mucking about with Ted.'

'Don't go on about it. I'll have a job by the end of the week.'

'Make sure you do or you'll have to see about selling that bloody contraption,' she threatened, pointing to the motorbike.

David felt stunned that she'd even suggested such a thing. His prized Matchless bike. No, he'd never sell it and his mum couldn't make him. He'd saved for years for the bike – granted, with money mostly acquired from her, but nonetheless it belonged to him. He enjoyed the freedom it gave him and he liked how it impressed the girls.

Having heard enough of his mother's nagging, David started the engine and sped off, leaving her calling after him. Bugger her, he thought, if she didn't allow his father to rule over her, she'd have no problem paying Errol his dues. But his dad was a tyrant in their home and not a day passed when David didn't secretly wish the man would drop down dead.

As the chilly September wind rushed against his face, stinging his cheeks, he pushed all thoughts of his mother and father from his head. But, try as he might, he couldn't shake the feeling of foreboding he had about Errol.

'Hello, mate,' David greeted Ted when he arrived at the man's garage.

'I wondered when you'd show your face,' Ted answered unhappily.

'What's the matter? You've got a face like a smacked arse.'

'You. You're what's the matter. I've had that thug Errol Hampton in here looking for you and I don't take kindly to being threatened cos you've landed yourself in shit with him.'

'Sorry about that, Ted, but it's all sorted now.'

'It had better be. Anyway, what have you done to upset the bloke?' Ted asked, his voice softening.

'Nothing much. I had a few games of cards with him and owe him a couple of bob.'

'Well, if that's all, it don't take much to upset him. I suppose that's why I haven't seen you for a while?'

'I've been keeping me head down. Ted, you don't need a lacky, do you?'

'Does it look like it?'

David glanced around the small garage and at the one car in sight.

'Sorry, mate,' Ted said, 'but I've barely got enough work to cover my rent. There ain't a lot of bikes in Battersea and even fewer cars. To tell you the truth, I've been struggling for a while now and have been thinking about signing up. They need mechanics in the army.'

'That's a mug's game, if you ask me.'

'Maybe, but we'll have to register in October or soon after anyway. Chances are we're gonna get called up sooner or later so I might as well join up now.'

David shook his head. He had no intention of fighting with the British army and thought anyone who volunteered needed their head testing. 'I'll register if I have to, but I'll find a way of getting out of any active service.'

'I'm sure you will, Dave, you're a slippery bugger. Me, on the other hand, I'm gonna do my bit. I'll be off soon.' With a wry smile he added, 'Will you miss me?'

'Yeah, like a hole in the head. But, seriously, mate, take care of yourself.'

'I will and do me a favour – check on my mum now and then.'

'Of course,' David answered but he knew he wouldn't bother. After all, Ted had a younger brother and two sisters so he didn't see why he should have to look out for their mother. He had enough on his plate with trying to keep his own old dear happy, let alone someone else's.

'Thanks. My mum would appreciate you popping in and she can give you news of what I'm up to.'

'No problem, Ted. I'd better be off. Look after yourself, you mad sod.'

'Yeah, you too, mate.'

David rode off, thinking Ted was a fool but he hoped his friend would be all right. It got him thinking – if he was going to avoid conscription, he'd need to find a way out of it, and soon.

5

Winnie snuck another penny into an empty pint glass she'd stored on a shelf under the till. It had been over two weeks since Errol had come calling for the money David owed him and she feared the man would soon be back again for more. She'd been squirrelling away a few pennies here and there from customer's orders and any tips offered. So far, although the takings appeared to be down a little, Brian's suspicions hadn't been raised. But the money Winnie had managed to stash was a long way off what was needed to repay Errol.

'Are you saving for Christmas?' Rachel asked.

Her voice made Winnie jump and she spun round to see the girl behind her, looking over her shoulder.

'Erm ... yeah, something like that. Do me a favour and keep it to yourself though.'

'Are you planning on another big day like last year?'

'I dunno, maybe.'

'I can put my tips in the glass too, Win, if it helps. I don't see why you should have to fork out for all the food and everything by yourself.'

'No,' Winnie answered abruptly.

Rachel looked taken aback.

'I'm sorry, love. I didn't mean to sound harsh. But no, thank you, you're not to contribute a thing to Christmas. You work hard all year and it's my way of saying thanks to you and our customers, well, them that ain't got a family to go to.'

'You're an angel, you are, Win. Everyone said that your Christmas last year was the best they'd ever had. It was for me too. I can't wait until this year's celebrations.'

'Yeah, well, you shouldn't wish your life away. Christmas will come round soon enough. I just hope I can get everything I need. Who knows, what with this bloody war an' all. In the meantime, there's plenty needs doing. You can serve Len, for a start.'

Rachel smiled and wandered down to the end of the bar. Winnie felt awful about lying but she didn't want to involve Rachel in the problem with Errol. The girl would only worry and that was the last thing Winnie wanted. She enjoyed seeing Rachel's smile, it was like a breath of fresh air, but that smile would be gone if Rachel knew the truth.

The pub door opened again and she felt herself tense. She couldn't relax knowing that Errol could breeze in at any moment and she still hadn't saved enough cash to pacify him. She sighed with relief when it was Terry who walked through the door.

'You're a sight for sore eyes,' she told him when he approached the bar.

Terry did a quick spin. 'I've got me Sunday best on,' he said and placed his thumbs behind his jacket lapels.

'But it's Friday and why ain't you at work?'

'I've got today and the weekend off so I'm taking my good lady out somewhere special.'

'This good lady being your girlfriend, Jan?'

'Yep.'

'Well, she's a very lucky girl. Where are you taking her?'

'First, I thought I'd take her to the tea rooms up the Junction for one of them posh afternoon teas. Then to the flicks.'

'I thought all the cinemas were closed.'

'Yeah, most of them are but The Globe is showing matinees. Do you think she'll like it, Win?'

'I'm sure she will, but I can't really say for sure because I haven't met her yet.'

'I know, but I've managed to talk her into coming in tomorrow evening. She's not all that keen but gave in on account of it being my birthday.'

'Oh, that's good. But isn't it the thirtieth of September tomorrow?'

'Yes, Winnie, it is.'

'Well, then, your birthday is on the tenth of January. I know that because it's on the same day as my sister's.'

'Yeah, but I don't know if I was really born then. That's the date I was dumped outside the orphanage so that's the one they gave me. So, from now on, I'm having me birthday on the thirtieth of September.'

Winnie chuckled. 'You are a card, Terry Card. But any reason for having it tomorrow?'

'Yeah — I want to show off my Jan and I can't wait until January to get her in here.'

Winnie chuckled again. She thought a lot of Terry and liked his sense of humour. 'I'd better bake a cake this evening, then,' she told him with a wry wink. 'But don't go thinking you'll be having another birthday in January.'

'Whose birthday is it?' Rachel asked as she came to stand alongside Winnie.

'Terry's — tomorrow. He's bringing Jan in to meet us.'

'Oh, smashing. But isn't your birthday in January?'

'Not anymore,' Terry answered, going on to explain.

'I see. Well, I hope you ain't expecting a present at such short notice,' Rachel said before walking away to serve another customer.

'It's serious, then, is it, with you and Jan? Do I need to be buying myself a new hat?' Winnie asked.

'Whoa, slow down. Not yet, Win, but I do really like her.'

'Well, no one could blame you for rushing into getting married. I hear there's a lot of young men and women tying the knot before being sent off to war.'

'I've no need to worry about that. I'm in one of them reserved occupations.'

'Well, yes, I suppose a baker is essential. What would we do without our bread, eh?' Winnie said, and then a thought crossed her mind. 'Terry,' she whispered and when he leaned in towards her, she continued, 'could you get my David a job with you in the bakery?'

Terry cleared his throat before answering and shifted from one foot to the other. 'I don't know, Win. It isn't really up to me. Yes, I run the place, but the owner, Mr Hope, he does all the hiring and firing.'

'You could put a good word in for him with Mr Hope. My David's a good lad, honest and hard-working.'

'Sure... I can, erm, ask, but I've got to dash now. I'll see you tomorrow night, Win.'

'Yes, see you, Terry, and I can't wait to meet Jan,' she said as he walked away. She could tell by his uncomfortable reaction that he wouldn't ask Mr Hope to employ David. He and her son weren't enemies but neither were they friends. Winnie was well aware that some people thought David lazy. He could be, but in her book having an idle streak didn't make you a bad person. They didn't know her boy like she did. Winnie was sure that given the right circumstances, David would come into his own and prove himself to be a grafter. The trouble was, he hadn't yet found anything to capture his attention. He needed a job he could get his teeth stuck into — one in which he could thrive. Maybe being a baker wouldn't be the career to do that, but it would keep him out of the army and that's all Winnie really wanted.

Jan Board peered out of the tram window and when she spotted Terry waiting to greet her, her heart skipped a beat. He looked quite dashing and his blond hair gleamed in the afternoon sun. She pictured herself running into his waiting arms and planting sweet kisses on his face, but in reality she knew she'd only be able to bring herself to offer a meek hello.

As Jan stepped off the tram, Terry walked towards her and she could feel herself blushing. She stood in front of him, peering at the ground as they waited for the crowd of travellers to disperse.

'Hello, Jan. You're looking lovely,' Terry said and bent down to kiss her quickly on the cheek.

Jan briefly looked up and met his bright blue eyes. Awkwardly, she tucked her long, brown hair behind her ear and half smiled before staring back down at the ground. Oh, why, oh why, wouldn't her mouth work? The words were in her head but she couldn't get them out. Hello. It was so simple. Hello. But nothing came and she remained silent.

'I've got a bit of a treat lined up for you. Would you like a fancy tea with cakes and everything?'

Again, Jan gave Terry a fleeting look and nodded her head.

'Great, come on, then,' he said, grabbing her hand.

It felt nice to walk along the busy street of Clapham Junction with her hand in his. She'd just turned twenty-six, but hadn't had a boyfriend before – her fanatical religious mother wouldn't allow it. If she knew about Terry, she'd be furious. So far Jan had managed to keep their relationship a secret, though her mother was beginning to ask some probing questions.

'Here we are,' Terry said and he held the door open for Jan to enter the swanky tea rooms.

Jan glanced around at the dark wood-panelled walls which were in stark contrast to the crisp, white linen tablecloths that adorned the rows of tables and chairs. A young waitress approached, smartly dressed in a black alpaca dress with white collar, cuffs, and pearl buttons sewn down the front. Her starched white cap matched the pristine apron tied around her waist. She showed them to a table where Terry was quick to pull out a seat for Jan, which she found very chivalrous. The quiet hum of voices and the clink of china almost drowned out the soft piano music. Jan couldn't see the piano but she thought it was behind a very large potted palm in the corner.

'Before you sit down, let me hang your coat up for you,' Terry offered, nodding towards a coat stand.

Jan swallowed, dreading revealing her old-fashioned dress that was going threadbare. She couldn't remember the last time she'd had any new clothes, and this dress was one of her mother's cast-offs. 'It's all right. I – I'll keep it on,' she said, quickly sitting on the chair. She knew her coat had seen better days too, but at least it looked tidy.

Terry looked puzzled, but as soon as he too sat down the waitress handed them the menu. 'We'll have the afternoon tea, please, with fish-paste sandwiches, scones and cakes,' he told her, then he looked over the menu to ask Jan, 'Is that all right for you?'

She nodded. It sounded delicious. They never had cakes and sweet treats at home as her mother thought they were frivolous.

'I popped into the Battersea Tavern on the way here. Winnie and Rachel are really looking forward to meeting you.'

Jan smiled, though her stomach knotted at the thought of her mother finding out. If she had even an inkling that Jan was frequenting a public house, there would be hell to pay. Her mother believed pubs were full of drunken men and loose women. They were places of debauchery and sin and not a suitable environment for a good God-fearing Christian woman.

'You are still coming with me tomorrow night?'

Jan nodded.

'Good. I've told them all about you. You'll get on well with Winnie. She's like everyone's mum.'

Good grief, Jan thought, hoping Winnie wasn't anything like her own mother, though she doubted that was possible. After all, surely nobody else could be like her!

The waitress returned with a trolley laden with a teapot, cups and plates. She placed the items on the table, followed by a cake stand with an assortment of sweet treats, along with scones and an array of sandwiches. Jan peered at the cakes and felt her mouth salivating. The raspberry jam smothered between two slices of Victoria sponge looked delicious, as did the lemon curd tart and cream horn.

'After you,' Terry said.

Jan would have liked to have put several cakes on her plate but, being polite, she started with a quarter piece of a sandwich. Even that was a treat.

'Have more than that,' Terry urged. 'You don't need to worry about watching your figure – I'll do that for you,' he added cheekily.

Jan grinned and placed a napkin across her lap. She ate another piece of sandwich and then reached out to take a cream horn, savouring the sugary puff pastry.

'You look like you're enjoying that,' Terry said with a chuckle.

'It's very yummy,' she replied and finished the last mouthful. She then went on to eat a lemon curd tart. The light pastry melted in her mouth and Jan thought it was sheer heaven.

'You like a bit of cake, don't you?'

Her mouth was still full and she nodded.

'Best make the most of it. My boss reckons there'll be food shortages soon.'

The cake now swallowed, Jan took a sip of tea and said, 'It won't make much difference in my house.'

'What do you mean?' Terry asked.

'My mother doesn't believe in having cakes or biscuits. She only gets the basic essentials like bread, eggs and cheese.'

'So what do you have for your dinner?'

'Bread and cheese or egg on toast.'

'What, that's it?'

'We have fish on Friday with a bit of mashed potato.'

'Don't you have any meat?'

'No. My mother won't buy any. She thinks she should give all her money to God and that He will provide for us.'

'I know you said your mum goes to church, but I didn't realise she had such strong views.'

Jan took a piece of Victoria sponge, but after just one bite she felt a bit queasy. She wasn't used to such rich food, and the thought of admitting the truth about her mother made her feel even worse. Yet she knew it was time to be honest with Terry. They'd been dating for a while now and if their relationship was going to last, he needed to know what they'd be up against.

She swallowed hard before speaking and hoped her revelation wouldn't make Terry run for the hills. 'I'm afraid I haven't told you everything about my mother,' she said quietly.

'At least you've got a mother. I was abandoned, dumped outside an orphanage.'

'I know, you told me, but sometimes, as awful as it sounds, I wish I'd been dumped too.'

'She can't be *that* bad.'

'Oh, Terry, she is. If I'm honest, I think she's a bit mad, and she seems to have got worse since my dad died ten years ago.'

'How do you mean?'

Jan dabbed the corner of her mouth with her napkin, placed it on the table and took a deep breath. 'She's obsessed with God and the Bible and is convinced the devil is putting temptation in our way. We don't have a wireless in the house because she thinks the devil will talk through it to lead us astray. She keeps the downstairs curtains drawn and the upstairs windows boarded up so that the devil can't see into the bedrooms.'

'Blimey, that sounds a bit extreme.'

'I know. My mother works hard as a housekeeper for the vicar but nearly everything she earns goes to the church, and she expects the same from me. I'm not allowed to wear any make-up and I only have a few clothes, mostly clothes that I've made myself or that are my mother's hand-me-downs. She doesn't allow me to have friends and certainly not a boyfriend.' Jan lowered her eyes and waited for Terry's response, secretly crossing her fingers under the table.

'Listen, you don't need none of that muck on your face. You're pretty enough without it. And your clothes look fine to me.'

She looked up, her smile one of relief. 'Thank you,' she whispered.

'There's no need for thanks, and as for the wireless, you ain't missing much, just a load of bulletins about the war. When it comes to food, if it's cake you want, it's cake you shall have and I'll bring you here as often as you like.'

She looked into Terry's sincere eyes and felt her own begin to well up.

'Don't cry, love. Your mother doesn't need to know about us,' he said, reaching across the table for her hand.

She fought to hold back her sobs. 'I can't believe you're so understanding. Most fellas would have run a mile.'

'Yeah, well, I ain't most fellas and we can't help who we was born to. It's you I want to see, not your mother, and if that means sneaking around, then so be it.'

At last Jan managed a watery smile and Terry said, 'Now, how's about another cuppa?'

Jan nodded and poured the tea, smiling as she did so.

'What would your mum do if she found out about us?'

'I don't know, Terry. Probably lock me in my room. Like I said, the window is boarded up so that the devil can't see in, and to keep me from seeing evil on the street. She's also put a big padlock on the door. The last time she locked me in, it was as a punishment for not singing clearly in church. I had a sore throat but it made no difference. She kept me in there for a week with just the Bible to read and bread and water to eat.'

'Bloomin' 'eck, that sounds over the top to me. It's a bit harsh. Where does she think you are now?'

'At work. As I've told you, I'm a companion for Mrs Savage in a big house by the park. She knows what my mother is like and is very understanding. She gave me the afternoon off so that I could see you.'

'That's good of her. But what about the evenings I've seen you? How have you got away with it?'

'Again, Mrs Savage has covered for me. She holds Bible classes at her home which Mother thinks I'm attending.'

'And tomorrow night?'

'That one's a bit trickier. I'm still working on it.'

'It'd be a right shame if you couldn't come for a drink on my birthday, but I wouldn't want to get you into trouble.'

'I'll try my best, Terry.'

'I hope you don't think I'm out of line asking you this, but have you considered moving out?'

Jan drew in another long sigh. 'Yes, I've thought about it a hundred times and more but I haven't found the courage.'

'For a young woman on her own, I suppose it can be pretty scary. Better the devil you know, eh?'

'Yes, probably,' she replied without enthusiasm.

They finished their tea and lightly chatted before jumping

into a black taxicab which took them to the cinema in the old Bolingbrook Hall. 'I hope you'll like the film,' Terry said. 'It's called *Jamaica Inn*, and it stars Charles Laughton and Maureen O'Hara.'

The names meant nothing to Jan, and after Terry had paid sixpence each for their tickets, they sat towards the back. Terry held her hand and she felt a shiver of delight, and then the lights dimmed. Jan was soon enthralled by the moving images on the big screen. It was the first time she'd been to the pictures and she found the film mesmerising.

When it came to an end, she couldn't believe how quickly the time had flown, and they stood for the national anthem, still holding hands. They made their way outside and she had to squint against the low light of the sun just beginning to set. Jan became worried about the time and said reluctantly, 'I'd better get home now.'

Terry hailed another cab and when they got out at Clapham Junction, he said, 'I'll walk you to the tram, and thanks, Jan, I've had a smashing day.'

'Me too,' she answered, her shyness lifting.

At the tram stop, Terry pulled her into his arms and with his finger under her chin, gently lifted her face. Jan could see the intensity in his eyes and her heart hammered when she realised he was going to kiss her. She closed her eyes and felt his warm lips on hers. The kiss was gentle and lingering. She should have felt embarrassed with all the people around, but Jan wished they could stay in that moment forever and that the kiss would never end.

'I hope I see you tomorrow,' he said huskily.

'Me too,' she answered and grudgingly pulled herself away to board the tram.

She took a window seat and as it sped off, she waved at Terry who blew her a kiss. She hadn't wanted to leave him and was missing him already. Her head filled with romantic notions of him, but as the tram approached her stop she came back to reality with a jolt. Now she had to face her mother.

David hadn't dared to ask his mother for more money as he knew she was saving all her spare change to pay off Errol. That meant his pockets were empty once again. It was Friday evening and he was bored as he ambled through to the kitchen to find his mum dusting a cake with icing sugar.

'You all right, Son?' she asked, wiping her hands down her apron.

'Yeah. Just a bit fed up.'

'The pub will be open soon. I'll treat you to a couple of pints, if you like?'

David thought about spending the evening in the pub but it had never really attracted a young crowd and he couldn't be bothered to listen to the old boys repeat their tales of when they'd fought in the Great War. Instead, he opted for a ride on his motorbike. 'Nah, though thanks for the offer. I'm going out for a bit.'

'Where you off to?'

'Nowhere special. I'm skint, so I'll just have a ride about.'

'Well, I hate to say it, but if you had a job you wouldn't be broke.'

David didn't answer but he knew she was right.

'Your father's been on at me again. He isn't happy with you hanging around the place all day. The sooner you find yourself some work the better. You know what he's like. He'll have me packing your bags and slinging them out the back door soon.'

'Yeah, all right, Mum. Don't keep harping on. I'll go down the labour exchange on Monday.'

'You make sure you do, or you'll be looking for somewhere else to live. Your father's words, not mine. If he goes through with his threat, there's nothing I'll be able to do to stop him.'

David huffed and marched from the kitchen. He'd heard enough of his mother's nagging and couldn't listen to her whining voice any longer. He went outside to his bike. Thankfully, there was still fuel in the tank, but he'd soon need some cash to fill it. It was looking more and more like he'd have to find himself a job and he scowled at the thought.

The sun was just beginning to dip and so was the temperature. He wished now that he'd worn his jacket instead of just a shirt and jumper. Nevertheless, it felt good to speed through the streets with the engine roaring between his legs, and he knew that heads were turning to admire him and his machine. As he came to the end of Stanmere Street, he stopped to check for traffic before turning onto the main road, but then a familiar figure strode confidently in front of his bike.

Stephanie Reynolds stood in the middle of the road with her hands on her hips, blocking his way. 'Hello, stranger,' she said tartly.

David's heart sank. This was all he needed – another person on at him about money.

'Have you been trying to avoid me?' she asked.

'No, course not. I've been busy.'

'Have you? I hope you've been busy working, cos I'm still waiting for my two quid.'

'Don't worry, you'll get your money. Now, if you don't mind, I've got things to do, so get out of my way.'

'But I do mind,' she snapped. 'I've heard your mother is paying back your debt to Errol because you ain't got any money to cough up. If that's true, how are you gonna pay me?'

'With respect, Steph, it's none of your business. You'll be paid and that's all you need to know.'

'That's not how I see it, Dave. If you can't pay me, you'd best own up now, or I'll have to have a word with my Errol.'

David was in no doubt that the woman would go through with her threat and so he softened his approach. 'All right, I admit I've been struggling, but I'll be working next week and I'll sort you out as soon as I get my first pay packet.'

'You'd better, because, as I said, if you don't, I'll tell Errol that you forced yourself on me.'

'I didn't. You know you were willing.'

'Maybe, but Errol will believe what I tell him.'

'All right, you'll get your money, but just give me a week or two.'

'One week, that's all you're getting,' she said, sauntering off.

He watched her shapely hips wiggling as she walked away and thought to himself that she was a right looker in a slutty sort of way. It was a shame he couldn't remember what she'd been like between the sheets. He was paying for something he had no recollection of and could only assume he'd enjoyed himself. It hadn't been worth it, but he did glean a small amount of satisfaction in knowing that he had one up on Errol. However, bumping into Stephanie had unnerved him.

It could have been Errol instead of her and he was the last person David wanted to see, so he cut his ride short and headed back to the pub. At least if he sat in the bar and had a couple of pints, he could surreptitiously watch Rachel.

'That's really nice, Win,' said Rachel as she looked at the cake Winnie was proudly showing off.

'I'll put it in the back kitchen. It's cool in there and will keep fresh for tomorrow night. I hope Terry likes it.'

'I'm sure he will. He loves your cooking. Talk of the devil ...'

The door opened and Terry walked in grinning like a man who'd won the football pools. Winnie dashed through to the back with the cake and Rachel greeted the man.

'Someone is looking very pleased with himself,' she said.

'I've had a smashing day.'

'Good. Your date with Jan went well, then?'

'Yep. She's a corker.'

'I'm looking forward to meeting the lady who makes you smile like that. She must be very special.'

'She is, Rachel. I reckon you and her will get on like a house on fire. I just hope she can come tomorrow.'

'Why wouldn't she?' Rachel asked as she handed Terry his usual drink.

'It's a bit of a long story but it's her mother. Don't let Jan know I've told you, but from what she's said, the woman is really strict and would do her nut if she found out Jan was seeing me.'

Winnie bustled up beside Rachel. 'What's all this?' she asked.

'Terry's girlfriend. Her mother doesn't want her seeing him,' Rachel answered.

'Have you met her mother?'

'No, Win, I think that's out of the question.'

'Maybe if you're introduced she'd see for herself what a nice young man you are. I'm sure if she met you there'd be no objections to you dating her daughter.'

'It isn't as simple as that. Jan said her mother is a bit mad.'

'In what way is she mad?' Winnie asked, frowning.

'She's a religious fanatic, and gives most of her money to the church, but as I said, don't let on to Jan that I've told you.'

'Mum's the word,' Win said.

'We're gonna keep it quiet that we're courting for now – you know, we're meeting in secret. It just means it might be a bit difficult for her to get out tomorrow evening.'

'She's a grown woman, surely she can stand up for herself and tell her mother what's what?'

'I don't think she's got the nerve, Winnie.'

'That's a shame, but as long as you're both happy. I hope she can make it tomorrow. It'd be lovely to meet her.'

'She'll try her best. But you will be gentle with her, won't you?'

'What do you mean?' Rachel asked.

'I told you, she's shy. She might be a bit, you know, over-whelmed.'

'Don't you worry; me and Rachel will take good care of her, won't we, love?'

'Yes, we certainly will,' Rachel answered, thinking it was sweet that Terry was so concerned about his girlfriend. He was proof that not all men were like Jim and David.

The door opened again and Rachel looked past Terry to

see David walk in. Instantly, her light mood changed and her jaw clenched. She tried to smile, for Winnie's sake, but the sight of him put her back up.

'Hello, Son,' Winnie said, clearly pleased to see him. 'Changed your mind, then? Fancy a pint?'

'Yeah, thanks,' he replied and came to stand beside Terry as Winnie poured his drink.

'You all right, mate?' Terry asked.

'Yeah. You?'

'I'm fine.'

Rachel listened to the curt and limited exchange between the two men, not surprised at their lack of conversation. It had never been said, but Rachel was sure Terry didn't think much of David. They were in complete contrast to each other and not only in looks. Terry was slim and blond, whereas David was broad and dark-haired. Terry was kind and caring, unlike David, who was selfish and spoilt. Rachel had often thought that Terry would have been a better son to Winnie. She wondered if Winnie thought so too, though Rachel doubted it. Winnie could see no wrong in her son, but if the dear woman knew the truth, it would break her heart.

'Did you have a nice ride on your bike, Son?' Winnie asked.

'Not bad. It's getting chilly now though.'

'You silly sod, you should have worn your jacket. And I wish you'd wear one of them crash helmets.'

'I don't need a helmet. I'm a good driver.'

'Maybe, but it's the other road users you need to be careful of. There was an accident up the junction last week, and one near the Prince's Head.'

'Mum, stop bloody fussing. You're souring me pint,' David hissed.

Rachel looked scornfully at David. How dare he speak to his mother in that tone, especially as she was footing his bill. Terry didn't look impressed either and Rachel could tell he was biting his tongue.

Winnie went to serve another customer but not before Rachel had seen the hurt expression on her face. She felt sorry for the woman. Winnie was nothing but nice and deserved better than a disrespectful son like David. It added to her hatred of him. Thankfully, David mooched off, picked up a newspaper, and went to sit in the corner.

'Anyway, Rachel, ain't it about time you found yourself a nice chap?' Terry asked.

'I'm fine as I am,' she answered, abruptly, taken aback by Terry's reference to her non-existent love life.

He held his hands up in the air. 'All right, I can take a hint – it's none of my business.'

'Sorry, Terry, I didn't mean to sound rude.'

'No, I should have kept me big gob shut.'

'It's all right, I'm used to it,' she said and smiled. 'Everyone's always on at me about settling down with a bloke, but I'm really not interested.'

'Like I said, it's none of my business, but I've always wondered why you're not seeing anyone.'

'Honestly, Terry, I wouldn't want to bore you with the details.'

'You couldn't bore me even if you tried.'

Again, she smiled warmly at him and thought Jan had done well to win his heart. Just like Jim had once won hers.

'I got hurt. It was a long time ago but I don't think I'll ever get over it,' she said, reluctant to talk about it.

'Sorry, love, that's horrible. Bad things shouldn't happen to a lovely girl like you. Do you wanna tell me who hurt you? I'll go and bash him up for you.'

Terry's remark was said with joviality but Rachel could still feel the pain from the memory of what she'd been through. No, she didn't wish any harm to come to Jim, but because of him she'd never trust another man again.

'Are you upsetting my barmaid?' Winnie said as she came alongside Rachel.

'Not intentionally,' Terry answered, looking worried.

'Of course he isn't. You know me, Win, I always bristle at the mention of a boyfriend.'

'It's no wonder. That Jim has got a lot to answer for. Go on, get yourself out the back and put the kettle on. I'm gasping for a cuppa.'

Rachel was grateful to be away from the curious look Terry was giving her. He could be like an old washerwoman sometimes, always wanting to know the gossip, and Winnie was more than happy to pass on to him anything she'd heard. Rachel guessed that Winnie would most likely be telling Terry about her unfortunate love life. It didn't make for pretty story-telling and she was glad she didn't have to hear it. Though she tried to push the memories of Jim to the back of her mind, his face would still haunt her dreams and she wished wholeheartedly that she'd never fallen in love with him.

6

Winnie had decorated the pub with colourful hand-made paper streamers that she always dragged out for special occasions and she had pre-prepared a few nibbles, including a large pork pie, Terry's favourite. She stood back and glanced around her empty pub, pleased with how it looked. But she sighed deeply, thinking it a shame that several of Terry's mates wouldn't be coming to the party as they'd already enthusiastically enlisted with the army. Many young men had, believing in glory, but Winnie knew the reality of war and the price these men would pay. She thought of Mrs Sandland's husband. He'd been unwell for years now, since returning from the trenches in France. He lived in his own world, stuck in his darkest moments, often screaming out in terror. Mrs Sandland doubted he'd ever recover. She often said it would have been better for him if he'd been killed instead of enduring never-ending misery and fear. Winnie hoped Terry's friends wouldn't succumb to the same fate as Mr Sandland, but these young men, some barely out of short trousers, seemed to think they were invincible.

She jumped when she heard Brian's thunderous voice. 'What the bleedin' hell is going on down here?'

Winnie quickly turned to see him standing behind the bar. 'It's Terry's birthday so we're having a bit of a do,' she answered apprehensively, hoping Brian wouldn't kick off.

'I don't suppose he's paying for all this fuss, is he?'

'No, but, well, I always like to do something nice for him. He's a good lad.'

'I couldn't care less if he's the Prince of bleedin' Wales – if he ain't paying for it, he don't get it.'

'But we're having a party, Brian. Everyone's coming, it'll be good for business.'

'I don't need you to tell me how to run my business. Now get this shit down and get back upstairs.'

Winnie was about to protest but, after seeing the angry look in Brian's eyes, she thought better of it and dragged a chair across the room. She climbed up to reach for the paper streamer.

'You'll do yourself a mischief standing up on that chair and then what good will you be to me?'

Thanks for your concern, she thought scathingly but she didn't say anything.

'Hurry up. I want you upstairs in five minutes,' he ordered before stamping away.

'Horrible, rotten sod,' she mumbled under her breath. He was so mean-spirited. What harm could a few streamers do? It was a good job Brian didn't know about the food she'd prepared, or that she'd given Piano Pete a couple of bob to play a few tunes later. The old piano had come with the pub and was probably older than she was. It needed tuning and two of the keys didn't work, but when Pete tinkled the ivories everyone in the pub usually joined in for a sing-along.

Once the streamers were down, Winnie begrudgingly trudged up the stairs to see what her husband wanted. She found him sitting in his armchair next to a roaring fire in the hearth, listening to wireless bulletins. The newsreader was talking about the Siege of Warsaw ending, another victory for the Germans. Winnie didn't want to hear it and wished Brian would turn off the wireless. It was too upsetting to think of the Germans winning and taking over Europe. As long as they stayed out of Britain, she could pretend they weren't really at war.

'You took your time,' he moaned. 'Go and get a bucket of hot water and a good pair of clippers. My toenails need cutting.'

Winnie baulked at the thought of attending to her husband's stinking feet but she carried out his instructions. First she soaked them in the hot water, then clipped his nails and threw the cuttings onto the fire, all the while trying not to breathe too deeply. The smell was stomach turning and once she'd finished, she rushed to wash her hands with carbolic soap. The dirty, lazy git, she thought as she scrubbed her hands. If he bathed more than once a fortnight and changed his socks more regularly, maybe his feet wouldn't stink like rotten meat. At least she didn't have to get into the same bed as them anymore.

She was just about to go back downstairs when she heard his booming voice again shouting her name.

'Winnie! Win, get in here – quick.'

Winnie stood at the top of the stairs and looked towards the ceiling. 'God give me strength,' she whispered, then traipsed back into the front room. She couldn't see Brian's face. He was reading the newspaper and spoke from behind it.

'Bring up some more coal for the fire,' he demanded.

Her eyes widened as her frustration reached breaking point. 'Bring it up yourself,' she snapped and stamped out, slamming the door behind her.

As she trod heavily down the stairs, she could hear Brian shouting for her. For once, Winnie ignored him and smiled to herself. That'll blinkin' show him, she thought, feeling surprisingly triumphant. The feeling was short-lived as it dawned on her that she'd have to face his fury later. But for now it was Terry's birthday and even without paper streamers, Winnie was determined that the Battersea Tavern was going to throw him a very jolly party.

Jan chewed on her thumbnail, deep in thought as she sat on an uncomfortable wooden seat at the small kitchen table, a slice of bread and a boiled egg in front of her.

'Gracious God, we have sinned against Thee. We are unworthy of Thy mercy. Pardon our sins. Bless our food for we eat and drink to Thy glory. For Jesus Christ's sake. Amen,' her mother intoned.

'Amen,' Jan parroted and quickly removed her thumb away from her mouth before her mother opened her eyes and saw. She looked down at her plate. The meal looked unappetising but under her mother's scrutinising eye she ate with feigned enthusiasm. Conversation was forbidden at the table so dinner was finished in silence. Jan cleared the table and as she placed the dishes in the sink, with her back to her mother, she found the strength to say, 'I'm going to visit Mrs Savage this evening.

I promised I would help her sew the patchwork quilts for the orphanage.'

'Why didn't you tell me this earlier?'

'I'm sorry. I thought I had and then I remembered that I hadn't.'

As she rinsed the plates under the cold tap, there was a long, quiet pause.

'You will be back here by ten,' her mother said finally.

Jan could have squealed with delight but she remained calm. 'Yes, Mother, of course,' she replied stoically.

'When you return, you will read the Bible for two hours. You must make up the time you are missing this evening.'

'Yes, I understand.'

'Good. In future, if Mrs Savage requires your time for anything other than Bible studies, she is to ask my permission. Is that clear?'

'Yes, Mother.'

As she dried the plates, her mother went to her room and at last Jan allowed herself to smile. In the morning at church she'd have to have a discreet word with Mrs Savage before her mother spoke to the woman. She couldn't bear to think of the consequences of her mother discovering the truth about her real whereabouts this evening. She had no idea what the consequences would be, but knew they'd be catastrophic.

Jan grabbed her coat from the understairs cupboard and as she buttoned down the front, she called, 'I'm going now. I'll be home at ten.'

She pulled open the front door and turned to see her mother coming back downstairs, her voice harsh as she said, 'Do not shout in this house. The devil will hear your raised voice and come for your soul. You must speak with grace at all times.'

'Yes, Mother. Sorry, Mother,' she said obediently, then closed the door quietly behind her.

She could have skipped along the street. It felt wonderful to be free and even better that she was spending the evening with Terry. She didn't have a birthday present for him but felt sure he'd understand and wouldn't be too disappointed.

Before long Jan stood anxiously outside the entrance to the Battersea Tavern trying to pluck up the courage to walk inside. She had no idea what to expect behind the doors and wished now that she'd arranged to meet Terry outside.

'Excuse me, miss,' a middle-aged man said.

'Sorry,' Jan answered and stepped to one side to allow the man to pass and go into the pub.

As he pulled the door open, Jan craned her neck to try and get a glimpse inside. The room appeared smoky and she couldn't see very much.

'You coming in?' the man asked, halfway through the door.

'Erm... err – if you know Terry Card, could you send him out here please?'

The man pulled the door open wider and Jan could see the back of Terry standing at the bar.

'Tel, there's a bird out here wants you,' the man called.

Terry turned around and smiled widely when he spotted Jan outside. The door closed, but opened again moments later as Terry walked out with his arms open. 'You made it,' he said as he scooped her into them.

'Yes, but I have to be home by ten.'

'Don't you worry, I'll make sure you're not late. Come

inside, Winnie and Rachel are waiting to meet you,' he said, taking her hand and pulling her gently towards the door.

'Wait – I don't know about this,' Jan said nervously, beginning to panic.

'It's all right. They don't bite. I'll look after you, I promise.'

She nodded her head, but bit her bottom lip.

'Good girl,' Terry said and gave her hand a little squeeze.

Once inside, Jan was greeted by a buxom, plump older woman who, she assumed, was Winnie, and an attractive younger woman, slim and blonde, who, she thought, must be Rachel. They were just as Terry had described and their welcoming smiles instantly relaxed her.

'We've heard all about you,' Winnie said. 'It's lovely to meet you and you're just as pretty as Terry said. What can I get you to drink, love?'

'I'll have a lemonade please,' Jan said, wishing she had a lovely pink dress like Rachel's. It looked like the latest fashion, calf-length, with a tie neck fashioned into a bow, and the skirt slightly flared.

'Terry said you had a smashing day out yesterday. I've never been to the tea rooms; is it posh there?' Rachel asked.

'Oh, yes, it's very nice.'

'Perhaps you two could go one afternoon. It would do you good to get out,' Winnie said to Rachel.

'Yes, I'd like that, if Jan would?'

'Yes, I would,' she answered eagerly. She thought it would be lovely to have the company of a woman her own age for a change. Mrs Savage was nice enough but the woman was nearly eighty and they had little in common.

'Now you're here, I'll get the cake out,' Winnie said.

She returned moments later, singing, 'Happy Birthday', and every customer in the pub joined in.

Jan looked around, taking in the friendly faces and soaking up the jolly atmosphere. This place wasn't anything like she'd expected. It was a far cry from how her mother had told her it would be. The pub wasn't full of sinners doing disgusting things. In fact, it felt just as welcoming as the church.

After the cake had been sliced and consumed, an elderly gentleman with an unlit roll-up in his mouth began to play the piano. The tune seemed to be familiar to everyone and they happily sang along. But Jan didn't know the words to 'Daisy, Daisy', and when that song finished, they started singing, 'My old man said, "Foller the van"'. It really was fun and Jan found herself clapping in time to the music. She'd never had such a good time.

'You can't beat a good old-fashioned knees-up,' Winnie said breathlessly when Pete on the piano was having a break. 'When is your birthday, love? Perhaps you'd like to have a party in here?'

'It's next March. I'll be twenty-seven on the thirtieth of March. But I'm not sure about a party. I've never had one before and I don't really know anyone to invite.'

Jan noticed that Winnie's smile seemed to have vanished and the woman was now looking at her in a peculiar way. She hoped she hadn't said something to upset her.

'You don't need to invite anyone. We'll do that for you, ain't that right, Win?' Rachel said.

Winnie didn't answer and was still staring at Jan with a strange expression on her face and it was beginning to make Jan feel uncomfortable.

'Erm … excuse me,' Winnie muttered and she hurried away.

'Is she all right?' Terry asked.

'I don't know. She looked like she'd seen a ghost,' Rachel answered. 'Oh, great. Now look who's just walked in.'

Jan turned round to see a haggard-looking drunk woman stumbling towards them. She immediately tensed and stepped closer to Terry. This appeared to be just the sort of woman her mother had warned her about.

The woman staggered up to the bar to lean on it. 'There she is, with a face that could sour milk. Look at her, the miserable cow,' she shouted at Rachel, her words slurred.

'Bugger off, Hilda. We're having a party and you ain't invited,' Rachel hissed.

'Says who?'

'Says me. Best you scarper before Winnie sees you in that state and bars you from the pub for good.'

'Don't tell me what to do, you ungrateful bitch. You don't know what I went through for you. None of you do!' Hilda yelled, throwing her arm through the air.

Rachel sighed heavily and softened her tone. 'Please, Hilda, don't make a scene. Just go home and I'll see you tomorrow.'

'What makes you think I wanna see you, eh? There you go again, thinking you're so bloody special. Let me tell you something – you ain't nothing. You couldn't even keep your fiancé happy. He didn't think you was special, did he? No, not when he was sleeping with our sister.'

'That's enough! Get out. Go on, get out!' Rachel shouted.

The pub fell silent and all eyes were on Hilda and Rachel.

Jan didn't like the sudden change in atmosphere and felt nervous. 'Can you take me home?' she whispered to Terry.

He swiftly placed his arm protectively over her shoulder and pulled Jan close before addressing the abusive woman.

'Hilda, it's my party and, like Rachel said, you're not invited. Off you trot, there's a good girl.'

'Don't patronise me,' Hilda said venomously. 'I was going anyway. You lot are boring me.'

With that she stumbled off and when the door closed behind her, it felt as if the whole pub sighed with relief. But her visit had marred the party atmosphere and everyone seemed more subdued now.

'Are you all right?' Terry asked Rachel.

'Yes, I'm fine, thanks. I'm used to Hilda. You know what she's like. A right Jekyll and Hyde. Sorry about her, Jan. That was my dear sister.'

'Oh, I see,' Jan answered, unsure of how to respond.

'I can't believe she brought that up in public,' Rachel said.

'What, about your ex-fiancé?' Terry asked.

'Yes. It's something I've tried to put behind me but it's difficult when she keeps mentioning it.'

'Winnie told me what happened. It wasn't your fault and you shouldn't feel bad about it,' Terry said softly.

'Yeah, I know. Thanks. Anyway, some party this is. Right, drinks all round, on me.'

Jan was intrigued to know what they were talking about and could see that though Rachel was filling glasses, she was close to tears. Jan quietly asked Terry about their conversation and Terry reiterated what Winnie had told him – Rachel had been due to be married to a bloke called Jim, but, on the night before their wedding, he took Rachel's sister to his bed. Rachel had been heartbroken and, to make matters worse, her sister had fallen pregnant. Jim abandoned the sister who was then ostracised for being an unmarried mother and she went into labour alone.'

'Oh, that's terrible,' Jan whispered.

'Yes, and sadly, she and the baby died in childbirth. Rachel was devastated. She couldn't bear to remain at home and left the borough, moving here to Battersea.'

'Oh, my goodness, how tragic,' Jan said. She knew that her mother would see it differently and would condemn Rachel's sister as a Jezebel. Jan couldn't agree with her mother's view of God. She preached fire and brimstone, often quoting the Old Testament, but Jan preferred to read and listen to the New Testament and the teachings of Jesus. He preached of love and forgiveness, not vengeance.

'I feel sorry for Rachel,' said Terry. 'She never dates now and keeps herself to herself. I was surprised when she said she'd like to go to the tea rooms with you.'

'It sounds to me like both of us could do with a friend,' Jan said thoughtfully, and looked down the bar to where Rachel was rinsing glasses. From what she'd seen of her, she thought they'd get on well together. Just as long as her mother didn't find out.

Winnie sat upstairs at the kitchen table with her face buried in her hands. It couldn't be possible – could it? Hardly a day had passed when she hadn't imagined this happening. Half of her wanted it to be true more than anything in the world, but the other half was petrified of the truth coming out. How would Brian react? Not well, she suspected. And David, would he accept it? She doubted it.

'What you doing up here?' Brian asked.

Winnie looked towards the kitchen doorway where her husband was standing but she couldn't bring herself to tell him what she suspected. 'I've got a stinking headache,' she lied.

'Huh, you ain't dying, so get back downstairs before some robbing bastard pinches my takings again.'

'But, Brian, my head is throbbing and Rachel is downstairs keeping an eye on everything.'

'You put too much trust in that girl. For all you know, it could have been her who stole the money.'

'Don't talk daft. Rachel hasn't got a bad bone in her body. She'd never steal from us.'

'Daft, am I?' Brian roared.

'I didn't mean it like that,' Winnie answered quickly, concerned that she'd set him off again.

'It's you who's bleedin' daft, if you think you can trust a barmaid. I ain't gonna tell you again – get downstairs and do your job. *NOW!*'

Winnie was quick to scrape her chair back and she hurried towards the door. Brian stepped to one side for her to pass, but as she did, he cuffed the back of her head.

'And don't come back up here until all the punters have left,' he warned.

As she plodded down the stairs, she could feel tears welling in her eyes. 'Pull yourself together,' she whispered quietly to herself. She drew in a long, steadying breath. 'And fix that smile on your face,' she ordered, before walking into the bar. Scanning the room, she couldn't see Terry or Jan and then Rachel approached.

'You all right?'

Winnie looked past the girl as she answered. 'Yes, I'm fine, thanks, love. Where's Terry?'

'He had to take Jan home. We've had right fun and games

while you've been upstairs. Hilda came in, shouting her mouth off, as usual.'

'You got rid of her, then?'

'Terry did. But I think she frightened the life out of poor Jan.'

'I don't doubt it. Your sister is enough to frighten the life out of Hitler. Perhaps we should send her to Germany. The Jerries might think twice about invading Britain if they know they'll have to come up against the likes of Hilda Duff.'

'Ha, Winnie, you do make me laugh.'

'She's a nice girl, that Jan, don't you think so?'

'Yeah, really sweet. And she's obviously besotted with Terry. You can tell by the way she looks at him.'

'Did you notice what colour eyes she's got?' Winnie asked.

'Brown, I think, like yours. Why?'

'No matter. Just curious,' Winnie said flippantly. But it did matter. It mattered a lot and now her suspicions were further confirmed. She tried to fight back the tears that were threatening to fall but it was no use and she turned away from the few remaining customers.

'Win, are you crying?' Rachel asked, her voice full of concern, which only made Winnie sob harder.

'Oh, blimey, what on earth's wrong?'

'Nothing. I'm fine.'

'You're obviously not. What is it?'

'Get rid of this lot. It's time they went home anyway. I'll be out the back making a cuppa,' Winnie answered and, sniffing, she trudged off.

In the kitchen, as she waited for the kettle to boil, Winnie felt she had to tell someone and, regardless of her husband's opinion of Rachel, she knew she could rely on her discretion. Ten minutes later, Rachel joined her in the kitchen.

'I've locked up. Now, what's got you all worked up?' she asked as she pulled out a chair opposite Winnie and sat down.

'You have to promise me that you won't say a word about this.'

'I promise, Win. You know you can tell me anything and it'll stay between us.'

'Yes, I know, love. And I need to tell someone because I don't know what to do.'

'Is it David? Has he done something to upset you?'

'No, no, not at all,' Winnie answered shaking her head. And unable to contain herself any longer, as tears rolled down her cheeks, she blurted out, 'I think Jan is my daughter.'

7

Late on Monday morning, David returned home from the labour exchange pleased with himself and hoping his mum would be too. He'd secured himself a position in a pillow-making factory and was starting work the next day. Not on the sewing machines — that was women's work — but in the packing department. The pay wasn't great but it would do for now to help keep Stephanie Reynolds off his back.

He found his mum in the kitchen and was looking forward to seeing the look on her face when he told her his news. 'Can you make me a packed lunch tomorrow?' he said as he sat at the kitchen table.

His mother didn't turn round from the stove and muttered, 'Yeah, all right.'

'Aren't you going to ask me why I need a packed lunch?'

'Eh?' she said, still stirring whatever she was cooking.

'I said, aren't you going to ask me why I need a packed lunch?'

'Oh, yes, I suppose. Tell me, then,' she said, though David thought she seemed uninterested.

'I've got myself a job. I'll be starting tomorrow in the pillow factory up Nine Elms.'

'Oh, right. Good. Well done, Son,' she said, still engrossed in her cooking and not bothering to turn round to give him her full attention.

He was disappointed in her reaction. Granted, he hadn't expected her to do cartwheels, but after all the fuss she'd made about him finding work, he thought she might have been a little more pleased. 'It's not bad,' he told her. 'Weekly pay, and a half-day on Saturday. I'll be in the packing department, though it shouldn't be too strenuous. I mean, how heavy can pillows be?'

'Nice. Just be careful of your chest with all that feather dust about.'

'It that it? Is that all you've got to say?' he asked, disgruntled.

'Sorry, Son. I'm away with the fairies this morning. That's really good news and your father will be pleased. Have you told him?' she asked, finally dragging herself away from whatever was so engrossing in the saucepan.

'No, not yet. The tight old git will probably want some of my wages for my keep.'

'Probably,' his mum said and then turned back to the stove.

'On account of me now earning, you couldn't lend me a couple of quid, could you?'

'Not really. As it is, you know I'm struggling to find the money for that Errol.'

'Please, Mum, just until the end of the week. I'll pay you back, I promise.'

With a huff she shook her head, but then walked across the kitchen, saying, 'I can stretch to a pound but that's your lot.' She rifled in her handbag and slammed the cash down on the table before returning to the stove again. David thought she was in a strange mood and assumed his father had been giving her a hard time again. She seemed subdued and not her usual cheery self.

'Great, thanks,' he said and collected the money, hoping that, come Friday, she'd forget about being paid back. Especially as a large chunk of his wage packet would be going to Stephanie Reynolds to keep her happy.

Realising he wasn't going to get any further conversation from his mother and satisfied with the pound in his pocket, David scraped his chair back and headed for his bedroom. Much to his disappointment, he met his father in the hallway.

'So, you're still out of work,' his dad said, eyeing him disdainfully.

'Nope. I start a new job tomorrow actually.'

'Not before bloody time. What are you gonna be doing?'

'I'm working in the packing department of a pillow factory.'

'Oh well, a job is a job, I suppose. Not that you'll be in it for long. The army will be calling you up soon. And a job in a poxy pillow factory ain't gonna keep you from doing your bit for King and Country. I just hope the army can make a man out of you.'

David ignored his father's remark and carried on towards his bedroom. Just before he closed the door, he heard his dad's voice again.

'I'll be wanting your keep on Friday. You've been living off your mother and me for long enough. It's time you paid your way.'

He closed the door quickly. What was the point in him

slogging his guts out in a factory when everything he earned was going to someone else – Errol, Stephanie and now his father too? At this rate, he'd be lucky if he had enough left from his wages to buy a bag of chips. Yet if it kept him from getting a good hiding, then he supposed it would be worth it.

Winnie was going through the motions of preparing Brian's breakfast, then washing and dressing, but she only had one thing on her mind – Jan. She'd barely slept last night; her mind had been filled with images of the baby she'd been forced to give up for adoption. It had been twenty-six years ago but the picture of the baby's sweet face was still clearly etched in her memory. Winnie had only seen her child for a minute before the midwife handed her to a nurse who hurried the child away. It had broken Winnie's heart but, at the time, she'd been only eighteen years old and unmarried and her parents hadn't given her any other choice. She'd hated them for what they'd forced her to do and had never forgiven them. Perhaps that had been the reason she'd so readily married Brian, to escape an unhappy home and to get away from her overbearing parents. Every time she'd looked at them, she'd been reminded of how unfairly and cruelly they'd treated her and Alma. That's what she'd named her precious girl – Alma. Though she knew her adoptive parents would have changed her name.

Winnie was grateful when Rachel arrived early for work. It would give them the chance to have a chat in private. She'd spilt her heart out to the girl on Saturday night and again after lunch on Sunday, yet still hadn't come to a decision about what to do.

'There's a fresh pot of tea made,' she told Rachel who followed her through to the back kitchen.

'You don't look like you slept much last night,' Rachel commented as she took her hat and coat off.

'No, I didn't. That's two nights running now. I'm exhausted thinking about it but I still don't know how to approach Jan or even if I should.'

'Sit down, Win; I'll pour us a cuppa.'

With a long day ahead of her, Winnie was glad to take the weight off her feet.

'Right, try and put the past behind you and look at the facts in front of you now,' Rachel suggested. 'Apart from Jan having her birthday on the same day as your daughter was born and the same colour eyes as you, there's nothing else to suggest she's your long-lost daughter?'

'No – but also yes. I can't explain it, Rachel. It's a feeling inside. I just *know* she's Alma. Look, this is me when I was her age. Can you see how alike we are?' she said, pulling an old, tatty black-and-white photograph from her cardigan pocket.

'To be honest, Win, it's difficult to tell from this. I suppose there could be a resemblance but you don't even know if Jan was adopted. Even if she was, her parents may not have told her about it.'

'I realise that and it makes talking to her all the more difficult. You're right; if she is my daughter and her parents never told her that she'd been adopted, can you imagine how much of a shock that would be?'

'Yes, it would. But from what Jan said, I don't think she gets on with her mother.'

'Terry said the woman's mad, and it makes things worse, Rachel. I had hoped Alma would go to a good home, a happy home, but it sounds far from that. Even so, news like this could still knock her sideways. But I can't do nothing. I have to know if she's my girl, and if she is, I need her to know that I didn't want to give her up.' Winnie could feel tears pricking her eyes again and tried to hold them in. She clasped her warm cup of tea in both hands and gazed into the liquid.

'If I found out that you were my mum, I'd be over the moon. Perhaps Jan will feel the same.'

'I hope so, Rachel, I really do. But what if she hates me for giving her up?'

'When she hears the circumstances, I'm sure she'll understand. Are you going to talk to her?'

Winnie sucked in a deep breath and lifted her eyes from her teacup. 'Yes, I think I am. I've got to. I have to know if Jan is my Alma. Oh, Gawd, I really hope she is. I've waited for nearly twenty-seven years to tell my girl how much I love her...' As her voice trailed off, tears fell freely. She pulled a handkerchief from the sleeve of her cardigan and blew her nose. 'I'm sorry, love. Look at the state of me, silly old moo.'

'Don't be sorry, Win. This is big – really big – and it's bound to stir up all sorts of emotions. If Jan does turn out to be your daughter, then I think she's a very lucky young lady.'

'Thanks, love. It means a lot to hear that. Now enough of this soppy sentiment, there's work to do and there's nothing I can do about Jan right now. I'll have to wait until Wednesday when Terry comes in with his washing. I'll have a word then and ask him to bring Jan to see me.'

Rachel took their cups to the sink. 'I know it sounds silly but I'm quite excited for you.'

'Yes, me too. Though if Jan is my Alma, I'm not sure how Brian and David will take the news. But I'll just have to cross that bridge when I come to it.'

'Please, Mother, let me out,' Jan called through her locked bedroom door. 'Mrs Savage will be expecting me this morning.' But Jan knew her pleas would be ignored and she was wasting her breath.

She'd returned home from the Battersea Tavern just before ten o'clock, careful not to upset her mother. All had seemed well until she'd gone to bed. That had been when she'd heard her mother turning the key in the padlock outside. Jan had flown out of bed, across the room, and shouted to her mother, but there'd been no response. And now, after another day and a second night imprisoned in her room, though she wasn't quite sure of the time, she could tell it was morning from the light that shone through a crack in the window boards.

Defeated, Jan slumped to the floor and rested her head against the door. How long would her mother keep her locked up for this time? And what had she done to deserve it? Surely her mother couldn't know about Terry or that she'd been in a pub? But what if her mother had spoken to Mrs Savage? The woman was happy to cover for her, but Mrs Savage had no idea that she'd told her mother she'd been sewing quilts with her on Saturday night. Her mother was bound to have seen Mrs Savage at church yesterday morning.

Jan's ears pricked up when she heard her mother's footsteps coming up the bare wooden steps and then across the floorboards towards the bedroom. 'Mother – Mother, are you there?'

'Do not speak to me. You have been seduced by Satan. You

will remain in there until your soul has been cleansed. The devil must be banished from you. You must be punished for your sins. God forgive you. I cannot set eyes on evil or your blackened soul. You have been contaminated by this unholy world. You've been led by temptation and will perish in the flames of hell!'

Jan's eyes widened. She didn't know what her mother was rambling on about but it was worse than normal. 'Please, Mother, I swear I haven't done anything wrong.'

'You speak with a forked tongue! It's Satan who puts these lies into your filthy mouth! You danced with the devil himself on Saturday night. I could smell him on your clothes.'

Jan gasped as she realised that she must have come home from the pub smelling of cigarettes and tobacco. But her mother hadn't mentioned anything about Mrs Savage so maybe she hadn't yet spoken to her. She'd be digging herself in deeper with more lies but she had to try to pacify her mother. 'No, no, not the devil, Mother,' she said fervently. Then she crossed her fingers as she added, 'When I was on my way home from Mrs Savage, I stopped to help an old man cross the road. He was smoking a clay pipe and that was what you could smell on my clothes. His strong tobacco must have lingered on the wool of my coat.'

Her mother's long silence indicated that she was considering Jan's explanation.

'Please, Mother. Have you spoken to Mrs Savage? Did you see her at church yesterday? I know she's old and gets confused, but she will tell you the truth. I was with her, I swear. The devil has no room in my heart, Mother. There is only room for God.'

Jan felt awful lying to her mother and terrible for involving

Mrs Savage, but it was the only way she'd get to see Terry. She longed to leave home, and her mother's actions this morning were making her more determined than ever to find a place of her own. In reality, Jan knew that what she earned as a companion to Mrs Savage wouldn't cover the cost of rent and bills, but surely there had to be a way. She couldn't stand living like this any longer and she knew it wasn't normal. What worried her most was, if she stayed much longer, she might be driven as mad as her mother.

8

On Wednesday, Rachel noticed that every time the pub door opened, Winnie looked over to see who had come in, and her face would drop with disappointment when it wasn't Terry. The woman had been ticking down the days, minutes and seconds until now, desperate to see Terry so that she could speak to Jan. Rachel really hoped that when she did, it would have a happy ending, especially for Winnie, but there was a possibility that a lot of people could end up being hurt.

When the door opened again, it was Rachel's face that dropped this time. Hilda walked in, though Rachel was pleased to see that, for once, her sister didn't look drunk. In fact, for a change, she was wearing a rather smart outfit and her hair was neatly waved.

'Don't say a word, just get me a drink,' Hilda said as she marched towards the bar.

'Where have you been, all done up to the nines?' Rachel asked.

'Wasting my time, that's where.'

'All right, there's no need to bite my head off.'

'Sorry, Rachel, I didn't mean to snap at you, darling. I've just had a wasted morning and I'm dying for a drink.'

Rachel wished her sister was reasonable like this more often. Without a drink in her, Hilda could be kind and caring but it was whisky that ruined her and Rachel was reluctant to pour her one. She knew that by the time Hilda reached the bottom of the glass and was ordering her second and then third one, her personality would change and the nasty Hilda would rear her ugly head.

'Do you want to tell me how you've wasted a morning?' she asked, hoping for a decent conversation before Hilda became aggressive or incoherent.

'It's me own silly fault. I got made a fool of – again.'

'How? Are you all right?' Rachel asked, genuinely concerned.

'Yes, I'm fine, but I've learned a good lesson. No man can be trusted. Rich or poor, they're all the bleedin' same.'

Rachel placed Hilda's whisky on the counter. Her sister picked it up and downed it in one.

'You'd better get me another,' she said, banging the empty glass on the counter.

Rachel heaved a sigh but fulfilled her sister's request. 'I take it a bloke has upset you, then?' she asked.

'No, not upset me but left me bloody furious. See, I've got this gentleman friend – or, I should say, I had this gentleman friend. He lived in that grand house near the river. I met him a couple of years back. His wife was one of them social reformers and was doing the Good Samaritan act on me. She was trying to drag me to church and get me off this stuff,' Hilda said, holding her glass in the air before knocking back the contents. Then she continued, 'The old girl used to call booze "the downfall of the working class". Anyway, she popped her clogs over a year ago and her husband was left to his own devices. He was a bit of a dithery old boy and didn't have a clue how to look after himself. So we came to an arrangement. I would pop in every morning, do him some food and have a flick round with the duster and he'd pay me. He never paid me much because he said I'd blow it on drink, but he promised he'd leave me a nest egg in his will, if I agreed to sort myself out.'

'You never told me any of this before,' Rachel said, astonished that her sister had held down a regular job for so long.

'I didn't tell you because I thought you'd say I was mad to look after him for hardly any pay but, to be honest, Rachel, I would have done it for free. I felt sorry for him. He was a nice chap.'

'You can be a bit soft sometimes and that's how blokes end up taking you for a ride.'

'Yeah, I know, but kindness costs nothing. And the few pennies he paid helped with the rent. I've got a couple of cleaning jobs but they pay better.'

'Really?'

'Yes, really. I bet you thought I was on the game, didn't you? I've heard the gossip. I know what they say about me, but I couldn't give two hoots what any of them think. Not my circus, not my monkeys.'

'No, Hilda, I never thought you a prostitute and I've never heard anyone suggest that you are. I have wondered how you pay the rent but assumed you made enough from the dress-making.'

'I don't sell my dresses, Rachel. I don't make enough of them. When I can afford a bit of material, the ones I do turn out I sell to Bill and Flo's market stall but that just covers the cost of the material and I give any extra to the Soldiers, Sailors, Airmen and Families Association.'

Rachel suddenly felt very humbled. She was always so quick to criticise Hilda for her drinking but without whisky spoiling her, Hilda had a kind and generous nature. 'That's really good of you. I feel bad now that I don't do anything for charity.'

'You're busy enough working here.'

'Yeah, but I could do something. You've inspired me, Hilda,' Rachel said, amazed by her sister's revelations. She was a dark horse and a woman of two extremes. Finding out about the cleaning jobs, the old man and the charity work made Rachel question if she really knew her sister at all. She'd spent so much time focusing on the vile, intoxicated Hilda that she'd forgotten about the sweet side of her character. 'Anyway, that aside, you haven't told me what made you so furious?'

'Oh, yeah – he died. The old boy went nice and peaceful in his sleep. Couldn't ask for a better way to go, really. Get me another drink, there's a darling.'

Rachel, intrigued now, poured Hilda her third whisky.

Hilda gulped down a couple of mouthfuls, belched, then continued. 'A solicitor contacted me and asked me to come to his office this morning. So off I trots, thinking this is it, I'm gonna come away a rich woman. Turns out the scheming old git had led me a right merry dance.'

'Why? What happened?' Rachel asked, leaning forward on the bar and hanging on Hilda's every word.

'He never left me a penny. Not a bleedin' thing – except this,' Hilda said. She fished in her bag and pulled out something wrapped in silk cloth and a piece of screwed-up paper.

Rachel picked it up and smoothed it out before reading the elegantly written words. She tried not to look amused at what the old man had penned.

'See what I mean. The self-righteous old fool.'

'I can understand why you'd be angry, but in all fairness, you carried on drinking so you didn't stick to your end of the bargain,' she said, thinking that the old man had a great sense of humour.

'I've been looking after him for a year. Every morning, come rain or shine, I'd be at his house, making sure he was fed and watered. I never asked for a thing from him but he made me believe that when he went off to meet his maker, I'd be looked after. I was stupid to believe him and when I got the letter from the solicitor, I got my hopes up. And this is the thanks I get – a painted egg! It's a diabolical bloody liberty.'

Rachel thought her sister had a point and could see why she felt let down but, as the man had explained in his letter, he didn't like to think of his legacy being frittered away on alcohol. Instead, he'd bequeathed what would have been Hilda's inheritance to the Salvation Army. He wrote that, however, he hadn't broken his promise and had left her a nest egg, albeit a painted one. Oh, the irony of it, thought Rachel. Hilda, sadly, was left penniless. 'What are you going to do now that you're not being paid to look after him anymore? Do your other cleaning jobs cover your rent?' she asked.

'Just about, but I ain't got a pot to piss in. You couldn't help me out, could you? Just until I find myself another little job.'

'Sorry, Hilda, I'm not flush myself.'

'I thought it would be a long shot asking you for anything. You've never done anything for me, you selfish cow.'

Here we go, Rachel thought, recognising the horrid side of Hilda beginning to emerge. As her sister had thrown whisky down her neck, Rachel had known she'd turn at any moment.

'Don't look at me like that,' Hilda snarled. 'Well, have you? Have you ever done anything for me apart from ruin my life?'

Before she could answer, Winnie walked over and stood beside Rachel with her arms folded. She glared at Hilda and warned, 'If you're going to start, I suggest you leave now before I throw you out. I'm in no mood for your shenanigans today.'

'Hark at you two, thick as thieves. Do you know that she walked away from our family because she was ashamed of what her fella did to our sister? I bet she ain't told you about that, has she?'

'Actually, she has. I know all about it and I won't have it spoken about it my pub. Either shut up or get out. I won't tell you again, Hilda.'

'Huh, my giddy aunt, listen to you sticking up for the little madam. Don't worry, I'm going before I vomit – you two make me sick.'

Hilda stamped across the pub and yanked open the door. Before leaving, she yelled over her shoulder, 'You wait, Missy. You'll find out the truth one of these days.'

'Before you ask, Win, I don't know what she's talking about,' Rachel said. 'It's always the same when she's had a drink. She goes on and on about me not knowing something or the other and how it will shatter me.'

'Take no notice, love. I don't suppose she knows what she's talking about herself. Are you all right?'

'Yeah, and thanks for intervening. Honestly, Win, I struggle to keep my mouth shut sometimes. And I wish she would stop bringing up Jim and the past.'

'There's no point in saying anything to her when she's like that. It would only make her worse and she probably wouldn't remember any of it when she sobers up.'

They both looked towards the door when it opened again and Rachel noticed that Winnie turned as white as a sheet when Terry breezed in.

'Oh dear, I've been waiting for this, but now I want to stick my head in a bucket of sand,' Winnie whispered.

'You don't have to say anything if you don't want to.'

'I must. I have to speak to Alma – I mean, Jan. If she's my daughter, then we both have a right to know.'

'Hello, ladies,' Terry said. 'I've just passed Hilda on the street. She didn't have a nice word to say about either of you.'

'Nothing new there,' Winnie said. Then, nervously, she asked, 'Erm, Terry, can I have a word, love? In private.'

'Course. I'll take my washing through to the back, shall I?'

'Yes, love, thanks,' Winnie said, smiling weakly.

Rachel tried to offer the woman a reassuring look and as Winnie headed to the scullery, she silently prayed that this would go well for her.

Terry pulled a chair out from under the table and dumped his bag of dirty washing on it. 'Here's what I owe you for last week's washing and today's,' he said, placing a few coins on the table. 'Now, what did you want to talk to me about?'

'Sit down, love. It's a bit, er, delicate,' Winnie answered, her mouth suddenly feeling dry. 'Can I get you a cuppa?'

'No, thanks. I'll have a pint in a minute but I want to know what this is about first.'

She sat opposite him and clasped her hands in front of her, resting them on the table. Her well-rehearsed words deserted her and she found herself struggling to know how to approach the subject.

'Something's clearly troubling you, Winnie. What is it?'

'Do you know if Jan is adopted?'

'She's never mentioned anything. Why?'

'Do you think she could be?'

'I don't know. Her dad died years ago and her mother's got a screw loose. It's a funny question, Winnie. What's this all about?'

'I need you to keep this to yourself, Terry, because my Brian and David don't know.'

'Yeah, yeah, I'll keep mum.'

Winnie drew in a deep breath, then said, 'I hope you won't think badly of me, but years ago, before I met Brian, I was young and stupid and got myself in the family way. I wasn't married, so as you can imagine, my parents were livid. They made me give my baby away.' She heard her voice breaking as she spoke and could feel tears brimming in her eyes. 'I didn't want to. I wanted to keep her, I swear, but I had no option.'

'It's all right, Winnie, I know how it is. I like to think that it was the same for my mum when she dumped me outside the children's home. I hope she didn't want to, and that she had no choice, just like you.'

'Of course, sorry, Terry. How selfish of me, I forgot about that. I'm sure it was the hardest thing your mum ever did and she probably thought she was doing the best for you. Believe me, no mother ever wants to give up her child.'

'Thanks, Winnie. That's what I like to think too. I don't

blame her for what she did. And you shouldn't feel bad either. But what's this got to do with Jan?'

Winnie looked at Terry with her watery eyes and, before she could answer, the penny must have dropped as he harped, 'You think Jan could be your daughter!'

'Yes, Terry, I do. She was born on the same day and she's got my eyes. I could be barking up the wrong tree but I don't think I am. I can't explain how, but I just *know* she's my girl.'

Terry sat back in his chair and exhaled long and loudly. 'Blimey, that's quite a claim.'

'Yes, it is. Do you think I could be right?'

'Anything is possible. Come to think of it, you do have the same eyes,' he said, smiling. 'And it would make my life a damn sight easier if you are her mother.'

'Oh, Terry, is that all you can think of?'

'I'm only kidding. But it would be really special if you turn out to be her real mum.'

Winnie felt so relieved that Terry had taken the revelation well and wasn't judging her past mistakes. She felt sure he'd help her to discover the truth. 'I need to speak to Jan about it and was hoping you'd bring her in to see me.'

'Yes, I will, but I've not seen her since Saturday. We'd planned on meeting last night but she didn't show up. I'm hoping it was because she couldn't get out and not because her mother has found out about us.'

'What would she do if she has?'

'I'm not sure, Winnie, but Jan told me her mother locks her in her bedroom with the windows boarded up. Jan told me her mother's illness has got a lot worse since her father died.'

'Illness or not, that ain't right. It isn't normal behaviour. It's no wonder Jan thinks the woman is mad. Perhaps you should go round there to make sure she's all right?'

'I'm not sure about that. What if her mother hasn't found out about us? If I go charging in with my size tens it would give the game away.'

'Yes, I suppose you're right. But if you don't hear from Jan soon, I think we should do something. Maybe Rachel could call on her?'

'That's not a bad idea. I'll give it until the end of the week, and in the meantime, don't you go worrying about what you told me. We'll get to the bottom of it. I really hope you are Jan's mum, cos that will make you my mother-in-law one day.'

Jan sat on the edge of her bed, hugging herself as she rocked back and forth. The boredom was getting to her, added to the frustration of not being able to get word to Terry. She'd tried to pull the nails from the boards over the window but had been left with split fingernails and bleeding fingers. She'd screamed, shouted and cried for help, but no one had come to her rescue. She'd kicked the door, hammered on it with her fists, and banged repeatedly on the walls. Still nothing.

Her mother had at least brought her a jug of water and half a loaf of bread. But when the door had been opened, Jan hadn't dared to try and escape. The sight of her mother brandishing a large knife and rambling about possession of the soul and exorcism was enough to force her to retreat to the far corner of her room. Although Jan had been scared, her mother had looked even more terrified. How could she be so frightened of her own daughter? There was no doubt about it, her mother had lost her mind!

Jan thought it was probably about five or six in the evening of her fourth day in captivity, though she couldn't be sure. It was difficult to tell, as the minutes and hours dragged by so slowly. But she knew she couldn't bear being locked up for much longer and had to find a way to escape. The window seemed the most feasible route, and she'd try removing the boards again. She scanned the room for something that would pull the nails out, but with sparse furniture and few belongings, there wasn't much that looked of any use. Even her shoes were downstairs by the front door. She felt helpless and tears began to streak down her face. She wished things were different. She longed for a normal mother, one who would have read her bedtime stories instead of psalms. A mother who would have taken her to the park to play instead of to church and Bible studies. A mother who loved her more than God.

As resentment built up in Jan, her anger turned to determination and she found a new inner strength. Gritting her teeth, she sat rod straight. She wouldn't allow this atrocious punishment. She refused to be caged in her room, especially as she'd done nothing wrong. Think, Jan, think, she told herself, knowing that she had to get out.

She walked resolutely to the window and pulled hard on the boards. 'Come on,' she growled, yanking harder. When there was no movement, she didn't give up and pulled at them again, this time with all her might. The boards remained fixed firmly over the window. Jan continued trying to remove them until, eventually defeated, she collapsed into an exhausted heap on the floor. Her strength had now waned and she realised it was going to be impossible to get them off. But there had to be another way out. There just had to be. Even if that meant confronting her mother.

9

On Friday afternoon, when the wages clerk toured the factory, handing everyone their pay packets, David smiled smugly at the brown envelope in his hand. He'd done nearly a full week's work and he had to admit it had been a doddle. The work was far from taxing and he'd soon discovered he could spend a good part of his day flirting with the factory girls. It was an added bonus that the supervisor spent more time reading his newspaper than he did on the factory floor. In the work's canteen, he'd found that there were none of the usual rules in place about men eating on one side and women on the other. All in all, it had been a good week.

'Fancy a drink, mate?' Kenny asked.

'Yeah, why not,' David answered, thinking it was the least he deserved.

'Do you want to go to your mum's pub, or the one round the corner from here?'

'We'll go to the one round the corner. I'm sick of the sight of my mum's place.'

Both men threw their jackets on and clocked out. Kenny was a few years older than David and had been quick to tell him about June, the woman on sewing machine number sixteen whom he was dating. David had taken it as a warning to steer clear of her, though, having seen her, he hadn't been enamoured. But he thought that June's friend Brenda was a looker and Kenny had said the woman was single.

'Are June and Brenda joining us?' David asked as he pulled his jacket collar up against the biting wind.

'No, mate. They won't go in a pub, not even in the saloon bar. But they'll be at the dance tomorrow night, if you want to come?'

'Yeah, all right, I will. Cheers.'

'Righto, the first drink is on you, then,' Kenny said as they walked into the pub.

David was grateful to be out of the cold. With his shoulders hunched and flat cap pulled low, he hadn't noticed Errol standing at the bar. When he saw him, his stomach dropped into his boots. He wanted to turn around and walk out.

'I'll have half a stout,' Kenny told the landlord, 'on him,' he added, nodding towards David.

'I'll have another, on him too,' Errol said, looking intimidatingly at David. 'Come into some money, have you?' he asked.

'No, not really,' David answered, trying to keep his voice steady as he fingered the wage packet in his jacket pocket.

'It's Friday, mate, pay day,' Kenny chirped. He didn't know Errol and was clearly oblivious to his reputation as the local hard man.

David swallowed hard, knowing what was coming next.

'Yeah, of course it is. Got yourself a job, then, have you, Dave?'

'Yes, but I ain't done a full week.'

'Still been paid, though?'

'Yeah, but not a lot.'

'A word,' Errol said gravely, indicating the door with a nod of his head.

David reluctantly followed him out into the chilly wind. He could feel his legs trembling.

'Let's have it, then,' Errol said, holding out his hand.

David pulled the envelope from his pocket, and before he could count out some money for Errol, the man snatched it away from him.

'That'll do nicely,' he said, looking inside. 'And I'll see you next week for the rest of what you owe me.'

'You can't take it all,' David protested.

'Are you gonna stop me?'

David hung his head.

'No, I thought not. I'll see you around. Off you go,' Errol said, shooing David away with his hand.

Knowing it would be futile to argue with Errol unless he wanted a good hiding, David sloped off back towards the factory to get his motorbike. His work all week had been for nothing and he was back to square one when it came to paying off Stephanie Reynolds. His father would be badgering him for money too, yet he couldn't tell the man he was skint because of paying Errol his dues. Christ, it was a mess. But he had one hope – his mother's purse.

Winnie had felt a sense of pride when she heard the back door click, knowing it was David returning home from work.

'I'll be back in a tick,' she told Rachel, and she dashed into the passageway to greet her son.

But she was disappointed to see the solemn look on David's

face. 'What's up, Son?' she asked as he began to trudge up the stairs.

'Don't ask.'

'Well, I did, so you'd best answer me.'

David stopped on the fourth stair up and turned to look down at her. 'I bumped into Errol and he took my wages.'

'Oh, no, and I expect he'll still come in here demanding more.'

'No doubt.'

'He's not going to stop until he gets every penny you owe him.'

'I know that, Mum, and I don't need you constantly chewing me ear off about it,' David snapped, throwing her a scathing look before thumping up the stairs.

Winnie knew she should be angry about the way David had spoken to her, but she could understand why he'd done so. Her poor lad had had a rotten time of it this evening already, with Errol taking his pay packet, and there she was, adding to it with her nagging. She heard his bedroom door slam shut and knew it was too late to placate him.

'Is everything all right?' Rachel asked when Winnie returned to the bar.

'Yes, fine,' she lied. 'No sign of Terry, then?'

'No, but I'm sure he'll be here any – and just like clock-work, here he is.'

'Thank goodness,' Winnie said, as he walked up to the bar. 'Any news on Jan?'

'No, not a dickie bird,' Terry answered. 'I'm getting worried now. I really think one of us should check on her.'

'Yes, me too. I'm sure she's fine, though. I mean, her mother wouldn't hurt her, would she?'

'I shouldn't think so, but what if she's been locked up again? It ain't right, is it?'

'No, Terry, it isn't,' Winnie answered. She turned to Rachel. 'Are you happy to go round and check on Jan? Terry will go with you, but he'll stay out of sight.'

'Of course I am. What do you think I should say if her mum comes to the door? I got the impression that Jan isn't allowed to have friends and I don't want to make matters worse for her.'

Winnie scratched the back of her head in thought. 'Maybe ask for Jan and if her mother wants to know who you are, you could say you're an old friend from school.'

'No, she can't say that,' Terry said urgently. 'I think her mother taught Jan at home.'

'Oh, right,' Winnie said, frowning in thought. 'What if Rachel says she's the niece or something of the woman Jan works for?'

Terry rubbed his chin, 'Yeah, that could work,' he said slowly. 'I don't know if the old girl has got any relatives but it's worth a shot. Mrs Savage – I'm pretty sure that's what Jan said her name is.'

'Good, that's sorted, then. You might as well go now, while it's quiet here,' Winnie told them, desperate to speak to Jan.

Rachel went through to the back to collect her coat and Winnie poured herself a drop of brandy. 'I hope she's all right,' she said to Terry.

'Yeah, me too,' he replied, his lips set in a grim line.

Moments later, haunted by a feeling of foreboding, Winnie watched them leave. Something wasn't right, she could feel it. And that feeling along with the knot of anxiety in her stomach strengthened her belief that Jan was indeed her daughter, Alma.

'What you doing by yourself? Where's Rachel?'

Brian's voice made Winnie jump. He was standing at the end of the bar and she looked at him in astonishment. He rarely came into the pub, and even less so when it was open.

'Well? I asked you a question,' he said impatiently.

Feeling flustered, she tried to remain calm. 'Erm, Rachel's just popped out. She'll be back soon.'

'What's she popped out for?'

'She had to nip home to get something – you know, womanly things.'

'Oh, right,' he blustered, 'but she ain't paid to be at home. You make sure you dock at least half an hour off her pay.'

'Yes, yes, I will,' Winnie answered, knowing full well that she wouldn't. 'Did you want something, Brian?'

'I was hoping Norris was in. I want him to have a look at the chimney.'

'Is it blocked?'

'How would I know, woman? Do I look like a bleedin' sweep?'

'All right, keep your hair on, I was only asking,' she answered, regretting that she'd asked the simple question.

Brian's face contorted in anger. He jabbed his finger towards her, then pointed towards the back. Winnie knew what he meant, and, ever compliant, she followed his silent instructions and walked through to the passageway. She knew what was coming and, as expected, Brian launched into a furious tirade of abuse.

'Don't ever speak to me like that again in front of customers. Who do you think you are? Do you think it's clever to show off in front of other blokes, not that it'd do you any good. You should take a look in the mirror. You're an embarrassment. A fat, ugly cow, and I don't know what I ever saw in you!'

She clenched her fists by her side and bit on her bottom lip. She wanted to yell back at him and tell him he wasn't an oil painting either, but that would only further provoke him.

'Get back to work and send Norris up when he comes in.'

Winnie didn't want to give Brian reason to shout at her again so she was quick to return to her post behind the bar. His words had penetrated deeply. She'd never considered herself any sort of beauty, but it hurt to hear her husband call her ugly and fat. Yes, she carried a few extra pounds, but she thought of herself as cuddly. And anyway, what did it matter to Brian? He hadn't made love to her in years. Not that she wanted him to – it was just that there were times when she craved a bit of tenderness. That was something she'd never receive from him.

She busied herself wiping down the bar and hoped that none of her customers would notice her unhappy face. She dragged the cloth across the already clean surface and thought back to the days when David had been a child. Brian was a better husband then. He'd always been demanding and there'd been times when he'd hit her, but when he was nice, he was really nice. Softer and even complimentary at times. They used to laugh together, have fun, and there'd been affection. But something in Brian had hardened and Winnie was convinced the catalyst had been when his mother, father, sister and three nephews were killed by the Spanish flu pandemic in 1918.

David had only been two years old at the time and Winnie could remember feeling terrified that the illness would claim his life too. She'd been so wrapped up in protecting their son that she hadn't noticed Brian's pain. She blamed herself for his unhappiness. Had she been a better wife, maybe things would be different now. Her husband had been devastated and she'd ignored his needs to concentrate on David's. Brian had never mentioned the names of his family since their deaths. It had changed him. He'd become reclusive and had stopped working in the pub, only venturing out to the bookies once a week. His loss had taken his joy and his love, destroying their marriage forever.

Jan lay curled up on her bed, shivering with just a thin blanket over her. The small glint of light that came through a crack in the boarded window had long disappeared, so she assumed it was about eight o'clock in the evening. Another long, cold and lonely night beckoned.

She'd tried to reason with her mother without success, so today she'd been braver. She had battled her physically. But attempting to wrestle her way to freedom had resulted in her being left with no water or bread and a nasty gash on her arm. Jan was coming to the conclusion that she'd never get out of her room and her bed would become her deathbed.

As she drifted into unconsciousness, she was suddenly roused by a muffled banging from outside. She held her breath and listened. There it was again – someone was knocking on the front door! She threw the blanket off and managed to hurry across the room to the window. If only she could see the street below.

'*Help ... help!*' she shouted but her voice felt weak.

Gathering her remaining strength, she frantically began to

pound the boards with her fists. Please, someone hear me, she prayed, oblivious to the pain in her hands.

'*HELP – I'm up here!*' she yelled, still thumping the boards as hard as she could.

She stumbled back to her bed and scrambled underneath it for a small wooden box that contained her Bible. Then she went back to the window and banged the box on the boards. '*Please – help me!*' she screamed hoarsely.

She kept knocking on the boards and crying for help until, finally, she gave up and fell to the floor in a heap, spent and weeping. 'Please, get me out of here,' she cried. 'Dear Lord, help me ... anyone ... someone ...'

As her body jerked with sobs, Jan's breath juddered when she heard a crashing sound and her bedroom door flew open. She squinted in the darkness, trying to focus, and saw what looked like a man coming towards her.

'Terry?' she muttered, unsure if she was hallucinating.

'It's all right, sweetheart, I've got you,' he soothed and pulled her onto her feet and into his arms.

'Terry – is it really you?' she asked, still not believing her own senses.

'Yes. Come on, I'm getting you out of here,' he answered and he urged her towards the door.

'But my mother – where's my mother?'

'Don't worry about her. You're safe now.'

Terry led her to the top of the stairs and held her hand as they went down. She could hear her mother screaming for the Lord's help and saw Rachel gripping the handle on the front-room door.

'My shoes – I need my shoes ...' Jan uttered, confused.

'Let's just get out of here,' Terry urged.

'Run! I can't keep her inside for much longer,' Rachel shouted over the screams from the other side of the door.

Once on the street, Terry scooped up Jan and she wrapped her arms around his neck. He pounded down the street, Rachel close behind them, and she could hear her mother calling her name. Terry didn't stop. He ran until her mother's voice faded into the distance. 'Is this a dream?' she asked, though the cold wind stinging her cheeks made it feel very real.

'No, darling, you ain't dreaming.'

She wasn't sure what was happening but her head began to swim and she felt distant, far away. 'I feel strange,' she whimpered, and then her world went black.

10

Winnie was out of bed, washed and dressed before the sun had come up. She'd hardly slept yet she was fully alert and couldn't wait to get round to Rachel's to see Jan. The poor mite had looked such a mess last night – pale, gaunt and exhausted. Mind you, from what Rachel had told her about how they'd found her, it wasn't any wonder that the girl had passed out.

'What are you doing up and dressed at this time of the morning?' David asked when he mooched into the kitchen.

'I could ask you the same question,' she answered, avoiding his question.

'I've got to go to work. Only a half-day today though.'

'Oh, yes, of course you have. I forgot you work on a Saturday now. Do you want a packed lunch?'

'Yes, please, Mum. It's not like I've got any money to spend in the canteen. Kenny, my mate from work, invited me out with a few of the others tonight but I'm scuppered without any cash.'

'I suppose you want me to lend you more?'

'If you could, Mum, that would be great. It doesn't seem right borrowing money off you now that I'm working but, well, thanks to Errol...'

Winnie gave him the few coins she had in her purse. 'You've worked hard all week. You deserve a night out.'

'Thanks, Mum,' David said softly and kissed her cheek. 'Come here, give us a cuddle,' he said and wrapped his arms around her. The sweet gesture made her smile. She liked being in his arms and wished he'd hug her more often. He was a good son, really, and had made a silly mistake with Errol that he now regretted. She'd made mistakes too when she'd been younger, only hers were much bigger and Jan might be the proof.

Quickly, she made his lunch and handed him the wrapped sandwich. She smiled fondly as she said, 'Go on, get yourself off or you'll be late.'

Once David had left for the factory, she made a fresh pot of tea for Brian and a bowl of porridge. She placed it on a tray and carried it through to the bedroom. As she put the tray on the table beside his bed, her husband was just stirring. He grimaced when he saw her looking at him.

'I thought you might like breakfast in bed,' she told him and nodded to the tray.

'You thought wrong, then, woman. Take it through to the front room.'

Winnie did as she was told and then gathered her coat and bag from the kitchen. She popped her head back round the door of the front room and saw Brian tucking into the warm oats.

'I'm off down the market. I'll see you later.'

Brian didn't lift his eyes from his bowl and Winnie closed the door, pleased that he hadn't questioned her. After all, it was early and the market would still be setting up.

Twenty minutes later, she tapped on Rachel's window.

'She's still sleeping,' Rachel whispered when she opened the front door.

'The rest will do her the world of good. Has she slept right through?'

'Yes. She was ever so restless, though. I think she was having bad dreams.'

Winnie noticed the dark circles rimming Rachel's eyes and her dishevelled hair. 'You don't look like you've had much sleep yourself.'

'Not much. I slept on the floor but every time Jan cried out in her sleep, it woke me. Oh, Winnie, the poor girl. You should have seen the state of her when Terry brought her out of that room.'

'I know. I wish we'd gone round there sooner.'

'Go in and sit with her. I'll make us a brew.'

Winnie quietly pushed the door open and sneaked inside. She gazed lovingly down at Jan, sleeping peacefully now, her brown, matted hair fanned out on the pillow. Oh, my angel, thought Winnie. She could have wrung Jan's so-called mother's neck for doing this to the girl.

Jan groaned and turned over in bed. She groaned again as, slowly, her eyes fluttered open. Then they widened and she sat bolt upright, looking terrified and confused.

'It's all right, love, you're in Rachel's bed,' Winnie said reassuringly and she sat down beside her.

'What ... what happened? My ... my mother –'

'Do you remember Terry breaking into your room last night? He carried you out but you passed out. They brought you here to rest.'

'Yes – yes, I think I remember. And my mother – she was shouting.'

'She won't be hurting you ever again. We'll look after you now.'

The bedroom door opened and Winnie noticed Jan flinch.

'You're awake,' Rachel said with a big smile. 'I'm making tea. I expect you're parched.'

Jan nodded. 'What happened last night?' she asked.

Rachel sat down on the other side of the bed before she answered. 'When I knocked on the street door, your mother answered it. I asked to see you and she quizzed me about who I was. When I told her I was Mrs Savage's niece, she said I was a liar and that I worked for the devil. She spat at me and said I'd never claim her soul and cursed me no end. Anyway, I heard something at the window upstairs and called to Terry. Your mother tried to close the door on us but Terry pushed it open and bundled your mother into the front room. He didn't hurt her, but got me to keep her inside. Blimey, Jan, she's got some strength, but I managed to hold the door shut long enough for Terry to get you out of there.'

'I remember some of it. I thought it had been a dream.'

'No, it was very real. To be honest, I was scared out of me wits so I can't imagine what it's been like for you. We bandaged that cut on your arm and bathed your hands. Thankfully, the wound isn't deep, so it doesn't need stitching, and it should heal in no time.'

Jan lowered her eyes but Winnie had seen that they were filled with tears. She desperately wanted to pull Jan into her arms but didn't want to smother her.

'I tried to fight my way out of the room, and – and her knife caught me. She can't help it,' Jan whispered. 'She's ill. I know she didn't mean it, but –'

'She's not right in the head, love, that's obvious,' Winnie said.

'She needs help,' Jan added and sniffed.

Winnie couldn't bring herself to have any sympathy for Jan's mother. 'You don't need to be worrying about her for now. Let's just concentrate on getting you better. We need to build your strength up and I've got just the ticket for that.'

'Oh, no,' Rachel said jokingly. 'Not Winnie's chicken broth. She swears blind it's the cure-all remedy for everything.'

'Don't you mock my soup, young lady. I'll have you know that a very wise Jewish woman gave me that recipe and she lived to be one hundred and two. So what does that tell you, eh?'

Winnie saw the young women exchange smiles and it warmed her heart. 'Has that kettle boiled yet?' she asked Rachel.

Alone again with Jan, Winnie took the girl's hand and, unable to contain herself any longer, she gently probed, saying, 'I know this might seem like an odd question, but did your mother ever say anything about adopting you?'

'No, of course not. I'm sure she's my mother, though many times I've wished she wasn't. I know what you must be thinking. A real mother wouldn't treat her own flesh and blood so badly, but, as I said, she's ill. She can't help herself.'

Winnie could tell that her question had upset Jan, and so she changed the subject. 'Are you hungry? You look like you could do with a good breakfast.'

'Yes, I'm famished. I've not eaten since –' Jan didn't finish her sentence as sobs began to wrack her fragile body.

Winnie couldn't help herself and impulsively pulled Jan into her arms. As the girl wept on her shoulder, Winnie could feel Jan's bones protruding through her thin clothes. Yes, the girl definitely needed feeding up – a good broth served with a spoonful of caring and a dollop of love. That was the Jewish woman's recipe and Winnie swore by it.

'There, there, there,' she soothed as she stroked Jan's greasy hair. Don't you worry, she thought to herself, your real mum's here now to look after you.

'I don't like leaving her there by herself,' Winnie said to Rachel as she opened the doors of the Battersea Tavern.

'I know, but she'll be fine and she'll probably just sleep. Terry will be going to check on her as soon as he's finished work.'

'I can't help worrying.'

Their conversation came to an abrupt end when Len came through the door, swiftly followed by Hilda.

'I'll see to her, if you like?' Winnie offered.

'No, you see to Len,' Rachel replied and she was pleased to see that her sister appeared sober.

'Hello, Rachel. Are you all right, darling? You look beat,' Hilda asked, lighting a cigarette.

'Yeah, I'm fine, just a bit tired. How are you? I haven't seen you since Wednesday.'

'That's because I've got myself a new fella, ain't I?' Hilda answered, looking very happy with herself.

Not another one, thought Rachel, hoping that her sister's latest relationship wouldn't end in heartbreak like the rest of them.

'No need to look so concerned,' Hilda said, grinning. 'He's different from the others.'

'I hate to point it out, but you say that every time.'

'I know, but he really is. He's got a good job, his own place and he thinks the world of me.'

'I'm sure he does, they always do, but they all end up taking advantage of you.'

'For Christ's sake, Rachel, why do you have to be so sceptical? Can't you just be happy for me? Ask me his name or something, what he does for a living. I came in here for a quiet drink and to share my good news, not for you to nag.'

'Sorry, Hilda, I just don't want to see you get hurt. Let's start again, shall we? What's his name, this new fella of yours?'

'Stanley,' she answered, 'Stanley Cooper.'

'And what does Stanley do for a living?'

'He's the new chap working for the Pru. I met him on Thursday when he called for my penny.'

'Blimey, I didn't know you're still paying that penny policy,' Rachel said. Although her sister had badgered her about taking out the insurance to cover funeral expenses, Rachel never had. She was surprised to hear that Hilda had kept hers up.

'I don't want a pauper's grave, which is what you'll end up in if you don't take one out. Anyway, Stanley and me got talking and we got on like a house on fire. He took me out to dinner on Friday and he's meeting me for a walk in the park later.'

'Rather you than me. It's freezing out there,' Rachel said, feeling cold just at the thought of being outside.

'That's all right, Stanley will keep me warm. But a large whisky will help too,' Hilda said with a chortle.

'I ain't being funny, Hilda, but do you think it's a good idea to have a drink before you go off to meet your new fella?'

'I'll only have the one. I need it to help me relax.'

Rachel fetched Hilda's drink but knew her sister wouldn't stop at one. She never did. Once her sister got a taste for it, she'd drink herself into oblivion.

'Ah, that's better,' Hilda said after she'd knocked back the whisky. 'Just one more, and then I'd best be off. I don't want Stanley to think I've stood him up.'

Rachel sighed heavily but poured her another which was quickly downed.

'One more for the road,' Hilda requested sheepishly.

Rachel could see her sister's eyes were looking glazed already. 'You'll be late for Stanley. Don't you think you should get going?' she asked hopefully.

'I've plenty of time yet and it won't do no harm to make him wait a few minutes. Keep him on his toes, that's what I say.'

Rachel didn't want to pour Hilda another drink but she knew she'd have to tread carefully. A third large whisky was sure to turn her sweet sister into a monster and she doubted Stanley would stand for it. But then, Rachel thought, it was only a matter of time before he'd meet the foul-mouthed drunk who'd inevitably hurl abuse at him. If not today, then another day, and, once again, Rachel would be picking up the pieces of a failed relationship that would result because of Hilda's drinking.

'I'm waiting,' Hilda said, snapping Rachel from her thoughts.

'Fine, I'll get you another whisky, but don't come crying to me when Stanley dumps you. Because he will, Hilda, as sure as day goes into night, Stanley will leave you when he sees what you're like with a drink inside you. And before you start having a go at me, I'm only talking to you like this because I care about you.' She braced herself, waiting for Hilda to make a scathing remark. Her sister's eyes narrowed and she glared at her, looking ready to attack. But then, to Rachel's surprise, Hilda raised her eyebrows and shrugged.

'You're right. Thank you. There's no use me denying it. I know I've got a problem with drink. And I know I can get a bit mouthy. The trouble is, I don't remember. I black out. But I can't seem to help meself. Whisky is the only thing that makes me feel happy and I'm so miserable without it.'

At last, Rachel believed she was finally making some headway with her sister. 'Admitting you have a problem is half the battle. But only you can stop you from drinking. Surely you'd be happy if things go well with Stanley? But if you turn up drunk, you'll ruin it.'

'Yeah, it's nice being with Stanley and he makes me laugh. But even when I'm with him, it's always there, niggling at me, the urge for a whisky. It'll never go away and I'm not strong enough to resist it.'

'Have you tried? I mean *really* tried.'

'Of course I have. Every day. But it always wins. I woke up this morning and thought to meself, right, that's it, no booze today. I had me date with Stanley to look forward to and I tried to focus on that. But here I am, in the pub, two drinks down and gasping for another. There's at least four more pubs en route to the park. I know I won't pass them without going in. That's the truth of it.'

'Oh, Hilda, I wish I could help you.'

'You can. Get me another drink and change the subject.'

'Hilda, please.'

'I don't want no more said about it. Now, are you gonna serve me or do I have to take my custom elsewhere?'

Rachel huffed, knowing that anything she said now would either fall on deaf ears or aggravate her sister. She didn't believe Hilda had tried hard enough and she couldn't understand how it was so difficult for her to abstain from drinking. If Hilda wanted to remain sober, surely it was a choice? How could she allow whisky to rule and ruin her life? Disappointed, Rachel slammed another glass on the counter in front of her.

'Enjoy,' she said sourly, 'I hope it makes you happy, because for the rest of us who have to put up with you, it's going to make us miserable.'

Poker-faced and without saying another word, Hilda picked up the glass and gulped down the contents. She threw some money on the counter and walked out, leaving Rachel flummoxed. It seemed her sister didn't care.

'Has Hilda gone?' Winnie asked.

'Yep.'

'Did she upset you again?'

'No, she behaved herself, but we were talking and I thought we were getting somewhere. She admitted she has a problem with drinking yet then she goes and orders herself another whisky. I don't get it, Win. Why does she do it?'

'Oh, love, she can't help it. I've seen it many times over the years. There's folk like Len who like a tipple, have a couple and go home. Then there's folk who like more than a couple now and then. But then there's those like Hilda who *have* to have a drink. They don't seem to be able to refuse it and come to rely on it.'

'Even if they know it's ruining their life?'

'Yes, I'm afraid so. I've seen many a man destroy his family because he's put the booze first. Some say drunkenness is a disease of the brain. I don't know about that but there's certainly them who can't say no to it and your sister is one of them.'

Rachel contemplated what Winnie said but couldn't

believe Hilda had a disease of the brain. No, her sister lacked self-control, but she wasn't ill. Rachel refused to feel sorry for her. She'd save her pity for someone who merited it. Someone like Jan.

David checked off the paperwork. The next consignment of packed boxes of pillows was ready to be loaded onto the delivery van. 'These are good to go,' he called to Kenny, who was skiving around the corner of the yard having a sneaky fag.

Kenny ambled up with his hands stuffed into his trouser pockets. 'I suppose I'd better give you a hand, then,' he said unenthusiastically but with a cheerful wink.

Kenny passed a box to David, who placed it in the back of the van, saying, 'You don't seem yourself today, mate.'

'I'm not,' Kenny answered. 'I told my June that I'm gonna sign up.'

Not another mug, David thought. First Ted and now Kenny. 'Didn't she take it well?' he asked.

'She's all right about me going away and said she'd wait for me, but I asked her to marry me before I go and she said no. She reckons it's too quick.'

'But she's gonna wait for you, so why the long face?' David asked, though he didn't really care and was only making polite conversation.

'She's a good girl, my June, and won't ... you know – unless we're married.'

'Oh, I see.'

'Yeah. I didn't say anything to her but between you and me, I've never slept with a woman and, well, let's face it, I could get killed. I don't want to die not knowing what it's like.'

David had a job not to laugh at Kenny but he kept a straight face. 'There're plenty of girls who will do it, mate. You've got time before you go and June need never know,' he said, blasé.

Kenny looked mortified. 'I couldn't do the dirty on my June,' he spluttered.

'That's your lookout, then, mate,' David replied unsympathetically.

'At least if I get killed, I'll die with a clear conscience. What about you? Are you signing up?'

'No, not me, not if I can get out of it.'

'How you gonna do that?'

'I don't know, but I'll find a way.'

'That bloke in the pub on Friday – Errol. He said he can supply medical exemption certificates for the right price.'

'Stay clear of him, Kenny. He's bad news,' David warned, though he was very interested to know how much Errol would charge for a fake certificate.

'Yeah, I've heard about him. I didn't realise who he was until you buggered off sharpish and then his dad came in. His old man seems like a nice bloke, nothing like his son.'

'If I was you, I'd give the whole family a wide berth. The Hamptons are a right dodgy bunch.'

'Maybe, but Errol could be your ticket out of conscription.'

The van was now loaded and it was time for a tea break, so they headed to the staff canteen. Kenny's mood was subdued, probably due to June's refusal to marry him, but David was happy for the quiet. He was deep in thought about Errol's certificates. He needed to get his hands on one, but as he still owed him money, he doubted the man would be obliging.

When they walked into the canteen, June was quick to

beckon Kenny over and David was pleased to see Brenda sitting next to her friend. Her blonde hair wasn't as light as Rachel's but she was just as slim and her tight grey jumper emphasised her large breasts. As David approached the table, Brenda looked at him from under her lashes and gave him a little smile.

'Good morning, ladies,' he said, keeping his eyes set on her.

'Morning, Dave. We was just talking about the band at the dance last week. Kenny said you're coming tonight. Is that right?' June asked.

He pulled an uncomfortable wooden seat out from under the table and sat opposite Brenda. 'Yeah, I was and I was looking forward to it, but me mum has been taken poorly, so I've got to work behind the bar in her pub,' he lied, not wanting to explain about Errol taking his money.

'Kenny said your mum's got the Battersea Tavern. Brenda's dad used to drink in there, didn't he?' June said, turning to her friend.

'Yes, that's right. Willy Judge. He passed away last year. Did you know him?'

Oh, yes, he knew Willy all right and was glad the giant of a man was no longer around. Willy would have had his guts for garters, if he'd known what his intentions were with his daughter. 'Yes, everyone knew Big Will. He was a good man, sorry for your loss.'

'Yes, he was. And he used to talk very highly of your mum. She came round after the funeral and brought a lovely cake. My mum was ever so touched.'

'Sounds like the sort of thing my mum would do.'

Kenny had gone to fetch the teas and came back to the

table to join the small group. 'Has June told you?' he asked Brenda. 'I'm joining up.'

'Yes, she has. I think you're ever so brave. When do you leave?'

'In two weeks. I'll write every day, if I can. You'll help June with reading my letters, won't you?'

'Of course I will. Keep 'em clean, mind.'

'Thanks, Brenda,' June said shyly. 'I've never been much good at reading and writing. I reckon we should all go to the dance again next Saturday, especially as Dave can't come tonight. It could be the last time we're all together for a while.'

'You'll come next week, won't you?' Brenda asked David.

'Yes, I'll be there, but only if you promise me a dance,' he answered with a cheeky grin.

'I might,' she replied teasingly.

'You've got to promise, or else I won't come.'

'All right, I promise, but you'd better not have two left feet.'

'Don't you worry, sweetheart, I've got all the right moves.'

Both women groaned and David chuckled. 'I can pick you up, if you like?' he offered, addressing Brenda.

'What, on that motorbike?'

'Yes. You can get on the back.'

'No thanks, it'd muck me hair up and my mother would have a fit if she saw me on that thing.'

'Yes, and the neighbours would have plenty to say about it an' all,' June added.

'You're scared,' he said, jokingly mocking her.

'No, I'm not,' Brenda protested.

'Prove it. Come for a quick spin round the block now.'

'Oh – I don't think so. My tea break is nearly finished.'

'See, I knew it. You're scared,' he goaded.

Brenda suddenly jumped to her feet. 'Come on, then,' she said defiantly. 'What ya sitting there for?'

'Mad as hatters, the pair of you,' Kenny said and laughed. June gasped, but they followed David and Brenda outside.

June looked worried as her friend climbed on behind David, but despite her obvious nervousness, Brenda gave her a reassuring smile.

'Hold on round here,' he told her, placing her hands around his waist. 'You might want to sit a bit closer,' he added.

As he turned the engine, revving it hard, Brenda clung on tighter. Then the bike jerked forward and he sped off with Brenda squealing in his ear.

'Slow down,' she shouted, which spurred him on to go faster.

He could feel her chest pushed up against his back and her warm breath on his neck. Then, once out of sight of the factory, he slowed the bike down and turned into a quiet, narrow street.

'Where are we going?' Brenda asked.

David stopped the bike and turned to look at her. He thought she looked sexy with her pink-flushed cheeks and windswept hair.

'What? You're looking at me strange.'

'I want to kiss you,' he said, feeling his groin stirring.

'No. I want you to take me back to work now.'

'Go on, just a quick peck.'

'No. Not here,' Brenda answered, looking around.

David smiled wryly to himself. She might be playing hard to get, but he was sure that he'd be getting a kiss after the dance next week and, if he had his way, a lot more besides.

11

On Tuesday, Jan was feeling much better, though her arm still felt a little sore. She'd made the bed and had prepared a light lunch for Rachel. Now she sat in the only chair, waiting for her new friend to come home from working at the pub. She picked up Rachel's book and began to read, but found she wasn't able to absorb the words. She had too much on her mind. Rachel had said she could stay for as long as she needed, but it wasn't practical when there was just a single bed in the small room. Yet she had no money and couldn't return to her job with Mrs Savage. Her mother was bound to look for her there and the thought of being found by her sent a shiver down her spine.

Jan rested the open book on her lap and stared into space. She wondered how her mother was and couldn't help but worry about her. She needed help, Jan could see that now, but she didn't know who to turn to. Rachel and Winnie hadn't shown any care or sympathy for her mother, not that she blamed them, and Terry had told her she should stay well away. But Jan felt awful leaving her mother alone, scared and unwell.

She must have been lost in her thoughts for some time

when she heard Rachel coming through the door. Jan was pleased to see her and Winnie followed in behind.

'How are you, love?' the kindly woman asked with a warm smile.

'Much better, thank you. I've made Rachel lunch, but I didn't realise you'd be here too.'

'Don't worry, I'm not hungry. I must say, you look a lot better.'

'I'll put the kettle on,' Rachel said after she'd thrown her coat and hat onto the bed.

'Would you like to sit down?' Jan asked, standing up to offer Winnie the chair.

Winnie shook her head and instead sat on the edge of the bed, patting the spot beside her. 'Come and sit here, love,' she said. 'There's something I want to talk to you about.'

Jan sat next to Winnie. The worried expression on the woman's face concerned her. 'Is something wrong?' she asked apprehensively, not sure if she wanted to know the answer.

'No, there's nothing wrong. But what I have to say will come as a bit of a shock to you.' Winnie paused, as though to gather her thoughts, then continued. 'You see, a long time ago – in fact, nearly twenty-seven years ago – I had a baby girl. I was only young and as I wasn't married, my parents were furious with me. They forced me to give my baby away, but I didn't want to, I swear. It broke my heart and there hasn't been a day gone by when I haven't thought about my daughter.'

Jan noticed Winnie's eyes fill with tears and she was curious to know why the woman was telling her this. 'It – it must have been awful for you.'

Winnie drew in a long breath and nodded. 'Yes, it was. I named my baby girl Alma. When she was taken away from me, I prayed that, one day, she'd come back. And – and Jan, I think she has. I think you could be my daughter – my Alma.'

Now the tears were flowing freely down Winnie's chubby cheeks and Jan stared at the woman in disbelief.

'I realise it's a lot for you to take in,' Winnie said and sniffed.

'What – what makes you think I'm Alma?' Jan asked, confused.

Winnie grabbed her hand and said earnestly, 'Your birthday. It's the same day I had Alma. And you've got my eyes ...' Winnie answered, her voice trailing off as she gave in to sobs.

Jan snatched her hand away and found herself reeling, too shocked to speak. Her mind raced. Could it be true? But neither her mother nor her father had ever mentioned anything about adopting her.

Winnie managed to compose herself and fished in her handbag for something. 'That's me when I was about your age,' she said, handing Jan a grainy photograph.

Jan studied the image of a young woman.

'See, it could be you in that picture.'

She looked closer. It wasn't a very clear photograph and she thought it could be anyone.

'I know it sounds mad, but I've got such a strong feeling about this. I'm sure you're my daughter. I can't explain it, but I just know it. But please, don't hate me for what I did. I've never forgiven myself for giving you up and have regretted it every day of my life.'

Jan continued to stare at the photograph and noticed that her hand was shaking. She didn't know what to say, but she knew she didn't hate Winnie. As the possibility of the woman being her real mother began to sink in, tears began to sting her eyes. In some way, she wanted it to be true yet, oddly, she felt disloyal to her mother.

'Do you think you could be my daughter?' Winnie asked gently.

Jan snapped her eyes away from the photograph and looked into Winnie's. They were very similar to her own. Brown and almond-shaped. 'I don't know,' she whispered. 'I suppose I could be.'

Rachel came in with a tray of three cups of tea. 'I thought you both might be needing this now,' she said, offering each of them a cup. 'I've stirred in lots of sugar. They say it's good for shock.'

Jan took one from the tray. The china cup clattered in the saucer.

'It's all right, give it here,' Winnie said and she held it for her. Just like a mum would do.

'Wouldn't it be lovely if Winnie was your mum?' Rachel said as she sat in the chair.

Jan thought for a moment before answering. Slowly, she nodded. 'Yes. I've always wanted a proper mum and I suppose it could explain why my mother is so cruel to me.'

'I'm so sorry, love. When they took you away, all I could do was hope you grew up with parents who loved you and looked after you well. I used to imagine what you looked like and what you were doing. It never occurred to me that your life would be so terrible. I feel awful, I really do.'

Now Jan took Winnie's hand. 'It's all right, I understand. It wasn't your fault,' she soothed.

'You've got a kind heart, Jan. Just like Winnie,' Rachel said.

Jan's thoughts were all over the place. Her mother had warned her that people who were not good God-fearing Christians were evil and wicked. She'd been forbidden to mix with anyone who didn't attend their church and had been told that the heathens of the world would lead her astray. Yet these women, Rachel and Winnie, had shown her more kindness and consideration in a few days than her mother had ever offered. Jan found herself coming round more and more to the idea that Winnie could be her real mother. 'I hope it's true. I hope you really are my mum.'

Winnie made a choking sound and Jan found herself being held in her arms. She wanted to stay there and never again have to face the wicked woman who had called herself her mother.

Winnie hadn't wanted to leave Rachel's. She'd have preferred to stay and talk to Jan. She wanted to know everything about the girl and to catch up on all the lost years. But instead, she was now in the kitchen preparing Brian's dinner. She'd bought a nice piece of belly of pork and was preparing boiled potatoes and cabbage to go with it. It was Brian's favourite meal and she hoped it would go some way to softening the blow she was about to deliver. Her stomach knotted again. The thought of telling Brian about Jan worried the life out of her but she had to come clean. Jan needed somewhere to live and Winnie had offered her a home. She'd blurted out the invitation to the girl without thinking it through properly. But whether Brian liked it or not, her daughter had to come first. She owed it to Jan and had twenty-seven years to make up for.

Winnie plated Brian's meal, placed it on a tray and carried it through to the front room. She'd been careful not to give him too much gravy because once she explained about Jan, he was likely to lob the plate at her. She paused for a moment outside the door and steadied herself. 'Right, you can do this. Do it for Jan,' she whispered and boldly walked in.

148

Brian was sitting in his armchair, as usual, his pipe on the table beside him. The wireless was on. Winnie thought it sounded like Sandy Macpherson playing his organ. She could never fathom what Brian found so interesting about the programme and she found the latest first-aid instruction bulletins even more boring. Yet Brian would listen to the wretched thing for hours on end.

'I've cooked your favourite,' she said to him as she handed him the tray.

Without showing any gratitude he took the meal and licked his lips. Winnie secretly hoped he'd choke on the cabbage. That would save her having to explain about Jan.

Brian looked up briefly. 'You not eating?' he asked. Even this simple question sounded more accusing than it did caring.

Winnie sat down in the other armchair. 'No, I'm not hungry. Actually, there's something we need to talk about,' she said.

'If you're going to start bending my ear again about painting downstairs, you can forget it. Get Rachel to wash the walls down. That'll do.'

'No, it's not about decorating. It's about my daughter,' Winnie said brazenly. There was no point beating about the bush. She wasn't prepared to hide Jan away or be ashamed of her, so she'd come straight out with it and now anxiously waited for Brian's response.

'What daughter? What are you on about, woman?'

'My daughter, Jan. I gave birth to her a couple of years before we met and my parents made me give her up for adoption. Now, though – she's back. I've found her and she's moving in with us.' Winnie's mouth felt so dry, she could hardly swallow.

Brian rested his knife and fork on the plate and moved

the tray to the table. He hadn't yet met Winnie's eyes so she couldn't gauge his reaction. Was this the calm before the storm? Then he picked up his pipe and lit a match, still not saying a word. Winnie found his silence deafening. She'd expected him to rage. To scream and shout. Possibly even a slap or two. But this indifference was unnerving.

With his head resting on the back of the chair, Brian's eyes closed as he sucked on his pipe. Well, that's it, thought Winnie, assuming her husband must simply have accepted the news. 'Right,' she said. 'Jan will be moving in first thing in the morning. I'll make sure she doesn't disturb you.'

As Winnie pushed herself out of the chair and stood up to cross the room, she heard Brian's ominous voice. 'If you think I'm having a pair of sluts living under my roof, then think on, woman.'

Winnie stood motionless facing the door as she realised Brian's silent compliance had been too good to be true.

'You and your bastard had better find somewhere else to live.'

Winnie spun round now, her temper flaring. 'Don't you talk about my girl like that,' she spat, finding the courage to stand up for her daughter.

'I'll talk as I see fit. I've no doubt the bastard is just as much of a slut as her mother is.'

'How dare you! I've been a good and faithful wife to you. I've not so much as looked at another man. And for what, eh? For you to treat me like dog's muck on the bottom of your shoe. I'm no slut and neither is my daughter. She's moving in here, so you'd best get used to it.'

Before Brian could retaliate, Winnie marched from the room, slamming the door behind her. Her legs were quivering but she felt empowered. 'That told him,' she said with a huff. However, she had a feeling that this wasn't the last of it. Brian's tone had sounded callous and his eyes had been dark and full of hatred. There was no way he was going to let this rest.

She wasn't going to back down, though. She went to the small box room past David's at the end of the hall. The room had become a bit of a dumping ground for anything that didn't have its own place and it needed clearing before Jan could move in. She pushed open the door and sighed at the sight before her. She had a bigger task on her hands than she'd anticipated. The single bed against the wall was stacked high with boxes and crates. And so was the small space between the bed and the chest of drawers. She had no idea where she'd put all the stuff, but, if needs be, she'd throw it out.

Rolling up her sleeves and with her mouth set in a determined line, Winnie made a start on clearing the clutter. She'd sorted through two boxes, all of which were for the bin, when she heard the click of the front-room door opening. She tensed, expecting Brian to storm down the passageway towards her. But to her surprise, she heard his slippered feet pad to their bedroom. Maybe it was asking for trouble, but Winnie thought it would be a good idea to have it out with him once and for all – and before Jan arrived. Her husband must still have plenty to say and she didn't want Jan hearing it.

She crept down the hallway and quietly pushed open the bedroom door. Brian was sitting on the edge of his bed staring at the wall in front of him. He didn't look round when she walked in or when she sat beside him.

'I'm sorry about how I spoke to you earlier and I'm sorry that I never told you about having a daughter. I've kept the secret all these years because I was so ashamed. But now I've met my girl again, I can't deny her and I wouldn't want to. She's had a terrible life and it was all my fault. She needs me and I'm going to do right by her.'

Brian didn't flinch or so much as bat an eyelid.

'I realise I've dropped a bit of a bombshell on you and that you've every right to be upset that I didn't tell you sooner, but what's done is done. And let's be honest, Brian, I've kept your secret for all these years. You're ashamed of what you did to your brother and I've respected your feelings and never told a soul. Well, this was my secret, something I was ashamed of. But I'm not anymore. Please, show me the same respect I've always given you.'

Finally, still staring ahead, Brian spoke. 'If you'd told me when we first met, I never would have married you. But now it looks like I'm stuck with a whore for a wife and her bastard child. Does David know?'

'No, not yet. I'll speak to him when he gets home from work.'

'I bet he's going to be so proud to know his mother is a slut and he has a dirty bastard half-sister. Well done, Win. You couldn't have brought any more shame onto this family if you'd tried. Christ knows what people are going to think about this. It's a fucking embarrassment. You're an embarrassment!'

'Please, Brian, don't be like that. Jan is a lovely girl and I'm sure her and David will rub along just fine.'

'Who's her father?'

The direct question took Winnie aback. She hadn't thought about Jan's father for nearly twenty-seven years. So far, Jan hadn't asked about him. 'He was nobody – nobody who mattered.'

'He mattered enough for you to open your legs to him!'
Brian barked.

Winnie hung her head as she tried to stop her eyes from
spilling the tears that were welling. 'He was my father's friend.
They were both stokers on the railway. After his wife died,
my dad quite often brought him home for his tea. Sometimes,
him and my dad would knock back the ale and he'd end up
kipping on the sofa. You know what my dad was like, Brian.
He hardly acknowledged I existed. But his friend, Rolf, he
would talk to me. He was always teasing me and mucking
about. I was just a kid and I thought I loved him. I believed
he loved me too, but once I told him I was with child, he
ran off. We never saw him again.'

'You're a liar! You weren't a kid. On my reckoning, you
was eighteen or nineteen when that bastard spewed out of
your belly.'

'I know, but it started with Rolf when I was thirteen. I
didn't know any better at that age. After a couple of years,
I tried to stop it, I swear I did. But Rolf threatened me. He
said he'd tell my father what had been going on. I was so
scared. My dad would have hit the roof and slung me out
after giving me a good hiding. I didn't feel I had a choice.'

'Of course you had a bloody choice, woman. And you had
a choice when you met me but you chose not to tell me.
How do you think I feel? Knowing another man has been
there – it turns my stomach. The thought of –'

'Come off it, Brian. All that sort of stuff is long behind us.
You haven't been near me for years.'

'Yeah, and that's how it'll stay an' all. I wouldn't touch you
now even if I was paid to.'

'I'm sorry, I really am,' Winnie cried, giving way to her tears.

'I bet you are. But you're only sorry cos your bastard has shown up and your disgusting secret has come out.'

'Please stop calling her a bastard. Her name is Jan.'

'I couldn't give a toss what her name is. She's still a bastard.'

Brian's coldness and lack of empathy came as no surprise to Winnie. She felt her strength returning and rose to her feet to address her husband. 'I won't have that word used ever again. I've told you all there is to know. I can't change the past and what happened. I'm her mother and if you don't like it, tough, there's nothing that can be done about it. But I'm going to do everything within my power to make a better life for my daughter. Don't stand in my way, Brian. You know I'll fight for my children. And you know I can easily tell people *your* secret.'

It was Brian who hung his head now and Winnie thought she'd won this battle. But then he made a low screaming, growling noise and leapt to his feet. She froze, fearing he was going to lay into her with his large fists.

'Don't tell me how things are gonna be under *my* roof!' he spat, his face just inches from hers.

She looked into his dark, raging eyes before closing her own, bracing herself for his punches.

'Don't forget your place, woman,' he yelled and then she heard the crunch of wood.

Opening her eyes, she saw he'd punched the wardrobe door and had left a gaping hole. He then sat back on the bed with blood dripping from his knuckles.

'Let me see to that,' she said and dropped down beside him, carefully taking his hand in hers to examine the wound. Brian allowed her to dab at the cut with her handkerchief but kept his head turned away and his eyes averted.

'I don't think it's too bad but I'll clean it up and bandage it,' she said softly.

She saw Brian nod his affirmation. She dashed to the kitchen, returning with a bowl of warm water, a clean cloth and a bandage. As she wrapped the cotton material around his hand, she said, 'I'll keep Jan out of your way and we won't speak of it again.'

Now his anger had been vented, her husband offered no objection. But she still had to tell David and had no idea how he'd react. She could only hope her son would take it better than Brian had.

'Fancy a drink?' Kenny asked David as they clocked out of the factory.

'No thanks, mate, I want to get home before it pisses down,' David answered. In truth, he would have liked a beer or two but he didn't want to risk bumping into Errol again.

'Can't say I blame you. I wouldn't fancy driving your bike in the rain and looking at the state of that sky, I reckon you'd better get a move on.'

'Yeah, see you tomorrow, mate,' David replied, looking over Kenny's shoulder towards Brenda, who was standing at the end of the line of workers waiting to leave. Their eyes met and she smiled at him, the sort of smile that confirmed what he already thought – she definitely fancied him.

As Kenny walked off, David lingered until Brenda came through the doors.

'Ain't you got a home to go to?' she asked.

'Course I have, but I was waiting for you. Do you want a lift?'

'No chance. I told you, me mum would have a fit if she saw me on that,' she said, pointing at the bike.

'I could drop you round the corner out of sight.'

Brenda waved at June as she passed then said, 'Go on, then. These shoes are killing me and I don't fancy standing at the bus stop in this weather.'

'Hop on, then. Your carriage awaits.'

'It's hardly a carriage,' she said as she wrapped her arms around his waist. 'And don't go so fast this time.'

David sped off, aware that the other factory workers were watching – some, especially the women, with disapproving looks. He didn't care what any of them thought, though Brenda's reputation would likely be sullied. But that was her lookout.

'Shall we stop at my pub?' he shouted.

'No, I've got to get home. I have to get the tea on for the little ones.'

'Can't your mum do it?'

'No.'

David didn't push any further. He got the impression from Brenda's abrupt answer that it was a subject she didn't want to talk about. He'd heard from Kenny that Brenda's mum had never got over losing her husband and hadn't left the house since his death. But he couldn't see why that would stop the woman making tea for Brenda's younger siblings.

It wasn't long before they were only a street away and he pulled into the kerb. 'Is this close enough to home for you?'

'Yes, thanks, Dave. And we made it just in time, it's just starting to spit down,' Brenda answered as she climbed off the back of the bike and ran her fingers through her tousled hair. 'I'll see you tomorrow.'

'Hey, not so fast,' he called and she turned back to him. 'Don't I get a kiss goodbye?' he asked.

She stepped closer and quickly placed her lips on his cheek. 'There you go and that's all you're getting – for now,' she said, and tossed her blonde waves back as she flounced off.

David sat grinning as he watched her walk away. He thought she was a sexy woman and he'd have liked to have paraded her in the Battersea Tavern, right under Rachel's nose. He thought seeing Brenda on his arm might make Rachel jealous and maybe she'd see him as a man instead of as a boy. He'd get Brenda in the pub one day, he thought, as he headed home. And Rachel's face would be a picture.

As he parked outside the back door, there was a sudden loud clap of thunder overhead and then the heavens opened. Heavy rain began to fall and he dashed inside. Once in the warmth, he shook the rainwater from his flat cap and then looked up to see his mum coming down the stairs, her face grim.

'I'm glad you're home, Son,' she said. 'I need to talk to you. Come up to the kitchen.'

'What about the pub?'

'Rachel's behind the bar.'

He followed his mother back upstairs and sat at the kitchen table. She placed a cup of hot tea in front of him before pulling out a seat opposite.

'Are you all right, Mum?' he asked, perturbed. She was normally so jolly but something was clearly bothering her.

'Yes, I am, and I hope you will be too.'

'What's that supposed to mean?'

'I've something to tell you and I don't want you getting upset.'

'Is my dad dead?' he asked hopefully.

'No, of course not. He's fine. Our family hasn't got any smaller. In fact, we've a new member to welcome. Your sister will be moving in tomorrow morning.'

David had been holding the hot cup of tea to warm his fingers but now he placed it back on the table and stared at his mother. Had he misheard? 'I don't understand,' he said, and waited for her to explain.

'You have a sister called Jan. She's a few years older than you and was adopted, which is why you've never met her. But she's back and is coming to live with us. It'll be smashing, David, and it'll give you the chance to get to know her.'

'Wahoo, slow down, Mum. You and Dad had a baby and gave her up for adoption? That doesn't make any sense.'

'No, Son, not me and your father. Just me.'

David jumped up, sending his chair falling backwards. He looked at his mother in disgust. 'You had a baby with another man?'

'I'm not prepared to discuss the details of my past with you. Suffice to say you have a sister and I hope you'll be as happy about it as I am.'

'She ain't my sister! Not a real, proper sister. She's your dirty secret, that's what she is. What's Dad got to say about it? I bet he ain't *happy*!'

'Your father has accepted it and she *is* your sister. Well, half-sister at least. Please, calm down, Son. Jan is a lovely lady and I'm sure the two of you will get on well.'

David paced the room now, his mind racing. His mother couldn't just throw this news at him and expect him to be fine about it. She'd lied to him his whole life, had told him he was an only child. And now, to find this out, well, it wasn't on. And what about his inheritance? He knew his dad had a few bob tucked away that would go to his mother. When, eventually, it came to him, would he have to share it? 'How could you do this to me?' he growled.

'Please, Son, try and see that this is a good thing. You've always wanted a brother or a sister and now you've got one. She's our family and we need to stick together.'

'No, Mum, she's *your* family, not mine or Dad's.'

David heard his dad clear his throat and looked round to see him standing in the kitchen doorway.

'You've told him, then, about your bastard girl.'

'Yes, I've told him and I've also told you not to use that word.'

'I'll use whatever words I choose. You've brought this on yourself and ain't in any position to dictate to me about right from wrong. The fact of the matter is, she's a bastard, there's no denying it, and I won't blame the boy if he wants nothing to do with her either.'

With that, Brian walked away and David could see his mother was close to tears but he couldn't feel sorry for her. Like his dad had said, she'd brought this on herself. Then, suddenly, he realised something – if he was to remain able to tap his mother for cash, he'd have to show her some support. He had to stay at number one in her eyes. He couldn't have his so-called *sister* becoming his mother's favourite child.

'I'm sorry, Mum. I've behaved badly, but it was just the shock. At the end of the day, whatever happened before I was born is none of my business. If Jan is my sister, she can't be that bad,' he said and walked over to the table and placed his hands on his mother's shoulders. 'Don't worry. I'll make sure she feels welcome.' And he would, to a point, but only to ensure he wouldn't be losing out himself.

12

The next morning, Rachel had woken up with a feeling that she couldn't shake, sure that something bad was going to happen. Now, as she walked alongside Jan on their way to the Battersea Tavern, she hoped her anxiety was unfounded.

She would have offered to help carry Jan's stuff, but the girl had nothing apart from a few bits and pieces she'd sorted out for her. Rachel had no doubt that Winnie would soon be spoiling Jan rotten and she was pleased. It would be nice to see someone other than David being spoilt by Winnie.

'I'm glad it's stopped raining. I broke my brolly and haven't got round to getting a new one yet,' she said, making small talk.

Jan didn't say anything and Rachel could tell she was nervous. 'Try not to worry. You'll be very happy at Winnie's. Take no notice of Mr Berry and ignore Dave as much as you can,' she advised with a half-hearted chuckle.

'Thank you. It just feels very peculiar to be going to live in a pub.'

'The Battersea Tavern is like a second home for most of the customers. They're a friendly bunch, you'll like them.'

'Terry said the same.'

'There you go, then, we can't both be wrong. Is he coming to see you today?'

'No, he said he's going to give me a couple of days to settle in and get to know my – Winnie better.'

'Winnie doesn't expect you to call her "Mum". You don't have to feel awkward about it.'

'Oh, thanks, Rachel. I was worried. I mean, I think I've got used to the idea that she could be my mother and I think she's lovely, but I'm not sure I could address her that way. Not yet.'

'Winnie's not pushy. She's just chuffed to bits to have found you after all these years. Look at her, she can't wait to see you.'

Rachel nodded towards the pub where Winnie was standing outside with a cardigan pulled around her and her arms folded across her chest.

'She's never come outside to wait for me to arrive,' Rachel said, chuckling.

When Winnie saw them approaching, her face broke into a wide grin and she hurried them inside. 'Come on, it's taters out here.'

'Well, it would be, in just a cardi,' Rachel said, then wished she hadn't, when she saw Jan looking embarrassed at wearing the oversized coat Winnie had given her.

'Rachel, get the kettle on while I show Jan to her room, and then we'll both be down,' Winnie said. She led Jan to the stairs at the back of the pub.

The water hadn't yet come to the boil when Winnie and Jan returned to sit at the small kitchen table downstairs. 'Do you like your room?' Rachel asked.

'Yes, it's very pretty with pink and mauve wallpaper, and I can see all the way down the street from the window.'

Her remark wasn't lost on Rachel and she was reminded of how Jan's old bedroom window had been permanently boarded over.

'Get the biscuits, love,' Winnie said to Rachel. 'Have you both had breakfast?'

'Yes, we had a bit of toast, but I'll never refuse a biscuit,' Rachel said as she reached for the tin.

'Jan, I suppose Rachel has warned you about my Brian?'

'She mentioned him,' Jan answered quietly.

'Brian can be an 'orrible old bugger, and it's probably best that you stay out of his way, but he'll do you no harm. My son, David, on the other hand, is a good boy and he's looking forward to meeting you when he comes home from work this evening.'

Rachel had to bite her tongue. She didn't think there was anything good about David and as she placed a pot of tea on the table, they heard someone knocking on the pub door.

'That can't be customers at this time of the morning,' Winnie said, rising to her feet.

'I'll go,' Rachel offered and she left Winnie to pour the tea. Whoever was at the door knocked harder. 'Hold your horses, I'm coming,' she called.

When she unbolted the door, she found Hilda shivering outside. 'It's a bit early, even for you,' she said disapprovingly.

'Don't be like that. I bumped into Terry last night. He told me about Jan and that she's been staying with you and is moving in with Winnie today. It sounds like the girl has had a terrible time of it, so I brought a few bits round that she might be able to use.'

Once again, Rachel was left humbled by her sister's generosity and she invited her inside. As Hilda brushed passed her, Rachel was pleased that she couldn't smell the reek of whisky on her. 'We're out the back. I've just made a pot of tea.'

In the kitchen, Rachel noticed that Jan looked horrified when she saw Hilda and she remembered her sister's drunken display at Terry's party.

'Hello. You must be Jan. I'm Hilda. Hilda Duff, Rachel's sister. I thought some of this might be of use to you,' she said, holding out a bag to Jan.

'You've met before,' Rachel told Hilda, giving her a look.

'Oh – I see. I suppose I'd had a drink. Sorry. It's no secret that I like a whisky or two. I hope I wasn't too awful. Anyway, have a look in the bag.'

'Would you like a cuppa?' Winnie asked.

'Any chance of a whisky?'

'No bloody chance at all,' Winnie answered firmly.

'In that case, I'd love a cuppa,' Hilda replied, pulling out a seat.

The four women sat around the table and admired the items Hilda had brought. The bag contained two dresses that looked brand new, a hat, scarf and glove set, all hand knitted, a hairbrush, a small bottle of lavender scent and a pair of lisle stockings with a suspender belt.

'I wasn't sure what size you are and I hope the dresses fit. I make them to give to a charity, but, at the moment, I think you need them more. If you're happy with them, I can always run you up another one or two,' Hilda offered.

'Thank you. I love them. I make my own clothes, but nothing like this. Mother would never allow bold colours or patterns. And stockings, well, I'm afraid you'll have to show me how to wear them. Mother preferred me to wear woollen tights.'

'You'll be sorry. Stockings are the bane of my life, always wrinkling round my ankles,' Winnie said.

Hilda pointed out a ladder in hers, saying ironically, 'Yes, but every woman should have at least one decent pair.'

'Did you knit this set yourself?' Rachel asked her sister as she looked at the hat.

'Yes, last winter, but it's been stuffed in the back of one of my drawers.'

'You did a good job, not a single stitch dropped,' Winnie said, examining the scarf.

'Jan, are you going to be working in the pub?' Hilda asked as they tucked into the biscuit tin.

'Oh – erm ... I don't know. I'll have to pay my way but I'm not sure I'm the right sort of person for bar work.'

Rachel had to agree but she kept her thoughts to herself. Jan was far too shy to be behind the bar and unless Winnie wanted some time off, they didn't really need an extra pair of hands.

'I think I should let Mrs Savage know that I won't be returning, but I'm worried about going there.'

'Don't worry, love, Rachel will pop round to see her and explain everything. Now, let's make you feel at home before we think about you working,' Winnie said.

'But if Jan wants to pay her way, and is good at sewing, she could use my sewing machine to make clothes and flog 'em to Bill and Flo on the market,' Hilda suggested. 'They're always looking for good-quality stuff and they pay a fair price.'

'I don't know about that,' Jan said, her eyes wide. 'I don't think anything I make would be good enough and I've never used a sewing machine.'

'As long as you follow a pattern it's a doddle and I can teach you. If you understand materials, seams and cuts, a sewing machine is just a quicker way of putting your stuff together.'

'Sounds like a good idea, Jan. If Hilda is willing to help you, I'd bite her hand off. Once you can use the machine, you'll be able to get a job in one of the clothing factories and I hear the pay is half-decent,' Rachel said, thinking that the idea of Hilda teaching Jan might keep her sister off the booze.

'If you're sure you don't mind, I'd love you to teach me, Hilda, but I haven't got any material or threads.'

'Make a list of what you need and we'll pop up the junction tomorrow,' Winnie suggested.

'Thank you. Thank you all so much. I'm quite overwhelmed...' Jan whispered as her eyes filled with tears.

Rachel found it all rather touching and had a job not to well up herself. It was lovely to see her sister sober and Winnie fussing like a mother hen. Everyone seemed content and she was secretly pleased to be having her room and bed back.

But Rachel had learned never to trust in happiness for too long. Something inevitably always came along to ruin it. And she still had that niggling bad feeling that something was waiting round the corner, ready to pounce.

Later that day, after dinner and when Winnie went downstairs to open the pub for the evening shift, Jan went to her room to write a list of what she'd need to get started on dressmaking. She sat on the pretty pink candlewick bedspread and ran her hand over the soft fabric. Again, it was something that would never have been allowed in her previous home. She couldn't wait to snuggle under it tonight in the knowledge that she was safe and out of reach of her mother. She shuddered at the thought of her. It was only now that she'd been away for a few days that the reality of the abuse she'd suffered was beginning to sink in. The more kindness Winnie and Rachel showed, the more she began to realise the depth of her mother's wickedness. It was ironic, really, considering what the woman preached about. But she couldn't help worrying about her and she knew that her mother was mentally unstable.

Jan dismissed any further thoughts about her and concentrated on the list in hand. As she scribbled, the list of items grew longer and she felt awful about asking Winnie to buy so much. But once she'd sold her first dress, she felt sure she could pay her back.

After putting the notepad aside, she gently opened her bedroom door and peeked down the hallway. She knew David's room was next door, with Winnie's and Mr Berry's at the other end. In between, there was a front room, a kitchen and bathroom. Mr Berry was probably in the front room. She'd been warned to stay out of his way, but if she was to use the toilet, it would mean creeping past. Thankfully, she'd noticed that the door was pulled to.

Jan quietly and swiftly padded along the hallway. Just as she was about to pass the front room, the door flew open and she found herself face to face with Mr Berry. He was much taller and broader than she'd imagined, which left her feeling very small. His dark, cold eyes bored into her and she was sure he snarled.

'Excuse me,' she whispered in little more than a croak.

Mr Berry stepped towards her and for a moment, Jan thought he was going to strike her. She closed her eyes in fear, waiting for the blow to come. But instead she heard him grunt and when she opened her eyes again, he was gone. She dashed to the bathroom. Her heart was beating so fast that it made her feel faint. Mr Berry certainly wasn't a friendly character. No wonder Winnie and Rachel had told her to stay out of his way! She didn't want to leave the sanctuary of the bathroom in case he was in the hallway again but she couldn't stay in there all evening and, reluctantly, she pulled open the door. Peeping outside, she was thankful to see there was no sign of the man so she ran along the hallway and into her room. Closing the door behind her, she leapt onto the bed and huddled against the oak headboard with her knees pulled up to her chest. That had been frightening! She didn't want to run into Mr Berry again in a hurry.

Half an hour later, Jan heard heavy footsteps coming up the stairs. They sounded like the steps of a man and she wondered if it was David returning home from work. But, still shaken after her run-in with Mr Berry, she remained sitting on her bed. The door of the next room slammed shut, making her jump. And then she heard a man humming a tune she didn't recognise. Yes, David must be home and, once again, her heart pumped. She hoped he'd be friendlier than his father. Then there were more footsteps on the stairs: slower and lighter. It must be Winnie coming up, she thought with relief. The steps approached her door and she was pleased when she heard Winnie's voice.

'It's me, love, can I come in?'

'Yes,' Jan answered, trying to hide the fear in her voice.

'David's home. I've kept his dinner warm and I can't wait for you to meet him. Do you want to come through to the kitchen?'

Jan nodded but she'd have much rather stayed in her room.

She followed Winnie into the kitchen and sat at the table. She tried to keep her hands from fidgeting as Winnie went to fetch David. Moments later, he walked in casually and instantly she saw the resemblance he had to his father.

'Hello, Jan. I've heard a lot about you.'

'Hello,' she answered nervously.

'This is a bit weird, isn't it? Me and you, strangers, but we're brother and sister.'

'Yes, I suppose it is.'

'You don't look much like me, but I take after my dad. Have you met him yet?'

'Briefly.'

'Do what I do and just ignore him,' David said and smiled.

Jan began to feel more relaxed and over a cup of tea she enjoyed listening to David talk about his job and his motorbike.

'Right, I'd better get ready. I'm taking a nice young lady out for a ride,' he said and winked at his mum.

'What, in this weather? Are you mad?' Winnie asked.

'No, I'll wrap up warm.'

'Who's the young lady? Do I know her?'

'No, Mum. She's a girl I met at work. Her name is Brenda and she's a machinist. You remember Big Will? Well, she's his eldest daughter.'

'Oh, yes, I remember Big Will. You couldn't forget him if you tried, God rest his soul. Oh, well, it's nice to know

Brenda comes from a good family. I've not heard you mention her before though.'

'That's because I haven't. Don't start with the Spanish Inquisition. It's early days yet, nothing to get excited about.'

'You cheeky bugger,' Winnie said warmly. 'But you saying that Brenda is a machinist has given me an idea. Our Jan is going to learn how to make dresses to sell, but I doubt she'll earn very much. Once she's confident using a sewing machine, you could ask about a job for her where you work.'

'I'm not sure if there are any vacancies, but I can ask. Mind you, there's talk about them stepping up production and making parachutes instead of pillows. Dad's calling for you.'

Winnie jumped up quickly, looking agitated, and she hurried from the kitchen. David scraped his chair back and took his cup and saucer to the sink. When he turned round, Jan was surprised to see that his expression had changed.

'I don't know if you really are my mother's daughter or not, but if you think you're getting your hands on any of her cash, then you can think again. You're a bastard and I'm only putting up with you because I have to. Stay clear of me or else, and if you repeat what I've said to my mother, you'll be sorry.'

He marched from the room, leaving her shocked and shaking. She had no idea why he'd turned from being friendly and good-humoured to threatening and vicious but the look in his eyes had scared her. She'd seen that same look in his father's eyes too. But what on earth had given him the impression that she was after his mother's money?

Winnie returned to the kitchen carrying Mr Berry's cup. 'He wants another,' she said, rolling her eyes. 'It wouldn't hurt the lazy sod to get off his arse every now and again.' Then she put a hand over her mouth, looking contrite before she spoke again. 'Oops, sorry. I don't suppose you're used to bad language.'

'It – it's all right,' Jan managed to say, but she was still reeling from David's harsh words.

'You look washed out, love. It's been a bit of a day for you, what with moving in here and meeting your brother. I know it's early, but you can go to bed any time you like.'

Jan swallowed hard before replying. 'Thank you, I am a bit tired. I think I'll retire now.'

'You do that. Night, night, love.'

'Goodnight, Winnie,' Jan said, and she hurried to her bedroom. She closed her door and wedged a chair under the handle. As much as she was already growing very fond of Winnie, she was regretting moving in. What with Mr Berry and his obvious contempt for her and David's menacing threat, Jan felt just as much a prisoner in her room as she had at her mother's house. No, she thought, that was silly. Her door wasn't locked from the outside and she was free to leave her room at any time. Yet, despite this, Jan knew she was going to have a very restless night's sleep.

13

'Are you still coming tomorrow night?' Kenny asked David as the factory horn signalled the end of another day. It was Friday evening and David was looking forward to seeing Brenda again at the dance. He'd seen her a couple of times in the week. On Tuesday, he'd taken her for a ride and, yesterday, he'd dropped her off home after work. She'd thanked him with a quick snog and now David was hoping for more.

'Yes, mate, I'm coming. Brenda is looking forward to it,' he answered.

'Good. It'll be the last dance I'll be going to for a while.'

'You'd better make the most of it, then. Perhaps your June will give you an extra special goodbye.'

'No chance of that. But at least I know I'll have her to come home to. A man can't ask for much more than a good woman.'

'Or two,' David said, and he winked at Kenny.

'Don't let June or Brenda hear you talking like that or you'll blow your chances. I reckon Brenda is like my June. She won't take no nonsense and she'll be expecting a ring on her finger before you get any hanky panky.'

'Maybe,' David answered, though he hadn't got the

impression that Brenda was in any way similar to her friend. In fact, he could tell from the way she'd kissed him yesterday that she was far from innocent. She knew exactly what she was doing and had obviously done it before.

David collected his bike and waited outside the factory gates for Brenda to offer her a lift. He felt sure his chivalrous gesture would earn him a few brownie points. As he looked for her face among the throng of people piling out, he felt a tap on his shoulder. His stomach flipped when he looked round to see Errol Hampton.

'I take it you're on your way to see me?' Errol asked and he took a drag on his roll-up.

'No, why would I be?'

'It's pay day and you owe me.'

'I'll come and see you tomorrow, Errol, and we can sort it out then.'

'No, we won't. There's nothing to sort out. Your wages belong to me so hand them over.'

'Be reasonable, Errol, you can't take the lot.'

'I ain't kicked your head in yet, so I'd say that's pretty reasonable. But that'll change if you don't give me your wage packet.'

'Please, Errol, you can't take it all. I've got other people to pay,' David said, panicking. He was terrified that the man would give him a hiding outside the gates and that would show him up in front of Brenda.

'I couldn't give a fuck. Have you forgotten that I'm your first priority, or do you need reminding?'

David was about to try and bargain with Errol when Brenda sidled up beside him.

'Who's this, then?' she asked, eyeing Errol up and down as she lit a cigarette.

'A mate of mine. I, erm, said I'd run him up to see his gran in Clapham; she's a bit under the weather. You don't mind getting the bus tonight, do you, sweetheart?'

'If I have to,' Brenda answered sulkily. 'I'll see you tomorrow,' she called as she stamped off.

Once out of sight, David delved into his coat pocket and reluctantly pulled out a brown envelope. His heart sank as he handed it over to Errol who readily accepted it.

Errol opened the packet, smirked, and pulled out two bob. 'Have a drink on me,' he said. He threw the coins at David before swaggering away.

Quickly, David climbed off his bike and scrambled for the measly amount. Anything was better than nothing, he supposed, but now he wouldn't be in a position to pay Stephanie Reynolds her blackmail money. He wasn't convinced that she'd accept another excuse. God, this was all he needed, he thought, straddling his bike again. It was bad enough being in debt to Errol but if Stephanie spouted her lies to the man, his life would get a whole lot more difficult.

Once home, David moodily stomped up the stairs. At least Errol had seemed satisfied with his pay-off for now, and then he was struck by a thought. It would mean the money his mother had kept by for Errol could now line his pockets instead. As long as Jan hadn't got her filthy hands on it. He was halfway up the flight of stairs when he looked up and saw the girl fleeing into her room. Good, he thought; she'd taken heed of his threat and was keeping herself away from him. But then his father appeared in the hallway and David knew the man would be expecting some of his wages. He had to think fast.

'You needn't think you ain't paying your keep. Five and six will do.'

'I've already given it to Mum,' David lied. 'Six shillings.'

'Fair enough. But in future, make sure you give it to me.'

'Yeah, I will,' he answered, relieved that he'd got away with it and confident that his mother would back him up.

Once in his room, David threw his coat on the bed and dashed back downstairs to the pub. He found his mother collecting glasses at the end of the bar. When she turned round and saw him, he was glad to see she looked like she was in a good mood.

'Hello, Son, I didn't hear you come in. Did you have a good day?' she asked.

'Yeah, great, until Errol turned up at the gates and demanded my pay packet.'

'Oh, no, not again!'

'Yep, he took the lot.'

'Oh, Son, I'm so sorry, love. But at least you're getting your debt paid back quickly.'

'Fat chance of that with the interest he's piling on top. The thing is, I had to fib to Dad. He was waiting for my keep, so I told him I'd given it to you. Six shillings. I'm sorry, Mum, but he put me on the spot and I didn't know what else to say. I hope I ain't dropped you in it.'

'No, you did the right thing. We could do without your father finding out about you owing Errol money. He'd do his nut and he's already fed up enough with the Jan situation. Don't worry, I'll square it with him.'

'What will you do when he asks you for the six shillings?'

'I've got a little bit more than that put by to pay Errol, but he won't come knocking now that he's had your wages. It's fine, love, I'll sort it with your father.'

'I know it's a bit cheeky, Mum, but I've been left skint again,' David said. He looked at his mother with sad eyes.

'I can't stretch to much, but I can give you a few bob. My bag is in the kitchen upstairs. There're a couple of florins in my purse. You can have them.'

David leaned down and quickly kissed his mother's cheek. 'Thanks, Mum, thanks so much,' he said. He darted back upstairs, but when he opened the kitchen door, he was sorely disappointed to find Jan pouring herself a cup of tea.

'Oh, I'm sorry,' she mumbled. 'I was just leaving.' She scampered across the room, leaving her cup and saucer on the kitchen side.

'You forgot your tea,' he said, watching her as, timidly, she walked back to fetch it. She really was like a little mouse and plain like one too. Her face was pretty enough but there was nothing striking about her and she was far too thin for his liking. Not like Rachel with her narrow waist and ample breasts. Or Brenda, equally as well proportioned.

'You'd better not have been in my mother's purse,' he warned, looking at the open bag on the table.

'No – I wouldn't do such a thing,' Jan protested, sounding mortified.

'Good. But we don't know you from Adam and you might be a thief, a liar, or both, for all we know. I bet when you saw my mum and the pub, you thought you was on to a right good thing. Well, forget it. It's all in my old man's name and, seeing as he ain't your father, you won't be getting a thing.'

'I ... I don't want –' Jan choked, her words unfinished as she fled the room in floods of tears.

David was pleased he'd put her straight and even happier when he opened his mother's purse and saw there was more than just two florins. The daft mare, he thought, and took the lot. There wasn't enough to keep Stephanie satisfied but at least he'd be able to impress Brenda tomorrow night.

When David had come into the pub, Rachel had avoided him and she was relieved when he'd left soon afterwards. Winnie had told her that he was dating a young lady called Brenda. She'd spoken with such pride but Rachel had instantly felt sorry for the girl. She thought Brenda had most likely been charmed by his good looks but had no idea what a sly and conniving young man hid under his attractive exterior. She had no doubt that David would break Brenda's heart just as Jim had broken hers. Still, at least with David's head turned, he was leaving her in peace.

'My Jan has been getting on a treat with your sister,' Winnie said when there was a lull between customers. 'Hilda said she soon got the hang of the sewing machine and her dresses look so professional. She's already knocked up a couple of simple ones, but I wish I could afford to buy her a machine of her own. I might see if I can get her a second-hand one for Christmas. I'd love to push the boat out and give her something nice. After all, I've got twenty-seven Christmases and birthdays to make up for.'

'I'm sure Jan doesn't see it that way. And from what she's said, I don't think she ever got more than a new Bible or pair of shoes for Christmas. She'll be happy with anything you give her.'

'Yes, I know, but I still want to make it special for her.'

The door opened with gusto and Rachel's mood slumped

when she saw her sister lurch in. Hilda looked the worse for wear and, despite Winnie singing her praises, Rachel felt disgusted. 'Been doing a good job with Jan, has she?' she seethed to Winnie. 'A good job at getting plastered, from what I can see!'

Hilda swayed towards the bar, saying hello loudly to everyone as she staggered past the tables. Bill, a regular in the pub when he wasn't working on the dress stall with his wife, Flo, was sitting in his usual corner, minding his own business. When Hilda saw him, she made a beeline in his direction.

'Hello, my lovely. Are you gonna buy me a drink?' she asked, steadying herself against Bill's table.

He looked at her with sympathy and stood up to take her arm. 'Come and sit down. I'll get you a drink.'

As Bill walked towards the bar, Rachel shook her head at him. 'I think she's had more than enough,' she sighed.

'Yes, she has. Just pour a very small whisky and add a dash of water. I'll see if I can persuade her to go home.'

'Thanks, Bill,' Rachel said, grateful that he was such a gentleman. She thought the man deserved a medal. When it came to Hilda, Bill had the patience of a saint. 'There you go. Good luck,' she said. She watched Bill take the watered-down drink to her sister.

It seemed that Hilda was so drunk that she didn't notice the water in her whisky and she drank half the glass. Then she leaned heavily on Bill and whispered something in his ear. Rachel couldn't hear what she said, and though Bill chuckled, she thought he looked embarrassed.

'The blinkin' state of her again. I've not seen her like it all week,' Winnie said and tutted.

'Me neither. If she's managed to stay off the booze until today, she's certainly making up for it now.'

'What you looking at?' Hilda screeched from the corner table.

'Oh, no, here we go,' Rachel moaned.

'Go out the back, love. I'll get rid of her.'

'No, it's too busy and I'm fed up with this. It's about time she learned how to behave herself and that's just what I'm going to tell her.'

Rachel heard Winnie's voice behind her. 'I don't think that's a good idea.'

Rachel marched off regardless, walking purposely towards her sister, who was glaring bleary-eyed at her.

'Bugger off, Rachel,' Hilda spat. 'Go and find your own friends. Oh – wait, that's right – you ain't got none.' Hilda cackled with wicked laughter and Bill lowered his head.

'Do you know why you ain't got no friends?' Hilda asked nastily, then she hiccupped.

'We're not discussing this now. You obviously can't control yourself, so it's time for you to leave,' Rachel replied firmly, pointing towards the door.

'Who do you think you are, Missy? You can't tell me what to do. Stop trying to humiliate me and go and do your job.'

'This *is* my job. Are you going to leave quietly or are you going to insist on making a scene again?'

'I ain't going nowhere. Me and Bill are quite happy here and we ain't doing no harm.'

Rachel had guessed that Hilda would kick up a stink when she was told to leave but she wasn't going to back down. 'I've asked you nicely, but if you still refuse to budge, I will physically throw you out if I have to.'

The threat made Hilda rise to her feet and she stumbled sideways but Bill supported her. 'Come on, then, let's see you try it. But you won't, will you? You've never stood up to anyone, not even your fiancé when he got my sister pregnant.'

Rachel gasped, horrified. How could Hilda spill her deepest and darkest secrets for all to hear and show her up like this in front of everyone?

'Yeah, that's right,' Hilda said loudly as she looked around the pub. 'Her bleedin' fiancé slept with my sister on the night before their wedding. Fancy that, eh. Bloody disgusting.' Then she turned back to Rachel, a sneer on her face. 'And then when my sister died giving birth all alone, what did you do? You ran away. Did you hear that?' she called.

No one in the pub answered and Hilda continued. 'Came here and started a new life like nothing ever happened. And I know you still hold a torch for Jim, even after everything he did. I bet you would have gone through with the wedding if I hadn't have stopped you.'

Rachel felt as though she'd been punched in the stomach and stabbed in the back at the same time. She couldn't meet anyone's eyes and had the sudden urge to push Hilda to the floor and spit in her face, but she felt Winnie gently tug her arm. 'Come away, love. Let me deal with this.'

'No,' she said, finding her voice. 'I'm sick of her running her mouth off when she's drunk, then pretending the next day like nothing happened.' Glaring at Hilda, she screamed, 'Get out!'

The pub was silent and all eyes were on Hilda, who looked across the room again, a twisted smile on her face. She seemed to be enjoying the attention. 'You'd throw me out, would you? That's choice, that is. You'd throw your own mother out.'

Confused now, Rachel spluttered, 'What? What are you talking about?'

'Yeah, that's right. Did you lot hear me? I'M HER MOTHER,' she declared loudly, looking triumphant before tumbling back into the seat next to Bill and giggling pathetically.

'No, you're not. You're my sister and I'm so ashamed of you right now.'

'Huh, typical of you, think you know it all. But you don't,' Hilda sneered.

'You're talking nonsense. Just get out.'

'It ain't nonsense,' Hilda shouted as she pushed herself to her feet again and staggered towards the door. 'You was the biggest mistake of my life. I'm your mother. Now put that in your pipe and smoke it. See ya.'

Hilda almost fell out of the pub, leaving Rachel reeling. She wanted to call her back and demand answers to all the questions flooding her head. She felt an arm over her shoulder. It was Winnie and the woman was gently leading her towards the bar.

'Go out the back, love. Put the kettle on and make yourself a cuppa. Take your time. I'll get Jan to come and sit with you.'

Rachel nodded and wandered through to the back, staggered at Hilda's announcement. Still dazed, she put the water on to boil. Could it be true? Could her sister really be her mother? Had her whole life been a lie? Shocked by Hilda's revelation, tears began to slip from her eyes. She considered chasing after Hilda so that she could get to the truth, but she knew it would be pointless. Hilda was in no fit state to talk. But she would be in the morning. And Rachel would insist on knowing everything.

14

Sleep had evaded Winnie for most of the night. She'd had Rachel on her mind and was worried because she knew the girl had taken Hilda's news badly. She'd sent her home early, though she wasn't sure that giving Rachel time to brood alone had been such a good idea. Rachel had said she'd visit Hilda first thing on Saturday and Winnie had offered to go with her, but the girl had insisted it was something she needed to do alone. Winnie glanced at her watch. The small face with gold hands and numbers was becoming more and more difficult to see. Moving her wrist further away, she could see it was just after nine. She wondered if Rachel was already at Hilda's.

'Good morning,' Jan said quietly as she came into the kitchen.

'Morning, love. Did you sleep all right?'

'Yes, like a log.'

Winnie looked at the girl's puffy eyes, ringed by dark circles, and didn't believe her. No doubt she was still worried about her mother, though not her real one, she thought. 'There's tea in the pot, would you like some?'

'Yes, please, but you sit there, I'll get it.'

Jan poured herself a cup and joined Winnie at the table.

'Right old shocking state of affairs, eh, love,' Winnie said, her hands resting on the table while she twiddled her thumbs. 'What with me telling you like a bolt out the blue that I think I'm your mum and now Hilda declaring she's Rachel's mum. You couldn't make it up!'

'Yes, but it's very different for Rachel. She thought that Hilda was her sister.'

'Yeah, that's true. She feels she's been deceived her whole life. Fancy having Hilda as a mother. I know she's been good to you, but the woman is partial to a drink and, well, you've seen for yourself what it does to her.'

'Hilda still isn't as bad as my mother,' Jan said, staring into her teacup.

Winnie felt a jab of guilt. If she'd been stronger and had stood up to her parents, Jan would have had a very different life. 'I told Rachel to take the day off but she won't hear of it, especially being Saturday. We normally get very busy.'

'I could help out,' Jan offered.

'No, you're all right, love, but thanks. You've got enough to do with your dressmaking, though I doubt Hilda will be taking you down the market today to meet Bill and Flo. Bill's often in here, though. In fact, he was here last night when Hilda kicked off, but it's no good me introducing you to him as it's Flo who does all the buying for their stall.'

'I've only got two dresses ready. I'll spend the weekend finishing off the others. But I think I'll have to do them by hand.'

'Yes, love, sounds sensible. I'd give Hilda a wide berth for a while – at least until the dust settles. Won't you be seeing Terry?'

'Yes, probably, but not until tomorrow evening. He's doing overtime at the bakery.'

Winnie yawned, then sipped her tea, studying Jan's face. She seemed tense and Winnie wondered if all this business with Rachel and Hilda had upset her. 'You needn't worry about Rachel. Once she gets over the shock, she'll be as right as rain, you'll see.'

'I'm not worried. I don't know Rachel well, but I can tell she's a strong woman. Stronger than me, that's for sure.'

'She is, but don't underestimate yourself, young lady. You've proven yourself to be strong too.'

'No, I'm not. I wasn't strong enough to leave my mother's. I should have left years ago.'

'But you survived it, which makes you stronger than most. Is that what's bothering you?'

Jan's head snapped up and Winnie thought she saw a flash of fear in her eyes.

'No, there's nothing bothering me.'

'Are you sure? I know you're worried about her, and I don't mean to be nosy, but if there's something else, you know you can talk to me about anything that's on your mind.'

'Yes, I know. Thank you.'

Winnie didn't want to push her, so she changed the subject. 'David's got another date tonight with Brenda. They've been courting for a week or two now. It'll be nice to meet her.'

Jan pursed her lips and stared into her teacup again.

'How have you two been getting on? It must be strange for you both, suddenly discovering you have a sibling.'

'Fine,' Jan answered shortly, still gazing at her tea.

'Has he mentioned the dance to you? Only I said it would be nice if he took you and Terry along one evening.'

'No, no … I wouldn't want to go.'

'Oh, Jan, you'd really enjoy it and David and Terry would take good care of you.'

'I said, no,' Jan snapped.

Winnie was taken aback and instantly Jan looked remorseful.

'I'm sorry, I didn't mean to talk to you like that.'

'It's all right, love. I realise I can be a bit pushy sometimes. You've had a lot to get your head round and I should imagine that the local Saturday-night dance is the last thing on your mind.'

'I'd – erm, better get dressed,' Jan said evasively. She pushed her chair back, leaving a half-drunk cup of tea.

Winnie thought she'd upset her and felt awful. 'Have some breakfast first. I can do you some toast and jam or there's porridge, if you'd prefer it?'

'No, thank you. I'm not hungry.'

'Oh, Jan, you're as thin as a rake. You really could do with a bit of feeding up.'

'I said I'm not hungry,' Jan repeated tersely.

Winnie sucked in a long breath. Something clearly wasn't right with the girl and she intended to get to the bottom of it. 'Sit back down, young lady,' she ordered.

Jan's eyes widened, but she meekly did as she was told.

'Right, there's obviously something or someone that's upset you. If it's my Brian, there's no need to be afraid to tell me. I know he can be a nasty git and I won't have him upsetting you.'

'No, Winnie. It's not Mr Berry. I did have one short run-in with him but he didn't do anything.'

'So who is it, then?'

'I'd rather not say.'

'Neither of us are budging until you do. So you may as well come out with it.'

Winnie noticed tears brimming in Jan's eyes and she felt the urge to hold her close but she managed to restrain herself. 'Come on, love. Whatever it is, we can sort it.'

'Oh, Winnie, I'm sorry, but I don't know how much longer I can bear living here,' Jan blurted out and now tears streamed down her cheeks.

'Why? Have I done something wrong?'

'No – of course you haven't. I've never had anyone show me the kindness you have,' Jan answered and she dabbed her wet face with the back of her hand.

'So what is it, then? Why don't you want to live here?'

'It's – it's David. He hates me.'

'Don't be daft, of course he doesn't. He hasn't shown you much attention cos he's busy working and courting, that's all.'

'No, Winnie, you don't understand. Please, just forget it. I've said too much already.'

Winnie could see that Jan was genuinely upset but she couldn't understand how David had made her feel this way. Her son had taken the news of Jan badly at first but he had quickly come round and she thought he was pleased to have his older sister living with them. 'I can't forget it. You'd better tell me everything,' she insisted.

Jan sniffed and shook her head. 'If I tell you, David will – I don't know what he'll do, but he threatened me.'

'My David? Never!' Winnie exclaimed incredulously.

'I knew you wouldn't believe me. I shouldn't have said anything.'

Winnie reached across the table for Jan's hand and patted the back of it. 'I'm sorry, love. I shouldn't have reacted like that. Now, start at the beginning and tell me exactly what that son of mine has said to you.'

It was painful for Winnie to hear Jan's reiteration of David's threats and accusations and she found it difficult to believe he could be so cruel. Yet he was his father's son after all and Brian had obviously rubbed off on him. It was bad enough that Jan had Brian to contend with and now with David being so vile, it was little wonder the girl wanted to move out.

'I won't lie to you, love,' she said after Jan had told her everything, 'I'm flabbergasted to hear my David's been behaving like this. But, trust me, I'll put a stop to it. You won't be getting any more bother from him, I promise.'

'Please, Winnie, you can't say anything,' Jan begged, ashen-faced. 'He'll – he'll –'

'He will apologise to you, that's what he'll do. At least he will, if he knows what's good for him.'

'But –'

'No buts. I'm really disappointed in my son. I expected better from him and I'm sorry you've been threatened and made to feel uncomfortable. This is your home and I won't have you driven out. Please stay, and leave me to deal with David.'

Jan wiped her nose on the cuff of her pale blue winceyette dressing gown. She looked so pale, so full of nerves, and Winnie was furious with her son. Jan had been through enough and she had wanted her daughter to be happy living with them.

'Well?' she pushed. 'Please say you'll stay.'

Jan nodded slowly and Winnie slumped with relief. 'I swear to you, no one is going to hurt you ever again and I'll make sure my son apologises. I'll see that he's civil to you in future.'

'Thank you.'

'Right, now that's sorted, how about some toast. Shall I do you a couple of slices with lashings of butter?'

'That sounds lovely,' Jan said softly and at last, the corners of her mouth turned slightly upwards.

Winnie cut thick doorstops of bread and placed them under the grill. She hummed a happy tune but it was all pretence as, inside, she was crying. David had let her down. She'd thought she could rely on him but he'd proved himself to be just as mean as his father. She'd always known he was lazy like Brian but until now she'd never thought he had his father's wicked ways too. David was a chip off the old block and it broke Winnie's heart.

Rachel's knuckles hurt from rapping so loudly on Hilda's door but she refused to give in and knocked again. Hilda rented a large room in a shared terraced house only ten minutes from her own. The neat net curtains and pretty painted flower box masked the mess that Rachel knew hid behind the door.

She heard Hilda's muffled voice shout, 'Go away.'

'Hilda, open this door,' she called sternly.

Moments later, Hilda did just that and Rachel barged in.

'Come in, why don't you,' Hilda said sarcastically as she passed her.

Rachel stamped across the room and stood in front of the hearth. Her eyes flitted around. Apart from Hilda's shoes strewn in the middle of the floor and her coat in a heap behind the door, the place looked unusually tidy. Hilda, on the other hand, looked like she'd been pulled through a hedge backwards. But Rachel wasn't here for an inspection and snapped, 'Would you care to explain to me about what you told me last night?'

Hilda rolled her eyes and sat at a small drop-leaf table in the recess of the bay window. She lit a cigarette and threw the spent matchstick into an overflowing ashtray. 'What are you talking about?' she drawled as smoke curled around her grey face.

'I'm talking about you telling everyone in the pub that you're my mother!'

Hilda rested her forehead in her hand, her elbow on the table. 'Gawd, my head hurts,' she muttered and closed her eyes.

'Never mind about your headache. What's all this nonsense about you being my mum?'

Hilda turned her head to look at Rachel through one half-opened eye. 'Did I really say that?'

'Yes, you did. It is true?'

'Sit down, Rachel, you're making the place look untidy,' Hilda answered with a weak smile. 'Jan gave me a hand cleaning up and I've been keeping it nice.'

'You haven't answered my question,' Rachel snapped, irritated.

'I said, sit down,' Hilda repeated.

Rachel drew out the one other wooden chair at the table and huffed as she sat, repeating, 'So, is it true?'

'Yes, darling, it is. But I'm so sorry you found out the way you did.'

Rachel felt as if all the breath had been punched out of her chest and her shoulders slumped. She peered at Hilda, shaking her head, unsure if she truly believed her.

'I should have told you years ago but I never found the right moment,' Hilda said and stubbed out her cigarette. 'My mouth feels like sandpaper. Be a love and make us a cuppa.'

'You're something else, you are,' Rachel said angrily. 'How can you be this blasé after the bombshell you've just dropped on me?'

'I knew you'd be all melodramatic, and don't talk so flippantly about bombshells dropping on you. Have you seen that barrage balloon in the park? It'll only be a matter of time before the Jerries are shelling us.'

'I don't care about the bloody war – shut up! Just shut up about it and tell me why you've lied to me all these years.'

'Huh, that's a fine way to talk to your mother,' Hilda said mockingly.

Rachel glared at her with her jaw clenched. If Hilda wasn't so infuriating, she might have burst into tears. 'You'd better start explaining,' she barked.

'All right, calm down. You've got a right to know the truth. But let's talk about it over a brew,' Hilda said, getting up to go and make the tea.

Rachel tapped her fingers on the scratched mahogany table as she waited for Hilda to return from the scullery. There'd still been doubt in her mind until now and though Hilda had confirmed the truth, she was struggling to accept it. Her thoughts tumbled over each other. It meant her mum was really her gran, her dad her grandfather and her brothers and sisters were her aunts and uncles. Hilda wasn't the only one with a headache – thinking about the family relationships made her head hurt too.

'I put an extra spoonful of leaves in,' Hilda said, carrying a tray into the room and kicking the door closed behind her. 'I could do with a strong cup this morning.'

Rachel waited for Hilda to sit down at the table and pour the tea. She managed not to raise her voice as she asked, 'Why are you only telling me now that you're my mother?'

'We thought it was for the best. I'll tell you why, but some of it's pretty ugly. Are you sure you want to know?'

'It couldn't be any uglier than what you said to me last night,' she answered, fighting to hold back the tears that she wished hadn't come. 'You said I was the biggest mistake of your life.'

'Flippin' 'eck, sorry. Having you did ruin my life but that weren't your fault. You never asked to be born. I messed up, not you.'

'What happened?' Rachel asked, calmer now and desperate to know the whole story.

'I was young and silly. I fell for a boy and got caught out. There's not much to tell.'

'Who was my father? Why didn't he marry you?' Rachel's questions came thick and fast. 'How did Gran end up bringing me up as her own? Why did you allow her to?'

Hilda ran a hand through her tangled hair. 'Christ, slow down. I can only answer one question at a time. I suppose it's only natural that you'd want to know about your father but there isn't much I can tell you. He was a young man, a soldier who'd been fighting in the trenches in France. Tom, his name was, Tom Casey. I worked in a café in Victoria and he was passing through on his way to see his family for a couple of weeks before being shipped back out to fight again. We got talking and when I finished work that evening, he was outside waiting for me. He ended up staying in Victoria for those two weeks and cos of that he never did get home to see his mum – never.'

'Why? What happened?'

'He was killed. Just like a lot of 'em were. I got one letter from him, but that was all. By then I'd worked out I was carrying you in my belly but I couldn't tell anyone, especially not my mum and dad. See, me and Tom had been meeting in secret. No one knew he existed. The trouble was, I was all set to marry Humphrey Jenner. He was quite a bit older than me and I didn't love him or nothing. But he was well off and had his own building company so my dad was really pushing me to marry him. He put a lot of pressure on me and, in the end, I agreed. Mum said I'd be better off with a man with money and that love was overrated. But I never forgot Tom.'

'How did you know he'd been killed?'

'I knew he lived just outside Canterbury and his name but that was all. I got the train out that way and set out to find his family. I couldn't, Canterbury was a lot bigger than I thought it was. In the end, I'd just about given up hope, but a few weeks later, a couple of soldiers came into the café and I asked them if they knew Tom. They didn't, but I told them where he was serving and they said his whole company had been killed.' Hilda paused and ran a hand over her face. 'So, that was that. I was left with you and could only hope Humphrey would accept you as his own.'

'I take it he didn't?'

'No, he was none too pleased, to say the least, and said he wanted nothing to do with me. Cor, the names he called me. Turned the air blue. By now I was six months gone and couldn't hide it anymore. I had no choice but to own up to my mum and dad. I had to tell them about Tom, and that Humphrey had washed his hands of me. Dad was furious with me at first but Mum managed to talk him round.'

'I still don't understand why I was passed off as their daughter?' Rachel asked.

'Well, with a baby on the way I had no chance of finding myself a husband or a job and you know what people think of unmarried mothers. Dad coughed up the money to see someone about getting rid of you.'

'Getting rid of me?' Rachel cried, appalled.

'I know it sounds awful, but believe me, I didn't want to. I cried me eyes out for days. Thankfully, it turned out I was too far gone, but then my dad said I'd have to give you up for adoption. My mum wouldn't hear of handing you over to a children's home. She said she already had thirteen of us so she doubted anyone would notice one more. And that's what happened. She made herself look pregnant and I was kept hidden away until you was born. Then my mum carried on as usual as if you were her baby and no one batted an eyelid.'

'Why didn't you tell me? Why didn't Mum – I mean Gran – ever tell me? Does the rest of the family know?'

'Oh, Rachel, darling, there were so many times when I wanted to tell you. It would rip me apart when I'd hear you calling her "Mum". I wanted to take you back and run off with you but I had no means to support myself with a young child. It didn't stop me trying though.'

'You eventually left home.'

'Yes, I found a job, but you should have heard the rows I had with Mum and Dad. They wouldn't let me have you, said I weren't fit to be a mother, and threatened to get the authorities on me. There was no proof that I was your mother so my hands were tied.'

'What about the rest of the family? Did they know?'

'Yes, some of them, but it was never mentioned – except when I'd come home again, wanting to take you away. They sided with my mum and dad, and in the end, as you got older, I realised it would be cruel to rip you away from the only parents you'd ever known. I sat back and watched them bring you up. I suppose that's why I came to Battersea with you. I'm still sitting back and watching you even now.'

Rachel sipped her tea which had now gone cold. She wanted to be angry with Hilda but in a strange sense, her fascinating tale felt as if it was about someone else. It hadn't yet sunk in that the hungover, stinking, dishevelled woman sitting opposite her was, in fact, her mother. 'Now I understand why you're always shouting about me ruining your life,' she said sadly.

'That's wrong of me and I shouldn't do it. It's that bloody whisky. I'd stayed off it all week and felt so much better but I let myself down again yesterday. You didn't ruin my life. I did a good job of doing that myself.'

'I just can't seem to take it in.'

'If I hadn't had you, I would have married Humphrey and my life would have been bloody miserable. So you did me a favour really. Yet, deep down, I resented that I couldn't be your mum and always had to take a back seat.'

'I suppose that must have been hard for you.'

'Yeah, and I didn't fall in love with anyone after Tom. I

think that's because I wouldn't let myself. I did marry, eventually, but that was only because I thought I should and it didn't last two minutes. I was too busy watching you.'

Hilda gave such a sweet, soft and loving smile, that it almost melted Rachel's heart. She realised things could have been a lot worse and sighed, thinking about Jan and how she'd been brought up by a tyrannical, mad woman. That could have been her fate too, or worse, especially being brought up in a children's home. Philosophically, she said, 'I wish you'd told me all this sooner, but what's done is done. We can't change the past. It is what it is, but I don't think I'll ever be able to look at my mum as my gran. I'm not sure that I can ever see you as anything other than my infuriating older sister, though that being said, I wouldn't be without you.'

To Rachel's astonishment, Hilda burst out crying. She wasn't normally one for showing her emotions, least of all tears.

'I kept it all to myself for so long,' Hilda gasped. 'The resentment has been building and building, till sometimes I feel like it's been eating me from the inside out. I'm glad you know everything now. I don't expect you to see me as your mum, but you'll have to put up with me trying to be.'

A thought sprung to Rachel's mind. Maybe this could keep Hilda off the booze. 'I think I could accept you as my mum if you stopped drinking,' she said hopefully.

'Oh, Rachel, you don't know how much that means to me. I'll stop drinking, darling, I promise I will, for you.'

Rachel hoped that Hilda meant it, but she had fallen off the wagon so many times in the past. Maybe now that the truth had come out it would give her the strength she needed. It was all Rachel could hope for, and only time would tell.

15

Later that evening, David felt happy that his dance moves appeared to be wooing Brenda. As he moved her around the dance floor, he pulled her in close, his hands slipping to just below the small of her back.

'Shall we get out of here?' he spoke huskily into her ear.

'Aren't you enjoying yourself?'

'Yes, I'm having a great time, but I want to be alone with you.'

'Oh, I see,' she answered, smiling teasingly at him. 'Where would we go? It's freezing outside.'

'Don't worry, I'll keep you warm. Come on, let's go,' he said and he pulled her towards their table where Kenny and June were sitting.

'Me and Brenda are gonna go for a ride,' David said. He picked up his half-glass of lager to swig it down.

'Rather you than me. It's bloody cold tonight,' Kenny said.

'Can I have a word?' June asked Brenda, ushering her to one side.

With the women out of earshot, Kenny lowered his voice. 'What are you playing at?'

'Nothing, mate.'

'So where are you planning on taking Brenda?'

'Just for a spin on my bike. She likes it.'

'Yeah, and the rest. I know your game. Just don't go breaking Brenda's heart or my June will blame me and I don't want to be on the end of a tongue-lashing from her.'

'Don't worry, Brenda's a big girl and she knows what she's doing.'

'Does she, though, mate? Does she know what you're like?'

He was saved from answering Kenny's question by the return of the women. Brenda had a face like thunder and June looked like she had the right hump.

'Are you coming, or what?' Brenda asked David, throwing June a filthy look.

'You'll ruin your reputation,' June snapped. She sat back next to Kenny with her arms folded. 'You should know better after what happened the last time.'

'I'll get our coats,' David told Brenda, hoping to avoid being caught in the middle of a catfight.

Brenda grabbed hold of his hand and pulled him towards the cloakroom. 'I'll come with you. There's an 'orrible smell around here. I think it's called jealousy,' she called over her shoulder and she didn't bother saying goodbye to her friend.

They weaved their way through the other revellers and David heard June's voice floating over the sound of the band. 'On your head be it,' she shouted. 'You'll be sorry.'

Outside, as they pulled on their coats, David turned to Brenda. 'What was all that about?' he asked.

'Nothing. Take no notice of June.'

'What did she mean about after the last time?'

'I told you. Nothing. She's just jealous because I want to

have some fun. She's such a stick-in-the mud and she's always worried about what other people think.'

'It sounded like there was a bit more to it than that,' David commented but in truth he didn't care what Brenda had done in the past. He doubted she was a virgin and that suited him.

'Just leave it, please,' she said, then changed the subject. 'Blimey, Kenny wasn't wrong though, it's bleedin' cold. Are you sure this is a good idea?'

They were standing next to David's bike. He cupped her face in his hands and looked into her dark blue eyes. 'Yes,' he said. He kissed her. It was a long, deep kiss. His groin stirred and she responded with equal ardour, moaning lightly and pushing herself against him.

'Oh, David,' she said huskily.

He pulled away, eager for them to be alone in private. Straddling his bike, he told her, 'Get on.'

Brenda sat behind him and as he started the engine, she nibbled his earlobe. Oh yes, he was sure he was going to get what he wanted from her and he raced towards Ted's house. His friend had an Anderson shelter in the back garden and Ted had told him it was kitted out with a camp bed and plenty of blankets. Ted's back gate was never locked and he knew they could slip in unnoticed. It was perfect – sheltered, private and reasonably comfortable.

'Where are we going?' Brenda yelled in his ear as the bike picked up speed along Falcon Road.

'You'll see,' he answered, the wind taking his breath away and making his eyes water. His hands felt numb with cold on the handlebars but David hardly noticed. He had one thing on his mind and the few beers he'd drunk at the dance were giving him a warm glow.

At the end of the main road, he turned right. He felt the back wheel slide out and the bike wobbled but he kept control and sped on.

'Slow down,' Brenda shrieked, tightening her grip around his waist.

But he opened the throttle, pushing the bike harder.

'David – slow down!' she yelled again.

He ignored her plea, enjoying the exhilaration of the speed and showing off what his bike could do. As they approached Ted's street, he leaned to one side and threw the bike around the corner. This time the back wheel skidded and he couldn't pull the bike upright. Brenda screamed as he lost control and they hit the tarmac hard. The bike was no longer under him and he felt himself tumbling over and over, his leg and shoulder scraping along the ground until he came to a stop on his side. 'Argh,' he groaned, grabbing his painful knee. His trousers had ripped and he could feel the dampness of blood on his leg. Thankfully, he could move and though he was sure he'd sustained many cuts and bruises, nothing seemed to be broken. He sat up, looking around for his bike.

The bike was several feet further down the street and bits of debris lay between him and his machine. Then he looked over his shoulder and saw Brenda lying motionless near the kerb. Quickly scrambling to his feet, he hobbled towards her, dropped to her side and took her limp hand in his. 'Brenda – Brenda, are you hurt?'

Her eyes slowly flickered open. 'My head hurts,' she groaned.

David noticed blood oozing from a gash above her ear. 'You've got a bit of a nasty cut. Can you sit up?'

She tried, but then her eyes widened and a look of terror spread across her face. 'I can't move,' she gasped.

'What? No, of course you can. Come on, sit up.'

'I – I can't. I can't move. Dave, I can't move,' she repeated, louder now. 'Oh, God, I can't feel anything. My legs – my arms – nothing's working. Help me – HELP ME!'

Brenda's screams and the shock of what she was saying sent David falling backwards. He sat on his rear on the damp ground staring at the paralysed woman in front of him. Her eyes were blazing with fear and her wailing filled the quiet night air. People were coming out of their houses. Someone placed a blanket over David's shoulders. A man knelt beside Brenda, trying to calm her, while another said help was on the way.

David staggered to his feet, unaware of the pain in his knee or the blood trickling down his shin. Brenda had quietened down and was drifting in and out of consciousness.

'You're all right, lad,' an elderly man said, offering him support. 'Best sit back down till the ambulance arrives.'

'No – no. I'm fine. I – erm, I have to get my bike,' he murmured, shaking the old man off. A crowd had now gathered around Brenda, obscuring his view of her. He looked along the street at the debris. His bike was probably broken beyond repair and in a daze he hobbled towards it, picking up the front number plate and a twisted mudguard. Someone was gently tugging on his arm, urging him to come back to where Brenda lay by the kerb. He ignored him, then found himself alone, looking at the mangled mess of twisted metal that was once his prized possession. He wouldn't be riding it home, he thought, limping further along the street, around the corner, and out of sight of the accident.

It felt a long walk home and the whole way, David replayed the moment of the crash over and over in his mind. Had he been going too fast? He hadn't thought so, he'd ridden just as fast before without incident. Had Brenda leaned too far over and sent them off balance? It was possible. Had the beer slowed his reactions? He doubted it. Maybe they'd hit an oil patch. Perhaps the tyres had lost their grip in the damp.

At last David reached the back door of the Battersea Tavern. He winced at the searing pain in his leg, grateful to be home. His mum would patch him up and no doubt offer him lots of tea and sympathy. He shuffled through the door, calling her name.

When she came through from the pub and saw him, her face drained of colour as she rushed forwards, helping him to lower his aching body onto the bottom step of the stairs.

'What on earth happened to you?' she asked, her voice full of concern.

'I had an accident on my bike. It's had it. I won't be riding it again.'

'David, your leg! You're bleeding!'

'It's all right, Mum, it's just a scratch, but it don't 'alf sting.'

'Can you get upstairs or shall I call your father to help?'

'No, I reckon I can manage. I walked home, after all.'

Holding on to the bannister and leaning on his mum's shoulder, he slowly and painfully climbed the stairs. In the kitchen, his mother washed and dressed his wound and quizzed him about the accident.

'I was on my way to Ted's and lost control on a corner.'

'What was you doing going to Ted's? I thought you was at the dance with Brenda.'

'I was. We were going to see if his mum had heard how he's getting on at basic training.'

'We? Was Brenda with you?' his mother asked, looking worried.

'Yes. She was on the back. I think she's in a bad way,' he admitted finally.

'What do you mean, you "think"? Where is she?'

'In the hospital by now, I suppose. Someone went to call for an ambulance.'

'You left her? You left her before the ambulance arrived?'

David met his mother's eyes and saw she was appalled. And it dawned on him that he should probably have stayed at the scene.

'Oh, David. What have you done?'

'I was in a bit of a fog and, anyway, there was nothing I could do to help her. There were loads of people with her. She was being looked after,' he answered, realising his excuses sounded feeble.

'Fog or not, you shouldn't have left her. Good God, David, what were you thinking?'

He knew it looked bad, especially considering Brenda's injuries. 'I don't know, Mum. I think it was the shock and I just had it in my head that I had to get home.'

Slowly, the seriousness of Brenda's injuries began to sink in. 'Oh, Mum, it was awful. The look in Brenda's eyes when she realised she couldn't move her arms or legs. It floored me, literally. I didn't know what to do ...' His voice trailed off as he pictured Brenda's terrified face.

'What? What do you mean she couldn't move her arms or legs?'

'I think she might have broken her back,' he said sheepishly, suddenly overwhelmed with guilt for leaving her.

'And you walked away?' she asked in disbelief.

The realisation hit him like a hammer blow to the head. 'What have I done? I wasn't thinking straight,' he mumbled, shaking his head.

His mother put her hand on his shoulder and David suddenly felt his emotions over-spilling. He crumpled, his face in his hands as he sobbed unashamedly.

'It's all right, Son, it'll be all right,' his mother soothed.

David reached out and wrapped his arms around her, burying his head in her flabby stomach. He stayed there for a few moments, then pulled away and looked up into his mother's sympathetic face. 'I've ruined her life. It won't be all right. And my name will be mud when it gets around that I left her there in the street. But I was in shock, Mum, I swear.'

His mother cleared away the bowl of bloodied water she'd used to clean his cuts and, resting her hands on the sink, she said, 'That's what we'll say. We'll tell the police and everyone that you'd taken a bump to your head and wasn't thinking clearly. The shock confused you. Yes, that's feasible. Poor Brenda, but maybe she's just bruised her back and will be back on her feet in no time. The doctors can do amazing things these days.'

'Maybe,' he said and sniffed, but he didn't believe Brenda would ever walk again. He'd seen this happen before to a teacher at his school. The man had been thrown from a horse and now lived in an institution, unable to move from the neck down. The same would likely happen to Brenda, he thought sadly.

'Someone needs to go and see Brenda's mother and tell her what's happened. Do you think you're up to it?'

'No way. I'm not going round there. Her mother is bound to blame me, but it weren't my fault. It was Brenda who was keen to drag me out of the dance. You can ask Kenny, he was there. And she was more than happy to get on the back of my bike. She leaned over too far when we went around a corner and it sent us over. It wasn't my fault that I lost control of the bike. It was Brenda's fault, but I doubt her mother will believe that, will she?'

His mum sucked in a long breath and sighed. 'No, I don't suppose she will. Anyway, I should think the police have been to see her by now. Maybe I should pop round in the morning, tell her how sorry you are for walking off but explain that you were in shock.'

'If you think it's a good idea?'

'Yes, I do. And I reckon you should go to the hospital tomorrow and see how Brenda is.'

'I can't. I feel so bad about leaving her and I don't think I can face her,' he lied.

'You must. Brenda's going to need a lot of help and support to get better. And I'm sure she'll understand.'

David shook his head. There was no way he was going to see Brenda. Though he felt sorry for her, he didn't want to be lumbered with a girlfriend who couldn't walk. He'd only been seeing her for a bit of fun. She wasn't his responsibility. And the chances were, she'd accuse him of driving too fast. But it would be her word against his and he'd deny the speed they were travelling at. His only priority was to make sure that his name was in the clear.

16

The next morning, with ten minutes to go until the pub opened for Sunday lunchtime, Winnie and Rachel were sitting in the downstairs kitchen enjoying a cup of tea. 'It's terrible, love. I didn't get a chance to tell you everything last night, what with sorting out David and seeing to the police. I dread to think what will happen to poor Brenda.'

'What did the police say about it?'

'Their investigations are ongoing but David swears blind he wasn't going too fast. I don't think there will be any action taken against him. It was just one of those things. Them bloody bikes ain't safe. I've always said so.'

'Any news on Brenda?' Rachel asked.

'No change. I went round to see her mother this morning. The woman was in bits and can't bring herself to leave the house, not even to visit her daughter in the hospital. Brenda's friend June is running between the hospital and Brenda's house to keep her mum up to date. The doctors have said it's early days but they don't expect her to make a full recovery. She'll be lucky if she can even feed herself.'

'Blimey, Win, that's awful. I think I'd rather die than be left like that.'

'Me too, but Brenda's mum doesn't see it that way, which is understandable. No mother wants to bury their own child.'

'I know, I saw my mum, I mean my grandma, have to do it enough times. I'll never forget the noise she made. It was like she was howling with grief. Awful, it was, Win, absolutely bloody awful.'

'I can imagine, the poor woman.'

'Is there anything we can do for Brenda's mum?'

'No, love. I'm the last person the woman wants to see. She's ever so upset with David and gave me a right ear-bashing about him. I tried to explain that it wasn't his fault but she wouldn't listen. She threw me out in the end but I suppose I can't blame her. If Brenda was my girl, I'd be looking for someone to blame. But she should be angry with that bloody bike, not with my son.'

Rachel said nothing and sipped her tea but Winnie saw the girl raise her eyebrows.

'Out with it,' she said huffily. 'You've obviously got an opinion, so let's hear it.'

'No, it's none of my business.'

'If you've got something to say, I'd rather you said it now and kept it between us,' Winnie said. She'd already prepared herself for some scathing remarks from her customers today but she'd hoped for Rachel's support.

'Look, I get it that David was injured and confused, but I don't think he should have walked away and I think it's bad of him not to at least visit Brenda in the hospital. It doesn't look good on his part. If it had been me who was courting him, I would expect more.'

'Yeah, I know. I'm not happy about it. He's upset me in more ways than one recently, but at the end of the day he's still my son and you've no idea what he's been through. Honestly, he was breaking his heart last night. I've not seen him cry like that since he was a kid. And it really brought it home to me – I could have lost him, Rachel. He could have been killed. Thank God he got off lightly, with just a sore head and his leg giving him jip.'

'Shame we can't say the same about Brenda.'

'I know, but David's had a massive shock. He feels terrible about what happened to Brenda and, to top it all, he's had to answer the police questions. Christ, Rachel, it's not like he did it on purpose or set out to hurt Brenda. I won't have my son treated like he's done something wrong. He's been hurt too, you know. Albeit not seriously, but he could have been. You wouldn't be so judgemental if I was having to bury him, would you?'

'All right, but you did ask what I was thinking. I didn't expect you'd give me a tongue-lashing for telling you what was on my mind.'

Winnie breathed in deeply and let out a long, slow sigh. 'I'm sorry, love. I didn't mean to bite your head off. I'm just tired. I lay in bed for most of last night thinking about what could have happened. I kept seeing my David, lying in the road, dead. To be honest, I'm glad he won't be riding that bloody contraption again.'

'There's no need to apologise. It's understandable you're upset.'

Winnie stood up, and touching Rachel's shoulder, she said, 'Come on, it's time to open up.'

★

Winnie plastered on her usual smile. Len was the first customer through the door and greeted her with a nod of his head before sitting at the end of the bar. She knew news of the accident would have spread through Battersea by now, but didn't expect Len to pass comment. He rarely did, always keeping himself to himself. She thought it was a shame that the rest of her customers weren't more like him.

Hilda breezed in next, thankfully sober. Winnie was pleased to see the woman was keeping her promise to Rachel but it had only been one day so far. She knew that being in a pub would be a testing time for Hilda.

'You all right, Win?' she asked, her voice full of genuine concern.

'Yes, love, I'm fine, thanks. You've heard the news, then?'

'Yeah, it's going around like a fire in a paper mill. How's David?'

'Sore, but he'll survive. Thanks for asking. What would you like to drink?' Winnie asked, doubtful that Hilda would refrain from ordering a whisky.

'Nothing, thanks, Win. I popped in to see if Jan wanted to come round and use my machine.'

Well, blow me down with a feather, Winnie thought. She called Rachel over. 'Keep Hilda company. I'm just nipping upstairs to get Jan,' she said.

Minutes later, she returned with Jan to see two more customers had come in. She knew John lived on the same road as Brenda and had been good friends with the girl's father before he'd died. Rachel went to serve them, but Winnie interrupted. She assumed John would have something to say and wanted to get it over and done with.

'I'll get these,' she told Rachel and turned to John. 'Your usual?'

'Yeah, two halves,' he answered coldly.

John was normally one of her friendly customers and she could always count on him for a cheery grin but his mood was definitely subdued today and she knew why. She placed the drinks on the counter and was tempted to lighten his mood by telling him they were on the house. But that would be like admitting guilt and she had nothing to be sorry for.

'David all right, is he?' John asked, smacking his lips together before taking a mouthful of beer.

'He will be.'

'Same can't be said for Brenda. Word has it that she'll be in a chair for the rest of her life. What's your son got to say about that?'

'He's very upset about what's happened to Brenda, we all are,' she answered defensively.

She was still smarting about discovering David's cruelty towards Jan and she had every intention of dealing with it, but not just yet. She'd have strong words with him when the time was right. But now she could guess that everyone would have an opinion about the accident. She was sure people would think it was their business and they'd have plenty to say. Winnie knew she'd have to defend her son, and she would – fiercely if need be – even if it lost her custom.

'David's got a lot to answer for. I hope the police bang him up for what he's done.'

'He didn't do anything wrong. It was a very unfortunate accident, John, and I'll thank you to keep your opinions to yourself.'

'Huh, accident, my arse. Everyone knows he'd been

drinking at the dance and her indoors heard he was bombing it down Falcon Road. Your son is responsible for what's happened to Brenda, no doubt about it, and you'd be a fool to stick up for him.'

Winnie placed her hands on her wide hips. 'Brenda knew he'd been drinking, but she still dragged him away from the dance, and did you know it was her who caused the bike to go over? No, of course you didn't, because you're all too quick to point the finger before you know the facts. Like I said, it was a very unfortunate accident and we're all sorry for what's happened to Brenda. Now, you're always welcome here, John, you know that. But if you continue to slander my David, I shall ask you to leave.'

'I'm going. The beer in here tastes stale,' John said and he slammed his half-drunk glass back on the counter. 'You're trying to shift the blame, but your son will get what's coming to him, you mark my words,' he added as he left.

Winnie blew all the air out of her lungs. John was likely to be the first of many confrontations she'd have to face over the coming days.

'I heard all that. Are you all right?' Rachel asked quietly.

'Yes, love, I'm fine. There'll be plenty more folk who will want to put their tuppence worth in yet. But they can say what they like about my David. I *know* it wasn't his fault and I won't let anyone say otherwise.'

'You're a good mum, Win. David's lucky to have you on his side.'

'Thanks, love. And now you've got a mum too and, by the looks of it, she's doing all right,' she said, and waved to Jan and Hilda as they left the pub arm in arm and chuckling together.

'It's still funny to think of Hilda as my mum. It must be the same for Jan too.'

'Yes, but the difference is you know Hilda and have done your whole life. You love her, it's clear to see. I love Jan. I've loved her since the day she was born. But Jan hardly even knows me, let alone loves me. Maybe she never will.'

'Stop being so maudlin. Everyone loves you, Win, and, one day, so will Jan.'

Winnie hoped so. She knew that as soon as David was up to it, she'd have to confront him about how he'd treated his sister. After all, she'd only just been reunited with Jan and hated the thought of losing her again.

'You're fast on that machine and I reckon you're better than me on it,' Hilda said, standing over Jan and admiring her work as she ran two pieces of material under the moving needle.

'Thanks, but I doubt that.'

'Look, I've been meaning to apologise about the other night. I'm sorry about the state I got myself into on Friday. It won't happen again.'

'It's nothing to do with me,' Jan answered awkwardly. She hadn't seen Hilda in the pub on Friday evening but she'd heard all about it from Rachel.

'You and Rachel are friends, aren't you?'

'Yes, though we haven't known each other long.'

'I suppose she's told you that I'm not her sister?'

'Yes, she did,' Jan said quietly.

'I don't want to put you in an uncomfortable position or get you to betray any secrets between you and Rachel, but how does she really feel about me being her mum?'

Jan took her foot off the treadle and sat back in the seat.

She looked up into Hilda's eyes and saw genuine concern. 'She was a bit surprised and felt deceived. I think she was angry at first, but she seems to have come round. She's not as upset as she was.'

'Good. I wish I hadn't told her the way I did, blurting it out when I was drunk like that, but that's water under the bridge now. Funny, innit, you two both discovering your real mums.'

'Yes, but I don't know for sure that Winnie is my real mother.'

'Does that bother you?'

'A bit. But other than confronting my other mother, there's no way to find out.'

'There must be records somewhere. Surely the hospital where Winnie had you. Or the people who arranged the adoption. What about your birth certificate? It would say on there who your mother is.'

Jan's brow creased. 'I've never seen my birth certificate. My mother must have it, but I can hardly go round and knock on the door to ask for it.'

'You don't have to. Speak to Winnie. Ask her if your birth was registered. I bet it was, cos I'm sure there's a two-pound fine for not doing it. The registrar's office will have a copy of your certificate.'

'Really? It would be nice to know the truth, but – but I don't want to upset Winnie. She's been so good to me.'

'Winnie won't be upset. You've every right to know who gave birth to you and I feel awful now for taking that right away from my Rachel. Both you girls deserve better than what you got from me and Winnie.'

Jan wasn't sure what to say, so she leaned over the sewing

machine and resumed stitching the seam of a nearly finished dress. She would really like to know if Winnie was indeed her biological mother but wasn't sure if she could bring herself to ask about her birth certificate. Especially as Winnie was so upset about David's motorbike crash. What if it turned out that Winnie wasn't her mother? The woman would be distraught. Nonetheless, she'd still like to know but decided it would probably be best to wait a while, at least until Winnie had got over the shock of David's accident.

A few hours passed and Jan was pleased with what she'd achieved.

'I'll take you down the market tomorrow. Bill and Flo will be impressed with these,' Hilda said as she examined Jan's stitching.

'I'd really appreciate that, thank you. I'd like to pay Winnie back for the materials she bought me and you for loaning me the use of your sewing machine.'

'Do as you see fit with Winnie, but don't go trying to give me any of what you earn for these dresses. I'm more than happy for you to come round any time you like. Anyway, you cleaned up the place a treat for me and having you here helps to keep me out of the pubs.'

'Thanks, Hilda, that's very kind of you. I'd best be off, then. Terry is taking me out this evening. I'll see you in the morning after you've finished work,' she said. She couldn't help but smile widely at the thought of seeing Terry.

'You like him, don't you?' Hilda asked.

Jan pulled on her oversized coat donated by Winnie. 'Yes, I do.'

'He's a good man. He'll treat you decent. And if he doesn't, he'll have me to deal with,' Hilda said, jokingly waving her fist in front of her.

As Jan headed back to the Battersea Tavern, she lowered her head and hunched her shoulders against the bitingly cold wind. The pub would be closed now and Winnie would probably be cooking something in the kitchen. She thought again about her birth certificate. Oh, how she'd love to see it. But she'd bide her time. Until then, with or without proof, she'd happily accept that Winnie was her mother. After all, if it wasn't for Mr Berry and David, she'd never been happier. If she could have picked a mother, Winnie would have been at the top of her selection.

17

On Monday morning, Winnie left Brian snoring in his bed and quietly tiptoed past, into the kitchen. She shivered and pulled her dressing gown around herself as she waited for the kettle to whistle. There was no sign of David up and about and she wondered if he was going into the factory today. She couldn't see why he wouldn't. His leg was cut and bruised and his shoulder was grazed, but he was perfectly capable of walking. Unlike Brenda.

Winnie shook her head at the thought of the previous day. It hadn't been pleasant. There were very few of her customers who'd had anything nice to say about David. She'd become sick and tired of trying to put them straight. Most were adamant that her son was culpable. She knew it looked bad on David's part but they hadn't seen how upset he'd been. She couldn't recall the last time she'd seen her son cry, but he'd had tears in his eyes on the night of the accident. That showed he wasn't the cold, callous monster that people were insinuating.

The kettle whistled and Winnie turned off the gas quickly before the high-pitched noise disturbed Brian. The longer he stayed out of the way, the better, she thought, pouring boiling water into the teapot. A sombre atmosphere tended to follow the man around and Winnie was determined to make today better than yesterday, if only for Jan's sake. Her daughter had only been with them a short time and had already experienced Brian's unfriendliness and a tirade of nastiness from David. Winnie herself had been upset yesterday and Jan must have noticed. It wouldn't do and though Jan had said she'd stay, Winnie feared the girl would up and leave if things didn't drastically change.

After making David a cup of tea, she tapped gently on his bedroom door and pushed it open. He was just stirring, obviously with no intention of going to work.

'Oh, Mum, it's still dark,' he moaned as he sat up in bed.

'You'll be late for work,' she warned him, placing his tea on the side. 'I've made you a cuppa. Come on, time to get up.'

'I'm not going in.'

Just as she had suspected, he planned on milking his minor injury for all it was worth. 'We both know there's nothing to stop you going to work,' she reminded him crossly.

'I know, but I've been thinking and I reckon I oughta make the most of this.'

'Oh, how's that?' she asked, disappointed. David was unlikely to get any sort of sick pay, so she'd be forced to find the money to pay off Errol again.

'I've got to register in a few days for conscription. I can't see how I can get out of it, unless…'

'Unless you play on your injuries and make out they're a lot worse than what they are,' she said, finishing off his sentence.

'Yes, that's right. I can try and get signed off on medical grounds.'

'But surely you'll be expected to join up once your leg has healed?'

'Probably. I'll just have to drag it out for as long as I can.'

'I don't know about this. I mean, don't get me wrong, the last thing I want is you being carted off to fight the Germans, but it don't seem right to feign an injury.'

'Have you got any better suggestions? Because I'd love to hear them.'

'No, I haven't. I asked Terry if he could find you work in the bakery but no luck there.'

'See, Mum. It's almost impossible to get round it. Errol's got fake certificates but he's unlikely to sell me one, so this is my only chance. Unless you'd rather I went to war? After all, I don't suppose you're bothered about me now that you've got your precious daughter.'

'Don't talk daft. I'd never put Jan before you and you know I don't want you fighting. Maybe you could get a posting in the offices or something?'

'You don't get a choice. They'll send me where they see fit and, knowing my luck, it'd be straight to the front line.'

'Oh, Son, I can't stand the thought of that,' Winnie said, beginning to think that David's plan was a good idea. 'All right, I'll go along with your leg injury, but you'd better be a good actor. You're going to have to do some lead swinging to make it work.'

'Don't worry about that. As it is, it looks pretty swollen and black and blue. I'll convince the doctor it's in a bad way.'

'Yes, now it does, but the swelling and bruising will go down soon. Perhaps you could pretend you've hurt your back too. Back problems are difficult to diagnose and it's hard to know for sure whether a back is genuinely bad or not. You remember Mrs Linton? She made out she had a bad back for years. Her husband used to do everything for her. The crafty mare used to sit on the sofa with her legs up and run her old man ragged. He worked all day at the power station and then would come home and do the dinner, washing, everything. She got away with it until her sister-in-law saw her with another bloke on Wandsworth Common. They were mucking about on the frozen pond and apparently there was nothing wrong with her back then!'

'Ha, yes, I remember her and I remember her husband throwing her clothes out on the street. I think it stuck in my mind because everyone was surprised that she could bend down and pick them up.'

'There you go. She fooled everyone for years. And it's common knowledge that you've had a motorbike accident. If you're going to fake injury, I think it would be best to play on a bad back.'

'It's worth a try. Can you get the doctor to come round and see me? I'll stay in bed and make out I can't get up cos it hurts too much.'

'It'll cost a pretty penny, but it'll be worth it. It'll mean I won't be able to pay much off your debt – hopefully, just enough to keep Errol happy. I'll go and see the doctor this morning before I open up. I'm sure he'll agree to a visit, especially if I throw in a few glasses of brandy. I've heard he's partial to a tipple. Gawd, David, I just hope this works, I really do.'

'Don't worry, I'm sure I can fool the man.'

'I think I can hear Jan getting up. I'll do you both a bit of breakfast, but you stay here and I'll bring it in to you. There's no need for anyone except me and you to know that your back is fine. I want Jan, your father and everyone else to believe you're bedbound for now,' she whispered so that Jan wouldn't hear through the thin walls.

David nodded, and also lowering his voice, said, 'It's going to get boring being stuck in here for a while. I could do with a newspaper or something.'

'Don't worry. I'll bring you everything you need, just as long as it keeps you out of reach of the blasted army.'

'Thanks, Mum. I don't know what I'd do without you.'

Winnie felt her heart warm but her son's treatment of Jan was never far from her mind. Though if he was laid up in bed for the foreseeable future, he wouldn't be able to harass her. She'd pull him on it, just not yet. Once he'd fooled the doctor and was out of bed, probably pretending to need crutches for a while, she'd tell him exactly how things were going to be and she had no intention of mincing her words.

Jan yawned and stretched before climbing out of bed and drawing back the curtains. The sun was just coming over the top of the rooftops on the left of the street, casting a pink and purple hue in the sky. There were only a few dark clouds, just small puffs and not enough for rain. She'd hoped the day would be a nice one and was looking forward to a trip to the market with Hilda. But then she heard David's bedroom door and tensed, listening for his footsteps in the passageway. She was desperate to use the bathroom but would hold on until after he'd left for work. With no idea of whether or not Winnie had spoken to him yet about the things he'd said to her, she thought it was best to stay out of his way for now.

She jumped when she heard a light tap on the door and stared at the chair she'd wedged under the handle, hoping it would hold tight and keep him out. Then she heard Winnie's voice quietly calling her name. She ran to the door, quickly pulling the chair away before opening it.

'Morning, love. I thought I heard you up. I'm making David some eggs and bacon. Would you like some?' Winnie asked.

Jan had never tasted bacon before. She'd had eggs twice a week but her mother had never cooked her bacon. She'd like to try it but was unsure about eating breakfast with David in the kitchen. 'Erm, no thank you,' she answered, disheartened.

'Are you sure? I'm cooking it anyway so it's no bother to bung in a couple of extra slices for you.'

'Isn't David going to work?' Jan asked, hoping with all her heart that he would be.

'No, love, he's not well. That accident has put his back out. The poor love can't get out of bed.'

'Oh,' Jan said, surprised, as she'd seen and heard him walking around until now. 'I hope he's all right.'

'I'll get the doctor out to him later. I'm sure he'll be fine but he'll be laid up for a while. He'll be having his breakfast in bed. So, do you want some?'

'Yes, please, I would,' she answered, secretly pleased to know she wouldn't be bumping into him, though she wouldn't wish him injured.

Winnie waddled off towards the kitchen and Jan pulled on her dressing gown, joining Winnie minutes later. The smell of the frying bacon twitched her nose and Jan felt her mouth salivating. The aroma was delicious and she hoped it would taste just as nice.

219

'There's tea in the pot, get yourself a cup and pour one for Brian too. He's bound to get out of bed once he realises I'm cooking breakfast,' Winnie said, turning away from the stove to smile at her.

Jan tried to return the gesture but her face must have given away her concerns.

'Don't worry, love,' Winnie said reassuringly, 'Brian never eats in here. He'll have a tray in the front room. You can enjoy your breakfast without having to see old misery guts across the table. Good job an' all. His 'orrible face would make the eggs wish they were still in the chicken and the bacon still on the pig.'

Now Jan smiled wholeheartedly. She found it funny the way Winnie spoke about her husband.

'There you are; you can't beat a fry-up to start the day. Get stuck in,' Winnie said. She put a plate on the table in front of Jan before taking a tray to David and one to Mr Berry.

Jan looked at the greasy pink meat and runny egg. It certainly smelt better than it looked. She picked up her knife and fork and sliced a bit of the bacon. Gingerly, she put it in her mouth. The saltiness made her taste buds dance and by the time Winnie returned to the kitchen, Jan had almost gobbled down the whole breakfast.

'Glad to see you enjoyed that,' Winnie remarked with a chuckle as she looked at the empty plate.

'Thank you, it was lovely. You sit down, I'll wash up.'

'Thanks, love, you're a good girl. You'd never catch my Brian or David with their hands in the sink. Have you got any plans for today?'

'Hilda's taking me to the market to meet Bill and Flo. Unless there's something you'd like me to do?'

'No, nothing. You'll enjoy the market. Oh, actually, you could get me a few pounds of spuds while you're there.'

'Yes, of course. I'm looking forward to seeing it. I've a vague recollection of my mother dragging me through it once but she thought the people who worked on the stalls were all talking about her and wanted to kill her. I was never allowed there after that,' she said sadly, thinking of the distant memory.

'I think your mother has been ill for many years, possibly her whole life. You should never have been with her. But, you're here now and that's all behind you. So, after the market, how about I take you to the hairdresser's for a wash and set?'

'Is there something wrong with my hair?' Jan asked, tucking a long brown wisp behind her ear.

'No, love, nothing at all. I just thought it would be a nice treat and I don't suppose you've ever had a proper style.'

'You're right, I haven't. Thank you, I'd really like that,' she answered, imagining herself with soft waves like Rachel's or a glamourous updo.

Once the washing-up was done and she had wiped down the table, Jan went to her room to get dressed. She stood in front of the window, excited about what the day would bring. The street downstairs was coming to life. The milkman's empty cart rattled around the corner, a couple of men were making their way to work and a few mothers stood on their steps, waving their children off to school. Jan thought it was very sad to see those who hadn't been evacuated carrying small gas masks. She hoped they'd never need to use them. It was a sobering thought, and one she quickly pushed to the back of her mind.

★

A couple of hours later, down at the Northcote Road market, Jan was arm in arm with Hilda and being pulled from one stall to another, both women oohing and aahing at the array of goods on display. Jan's ears filled with the sounds of coster-mongers vying for business as they called out their prices and housewives bartering and chatting. The place felt so vibrant, making her appreciate the freedom she now had.

'It seems strange with all the kids being billeted. Normally, there are mothers dragging their little 'uns around with them or pushing prams. Still, I suppose it's for the best,' Hilda said.

Jan didn't know any different, but Hilda was right, there was a distinct lack of children around.

'Here we are,' Hilda said as they approached a clothing stall. 'You'll like Bill, he's a diamond. Flo's all right, but she can be a bit of a cold fish sometimes.'

'Are you sure they'll want my dresses?'

'Most definitely. They're really good quality. Look, Bill is waving at us.'

'Hello, Hilda, nice to see you. Who's this young lady?' he asked with a jolly smile.

'This is Winnie's daughter, Jan. She makes dresses and wants to sell them.'

'Do you, indeed? Have you got any to show us?'

'Yes, I have,' Jan answered shyly, pleased that he was show-ing an interest. She began to pull one from her cloth sack, but Bill stopped her.

'Just a minute, pet, Flo will want to see these too,' he said and called to his wife.

A tall, slender woman approached. Her dark hair, scat-tered with grey, was piled in a neat bun on top of her head. With her thin features, it gave her a harsh look. She didn't seem quite as friendly as her husband and she eyed Hilda suspiciously.

'This is Jan, Winnie's daughter. She makes dresses,' Bill said, nodding at his wife.

'Winnie from the Battersea Tavern? I didn't know she had a daughter.'

'Yeah, well, she has,' Hilda said. She nudged Jan in the side. 'Show Flo your dresses.'

Jan felt rather nervous under Flo's scrutiny and rummaged in the sack for a dress. Flo took it and examined the seams, tugging roughly on them. Then she held the dress up and studied the design. Her face gave nothing away. Jan couldn't tell if the woman liked it or not.

'She's done a good job,' Hilda said. 'You won't find better quality around here.'

'Yes, she has,' Flo agreed. 'A very simple cut but well made. It'll sell. I'll give you two shillings.'

Jan was disappointed with the offer but was about to accept when Hilda cut in. 'Come off it, Flo. That hardly covers the cost of the material. Six shillings, that's fair.'

'Four, and that's my final offer.'

'Five, and you've got a deal. Jan's got four dresses and she'll have more next week.'

Flo sucked in her cheeks, making her pointed nose look even longer. 'Five a piece it is. It's a good job you have Mrs Duff looking after your interests, young lady.'

'It is,' Jan answered, thinking she could pop with excitement. For a moment, she'd thought that Hilda might have blown the deal and couldn't believe she'd so brazenly driven up the price.

She handed over the rest of the dresses and, after Flo had

inspected them, she counted out the payment. The spindly woman wasted no time in putting the dresses on display. It gave Jan a feeling of pride to see her work on show for everyone to see and she couldn't wait to make more.

'Are you popping into the pub later?' Hilda asked Bill.

When Flo threw him a disapproving look, Bill was quick to say no.

'All right. Well, if we don't see you before, we'll see you next week. Ta-ta,' Hilda said. She hooked her arm in Jan's and they headed back through the busy market.

'Thanks, Hilda. I would have taken two shillings, if it wasn't for you.'

'Never sell yourself short. You'll learn, just stick with me, kid. Now then, shall we stop for some more material on our way back?'

'Yes, and I need some potatoes for Winnie.'

'Righto.'

'Erm, Hilda, I hope you don't mind me mentioning it, but Flo called you Mrs Duff. I didn't know you'd been married.'

'It was a long time ago and didn't last long. After he left, I never got around to changing my name back to Robb. I suppose I should really.'

'I'm sorry, it's none of my business.'

'It's all right, I don't mind talking about it. I hardly even think about it these days. It was my own fault he left – or the fault of the whisky. But the bugger ran off with everything I owned. Even my brassieres! Between you and me, I kept his name cos I like being a Missus. It gives me an air of respectability.'

Jan hadn't taken in Hilda's last comment. She was too busy trying not to scream or pull away from Hilda and run in the opposite direction. She was sure she'd spotted her mother walking towards them. The woman was lost in the crowd now, but she'd been there, as plain as day. Frantically, she scanned the sea of faces, terrified of seeing her mother's there again.

'What's wrong? You look like you've seen a ghost,' Hilda said.

'I ... I'm sure I saw my mother.'

'Where?'

'She was right there in front of us.'

'Come on,' Hilda said and she pulled her into a curtain shop.

Jan stood behind Hilda and peered through the window, looking up and down the street.

'Any sign of her?'

'No,' she answered, fighting back tears.

'Look at you, you're shaking. Let's get you straight back home. We can pick up some material tomorrow.'

'I ... I don't think I can go back out there,' she protested fearfully and gulped.

'Don't worry. I'll be with you every step of the way and I swear I won't let that woman near you.'

Hilda held her hand towards her and Jan took it, allowing herself to be led outside. 'I promise you'll be safe with me,' Hilda reassured her as they hurried home.

Jan could feel her heart pounding even faster than their footsteps. No matter what Hilda said, she wouldn't feel safe until she was back in the Battersea Tavern and under Winnie's protective eye.

18

Rachel's rare night off had been wasted. She'd spent most of the evening feeling bored and she hadn't slept well either. Her dreams had been punctured with images of Jim. She'd woken up several times, wondering where he was now, what he was doing, and if he had joined the army. She hoped he still thought of her and that he regretted the fact that they'd never married. Though she harboured anger over his actions, she couldn't hate him. Yes, she hated what he'd done and that her sister, who was really her aunt, had died. She hated that he'd ruined any chance of them marrying. She hated that he'd lied to her. Yet part of her still loved him and always would, though she'd never admit it to anyone.

She'd been grateful when morning came and it was time to get up for work. She was tired but anything was better than being tortured by thoughts of Jim and work would take her mind off him.

As Rachel made her way to the Battersea Tavern, she again had a terrible feeling that something awful was going to happen. She'd felt it for weeks now. She'd thought when she'd discovered that Hilda was her mother that the feeling would go away. But it hadn't. And neither had it when David had had his accident. She'd told herself she was being silly and that maybe it was the war hanging over them that had given her this sick feeling in the pit of her stomach, but something kept niggling at her, telling her fate had it in for her. She stepped into the road, not paying attention, and had to leap back when a car sped around the corner.

'Idiot,' she screamed down the street after the car had passed. That had been close but it hadn't hit her and the feeling of foreboding remained.

Once in the warmth of the pub, Rachel tried to dismiss her worries and joined Winnie for their usual morning cuppa. She noticed the woman seemed distracted, deep in thought, her brow creased. It seemed she wasn't the only one with things on her mind.

'Penny for 'em,' Rachel said.

'Oh, my thoughts are worth more than a penny. Do you reckon you can afford them?' Winnie replied.

'Don't I get a discount?' she asked.

The women smiled warmly at each other and Winnie told her about Jan returning from the market in a right old state. 'She thinks she saw her so-called mother.'

'Blimey, poor Jan. I'm glad Hilda was with her.'

'Yes, me too. But I couldn't persuade her to come to the hairdresser's after that. She stayed in her room all day, only coming out for a quick sandwich.'

'It'll take time to build up her confidence, but she'll get there.'

'Yes, I think you're right. But to be honest, I'm not convinced that her mother was even there,' Winnie said in a hushed voice.

'What, you think she was making it up?'

'No, nothing like that. I think she *believes* she saw her mother, but I reckon it was her mind playing tricks on her. She said her mother looked straight at her. Well, if that's the case, the woman wouldn't just have vanished without confronting her, would she?'

Rachel raised her eyebrows. 'No, I doubt it. I've met the woman. She ain't the sort to have seen Jan and not said something.'

'See, that's what I mean. Maybe I'm worrying over nothing but I can't have the girl scared out of her wits over a figment of her imagination. I don't know, maybe I'll have a word with Terry and see what he thinks.'

'Good idea. Or I can talk to her, if you like?'

'You can try. It won't do any harm. By the way, I didn't tell you – the doctor came in to see David yesterday. He said David has probably slipped a disc and should rest it for as long as required. If it's no better in a week or two, I'm to call him in again.'

'Oh, right. Sounds painful,' Rachel said sceptically.

'It is. The poor love can hardly move. It's as much as he can do to get to the bathroom, even with me helping him. I can't see him improving in as little as a week or two.'

Rachel didn't believe a word of it and thought David was pulling the wool over Winnie's eyes. She'd seen him after the accident and he'd been walking perfectly well with only a slight limp from his knee wound. This was more likely to be David getting out of going to work, as usual. And gullible Winnie was falling for it.

'Bugger me, is that the time?' Winnie said as she looked at her watch. 'It's eleven thirty-five. We're late. Len will have something to say about that,' she chuckled, pushing her chair back and smoothing down the front of her well-worn dress. 'I might get Jan to knock me up a couple of new dresses. Mine are nearly threadbare and you know how Brian insists I keep up appearances. He's a stickler for putting on a good show. Me, I couldn't care less what people think of me but him, well, he's always been bothered about that sort of thing.'

'You always look lovely,' Rachel told her, 'but that's a good idea to ask Jan. I think I will too. I could do with something a bit more fashionable,' she said, looking down at her drab, grey, straight dress. It did nothing to accentuate her slim waist and the colour dulled her complexion. It wasn't her most flattering outfit, but it had suited her mood this morning when she'd dressed.

Once Winnie had unlocked the door, Len came through, grumbling about poor time-keeping and punctuality. 'It's just bad manners,' he moaned as he sat in his usual place at the end of the bar.

Rachel tried not to smile and instead looked sincere. 'I quite agree, Len. Sorry, it won't happen again,' she said as she placed a bottle of stout and his tankard in front of him.

Her eyes lifted towards the door when it opened again and a tall man walked in, a man she'd never seen before. His light brown hair showed under his trilby hat and his raincoat billowed behind him, exposing a sharply cut, smart three-piece suit. He didn't look like their normal customers. This man reeked of class and she wondered if he was lost.

'Good morning, sir, can I help you?' she asked in the best-spoken voice she could muster.

'Good morning,' he answered, doffing his hat and smiling, showing his white teeth. 'I'll have a large brandy, thank you.'

Rachel prepared his drink, curious to know what business he had in the Battersea Tavern. 'I don't think I've seen you in here before,' she said, placing his drink before him and resting her hands on the bar.

'No, you haven't. Had I known the attraction of the place, I would have visited sooner,' he replied, his brown eyes boring into hers.

She could feel her cheeks flush and found herself flustered. She pulled her eyes from his gaze, searching for something to say, but nothing came.

The good-looking stranger broke the silence. 'I'm Arnold Sanders; pleasure to meet you.'

'And you,' she answered coyly. 'Rachel, Rachel Robb.'

'This is a very fine establishment you have, Miss Robb.'

'Oh, it's not mine. I just work here.'

'I'm sure you are a very fine asset. Would you allow me to buy you a drink?'

'Oh – err ... I don't normally.'

'Please, Miss Robb. I'd be honoured and grateful if you'd care to partake in a small glass and keep me company for a moment. That is, of course, if you're not too busy.'

Rachel nearly giggled at the words he used. He sounded a proper nob. She glanced around to see that there was only Len supping his stout, and Winnie, slowly edging towards them and looking bemused.

'Thank you, but –'

Winnie was now standing beside her. 'Rachel would love a glass of sherry and she'll be happy to keep you company for a while, won't you, love?'

Rachel looked wide-eyed at Winnie and could feel herself blushing. The woman was at it again, matchmaking.

'In fact, I'll get the sherry for you,' Winnie added and sloped off.

'It seems you're stuck with me,' Arnold said, his amusement clear. 'I do hope I haven't put you in an uncomfortable position?'

'No, it's fine,' she answered as her stomach fluttered.

Arnold removed his hat and placed it on the bar and Winnie returned with a small glass. 'You're not from Battersea, are you?' she asked.

'No, I've recently moved to the area from Winchester in Hampshire.'

'What brings you here, then?' Winnie questioned.

'My father recently passed away leaving me a property near the park. As I work in London, I thought it made practical sense to live here too.'

'Sorry about your father. What work do you do?'

'Winnie,' Rachel said through gritted teeth, 'I'm sure Mr Sanders came in for a quiet drink and not to undergo an interrogation.'

'It's fine.' Arnold laughed. 'I'm happy to answer any questions and I'm delighted to have the pleasure of two beautiful women to talk to. Would you like a sherry too?'

'Don't mind if I do,' Winnie replied and she went off to get one, leaving Rachel cringing.

'I assume that's the landlady,' Arnold commented.

Before Rachel could answer, Winnie was back, and she began probing the man again. 'So, you was just about to tell us what work you do.'

'Yes, I was, wasn't I? It's quite boring, really. I work in building design for a large company in the city.'

'What sort of building design?'

'All sorts, from social housing to the commercial sector. I fine-tune details on architectural plans. As I said, all quite boring. Not nearly as exciting as running a public house.'

'Oh yes, it's full of excitement here,' Winnie said sardonically, indicating Len at the other end of the bar.

Arnold laughed and threw his head back. 'Indeed. It's very much like my office.'

Winnie sipped her sherry and then walked down to the end of the bar, leaving Rachel alone with Arnold. Rachel had to admit she found him attractive, but he wasn't her sort. He was too posh, from a different class. However, she didn't want to appear rude, so she searched for something to say. 'It must be nice to have a house near the park.'

'Yes, it is,' he said. He finished his brandy, then added, 'Now, if you'll excuse me, I'm afraid I must be off. The removal men will be arriving shortly with my furniture. It truly has been a delight to meet you and I shall very much look forward to seeing you again.'

His eyes bored into Rachel's and she quickly averted her own. She doubted he meant what he'd said about looking forward to seeing her again but she hoped he had. Reluctant to admit it, he'd made her stomach flutter, an experience she hadn't felt since Jim.

'Well, I say,' Winnie declared after he'd left. 'He couldn't take his eyes off you!'

'Yeah, well, he's wasting his time.'

'You keep telling yourself that but I saw the way you looked at him. Admit it, you like him.'

'It doesn't matter if I do or don't. I'm never getting involved with another man and you know my reasons why. I couldn't go through it again, not after what happened with Jim.'

'Oh, love, you can't live your life afraid of having your heart broken again. He seemed like a nice enough chap and obviously has a few bob.'

'Even if I do like him, he isn't my sort. A bloke like that would never be interested in someone like me.'

'Ha, I knew it! I knew you liked him. And don't talk nonsense. You're a beautiful and kind woman. He'd be lucky to have you.'

Rachel wasn't convinced. She believed men of Arnold's class would only want to be with a woman like her for one thing and it wouldn't involve marriage. But she couldn't deny the effect he'd had on her. If he was to frequent the Battersea Tavern, she'd have to be on her guard. It wouldn't do to fall for someone like him. No, the last thing she needed was to end up smitten with Arnold Sanders.

19

The next day, every time Winnie thought about Rachel and that Arnold bloke, she found herself chuckling. She'd never seen Rachel blush like that before; it was clear the girl felt attracted to him. She hoped he'd come back in again soon. It would be nice to see Rachel finally put her past behind her and allow herself to fall for another man. And if she was to date someone, a wealthy gentleman would be all the better.

'Hello, love,' she greeted Hilda when she came in. 'You're looking well,' she added, thinking that the woman's skin appeared clearer and her eyes were brighter than usual. Abstaining from the alcohol seemed to be doing Hilda the world of good.

'Hello, Winnie. Thanks, I feel great too. I must admit, coming in here is a challenge but I promised my girl I'd stay sober so that's what I'm going to do. Anyway, is Jan around? I didn't see her yesterday and thought she'd be banging my door down this morning to get at my sewing machine.'

'She's in her room. That scare with her mother in the market really got to her. I can try again, see if I can coax her out, but don't hold your breath.'

'Shall I go up and have a go?' Hilda offered.

'Feel free. I've had no luck this morning, so you may as well give it a try.'

Winnie lifted the bar hatch to allow Hilda through. 'Top of the stairs, turn left and it's the last door at the end of the passageway. Mind you don't disturb David. He's in his bed. The poor love has put his back out and mustn't move. Doctor's orders.'

'Oh, right,' Hilda answered. 'I'll be as quiet as a mouse.'

'Where's Hilda going?' Rachel asked, sounding a little alarmed.

'To see if she can persuade Jan to come out of her room and go round to hers to do some sewing.'

'They're spending a lot of time together.'

'Yes, they are,' Winnie said, wondering if Rachel felt jealous. After all, she'd only recently discovered that Hilda was her mother. 'You don't mind, do you? Having Jan around seems to help Hilda stay off the booze.'

'No, I don't mind. Why should I?' Rachel answered shortly.

'I think you do. And it's only natural that you should feel pushed out.'

'I told you, I don't. But Hilda did say she'd try and be more like a mum to me and I've hardly seen her.'

'She's probably giving you some time to come to terms with it all and trying to sort her own life out. I shouldn't worry, love. She's doing ever so well and, no doubt, she'll soon be getting on your nerves again.'

'I sound like a spoilt child. Take no notice of me. I'm really pleased that they're helping each other.'

'That's more like it and this will put a smile on your face,' Winnie said, indicating the door where Arnold Sanders had just walked in again. His eyes were fixed on Rachel and when she saw him, Winnie noticed her cheeks redden. 'I'll leave you to serve him,' she said, then winked.

Moments later, she was pleased to see Jan following behind Hilda and had to admit to herself that she also felt a tad jealous. She'd really tried to get Jan to come downstairs this morning but the girl had refused to budge from her room. Yet Hilda had been upstairs just minutes and had somehow persuaded Jan to change her mind. She wished she was closer to Jan, but she knew it was going to take time to form any sort of mother-and-daughter relationship.

'I'll have her back before teatime,' Hilda said breezily.

'Just a minute,' Winnie called to them as they went to leave the pub. 'Do you mind if I pop round when we close? I'd love to see what you're doing.'

'You're always welcome, especially if you bring some of them cakes you've made,' Hilda answered cheekily.

'I told her you was baking until late last night,' Jan chipped in. 'I could smell it.'

'Well, there's no shortage of cakes in my larder. Perhaps Rachel would like to come too, but she might have other plans,' Winnie said, looking down the bar to where Arnold was flirting with the girl.

'Who's that?' Hilda asked. 'He looks proper posh.'

Winnie leaned over the bar and lowered her voice. 'He is and he fancies Rachel something rotten.'

'Does he indeed? Well, if he's going to court my daughter, he'd better treat her right or he'll have me to answer to!'

'Quieten down,' Winnie hissed. 'We don't want the bloke scared off before he's even taken Rachel out.'

'I was only saying.'

'Well, don't. It's about time the girl showed a bit of interest in a man and she won't thank you for sticking your oar in.'

Hilda sighed, then agreed. 'I suppose you're right. But I mean it, he'd better be good to her. Anyway, we'll see you both later – that is, if you can drag her away from him.'

Winnie thought she'd take advantage of the pub being quiet and nipped upstairs with the intention of seeing if David wanted anything. As she reached the top of the stairs, her heart sank when Brian appeared in the hallway, scowling at her.

'Do you think you own this gaff?' he asked, snarling.

'What are you on about?'

'I'm on about you inviting all and sundry upstairs. It's bad enough that I've got to put up with your illegitimate daughter living under the same roof as me. And now I find the likes of Hilda Duff wandering around my hallway.'

'She popped up to get Jan, that's all.'

'I don't care for what reason she was up here. Just don't let it happen again,' he shouted.

'All right, keep your voice down, you'll disturb David,' she said and rolled her eyes at him as she walked past towards the kitchen. She thought the silly old sod was overreacting, as usual.

She'd only taken two steps when she felt a sharp tug on her scalp and yelped. Brian had hold of a handful of her hair and was dragging her to the front room. She reached up and tried to prise his hand away. 'You're hurting me, get off!' she cried.

He forcibly slung her into the room and slammed the door closed. Winnie stumbled but stayed on her feet. She realised Brian was raging and her pulse quickened.

'You're getting a bit too big for your boots lately, woman. It's time I put you back in your place.'

He stamped towards her and her first instinct was to cower

in the corner. There'd been a time when she would have crouched down with her hands above her head and begged Brian not to hit her. But something inside her snapped and she stood her ground.

'Go on, then, hit me. But I swear, I'll give as good as I get,' she spat and clenched her fists by her side with her chest pushed forward.

Brian began to laugh. 'You're full of yourself, all five foot of you. I'm not going to waste my energy on you, but believe me, if I wanted to put you on your fat arse, that's where you'd be. Now I'll tell you again, I don't want all and sundry up here in my private quarters. If it happens again, you'll be sorry. Do I make myself clear?'

'Yeah,' Winnie said, just wanting this to be over with.

'Good, now make me a cup of tea. I SAID NOW!'

Winnie's heart hammered and she felt light-headed. She could feel herself shaking from head to toe but she'd had enough of bowing down to him and doing his bidding. She had a daughter now, one whose respect she wanted to gain. She'd never earn it if she didn't stand up to her husband. 'I'm busy,' she said. 'If you want tea, you know where the kettle is.'

Brian's eyes bulged and the veins on his neck looked like they might explode. He marched towards her, his eyes black and filled with fury. Winnie, scared but staunch, remained on the spot. He grabbed her hair again, yanking her forwards and pulling her towards the door. She struggled but he tightened his grip until she was sure he was ripping her hair from its roots.

'Let me go,' she screamed, the pain making her cry.

They were outside the kitchen now. 'Get in there and make me a drink,' he seethed, tugging her through the door.

Winnie kicked hard at his shins but twice her foot only

scraped off his trouser leg. The third hefty kick landed on his bone but he didn't flinch. 'I hate you,' she fumed, and kicked again.

This time she felt him jerk and he let out a small groan of pain, at last letting go of her hair.

'Bitch,' he spat, and Winnie saw his large fist coming towards her.

She tried to move away, but she wasn't quick enough and he whacked her on the side of the head. The blow was hard and dazed her. The room spun and she fell to the floor, landing in a heap, her legs akimbo.

'Are you going to do as you're told now?' he asked, sneering as he looked down at her.

Winnie shook her head to clear it and managed to return his glare. She'd come this far and wasn't going to back down now. She'd stand her ground, whatever it took, not for her but for her daughter. 'Do your worst, Brian. I've had it with you. You can knock me about all you want but I'll never, *never* cower to you again. And I'll never make you a cup of tea, not for as long as I live.'

'Huh, we'll see about that,' Brian said and pulled his booted foot back.

She turned her head and body and wrapped her arms around herself protectively. Then, as Winnie braced herself, a voice screamed, 'GET OFF HER!'

Her eyes snapped towards the kitchen door to see Jan standing there, looking horrified. The shock of hearing her screeching voice seemed to stop Brian in his tracks. He glared first at Jan, and then at Winnie. 'Now your bastard child can see what a useless, snivelling, fat cow you really are,' he said, and spat in Winnie's face.

As his saliva dripped down her cheek, she saw Jan run across the room and grab at Brian's arm. 'Leave her alone,' the girl shouted with a look of determination on her face.

Brian shrugged her off. 'Get your dirty hands off me,' he growled.

When she stumbled backwards, Brian pulled his arm back and leaned forwards towards Winnie. She could see he was going to punch her again but was stopped when Jan leapt on his back.

'I said leave her alone. Don't hurt my mother!' Jan screamed, before falling off Brian and to the floor.

Winnie scrambled to her feet, desperate to get in between her husband and Jan, but before she could, Brian began to walk away.

'I've had enough of this shit. You two deserve each other,' he said with disgust as he left the room.

Winnie rushed to help Jan, and despite her own pain, she placed an arm around her waist to gently ease her up. She could feel her trembling and saw tears trickling down her pale face.

'Oh, love, I'm so sorry,' she said and pulled out a chair at the table for her.

'It wasn't your fault,' Jan whispered, her eyes fixed firmly on the kitchen door.

'Don't worry. He's run out of steam now and I heard him go out. He'll bugger off to the bookies. He won't come back for a while. Are you all right?'

'Yes, I think so. Are you?'

'I'll live, thanks to you. That was really brave of you, but you should have stayed out of it. I'd have felt awful if you'd been hurt.'

'I couldn't stand by and let him hit you. Does he do that a lot?'

'Not so much these days, love. I used to think it was my fault; that I'd done or said something to start him off and I'd just take it. I realise now I hadn't, and today, believe it or not, what you saw was me standing up to him.'

'Oh, Winnie, that's terrible. Why do you stay with him?' Jan asked, drying her eyes on the cuff of her coat.

'Gawd only knows. I should have left him years ago – but you don't, do you? You make your bed and you lie in it. When I took my wedding vows, I believed and still do that they are for life. For better or worse.'

'I understand. I put up with my mother for far longer than I should have.'

'Well, from now on, neither of us will stand for being bullied.'

Jan smiled faintly, then Winnie asked tentatively, 'Did you realise what you said when you was screaming at him to get off me?'

'What?'

'You told him to leave your mother alone. You called *me* your mother.'

Jan looked down at her hands. 'Did I? Do you mind?'

'No, love, I'm chuffed to bits. It means the world to me that you think of me as your mum,' she answered, and feeling her eyes well up, she quickly changed the subject. 'What was you doing back here? I thought you'd gone off to Hilda's?'

'I had but I'd forgotten a dress pattern that I drew out last night so came back for it. Then when I came upstairs, I heard you crying out and...' Jan's voice trailed off and Winnie could see she was becoming upset again.

'Well, we showed him, didn't we, eh? He'll think twice before he tries something like that again,' she placated, trying to sound jolly. 'Now, seriously, don't let this upset you. There'll be no more trouble from him, I promise. You get off with Hilda and leave him to me. I won't come round to Hilda's today. I'll deal with Brian instead.'

Jan nodded but Winnie was worried that this would give her more reason to move out. She wasn't sure how she was going to *deal* with Brian, but she'd made a promise to her daughter. And come what may, she couldn't let Jan leave, not now that they'd been reunited after all these years. 'Oh, and tell Rachel I'll be down in a while. I doubt she would have heard anything but if she did, tell her I'm fine and I'll fill her in later on what happened.'

David heard a tap on his bedroom door and squeezed his eyes shut, pretending to be asleep. He'd heard the commotion, guessed his father was giving his mother a slap, but he wasn't going to get involved. After all, he reasoned, he was supposed to have a bad back and helping his mother would give the game away.

'I've brought you a cuppa and a ham sandwich,' his mother said as, quietly, she sneaked into the room. 'Are you awake?'

He groaned and rolled over, slowly opening his eyes. Surveying his mother, he could see she'd obviously straightened herself out and he didn't notice any cuts or bruises. That didn't mean his father hadn't hit her. There'd been many times when she'd nursed a sore arm, leg or stomach. The sly git didn't always leave her with visible marks.

'Thanks, Mum, I'm starving,' he said and sat up, rubbing his eyes and faking a yawn as if he'd just woken up.

She placed the small tray on the side. 'Did you hear your father creating a fuss again?' she asked, her voice light-hearted.

Typical of her, he thought, always playing it down. 'No, I've been asleep,' he lied. 'What happened?'

'Nothing much. He was going to hit me but Jan jumped in and stopped him. Fancy that, eh! There's nothing of her, bless her, but she's a brave little thing.'

Yeah, fancy that, thought David, but he already knew everything that had happened. He'd heard it all. His mother's cries of pain, his father's venomous threats, and Jan, the hero, rushing in to save their mother. He had hoped that his father would have given Jan a slap too. It might have made her think twice about her living arrangements and sent her on her way. But it hadn't turned out how he'd expected and now Jan was in even bigger favour with their mother.

'Oh, Mum, you should have called me. I would have come running if I'd known that Dad was on at you.'

'I'm glad you didn't. I wouldn't want to see either of my kids getting hurt. Neither of you should have to intervene. I've had it with your father and I've realised it's time I stood up for myself, and for Jan. She wouldn't think much of me if I allowed him to get at me like he does. But it won't happen again. I'm going to put a stop to it. Enough is enough.'

'Oh yeah. How?' David asked sceptically.

'Don't worry, I've got something up my sleeve that I should have pulled out a long time ago,' his mother said with a wry smile as she placed the tray on his bed now. 'Here, eat your lunch. I'd best get back downstairs. I've left Rachel by herself.'

'I feel terrible just lying here when's there's nothing wrong with me and you're doing everything,' David fibbed and bit into his sandwich.

243

'I'm sure you do, Son, but we've got to keep up the façade. You can't be seen out of that bed, not if you're going to avoid National Service.'

'But when Dad and Jan are out, couldn't I stretch my legs, maybe listen to the wireless?'

'No, it's not worth risking it. I've had word sent to the factory and I'll be taking your medical certificate in to the army offices tomorrow. There's always the danger they could send someone round, an inspector or something? Just stay put and don't get up.'

'With thousands of able-bodied men to register, I can't see that happening, but if you think it's for the best,' David said, relieved that he wouldn't have to leave the comfort of his bed to face accusing eyes. He wasn't stupid. He knew there would be plenty of people with lots to say about what had happened to Brenda. Kenny and June, for a start. In fact, he was pretty sure that his name would be dirt with most of the workers in the factory. He wasn't going to return there but he wasn't fussed. He hadn't liked the job anyway; it was boring.

'And don't worry about Errol. I'll make sure he's paid,' his mum said as she left the room.

David knew his mother would cough up to pay back Errol, but she didn't know about Stephanie Reynolds and he could hardly tell her. Would Stephanie keep quiet? She'd be sure to hear about him being laid up with a bad back. Would she wait for him to recover and then collect her blackmail money? Or would Errol be waiting in the wings to give him a good hiding for sleeping with his girlfriend? Either way, he had more than just National Service to avoid so the longer he could get away with a back injury, the better.

20

The next morning, Jan was sitting in the downstairs kitchen while Winnie made a pot of tea. Rachel would be arriving for work at any minute and Hilda had said she'd come round as soon as she'd finished her cleaning job. Jan would have preferred to have waited in her bedroom until Hilda arrived but she didn't dare stay alone upstairs. Mr Berry was there and after the confrontation with him yesterday, she had an uneasy feeling and she was petrified that he'd attack her.

Winnie seemed to sense her fear. 'You won't be getting any bother from Brian. Not ever again,' she said adamantly.

She wanted to know how Winnie could be so sure, but she didn't feel it was her business to ask. Instead, she said nothing and just hoped it was true.

'I can see you're not convinced, but believe me, my girl, he won't so much as look at you sideways. Or me, come to that. He ain't a fool, he knows when he's been beat.'

'But... we didn't *beat* him. He walked away but he could have really hurt us both.'

'No, we didn't beat him in that sense, but I've had a word

with him and he understands it would be in his best interest to toe the line from now on.'

'Oh – but are you sure he will?' Jan asked, still more than curious to know what Winnie had said to the brute.

'Yes, I'm *very* sure. He'll be as meek as a baby deer, you'll see.'

They heard a knock on the front door of the pub and Winnie said it would be Rachel. 'Pour the tea, love. I'll let her in,' she said, waddling off.

Jan held the tea strainer over the cups and noticed her hand was unsteady. She took a deep breath and reminded herself that Mr Berry was no longer going to be a problem. And with David dubiously stuck in his bed, she hoped to feel safe living at the Battersea Tavern. If anything, the thought of the streets outside was far scarier. If she could have cocooned herself in the small back kitchen with Winnie and Rachel, she would have. But Hilda was due any minute and Jan would have to face her fears or ashamedly admit that she was scared of the world outside. A world where her mother lurked. She shivered at the thought of possibly bumping into her again.

'Good morning, Jan,' Rachel said as she breezed in. 'It's nice to see you downstairs with us. I hope you're going to make this a regular thing?'

'I might, seeing as I've found the biscuit tin,' she answered with a smile, pleased to see her friend.

'Winnie keeps her best biscuits downstairs. They just get plain old digestives upstairs.'

'Shush, don't tell all my secrets,' Winnie warned with a chuckle.

'Are you both all right after yesterday's events?' Rachel asked.

'The side of me head is a bit sore but I only noticed when I was brushing my hair this morning. Apart from that, we're as right as rain, ain't we, love?' Winnie replied. She looked at Jan to chip in.

'Yes, that's right. We are,' she confirmed.

'I wish I'd heard what was going on. I would have come up and helped. But we never hear nothing down here that goes on at the back of your flat,' Rachel said, shaking her head.

'Well, I'm glad you didn't and from now on, Brian will be keeping his head down. I've made sure of it,' Winnie said.

'How have you done that? Have you chopped it off?' Rachel asked.

'No, but it's tempting. I've reminded him of something that he would rather forget about. When you've been married for as long as we have, you have all sorts of secrets and I've got one of his that he'd rather I kept to myself.'

'Do tell,' Rachel said, voicing Jan's thoughts.

'No, it wouldn't be a secret if I told you. But if that man steps out of line again, I'll be shouting it from the rooftops. Anyway, enough about him. Tell us what happened with Arnold last night. I noticed he waited for you to finish work.'

'Oh, Winnie, he's such a gent. He said he didn't want me walking home alone in the blackout. I told him I do every night and it's perfectly safe, what with the wardens and everything. But he said from now on, he'd escort me to my door and wouldn't take no for an answer.'

'And did he try and get behind your door?' Winnie asked, her eyes narrowing.

'No, not at all. I thought he might and I would have told

him where to go but he was as good as gold. He didn't even try to kiss me.'

'Well, I never. A true gent.'

'That remains to be seen. He's asked me out for a late lunch today,' Rachel said, her eyes shining and her cheeks pinking up.

'Has he indeed? And are you going?'

'Of course. I mean, a girl's got to eat, hasn't she?'

Winnie roared with laughter and Jan joined in.

'Jan, what about Terry? When are you seeing him next?' Rachel asked.

'Oh, I'm not sure. I think he wants to take me out this evening but I don't know if I want to go,' she answered awkwardly.

'Why not, love?' Winnie quizzed.

Jan felt put on the spot and didn't want to confess that she was terrified of seeing her mother, but she didn't like to lie to these dear women either. 'I just – erm, err, it's cold and I'm very busy with my dressmaking and –'

'Do I look like I just fell off the last turnip truck, young lady?' Winnie asked.

'No – no, of course not,' she stammered, unsure of what Winnie was getting at.

'Good, then don't treat me like an idiot. Now, what's the *real* reason for you not wanting to go out with Terry?'

Jan lowered her head, tears filling her eyes. She thought Winnie was a wise woman and felt awful for fibbing and even worse for getting caught out. 'I'm worried about seeing my mother,' she admitted.

'I thought as much. It's unlikely, and, even if by some slim chance you did, Terry wouldn't let you come to any harm.'

'I know. I'm being silly, but the thought of it terrifies me. I'm not even looking forward to going round to Hilda's this morning.'

'After the way you jumped on Brian's back, I should have thought you'd be fearless now. I've seen you in action and I'm telling you, it's your mother who oughta be scared of you.'

Jan chuckled, albeit half-heartedly. 'Thanks, Winnie. I don't know why I'm so worried about it. As you say, Terry wouldn't let anyone hurt me. And maybe you're right – maybe I can stick up for myself.'

'Too right you can,' Rachel said. 'Tell you what, I'll show you how to wear a bit of lippy and mascara, if you like? Not too much, you wouldn't want people thinking you're brassy. But you'll look beautiful for your date tonight and it'll make you feel better.'

Jan wasn't sure about wearing cosmetics but thanked Rachel. She could always wash it off before she went out. Someone hammered on the door. It was loud and made her jump.

'That'll be Hilda,' Rachel said and went to let her in.

'Morning, ladies,' Hilda said breathlessly when she joined them in the kitchen.

'Have you been running?' Winnie asked.

'Yeah, all the way from the Latchmere. I was just putting out the rubbish at my cleaning job and I saw this old paper. Look, have you seen it?' Hilda said, frantically waving the creased-up *Daily Mirror* in front of them.

'Yes, love, I know. It's tragic, absolutely tragic,' Winnie said sadly.

'I can't believe it, Winnie. The Germans have sunk the *Royal Oak*. Hundreds of men drowned right off the coast of Scotland. I didn't realise the Jerries are so close. They're coming for us, ain't they?'

The alarm in Hilda's voice must have been contagious because Jan now found herself searching Winnie's face for reassurance.

'Don't worry, love, that news is days old. Our boys won't let the Germans in. The crafty shits have got away with getting one of our navy fleet, but they'd never get on land, never. Huh, I'd like to see 'em try. Now, calm down, stop overreacting and have a cuppa while I open up. Yes, there's a war on but my customers will still want their ale.'

Jan felt reassured, and Hilda seemed happier too as she pulled out a chair and asked, 'Am I the only one who's worried about this war?'

Rachel scraped her chair back and shrugged her shoulders as she rose to her feet, 'I doubt it, but I don't see the point in upsetting yourself. There haven't been any bombs dropped, and maybe there never will. I reckon it's a phoney war. That's what a lot of our customers are saying. Talking of which, I'd better go and help Winnie.'

'Sorry about that, Jan,' Hilda said and she poured her tea into a saucer before slurping it. 'Winnie's right, I do overreact sometimes. I walk about with me eyes closed most of the time, so this news came as a bit of a shock. I'll finish this cuppa and then we can get going. You can update me on Rachel and that fella.'

Jan thought it was a strange way for Hilda to drink her tea out of the saucer, but she'd found there were many things that were very different to how they'd been at her mother's. For instance, no one said grace before eating. Belching wasn't thought of as a sin. And bathing didn't have to be done in pitch-blackness.

'Are you ready?' Hilda asked.

Yes, she was. She was still worried about coming face to face with her mother, but as Winnie had reminded her, she could stick up for herself and had proven it. She hoped she wouldn't have to prove it again.

Later that day, as Winnie saw the last customer out, Arnold Sanders turned up with a bunch of flowers in his hand.

'For you,' he said to Winnie, offering them to her as he doffed his hat.

'Get off with you, you daft bugger, and give 'em to Rachel. She's just gone to powder her nose. I'm closing up, but come in; you'll catch your death out there.'

'Thank you, Winnie, but I don't mind waiting outside for Rachel.'

'I said, come in, didn't I? Now, make yourself useful, young man, and take that crate of empties down to the cellar for me.'

Arnold clicked his heels together and pretended to salute. Winnie noticed his shiny, expensive shoes, the sort only a bloke in the City would wear. 'Hang on, love, just leave the crate on the bar. You'll scuff your shoes on the steps and it's a bit dusty downstairs.'

'It's no bother, Winnie,' Arnold insisted and he took the crate. 'Would you like to come to lunch with us?' he asked.

'No, thanks. I've got a mountain of ironing to get through this afternoon.'

Arnold went to the cellar and Rachel came into the bar, her cheeks matching the colour of her coat. 'Did I hear Arnold's voice?' she whispered.

'Yes, he's taken that crate downstairs for me. He's got you a lovely bunch of flowers, look,' Winnie said, pointing to the bar where he'd left them.

'Oh, blimey. I haven't got a vase at home.'

'He don't need to know that. Just accept them graciously.'

Moments later, Arnold returned from the cellar, beaming at the sight of Rachel. 'Good afternoon, Miss Robb,' he said as he brushed dust off his fine wool coat.

'Mr Sanders,' Rachel replied, smiling.

'Shall we?' Arnold offered his arm to Rachel. She readily accepted, hooking her arm through his.

'Are you sure you won't join us?' he asked Winnie.

'I'm sure, but it's very kind of you to ask. Go on, bugger off, the pair of you, and have a good time.'

Arnold picked up the bunch of flowers as they left and Winnie locked the door behind them. Her feet were killing her and she couldn't wait to get upstairs and put them up for a while. But first she'd check on David. He was bound to be hungry and thirsty by now. She hadn't had a chance to nip upstairs for the past couple of hours.

She tapped on his door before pushing it open, and asked, 'Are you ready for a cuppa?'

He was sitting up in bed reading the newspaper. 'Cor, not half. I am, thanks.'

'I won't be long,' she said and she smiled warmly at him. She didn't feel easy about deceiving the authorities over David's injuries but she'd much rather have her son in his warm bed than out in the field somewhere and under fire from the Germans. She thought of all those poor men who'd lost their lives when that blasted German U-boat had torpedoed the *Royal Oak*. Reports said eight hundred were dead.

Eight hundred grieving mothers. Eight hundred mothers with shattered hearts. She couldn't imagine their pain and hoped she'd never have to experience it.

After taking David his lunch, Winnie finally got to sit in the front room. Wearily, she warmed her feet in front of the fire. Brian had got a roaring one going and she noticed the coal bucket was full. Normally, it was a job he left to her. He was listening to the wireless as he puffed on his pipe, his eyes closed.

'Did you make me a cuppa?' he asked.

'Nope,' Winnie answered, proud of herself. She'd said she never would again and she intended to stick to it. She'd show him she wasn't a pushover anymore. She had to; she had a daughter to set an example to. 'Things are going to be different from now.'

'All right, woman, no need to harp on. I needed telling and you made your point – very impressed I was too. Now leave it. Do you want a cuppa?'

Winnie could have fallen out of her chair with shock. 'Err, yes, please. There's tea already made in the pot. You only need to pour it,' she replied, but her suspicions rose. Was this just an act to lull her into a false sense of security before an attack, or had her threat to spill the beans about his secret had the desired effect?

Brian placed his pipe in an ashtray beside him and stood up, asking uncomfortably, 'Do you take yours with sugar?'

She was about to say scathingly that, after all these years of marriage, surely he should know whether or not she took sugar, but not wishing to antagonise him, she bit her lip, instead politely answering, 'No, thank you.'

Shortly afterwards, Brian returned from the kitchen

carrying a tray and two teacups. She half expected him to launch it at her but he placed it gently on the side table and handed her a cup. He must really want her to keep her mouth shut about what she knew, Winnie thought, thanking him as she accepted the tea.

'Will you be cooking our supper tonight?' Brian asked and sat back in his armchair opposite her.

'Yes, of course. Sausage, egg and chips all right for you?'

'It'll do,' Brian answered, but Winnie knew he'd never been keen on sausages.

While Brian seemed to be in an agreeable mood, Winnie thought she'd try her luck. 'The pub could do with some new curtains. It's all very well covering the windows with cardboard and taping them up, but if we had some decent blackout curtains, it'd look a lot better.'

'How much?'

'I'm not sure. I'll price them up and let you know,' she answered. She'd had an idea to get the material cheap and ask Jan to run up a few pairs of curtains on Hilda's machine. Brian need never know and she'd tell him the cost of ready-made curtains, splitting the difference to use the money to pay Errol.

'Fine, you do that. How's David?'

'No better,' she answered with a sigh.

'It's early days, I suppose,' he replied.

His answer left her surprised. Brian didn't normally participate in small talk, so before sipping her tea, she continued their rare chat, saying, 'That sinking of the *Royal Oak* was awful. Such a tragic waste of young lives.'

'Bloody Hitler and his armies. If I was a younger man, I'd

be champing at the bit to shoot the bastards. Soon as David's well enough, he can do us proud.'

'Oh, no, Brian, you can't mean that? You made out you were half deaf to get out of active service during the last war, yet you expect our son to sign up?'

'I had this place along with you and a baby on the way to think of. That boy ain't got any responsibilities and should do his bit.'

'How can you say that? What if something happened to him? He could be killed.'

'If he died while fighting for our king and country, it would be with honour. Better that than half killing himself on that stupid bike.'

'The bike is beyond repair, he won't be riding it again. And the way his back is, I can't see him being fit and able for National Service for a long time yet. Hopefully, the war will be over by then.'

'We'll see about that. I reckon this war is going to drag on for a long time yet. And mark my words, there'll be food rationing soon.'

'Oh, I hope not. It's bad enough with the petrol being rationed and the blackouts,' Winnie tutted.

'I'd get used to the idea, if I was you. You've always been good in the kitchen, so if you want to carry on making decent meals, maybe you should stock up.'

Winnie was too taken aback to respond. Instead, she carried on drinking her tea. This was the longest reasonable conversation she'd had with her husband in years. And she couldn't remember the last time he'd complimented her cooking, though the talk of David joining up unnerved her.

'I know it's only mid-October and a bit early to be

thinking about it, but I suppose you'll be wanting to throw a Christmas lunch party for half of Battersea again?'

'Yes, I was going to,' she answered, hoping he wouldn't moan about it as he had for the past seven years.

Then he spoke again, unprompted this time, and what he said caused her to splutter on her tea.

'There's fifteen shillings in my pot. You'd better take it and buy yourself a new dress for Christmas.'

Winnie was almost speechless with shock, but then managed to say softly, 'Thank you. I could do with one.'

'Well, then, best get yourself one. Get a red one. Red suits you.'

'Thanks,' she said, but her suspicions were rising. What on earth was Brian up to? This was so out of character. Yes, she'd warned him that she'd reveal his secret if he ever showed any signs of violence to her or Jan again and he'd reluctantly backed down. But she hadn't demanded conversation, presents or niceties.

'You throw a good Christmas lunch. I bumped into Reggie Charter yesterday. He was waxing lyrical about last year's knees-up. I said him and his boy would be welcome this year, but he'll be coming alone. His lad has already gawn off to France.'

'Poor Reggie, he must be worried sick. I know I would be, if our David was there.'

'Yeah, you would an' all. You was bad enough when he went camping that weekend with the Tuckers from down the road. Do you remember, you asked me to go and fetch him back from the New Forest?'

'Yes, I remember,' she answered, chortling at the memory.

'But you wouldn't go and instead made me drink a few glasses of brandy to calm my nerves.'

'That's right and it made you as drunk as a skunk,' Brian said and he laughed. 'Singing your bleedin' head off to all the customers. We closed early that night, thanks to your dulcet tones.'

'Don't remind me! I can still see Len with them handkerchiefs hanging out of his ears and the look of anguish on his face,' she said as tears of laughter streamed down her face.

Brian was rocking with laughter too. 'And do you remember when the copper came in? You pinched his helmet and he chased you out the pub and dragged you back, still singing. I begged him to do us all a favour and arrest you but he said they couldn't have put up with you singing all night in the station. He couldn't get out the pub quick enough.'

'Oh, don't. I was so embarrassed the next day, especially when Len stuck them posters up outside.'

'Ha, yeah, I'd forgotten about them. What was it they said?'

'Winnie the Wonder Warbler. Come and see Battersea's only operatic performer, live in the Battersea Tavern. Ideal entertainment for the deaf. Warning: don't wear your spectacles, she'll shatter them,' she reminded him, and dabbed her wet eyes.

'That's right, and he'd drawn a picture of you to look like a Greek goddess. Mind you, it wasn't very flattering.'

'No, it wasn't. You made him take them all down.'

'Too right, I did. I weren't having my wife made a laughing stock. You're better than that.'

Winnie smiled and finished her tea. It had all happened years ago, fifteen or so. At the time, when Brian had demanded Len rip down every poster, she'd assumed he was just being a miserable beggar. She hadn't realised he'd been protecting her honour. She pushed herself out of the chair. 'I'd better get that stack of ironing done; it won't do itself,' she said and headed to the kitchen.

In her head, Winnie replayed the conversation with Brian. It had been like the clocks had turned back and, to her astonishment, she found she'd enjoyed his company. Surely it wasn't the threat of revealing his secret that had made him so amiable. If anything, that should have made him morose. Whatever had caused it, it was nice to have a bit of harmony between them. But would it last? Only time would tell.

21

It was less than a week since Rachel had first met the charming Arnold Sanders and though she'd fought to keep her feelings in check, she'd soon realised she wasn't winning. He had an ease about him that relaxed her, a confidence she admired, impeccable manners and good humour. Not to mention his devastating good looks! At first, when he'd shown an interest in her, she'd questioned his motives, but he'd proved himself to be honourable and had treated her with respect. In fact, he'd seen her home every night after work and hadn't once overstepped the mark. They'd shared a gentle kiss last night which had left her tingling, and now, as she wiped down the bar in the Battersea Tavern, her stomach fluttered at the memory of his lips lingering on hers.

'Oi, Miss Dolly-day-dreamer,' Winnie called, snapping her from her thoughts.

'Sorry, Win, I was miles away,' she answered, turning to see the woman emptying an ashtray.

'I can guess exactly where you was in that pretty little head of yours. Did you have a nice lunch?'

'Wonderful. Arnold had a taxicab waiting and took me

over the river to this posh little restaurant overlooking the Thames. He's so sophisticated. Not like me, I felt like a fish out of water. He knows all about wine and foreign food. I couldn't even pronounce some of the things on the menu so I ordered Dover sole. And then we had a stroll along the Embankment.'

'Sounds smashing, love. Is he coming in later?'

'Yes, to walk me home. Erm – I was wondering –'

'If you can take an evening off to go out with Arnold?' Winnie jumped in, finishing the sentence for her.

Rachel didn't like to ask, but Arnold had invited her to the theatre. She'd never been before and was keen to go but was worried about leaving Winnie to work alone.

'I can't expect you to work every night, it's not fair. You need to have a social life, so I'll make arrangements for you to have Wednesday and Saturday evenings off. You won't lose any pay.'

Rachel hadn't been expecting her time off to be a regular thing. She had the occasional Monday night off but that was only if the pub was quiet. But if Winnie was offering, and if it was possible, she wouldn't turn it down. 'What arrangements? If you're thinking of asking Jan, I'm not sure she'd enjoy it.'

'No, I wouldn't ask Jan. But Brian knows how to pull a pint.'

'Mr Berry!' Rachel exclaimed. 'I know you said he's been nice to you lately but he wouldn't work the bar, would he?'

'I don't know; he might. There's no harm in asking. See, the thing is with men like my old man, they're bullies. I've stood up to him and now he knows I won't stand for it, he's backed down.'

'Maybe he respects you, Win?'

'Maybe. Or maybe he just wants me to keep me mouth shut. But whatever, I'll ask him to work a couple of nights.'

Rachel's eyebrows lifted in surprise. 'Well, if you're sure.'

'I am. We can't have the Battersea Tavern getting in the way of true love,' Winnie teased.

Rachel could feel her cheeks burning. 'I wouldn't go as far as to say it's true love, not yet, but I do think a lot of him,' she said, realising she hadn't thought of Jim now that Arnold filled her mind nearly every minute of every day. She'd never have believed a good-looking man would turn her head again, not after what Jim had done to her, but Arnold had, and she smiled.

The door opened and she was pleased to see Terry walk in.

'Hello. Are you here for a drink or to see Jan?' she asked.

'Both. I've got the afternoon off so I thought I'd pop in and see Jan. She said she'd be happy to stay here in the pub tonight an' all.'

'Aw, that's nice. You can meet Arnold, he'll be in later.'

'I'm looking forward to it. Will I need to bow? I hear he's a bit upper class.'

'Don't be silly. He's not like that. You'll like him.'

'Good. Any bloke who makes you smile can't be bad.'

Again, Rachel could feel herself blushing but she couldn't deny the effect Arnold had on her and yes, he certainly made her smile.

Winnie walked over and greeted Terry, then asked, 'Shall I give Jan a shout, let her know you're here?'

'If you wouldn't mind, thanks.'

'No problem. I'll check on David while I'm up there.'

'How is he?' Terry asked, though Rachel thought he was only enquiring to be polite.

'No improvement yet,' Winnie answered. 'I'll send him your regards,' she added as she walked off.

Terry lowered his voice and leaned in towards Rachel. 'Call me a cynic, if you like, but it's a bit of a coincidence, him suddenly hurting his back when he's supposed to be registering with the army soon.'

'Funnily enough, I thought the same,' she whispered. 'Only don't let Winnie hear you talking like that.'

'I won't. She thinks the sun shines out of his backside. To tell you the truth, he's better off hiding in his room. He ain't very popular at the moment. I've heard that folk ain't happy about what happened to Brenda.'

'I know. Winnie's had cross words with quite a few of our regulars. It's really awkward for me. I feel I want to back her up but I can't, not when it comes to David,' she said, still incensed at him for stealing from his mother.

Their conversation ended abruptly when Winnie came back in, followed by Jan who was wearing a light-coloured lipstick and a bit of mascara. The girl beamed when she set eyes on Terry and Rachel wondered if that was how she looked when she saw Arnold. Probably, but it was uncontrollable and it felt good to be this happy again. She was enjoying every moment of courting Arnold. And to top it all, Hilda had stopped drinking. Then there was the added bonus of finding she had a new friend in Jan and even Mr Berry was treating Winnie well. Life was the best it had been in a long time, so why did she still have a heavy feeling that something terrible was going to happen?

★

Once the morning customers had left, Winnie trudged up the stairs and into the kitchen, surprised to find Brian making a pot of tea.

'I thought you'd like a cuppa,' he said awkwardly.

'I would, thanks, but I don't have time. I've got to fix David his lunch and then pop out for some shopping.'

'Well, there's tea in the pot if you change your mind. I'm off out myself but I'll be back for dinner.'

'Okey-dokey,' she said breezily, guessing he'd be going to the bookies in Peckham. She just hoped he wouldn't blow too much money on gambling. If he did, she could say goodbye to blackout curtains for the pub.

Once he'd left, Winnie ladled broth into a big bowl and tore off a chunk of bread, then carried it through to David's room.

'It's only me,' she said, pushing open his door.

'That smells nice, Mum, thanks. I'm starved.'

'There's more in the pot, if you want it, but I'm off out, so you'll have to wait for me to get back.'

'Where're you going?'

Winnie sighed before answering. 'To pay off some of your debt.'

'Has he been in?'

'No, not yet, but it's only a matter of time. I'm going to ask your father to do a couple of shifts in the pub, and I don't want Errol calling in looking for his money.'

David's eyes widened. 'You're gonna ask Dad to work downstairs?'

'I am. Rachel needs time off to spend with her new fella and I don't see why your father can't pull his weight a bit.'

'Rachel's got a boyfriend?'

'Yes. A lovely chap called Arnold. He's right posh an' all,' she answered and noticed David appeared to look rather perturbed by the news. 'You're not still holding a torch for her, are you?'

'No, course not,' he said unconvincingly, adding, 'I can't see my dad agreeing to work downstairs.'

'I think he will. He's a changed man of late.'

'Huh, we'll see about that.'

'You'd be surprised. He was just in the kitchen making a pot of tea.'

'No way! Blimey, Mum, what have you done to him?'

'Scared the bloody life out of him,' Winnie chuckled. 'Anyway, I'd best get off. I'm not looking forward to this.'

'I'm sorry I've put you in this position, Mum, and thanks.'

Winnie smiled softly at her son. He was a good lad, really, and it was nice that he appreciated what she was doing for him.

Winnie wrapped a scarf around her head, pulled on a cardigan over the one she was already wearing and picked up her shopping bag. She'd have liked to have bought herself a new coat but Errol had to be paid off first. When she stepped outside the back door, she was pleased it wasn't as cold as she'd anticipated.

'Good afternoon, Mrs Lloyd,' Winnie said to a passing neighbour in the street. But Mrs Lloyd ignored her and marched on past. Winnie knew it was because of the David-and-Brenda situation and would have liked to have given the woman a piece of her mind but she had more pressing matters to deal with.

Fifteen minutes later, she stood outside Errol Hampton's

house and knocked on the door. When Errol's mother pulled it open, Winnie swallowed hard. Carmen was known to be a hard woman and Winnie knew she'd have to tread carefully. She hadn't seen Carmen Hampton in years and was surprised to see her jet-black hair was now interspersed with a distinctive white streak across the front. She'd once been a beautiful woman, probably of Gypsy heritage, but age had savaged her good looks and her face was drawn and haggard.

'Mrs Berry, what do you want?' Carmen asked, looking down her nose suspiciously.

'Good afternoon, Mrs Hampton. I'm sorry to disturb you, but I'd like a quick word with Errol.'

'Why? What business do you have with my son?'

'My son has had an unfortunate accident and is bedridden. He's asked me to pass on a message to Errol.'

'He ain't here. You can pass it on to me and I'll make sure he gets it.'

Winnie stuttered, 'I'd – erm –'

As she searched for the words, the door opened wider and she saw Errol come to stand behind his mother.

'What's going on?' he asked.

'She's got a message for you from her son,' Carmen answered.

'All right, Mum, I'll deal with this,' he said, and stepped in front of her.

Winnie had a quick glimpse of inside. The house looked lavishly decorated and even had carpet in the passageway and up the stairs. It was very unusual in the run-down houses in this part of Battersea, but it was no secret that Carmen's husband, Have-it Harry, was an accomplished thief. No doubt the luxuries in their home had been acquired from the stuff he'd stolen.

Carmen huffed and went back inside and Errol stepped onto the chalked step, pulling the door closed behind him. 'You've got some front to come knocking on my door.'

'You want your money, don't you?' Winnie asked, feeling more nervous than she sounded.

'Yeah, I do.'

Winnie fished in her purse and handed him the cash she'd saved, less what she'd had to fork out for the doctor.

'Is this it?' he asked, looking at the coins.

'I'll get you more next week.'

'You make sure you do. But don't come here again, I'll come to you.'

'I'd rather meet you. How about outside the Latchmere baths, same time next week?'

'Fine, but if you don't turn up, I'll come calling.'

'I'll be there.'

Errol grunted, turned on his heel, opened the front door and slammed it shut in her face. She didn't care, glad that it had been sorted, and breathed a sigh of relief. It was done, over with for now, and she could relax, safe in the knowledge that he wouldn't be making an appearance in the Battersea Tavern. Her next mission was to ask Brian to work the bar.

22

On the Saturday evening, Rachel felt Arnold's hand on the small of her back as he led her through the theatre lobby and out onto the street.

'That was wonderful,' she exclaimed. 'I can't believe you managed to get us tickets. All the theatres are supposed to be closed.'

'Indeed. This blasted war is quite an inconvenience. But I'm glad you enjoyed it. I should imagine a stage show is a pleasant change from working in the pub?'

'Oh, Arnold, it really is, though I still feel guilty about not being there.'

'You said Winnie's husband is working at the bar, didn't you?'

'Yes, he is, but Lord knows how Winnie got him to agree.'

'Well, I shouldn't worry. It all sounds like it's in hand, so you, my dear, have nothing to feel guilty about.'

'I suppose you're right.'

Arnold stepped into the road and hailed a passing taxicab. When the black Austin pulled over, he opened the back and Rachel climbed in.

'Where to, Gov?'

'Battersea, my man, Prince of Wales Drive.'

The cab driver set the taximeter and the taxi sped off.

'Isn't that where you live?' Rachel asked.

'Indeed, it is. I thought you might like a nightcap before I take you home. The night is young and I'm enjoying your company.'

She didn't answer as her mind raced and she suspected Arnold had an ulterior motive for taking her to his house. Well, she thought, if he thinks I'm going to sleep with him, he can think again, resolute that he wouldn't use her as she still suspected might be his intention.

They pulled up outside a grand house and Arnold payed the driver, tipping him generously. After taking her hand and helping her out of the cab, Rachel looked up at the impressive building as Arnold found his key.

'You're gaping, dear, but there's no need. I don't own the whole mansion, just a modest apartment on the first floor.'

'Even so, it's quite a place. It makes my little room look like a mouse hole. And I can see from here that you've got a balcony.'

'After you,' he said, gesturing with a sweep of his arm through the heavy wooden double doors.

Rachel walked in and was immediately struck by the size of the hallway. She peered around, feeling out of place. She'd felt that way too in the theatre. Many of the other women had been dressed in their finery with fur stoles and glittering jewellery. She'd worn her best burgundy skirt with matching jacket, but felt that she had looked more like one of the usherettes.

Once inside Arnold's apartment, she was surprised at how

old-fashioned some of the furniture appeared and though she could tell it was good quality, there seemed to be a mismatch of pieces. He invited her to take a seat on one of the three sumptuous sofas.

'As you can see, I haven't yet had my father's things removed. I'm afraid you might find the place in disarray.'

'It's smashing and those big bay windows must give you a lovely view over the park.'

'Yes, they do – though, unfortunately, of the barrage balloon too. A constant reminder of the fact that we are at war. I'm sorry, I don't mean to sound so dour. Where are my manners? What can I get you to drink?'

'Just a small sherry for me, please.'

Arnold poured their drinks from an array of bottles on a large silver tray and handed her a fine crystal glass.

'This is funny, you serving me a drink,' she said.

'Yes, quite. I hope you don't think I'm talking out of turn, but you could do much better than working in a pub.'

Rachel shot him an indignant look. 'But I enjoy working in the Battersea Tavern and Winnie is like family to me.'

'I'm sure she is and I think she is a wonderful woman, but don't you feel that being a barmaid is beneath you?'

'No, Arnold, I don't. I didn't have the sort of privileged upbringing you obviously had. My family were poor. I had to share a bed with my sisters and we had old coats as coverings instead of blankets. We had bread and dripping for breakfast and were lucky to have a bit of scrag end and rotten veg stewed up for supper. I consider myself lucky to have my job at the pub and, frankly, where I work is none of your business.'

Arnold looked contrite and said quickly, 'I apologise if I've upset you, it was quite unintentional. I didn't put that very well, and what I meant to say was that I believe you could do better for yourself. Work in an office, maybe, or something along those lines. Anyway, am I forgiven?'

One look into his eyes, and Rachel felt herself melt. 'I suppose so,' she said and then her pulse quickened as Arnold took the sherry glass from her hand, reached past her and placed it on the gilt table beside the sofa. There was no mistaking the passion in his eyes and she knew he was going to kiss her.

As their mouths met, he reached his hand round to the back of her head and placed his other on her thigh. She sensed his breathing becoming heavier and though it felt good, she pulled away.

'I'm not that sort of girl,' she said.

Arnold cupped her face in his hands and began kissing her again. 'I want you, Rachel, you're beautiful,' he said huskily.

She could feel her body responding to his ardour but she pulled away again. 'No, Arnold. I won't do anything like that.'

He took a long breath and jumped up from the sofa. 'I understand. Come on, I'll take you home.'

Rachel could see he was disappointed and she felt hurt that he'd obviously had an agenda in bringing her here. She'd hoped he'd prove her wrong but she'd been right to keep her guard up. Now she'd made it clear that she wouldn't sleep with him, she wondered if he'd want to see her again.

Arnold hailed another taxi, and once he'd paid the fare and they had alighted outside her own front door, he pulled her into his arms. 'Rachel, oh, Rachel, what's a man to do?'

'I don't understand,' she said, content to feel his arms engulfing her and the warmth of his body. 'Do you still want to see me?'

'Most certainly, my dear. I shall be at the pub tomorrow to walk you home as always and then we can make plans to go out on your next evening off.'

Relief washed over her and she held him tighter.

'I'm sorry I tried to take advantage of you. You said you're *not that sort of girl* and I respect your wishes. I find them admirable. Now, sleep tight, my dear,' he said and lightly kissed her cheek.

Rachel offered him a final wave goodbye, closed the door and leaned against it, swooning in his wake. He'd alleviated her fears of him using her and now she knew it was going to be easy to fall in love with him. After the devastation with Jim, she'd believed that no man would ever win her heart but Arnold had and she felt she was walking on air.

Winnie lay in her bed just a few feet away from Brian's. She knew he was still awake as he wasn't yet snoring. He'd readily accepted her request to work behind the bar for two evenings a week and had agreed that Rachel's pay should remain the same. And she'd been pleased that he hadn't lost his charm behind the bar. He'd been friendly with all their customers and had thrown out one bloke who'd said something derogatory about David. In fact, she'd enjoyed the jolly atmosphere and had laughed more than she had in ages. But still there was the fear that this was all an act and, any day soon, he'd revert to being a bullying and hateful husband.

'Thanks for tonight,' she whispered in the pitch-darkness.

'I had a good time,' he responded.

'Yeah, me too. It was like the old days.'

'We made a good team, you and me, everyone used to say so.'

Yes, they used to, but their customers had no idea what went on behind closed doors. Winnie had always been good at putting on a front and covering her bruises. And although Brian's violence hadn't been a regular thing, it had been sufficient to keep her compliant.

'I'm keeping to my end of the bargain, so I trust you'll keep to yours?' he asked.

'I said I would.'

'Good. Night, Win.'

'Night,' she replied and turned her back to his bed. She had to remind herself to not be fooled by Brian's good behaviour. He wasn't being nice because he wanted to be. He was playing her, being sweet to keep her quiet. Christ alive, she thought, he must *really* want to keep his secret from getting out. But she couldn't blame him. If people discovered the truth, they'd likely ostracise him and the pub. He'd get abuse thrown at him and wouldn't be able to show his face in public. It was no more than he deserved. What he'd done had been despicable but Winnie was under no illusion that if people knew, she, as his wife, would be tarred with the same brush. That's why she'd never told anyone. She'd had to protect herself and their son, so she'd carried the burden of what Brian had done for years. In all truth, she'd still prefer it that people never found out, but if Brian stepped out of line again, she would have to be prepared to talk openly about what she knew and somehow accept the backlash. She just hoped it wouldn't be necessary, for her sake and her children.

23

On Wednesday, David waited until he heard everyone leave before he climbed out of bed. He thought it was all very well feigning a bad back, but the boredom felt relentless. The wireless his mother had put in his bedroom did little to entertain him and he'd read the newspaper from cover to cover. At least now with the flat empty, he could have a sneaky wander around. Stretching his arms above his head, it felt good to be on his feet.

Quietly, he opened the bedroom door and peeked along the hallway, pleased to see it was all clear. Jan had left early; he'd heard her go. His mum would be downstairs and had told him that his father was going shopping today to buy paint for the pub. Quietly tiptoeing into the kitchen, he went straight for his mother's tin and took it from the shelf to look inside. He found two florins and half a crown which he helped himself to. If his mother questioned him about the missing money, he'd deny it and, hopefully, her suspicions would turn to Jan.

Next, he looked in the larder but there were no freshly baked cakes. He wasn't hungry but had fancied a slice of his mum's jam sponge. With a scowl of disappointment he went through to the sitting room where he could smell the lingering aroma of his father's pipe. It was unusual for his father not to be in the room with the wireless on, but whatever his mother had threatened him with seemed to have had a profound effect. He wanted to find out what it was. It would come in handy to have a hold over his father too, one he could use if the bastard turned on him again.

David wandered over to the window and peered through the clean net curtains to the street below. It looked cold outside but he'd have liked to venture out, regardless of the weather. Of course he couldn't. He had to maintain this façade of having a bad back. Anyway, his mother had warned him that he could face a hostile reaction from the locals. Apparently, they were still smarting over the business with Brenda. The girl remained in hospital with no change in her condition. It was sad but it wasn't his fault and he hoped people would eventually forget about it. From what he'd been reading in the papers, they should be more worried about Hitler and his troops who were marching across Europe.

He stretched his arms again and yawned. Being bored and in bed all day was tiring. He left the sitting room and ambled back along the hallway, passing his own room and going into Jan's. Glancing around the small room, he could see his mother had done a good job of clearing it and now it looked quite pretty. Jan's bed was neatly made and her clothes were folded tidily on a seat in the corner. A few scribblings were scattered on the bed. He picked one up, uninterested when he saw it was a design for a dress. He knelt down and looked under her bed. There was nothing except a pair of slippers. And there wasn't anything of interest in the chest of drawers.

He wasn't sure what he'd hope to find but maybe something incriminating that he could use against her. Unfortunately, it appeared her room was just as uninspiring as she was.

Returning to his own room, he stashed the coins he'd pinched in his jacket pocket. His mother was due to meet Errol and he knew she'd already saved some money to pay him. If she carried on at this rate, by the time he could leave his room, his debt would be clear and then he'd only have Stephanie Reynolds to worry about. At least she'd kept her mouth shut so far but he wasn't sure she would indefinitely. Stephanie must have heard about his accident and would know he wasn't working. The woman was probably biding her time and would pounce on him the minute he was back on his feet. Well, he had time on his side at the moment and he intended on adding to the few coins in his jacket pocket. Eventually, he might have enough to keep her quiet until he could find another less expensive way of buying her silence.

After the lunchtime shift, Rachel had just left and Winnie was about to lock up, keen to get to the Latchmere to meet Errol. She heard the back door close, assuming Brian had returned with the paint to smarten up the bar. As she walked across the pub, she heard his voice behind her.

'I wasn't sure you'd like the colour I chose, so you'd better come with me and have a look for yourself.'

Winnie gulped, her mind racing. She couldn't go shopping with Brian and leave Errol waiting, but what excuse could she use?

'Come on, grab your coat. It's cold outside,' he urged.

'You go, Brian. I'm sure whatever colour you've chosen

will be suitable. Some sort of deep red for the back and side walls. The wallpaper on the others doesn't need painting over.'

'No, I'm not taking responsibility for getting the wrong colour.'

'Can't we wait until tomorrow?'

'Why? Have you got something better to be doing?'

Yes, she did, but she couldn't tell him that. 'No, but I'm worn out and ain't in the mood for paint shopping.'

'You've been on at me all bleedin' year about decorating the pub and now you can't be bothered. If that's the case, I won't be doing any painting.'

'It's not that I can't be bothered, I'm just knackered and me feet are killing me. Surely we could go tomorrow instead?'

'No, Win, you know I always go to the bookies on Thursdays and by the time I've caught the bus home from Peckham, it'll be too late. All this time standing here arguing about it, we could be halfway to the shops by now.'

She was running thin on excuses and didn't want to rile Brian. He'd been on his best behaviour and she wanted to keep him that way. 'All right, I'll finish locking up.'

'I'll get your coat.'

Winnie's heart hammered as she bolted the doors. Not only was she going to leave Errol standing but Brian was about to discover she'd given her coat to Jan and she knew he'd be none too pleased about it. It had been second-hand but had still cost a few bob.

'Don't worry about my coat,' she called up the stairs. 'I've got a thick cardi on and should be warm enough.'

Brian came to the top of the stairs. 'Trust me, it's brass monkeys out there, you'll need a coat. But where is it? It ain't on the coat stand.'

'I – erm, lent it to Jan. The poor mite didn't have anything and she's hardly got an ounce of fat on her to keep her warm. I wasn't expecting to need it today.'

'Right,' Brian said, tight-lipped as he came back down the stairs, 'you'd better wear my donkey jacket.'

'I'm not wearing that thing,' she replied. 'What would the neighbours say!'

'Who gives a toss what you look like, as long as you're warm, but suit yourself.'

'You've had a change of heart,' Winnie said. 'Since when have you not bothered about what the neighbours think?'

'Since it dropped to nearly freezing outside and my wife lent her bleedin' coat out.'

Winnie kept quiet. As they headed for the hardware store, she checked her watch surreptitiously. Even if they ran there and back, she'd never make it in time to meet Errol. Perhaps she could catch him later. He'd made it clear that he didn't want her knocking on his door again but she would need to know where to find him, so didn't have much choice. She shivered, the cold wind nipping as it blew through her cardigan. She'd need to buy herself another coat, but every spare penny was going to pay off Errol. David bloody Berry, she thought, I could ring your blinkin' neck!

Hilda looped her arm through Jan's and laughed heartily. 'Did you see the look on Flo's face when Bill said he'd pop round to have a look at the broken lock on my window?'

'Yes, I did. She didn't look happy about it.'

'Silly old cow. There's nothing going on with me and Bill, we're just mates. I reckon he fancies me, but Bill is a good bloke and would never do anything to upset Flo. I wish there were more men around like him.'

'He does seem very kind,' Jan replied, thinking Hilda liked the man a lot more than she was letting on.

'He's always been good to me. Flo's a lucky lady to have such a good husband, but she doesn't appreciate him.'

'I don't know about that, but I'm glad she was pleased with the dresses I made.'

'Yeah, she was an' all! She said your dresses sell like hot cakes and she can't get enough of them. That's a big compliment coming from Flo.'

Jan smiled, proud of herself and grateful to Hilda for helping her.

'How do you fancy a trip to the high street? There's a new haberdashery shop opened and I've heard they've got some lovely buttons.'

'Yes, I'd like that,' she answered with gusto. She had a dress style in mind and a few fancy buttons would finish it off nicely.

'And we could have a bowl of pie and mash in Maggie Brown's.'

'I've seen the place but never been in.'

'Cor, you don't know what you're missing. A lovely load of liquor with lashings of vinegar. It's the best meal – and cheap too.'

'Is it as nice as bacon?'

'Better, but don't let the green colour put you off.'

'Green! It sounds funny, but I'll try not to let it,' she answered with a smile.

'It's just parsley sauce. Come on, then, though you'll have to drag me past every pub kicking and screaming. I'm dying for a drink but I made a promise to my girl and I'm gonna try me best to keep it. Talking of Rachel, how's she getting on with that Arnold fella?'

'Wonderfully! She's walking around with a silly smile on her face and talks of nothing else.'

'Huh, good for her. But I hope he don't go breaking her heart. She makes out she's tough but that Jim left her fragile.'

Jan couldn't imagine how Rachel must have felt when she'd discovered that the man she loved had seduced her sister. She knew that if Terry was seeing another woman behind her back, it would devastate her and she wasn't sure she'd be able to cope. Hilda interrupted her thoughts as she began to tell her about jellied eels.

'I'm sure you're gonna love it,' Hilda said, sounding keen to get to the pie and mash shop. They were almost racing along the street now, but as they hurried under the railway bridge on Falcon Road, Jan froze when she saw a familiar face approaching them.

'What's wrong?' Hilda asked.

'My mother — that's my mother!'

'All right, don't panic. Just keep walking.'

She could feel Hilda tugging her arm but her legs wouldn't work. She stood, rooted to the spot, as her mother's mean eyes fixed on her.

'Don't worry, I won't let the woman hurt you,' Hilda reassured her, but still Jan couldn't move and now her mother was just feet away.

'Oh — no — no,' Jan cried as her mother fell to her knees in front of them.

She grabbed Jan's hand, staring up at her with crazed eyes. 'Child, redeem yourself. Beg our Lord for forgiveness and relinquish the devil in your heart. I implore you, turn your back on evil and come back into the fold. You are God's child. He *will* forgive your sins.'

'Let her go, you mad woman,' Hilda spat and in a bid to release her, she grabbed Jan's hand too and tried to uncurl her mother's fingers.

Her mother's face twisted as she garbled on. 'She works for the devil! Your soul will burn in eternal flames within the furnace of hell! Turn your back on her for she is Satan in disguise!'

Jan felt tears beginning to prick her eyes, but suddenly realised that they weren't tears of fear. They were tears of pity – pity for the woman kneeling on the cold, hard pavement. Nonetheless, she had to stand up to her. 'Leave me alone,' she said and pulled her hands from her mother's vice-like grip. 'Hilda is not the devil. She's my friend.'

'She is unholy and carries the Beast within her. I am your mother. You will do as I say and come home.'

'You're not her mother, you silly cow,' Hilda said harshly. 'We know you adopted her so bugger off and leave her alone.'

'LIES! LIES! LIES! You see, Jan, they feed you lies! Of course I'm your mother. You spewed from my womb and drained my life. I should have known then that the blood I lost was a sign from God. He was warning me that I had birthed the spawn of the devil!'

'You're – you're really my mother?'

'Of course I am! Do not believe these people. Just as He walks among us, so do slaves of Satan. SHE is a slave of Satan. SHE wants your soul!'

'I've heard enough of this codswallop,' Hilda said and she grabbed Jan's arm. 'Come on, we're going. Your mother or not, she's got a screw loose and is by no means a good Christian woman.'

As Jan was pulled along the street, Hilda turned to her mother and shouted, 'You oughta be ashamed of yourself. People like you give the Church a bad name.'

When they hurried the short distance to other side of the bridge, Jan glanced over her shoulder and was relieved to see her mother wasn't chasing after them. She was standing with her arms held in the air and looking upwards towards the sky. Jan couldn't catch what she was shouting, but people were staring at her, one woman giving her a wide berth as she passed. It was clear that her mother was insane, yet if what she'd said about giving birth to her was true, then both she and Winnie were in for heartbreak.

As if reading her mind, Hilda said gently, 'Take no notice of all that crap about you and her womb and blood.'

'But she sounded adamant. I've no reason not to believe her.'

'Yes, you have. You've a very good reason – Winnie.'

'I don't want to hurt Winnie, but I can't live a lie.'

'Well, it's up to you, but from what I heard, your so-called mother was spouting a load of nonsense. She lives in some sort of mad fantasy world, where she *thinks* she's your real mother. I reckon you should keep this to yourself and stay well clear of her.'

'It doesn't seem right. I think she needs help.'

'Judging by the state of her, surely someone in her church will sort her out?'

'Yes, she's definitely worse. Perhaps the pastor will notice. Oh, I do hope so, Hilda.'

'Right, then. You don't want a mother like that, you want a

decent one and you've got that in Winnie. And Winnie wants to be your mum, so why not let her?'

'I don't know,' Jan sighed. 'I suppose it would be easier to say nothing. I'm very fond of Winnie and wouldn't like to see her feelings hurt.'

'There you go, then. We'll keep this between us and everyone will be happy.'

Jan thanked Hilda for sticking up for her, but walked the rest of the way to the haberdashery in silence, battling with her conscience. If her mother was telling the truth, remaining silent would be living a lie. But was it? Winnie may or may not have given birth to her, but, in a short time, she'd been more of a mother to her. She hadn't hurt her, starved her, or locked her in her room. She'd shown her nothing but kindness and love. Yes, love. That thought sealed Jan's decision. From now on, she would consider Winnie as her real mother; she had already come to love her in return.

24

Rachel was thinking about Arnold as she walked home and she was looking forward to spending another evening with him. He'd told her he knew of a few clandestine theatre houses that were flouting the Government rules and remained open. He'd said he'd like to introduce her to the opera or the ballet but she was bluntly honest with him and said it wasn't her cup of tea. In truth though, she'd declined his offer because she didn't have anything suitable to wear. Instead, he said he'd take her to an intimate bistro he knew near Marble Arch and that the Christmas trees displayed at Selfridges were quite spectacular this year and worth a visit.

As she neared home, she spotted Hilda hanging about and instantly felt herself tense. Normally, Hilda only came round when she was drunk. As Rachel approached, she could see that she seemed sober but looked twitchy and bothered.

'Thank God you're home, I've been waiting ages for you.'

'I had a cuppa with Winnie before I left. Are you all right?' Rachel asked, pleased to see that Hilda was still keeping her promise to stay off the booze.

'Yes, darling, I'm fine. But let's get inside.'

As Rachel opened the front door, she glanced again at Hilda. She could tell something was definitely troubling her. Once inside the room, Hilda, looking pensive, flopped onto the side of the bed and then lit a cigarette. Worriedly, Rachel asked, 'Are you going to tell me what's wrong?'

Hilda took a long pull on her cigarette, blew the smoke up into the air and then whispered, 'Winnie isn't Jan's mum.'

On hearing this, Rachel slumped onto her chair, upset for Winnie. She knew the news would devastate the woman. 'How do you know?'

'Me and Jan bumped into her mother yesterday,' Hilda answered, her voice hushed.

'There's no need to whisper, no one will hear you.'

'Yeah, right, I dunno why I am. Probably cos it's a secret.'

'What do you mean? And what on earth happened when Jan saw her mum?'

'Oh, Rachel, it was horrible. Her mother is as mad as a hatter. Poor Jan was terrified at first but then she seemed to pull herself together and was all right. But I told the woman that she weren't even Jan's real mother and she emphatically denied it. Talked about blood and her womb and all sorts.'

'Blimey, this ain't good news, but are you sure she was telling the truth?'

'Yeah, there was something about the way she reacted. She was adamant that she's Jan's mother,' Hilda said, taking another pull on her cigarette before continuing. 'I managed to persuade Jan to keep it to herself. I did the right thing, didn't I? I mean, there's no point in upsetting Winnie and Jan seems happy living at the pub. What do you reckon?'

Rachel sucked in a long breath, then asked, 'You're sure Jan won't say anything to Winnie?'

'I don't think she will.'

'In that case, it's probably for the best. But I wish you hadn't told me. I don't like deceiving Winnie,' she said. She was full of regret about keeping David's secret and now she had another.

'I'm sorry, but I wasn't sure I'd given the right advice to Jan and didn't know who else to talk to.'

'Never mind. I hope Jan is all right.'

'I think she is, but you know how quiet she can be. She don't really say much. I took her for pie and mash and she seemed fine. She didn't mention it again and I think that's how she prefers it.'

'Winnie will be devastated if she finds out. Do you think I should tell Jan that I know?'

'No, I wouldn't, if I was you. You're close to Winnie and she might worry that you'd tell her.'

'Yes, good point. Christ, what a mess. But I suppose as long as you, me and Jan all keep quiet, Winnie's feelings will be spared. I'll go and make us a drink,' she offered.

'Thanks, love.'

While in the scullery, Rachel's thoughts turned. It seemed wrong to keep this from Winnie, but telling her would break her heart. With a sigh she poured two cups of tea and then carried them back to her room, inwardly praying that this was the last secret she'd have to keep from Winnie.

Hilda poured her tea into the saucer and gently blew on the hot liquid. They both sipped their tea, then Hilda broke the silence, saying, 'Cor, I needed this cuppa. I've flown round both me cleaning jobs today to get here as soon as I could. Anyway, tell me, how's Arnold?'

Rachel felt herself smiling and didn't care if she looked a fool. 'He's perfect and he's taking me up town tonight.'

'That's nice, darling,' Hilda replied with a soft, loving smile.

'In fact, now you're here, could you wave my hair for me?'

Hilda seemed happy to oblige and as Rachel's hair was manipulated into a flattering style, she thought how nice it was to be spending time together like this. In her eyes, Hilda would always remain her older sister but, right now, they seemed like any other normal mother and daughter. Rachel felt a surge of emotion. Perhaps one day she would come to love Hilda as her mother.

That evening, Winnie was on tenterhooks, dreading the thought of Errol walking through the pub door. After choosing the paint, she'd told Brian she had shopping to do, leaving him to carry it back to the pub. She'd hurried to Errol's house, breathless as she knocked on the door, but nobody was at home. After hanging around for over half an hour, shivering in the cold while she waited to see if Errol or his mother came home, she had to scurry off. She couldn't wait any longer as she had to open the pub.

An hour passed. With only a few customers in, Winnie turned to Brian, saying, 'It's quiet tonight. I'm sure I can manage by myself. You can go upstairs, if you like.'

She was disappointed when he declined.

'There's no need for both of us to be down here,' she said.

'I don't mind. There's nothing much on the wireless I want to hear.'

Typical, Winnie thought. All these years she'd moaned about him not pulling his weight and working in the pub, and now she couldn't get rid of him. Another half-hour passed, and when the door opened, her heart sank. Her greatest fear had been realised. Errol Hampton walked in.

'I'll serve him,' Brian said before Winnie could stop him.

A customer called out for another bottle of beer and, reluctantly, Winnie went to see to him. She saw Errol talking to Brian and hoped he wasn't saying anything about David's debt.

Suddenly, Brian turned his head to glare at her and his infuriated expression told her all she needed to know. 'Come here,' he screeched.

Reluctantly, she walked to his side.

'Is it true?'

'Please, Brian, not here. Let's go out the back and talk about it.'

She saw Errol smirking and wanted to slap the wicked grin off his face but Brian was screaming at her again.

'I asked you a question, woman. Is it true? Have you been paying off David's debts?'

Winnie, wide-eyed and terrified, stared at her husband's angry, contorted face. 'I – erm, I ...'

'So it is true, then,' he said. He leaned in closer to her face and warned, 'I'll deal with you later.'

She flinched as he stamped past her and she heard his heavy boots pounding up the stairs.

'Get out,' she snapped at Errol. 'You won't be getting any money from me tonight.'

'You'll regret that,' Errol warned, then gulped down the rest of his drink, slammed his glass on the counter, and left.

Winnie's eyes flitted around the pub to find her customers were all staring back at her. No one said a word. She flew out the back and upstairs to hear Brian and David shouting at each other. As she reached David's room, she was horrified to see her husband dragging David out of his bed and across the floor.

'Stop, stop! Please, Brian, stop,' she pleaded and tried to wrestle him off her son.

Brian shoved her to one side. 'I'll kill the lazy bastard,' he roared, raining blows down on David who'd curled up into the foetal position. 'How fucking dare he allow you to pay off his debts with *my* money!'

'Stop, or I'll tell everyone what you did. I swear I will!'

Her threat had the desired effect and Brian, now gasping for air, released David. 'You bitch,' he spat at her.

David had climbed to his feet and edged towards her. 'He was gonna kill me, Mum, I know he was.'

'It's all right, Son. He's going now,' she assured him, glaring at Brian though her heart was pounding.

He returned her look with venom and, with his fists still clenched by his side, spun on his heel and marched out of David's bedroom. Winnie felt she could breathe again but then heard his poisonous voice.

'What you looking at?' he shouted. 'Want some, do ya?'

She ran onto the landing to see Brian leaning ominously over Jan who was backed up against the bannisters.

'Leave her alone,' she screeched, rushing towards them.

'The fucking lot of you are taking liberties and I ain't having it.'

'Do your worst, then, Brian, but you'll regret it,' she answered defiantly, aware that David was standing beside her.

Brian lifted his arm and in that second Winnie was convinced he was going to punch Jan. Quickly, she blurted,

'David, your father stole the money to buy this pub from his dead brother's widow and her six children.'

Brian turned to look at her and his lips pulled back in a threatening snarl but Winnie wasn't finished yet.

'His brother had done well for himself and Brian was jealous of him. All your father had managed to achieve was running up debts to anyone who was stupid enough to loan him money.'

'Shut your mouth, woman!'

'No, I won't. I've kept my mouth shut for far too long. It's about time people found out what a sly and despicable man I'm married to.'

Brian stepped towards her but David was quick to jump between them. 'Don't even think about hitting my mum,' he warned.

Winnie moved David to one side, her tone harsh as she spoke to Brian. 'The only way you'll shut me up is by putting me six feet under. I suggest you collect your things and leave before there's a lynch mob out for you.'

Brian glared at her for another few moments, then, much to her relief, he stormed off into their bedroom.

Winnie turned to Jan, saying quickly, 'Get yourself downstairs and wait in the bar for me. You'll be safe there. And for Christ's sake, don't tell anyone about what's been going on up here.'

Jan, looking as white as a sheet, nodded and slipped away.

Then Winnie turned to David. 'Thank you. Now, you'd best get yourself back into bed. You're not supposed to be able to walk. Don't worry about your father. I'll make sure he goes.'

'I'm not leaving you alone with him.'

Before Winnie could protest, her bedroom door flew open and her husband came out carrying a moleskin bag. Without so much as throwing her a look, he stamped down the stairs. She heard the back door slam.

'He's gone,' she said with relief and a deep sigh.

'What if he comes back?'

'He won't. I know your father. He's too scared I'll carry out my threat to tell everyone what he did. It's eaten away at him for years, but he never did anything to put it right, leaving his brother's wife to live in poverty.'

'So, it's true, then, what you said?'

'Every word and more besides. I hated him for what he'd done but there was nothing I could do about it. I was already carrying you when I discovered the truth and, after having to give Jan up, I couldn't face losing another child. I had no money or home without your father and so, to keep you, I stuck with him.'

'What do you mean? More besides?'

She didn't want to be bombarded with questions and said, 'Not now, David, I've got to get downstairs. Go on, back to bed. We can talk about it later.'

Thankfully, David did as she asked. Smoothing her hair and dress, Winnie went downstairs and into the bar. Scanning the smoky room, she saw Jan sitting nervously at a corner table, and called out across her pub, 'Sorry about that. Is everyone all right?'

'Yeah, we are, Win, but are you?'

'Yes, Bert, all shipshape and ready for business. Who wants another drink?'

Bert came to the bar. 'I'll have another,' he said. 'It's the best entertainment in here that I've seen in yonks.'

'You cheeky beggar,' she replied warmly.

After serving him, she beckoned Jan over. The girl was clearly terrified and looked close to tears. 'He's gone. He's packed his stuff and left. That's the last we'll be seeing of him. It's just you, me and David now.'

Jan smiled feebly.

'Don't worry about David, I'll be dealing with him next,' she whispered, 'and please, don't mention to anyone that you saw him walking.'

Jan nodded.

'Thank you. Do you want to stay down here with me?'

'Erm – no, I'll go to my room.'

'All right, love. I'll give you a knock later. I'll try and close up early.'

Winnie served another three customers, quietly bringing her thoughts into order. Brian was gone. He'd been fine for a while, but as soon as he found out about David's debt, he'd reverted to form. If he had stayed, she'd be walking on eggshells again, worried something would upset him and that she'd get a backhander. She was better off without him. No more jumping to his orders. No more living on jangled nerves. He really had left. Hopefully, she'd never set eyes on him again.

25

The following morning, Jan sat in the back kitchen while Rachel made tea. She'd had a challenging few days, what with bumping into her mother and discovering the truth about her birth and then, last night, fearing Mr Berry was going to attack her. The worry of it all had taken its toll and she'd slept very little.

Rachel brought the teapot to the table and pulled out a seat. 'Tell me again what happened,' she said to Winnie.

'I'm not going over it for a third time. I've already told you. Suffice to say, Brian has gone now, so it's down to me to run this place.'

'But isn't it all in his name?'

'Yes, and maybe I should get some legal advice. I don't want him trying to sell the pub. Granted, I've never liked how he came to own it, but I've put blood, sweat and tears into the Battersea Tavern and it's my home.'

'You and this pub go hand in hand, Win. The place wouldn't be the same without you. I'm still shocked, though. I can't believe he'd swindle his own family out of money.'

'I know. I suppose his brother's wife has the same surname

as me, and maybe I should try to find them and see if they're all right, but I've no idea where she is and I wouldn't know where to start. I never met her, but she must have struggled to bring up six kids with no means of supporting them. That was thanks to my old man.'

'How did he manage to do it?' Rachel asked.

Jan listened with intrigue.

'I don't know all the ins and outs, but from what I do know, his brother was quite well off, but ever so poorly. His wife wasn't coping with caring for both him and the children. To make things easier for her, he went to stay with his mum. When Brian saw that his brother was at death's door, he drew up a will, leaving everything to himself and managed to get his brother to sign it. I don't suppose his brother had any idea what he was putting his name to. Brian even managed to pass himself off as his brother and get the will endorsed by a solicitor. Brian also wrote some fake entries in his brother's diary, stating that his wife had been having an affair, and that he was infertile so the children weren't his. He slipped the diary under his brother's bed, knowing that his mother would find it.'

'My God, that's unbelievable!' Rachel said.

'Yeah, well, a couple of weeks later, his brother passed away. When their mother found the diary, all hell broke loose. Brian had lodged a false will with a solicitor and because the rest of the family now believed his wife was a slut, they didn't contest it.'

'You'd have thought the wife would have tried.'

'Yeah, but maybe she didn't think she'd be believed. Perhaps she didn't have the money to pay for a lawyer to take up her case.'

'Poor cow.'

'Anyway, Brian got away with the lot. He sold the house and the business to pay off his debts and had enough left to buy this place.'

'Blimey, Win, that's really devious.'

'Tell me about it! I had no idea what Brian was up to. When he brought me here, I asked him how he'd afforded to buy it. I'm surprised he told me, but he did and I couldn't believe it. I told him I didn't want anything to do with it. I begged him to sell the pub and give his brother's wife the money back but he wouldn't hear of it.'

'You didn't think of leaving him?' Jan asked now.

'How? It was during the Great War, and I was five months pregnant, with no money of my own and nowhere to go. I kept trying to talk Brian into selling this place and giving the proceeds to his sister-in-law, but he became violent. He gave me a good hiding and told me never to mention it again. I should have stood me ground and walked out but I had David and I don't mind telling you that, by then, I was scared stiff of Brian.'

'Blimey, Winnie. All I can say is I'm glad he's gone.'

'So am I. I kept quiet all these years, and eventually managed to put it out of my mind, but now it's reared its head again I feel so guilty that I didn't open me mouth before.'

'You shouldn't. It wasn't your fault. And what's done is done. You can't change the past and, like you say, you've worked hard for this pub,' Rachel said.

'Thanks, love,' Winnie said. She reached across the table to pat the back of her hand.

Jan was surprised when Winnie then turned to her and said, 'I hope you don't think badly of me because of this?'

'No, of course not,' she answered emphatically, shaking her head. How could she? She was living a lie herself, deliberately deceiving Winnie, though it wasn't for financial gain.

'Good. I don't want you thinking that I'm as wicked as my husband.'

Jan would never think such a thing. She'd been at the receiving end of Mr Berry's wrath and would have robbed a nun if he'd ordered her to! If anything, she felt sorry for Winnie. It couldn't have been easy for her to have lived with this knowledge for all these years.

'Right, let's get this pub open. I'm surprised Hilda isn't here yet. She should have finished work by now.'

'Yes, me too. Did you make any arrangements with her?' Rachel asked Jan as she cleared away their teacups.

'Yes. I expected her to be here by now too. Oh well, I'm sure she'll turn up soon,' she answered, but with Hilda's words that she was dying for a drink ringing in her head, Jan worried that she'd succumbed and was now nursing a hangover.

The moment Winnie unlocked the doors, Len ambled in.

'He's gawn, then?'

'Yes and good riddance,' she answered.

'Never liked the man and never will. I've always known there weren't nothing wrong with his hearing when he used that to get out of serving in the last war. He should have been in the trenches with the rest of us. I'll say no more. My usual please.'

Winnie smiled to herself as she fetched Len's tankard and his bottle of stout. It seemed her most regular customer was a good judge of character. She hoped the rest of them would be just as loyal to her.

Terry came in next, his face screwed up in consternation. 'I can't stop, I just wanted to make sure you're all right?'

'You've heard, then?'

'Yeah, it's going through Battersea like a dose of salts. Is it true?'

'If you mean has Brian left, yes, it's true.'

'Blimey, Win, I'm sorry.'

'I'm not,' she answered firmly. 'How did you hear about it?'

'You know what the gossip is like. Mrs Jacobson's old man was in here last night and told her there was a bit of a palaver going on upstairs and that Mr Berry had walked out in a right two and eight. She told the milkman who said he'd seen Mr Berry in the Fishmongers Arms and he was ranting about how he was never coming back to Battersea again cos the place stinks.'

'Well, Battersea does stink, so you can tell the gossips it's all true. But if anyone sees him in the area, you will let me know, won't you, love?'

'Yeah, Win, no problem.'

'Do you want to see Jan while you're here?'

'I can't, I've got to get back before they notice I'm gone. But I'll be in later to see her.'

'Okey-dokey, see you tonight.'

Rachel came up from the cellar carrying a large bottle of brandy. 'Was that Terry I just saw leaving?' she asked.

'Yes. He popped in quickly to make sure I was all right.'

'Aw, bless him, he's a good egg. Word is out already, then.'

'I guessed it would be. Oh well, it'll give folk something to talk about other than this bleedin' war.'

'Still no sign of Hilda, then?'

'No, love, not yet. Try not to worry, I'm sure there's a perfectly reasonable explanation for her whereabouts.'

'Yes, probably, but I hope she hasn't started drinking again.'

Winnie gave Rachel's hand a gentle squeeze and offered her a warm smile but words failed her. In truth, she was beginning to think that Hilda had fallen off the wagon. If she had, it was sure to disappoint Rachel.

'I've had this awful feeling for weeks now, you know, like something bad is going to happen. I hope it's nothing to do with Hilda,' Rachel said, sounding heavy-hearted.

'It's more likely that you're expecting Arnold to let you down.'

'No, it's not that. It started before I met him.'

'Maybe it's the war, love. I know you say you ain't worried, but you must be, deep down.'

'Maybe,' Rachel answered without conviction.

'By the way, I've guessed you've worked it out, but you won't say anything about my David acting out his bad back, will you? The doctor has signed him off and that's how I want to keep it.'

'It's nothing to do with me.'

'Thanks, love. I feel awful about encouraging him to lie about it, but I couldn't cope with him being signed up. I've had more than my fair share of sleepless nights and I'll probably have more to come until I get this pub in my name. As soon as Christmas is over with, I'll go and see Miss Vickers. She works in a solicitor's office up Lavender Hill, so hopefully she'll be able to tell me what I should do.'

'Good idea. But are you sure you shouldn't go to see her sooner rather than later?'

'I'm sure. I know Brian. He'll be licking his wounds

somewhere and I can't see him putting this place up for sale yet. He's too astute. With the war on and the threat of bombs dropping, I think the pub will have gone down a lot in value. He's wily enough to wait until the war is over and prices go up again,' Winnie told her. She just hoped she was right. Brian had always been a miser and she knew he had money stashed away, enough to keep him going for some time, long enough for her to get the necessary paperwork in order. And though money was important to him, so was his reputation and she didn't believe he'd have the audacity to show his face for a good while yet.

Later that evening, Rachel was enjoying the light and cheery atmosphere in the pub. With Winnie's husband gone, it felt like a heavy weight had been lifted. Even Jan had come downstairs and was partaking in a small sherry with them.

'To us,' Winnie toasted, and they clinked their glasses. 'Who needs a man about the place, eh?'

'What's all this?' Terry asked when he walked in and joined them.

'Winnie was just saying that we women don't need men,' Rachel answered.

'That's not what I was saying at all, Terry. Take no notice of Rachel.'

He sidled up beside Jan who blushed and looked embarrassed when he lightly kissed her cheek. 'I don't know about women not needing men, but you'll do all right without Mr Berry,' he said to Winnie as Rachel poured his drink.

'Right an' all. But poor Rachel has given up her nights off for now. It won't be forever, though. My David will be a help, once he's back on his feet.'

Rachel and Jan exchanged a quick, knowing glance and Rachel swiftly changed the subject, 'Arnold is coming in later. He said he's looking forward to a night in here.'

'Good. I hope he enjoys himself. He should do, my customers are the salt of the earth,' Winnie said. 'Mind you, it's a bit different from those fancy places he takes you to.'

'Yes, you're right there, Win, but I can't relax in them expensive restaurants. Arnold fits in well cos he's posh, but I swear he laughs harder when he comes here.'

'Perhaps I can persuade Pete to bang us out a few tunes on the piano later. Show your Arnold a proper Battersea Tavern night,' Winnie said.

'I don't know if he's ready for that yet,' Rachel guffawed.

The pub began to fill with customers, many asking after Mr Berry. Winnie and Rachel confirmed that he'd left, but neither explained why. Some made disparaging comments about the man, others just lifted an eyebrow. Only a couple appeared to be genuinely sorry to see him gone.

In between serving drinks, Winnie whispered to Rachel, 'Huh, and Brian thought he was so popular. Seems not.'

'People ain't stupid,' she replied.

Shortly afterwards, Rachel looked up as the door opened and was delighted to see Arnold smiling at her. However, a tall, slender and attractive woman followed in behind him. As she approached the bar with Arnold, she glanced around with a look on her face as if she could smell something foul under her nose. Rachel thought she looked like a right stuck-up cow and wondered who she was.

Her question was answered when Arnold came to stand beside Terry and Jan at the bar and said, 'Good evening, my dear. This is my delightful, older sister, Felicity, who unexpectedly called on me this evening, no doubt checking up on me.'

'Pleased to meet you,' Felicity said, 'and I'm only a smidgen older than my utterly outrageous brother. I've heard much about you, Rachel. I trust you're keeping Arnold in order?'

Rachel looked at Felicity, unsure of how to answer or what to say. She couldn't work out if Felicity was talking in jest or if it was a serious question. Thankfully, Arnold interrupted.

'I do not require *keeping in order*,' he said, adding, 'and if I did, Rachel would do an excellent job of it.'

Felicity looked at her dubiously and Rachel decided that she didn't like the woman. There was none of the warmth or good humour that Arnold exuded. In fact, the only similarity between them that Rachel could see was their brown hair.

'What would you like to drink?' Rachel asked with a false, sweet smile.

'Nothing, thank you, though I'm sure Arnold will partake in an alcoholic beverage. He rarely declines an invitation to be frivolous.'

'Indeed,' Arnold said, smiling. 'A large brandy, please. I need one to calm my nerves, you understand. You see, dearest Felicity has the unique skill of being capable of belittling me in one sentence. She's quite adept at it and I'm always braced and ready for it when in her charming company. Hence, the requirement for a very large brandy, thank you.'

Again, Rachel was left at a loss for words. She sensed there was some obvious friction between the siblings and though Arnold spoke as if he was joking, she felt there was truth in his words and feared Felicity would say something scathing. The brandy was kept at the other end of the bar and as she went to get Arnold his drink, she was pleased to be away from Felicity's scrutiny.

'Who's she?' Winnie whispered as Rachel poured the drink.

'His sister, Felicity. She seems like a right pretentious cow.'

'Do you want me to help?'

'No, it's fine, thanks, Win. It's fairly busy tonight, so I won't have to hang around her too much.'

'All right, love; just give me the nod if you change your mind.'

Rachel carried the drink back but was then beckoned to the end of the bar again by another customer. She served three half-pints, then Jan caught her eye and gestured for Rachel to follow her. Jan walked over to the piano, out of anyone's earshot, and said quietly, 'I think you should know that I heard Arnold and his sister talking and it wasn't very nice.'

'What, about me?'

'Yes, sorry.'

'What were they saying?' Rachel asked, her stomach now in knots.

'That Felicity said you're nothing but a common barmaid and she couldn't see the attraction. Arnold told her that you're quite exquisite. Felicity told him that he's only seeing you to get back at someone called Josephine. She said that he must be aware that taking a servant girl to Maestro's and – some other place, but I can't remember the name – would cause talk and it would get back to Josephine.'

'Josephine – who's Josephine?'

'I don't know, but Arnold told her she was being ridiculous and that he didn't care what Josephine or anyone else made of it.'

Rachel thought for a moment and assumed Josephine must be an ex-girlfriend and was pleased that Arnold had said he didn't care. 'At least he isn't seeing this Josephine now.'

'Sorry, Rachel, I hate to tell you this, but that's not all and you have a right to know. Felicity told him that as he had sent Josephine flowers, and several letters begging her to come back, he must still care about her.'

Rachel felt the air had been punched out of her and tears stung her eyes. Arnold had been so genuine; she couldn't believe she'd been used to make his old flame jealous. 'Did he deny it?' she asked hopefully.

'Sort of. He told Felicity that he hadn't written to Josephine since he'd met you and then told her to shut up about it.'

'That's not so bad, then.'

'The thing is, Felicity didn't shut up. She said he was a liar; that he *had* written to Josephine, and then she went on about how their mother would have been outraged at him courting a common tart and that if their father was still alive he'd have cut him out of his will. Arnold laughed and said it was a good job they were both dead and he didn't see why she was making such a fuss. He said he would continue to take you to the theatre or to decent restaurants, but he had no intention of introducing you to his work colleagues or bringing you to any of their society events.'

Rachel glanced over to the bar, but saw that Felicity and Arnold had gone to sit at a table by the window. He looked tense and Felicity haughty. As Rachel brushed away a tear that had rolled down her cheek, Jan gave her arm a gentle squeeze, asking her, 'What are you going to do?'

She wasn't sure, but she was tempted to march over and pour Arnold's drink over his head. She'd already felt inferior and not good enough to mix in Arnold's circle and now she knew he felt the same too. Yet in all fairness, she had no desire to attend his society events or meet the people he worked with and she loved it that when they went out it was just the two of them. Before she could think further, the door flew open and Hilda lurched in.

'Oh, no,' Jan exclaimed.

'This is all I need,' Rachel said, shaking her head in disgust at the drunken state of her so-called mother.

Hilda staggered towards the bar. 'Where's my girl?' she slurred, her head wobbling as she looked around the pub.

Quickly, Rachel went to her, hoping to get her out before she caused any more of a scene.

'Ah, there you are,' Hilda said, and patted Rachel's cheek.

The smell of her breath made Rachel turn her face. 'You've been drinking,' she hissed accusingly.

'Just a couple.'

'You've had more than just a couple. Oh, Hilda, you promised me you wouldn't do this again.'

'What? I ain't done nothing.'

'If you say so, but I don't want you coming to see me in this state.'

'Don't flatter yourself. What makes you think I'm here to see you? Bloody typical, that is. You don't 'alf rate yourself.'

Rachel could see exactly where this was going and knew that Hilda would find anything she said, inflammatory or not, cause for an argument.

'I wanna drink,' Hilda slurred and moved closer to the bar.

Rachel glanced at Winnie and saw that she was standing with her hands on her hips, glaring furiously at Hilda. Then, to her horror, she saw that Arnold had now walked up to the bar too and that Hilda was making a beeline for him.

'Hello,' Hilda said, steadying herself on the bar.

Arnold looked uncomfortable but politely smiled at her before asking Winnie for another brandy.

'You're Rachel's bloke, Arnold, ain't ya? I'm her mother, you know. Are you gonna buy me a drink an' all? I know you can afford it. Rachel reckons you're loaded.'

Arnold looked over his shoulder to Rachel who was cringing with embarrassment. She quickly moved to stand between them, saying quietly, 'I'm sorry about her behaviour.'

But Hilda heard and screeched, 'How dare you apologise for me! Ashamed of me, are you? Well, let me tell you something, Missy —it's me who oughta be ashamed of you!'

'That's enough,' Winnie barked.

The pub had fallen quiet and Rachel knew that having an audience would spur Hilda on.

'What's the matter, Winnie? Ain't I permitted to speak as I find? I thought this country was all about free speech. Ain't that why we're fighting the Jerries off?'

'You won't be getting a drink in here, Hilda, so you might as well go home.'

'Oh, that's choice, that is! Little Lord bleedin' Fauntleroy here can have a drink but you'd sling out the mother of your own barmaid? Preferential treatment, that's what it is. Just cos he's got a few bob. Well, *Arnold*, just so you know, my girl don't love you. She's only ever had eyes for one man and she couldn't keep hold of him. He slept with my sister the night before he was gonna marry Rachel. No woman in her right mind would have gone through with the wedding after that, but my Rachel was going to. See, that's how much she loved him. But you −' Hilda eyed him disdainfully up and down − 'she's only after your money.'

'I said, ENOUGH,' Winnie barked again. 'Just get out, Hilda. You're a nasty piece of work and no one wants you here.'

Rachel hung her head in shame, filled with despair at what Arnold and his snooty sister must be thinking. She couldn't bring herself even to look at him and knew that if she retaliated against Hilda, it would only make matters worse.

Hilda began to laugh, a low cackle at first. Then her laughter turned into a roar and she doubled over, holding her sides as she chuckled. 'It's bloody ironic, ain't it?' she said loudly. 'She don't want me here cos she's worried I'll show her up in front of her fancy man and you don't want me here cos you're jealous of me. Go on, Win, you can admit it. You're jealous of Jan spending more time with me than she does with you.'

'No, Hilda, you're talking nonsense. I'm happy that you're helping out my Jan. Now, I won't ask you again, please leave or I'll call the police.'

'And what crime are you gonna report? Oh, forget it, I'm going, but you can climb down from your ivory tower, the lot of you, especially you, Winnie Berry. I'll tell you something − Jan ain't *your* Jan. She ain't your daughter and she knows it. Go on, ask her!' Hilda shrieked.

Rachel looked at Winnie and saw that the colour had drained from her face and she was shaking visibly. Then she looked at Jan, who was huddled into Terry, her face buried in his chest. The pub was so quiet; the only noise that could be heard was the sound of Jan's soft crying.

Hilda broke the silence. 'See ya,' she called merrily as she turned to leave. 'Oh, and, Rachel, good luck with bagging yourself a rich fella. I hope his pockets are as deep as you think they are.'

The door closed behind her and Rachel dashed behind the bar. She placed her arm around Winnie's waist and urged her towards the back kitchen. 'Take no notice of her. You know what she's like when she's drunk.'

'She said Jan isn't my daughter – is it true?' Winnie asked and looked up at her with watery eyes.

Rachel couldn't lie and she nodded slowly. 'Yes, I'm afraid so.'

She heard a sob catch in Winnie's throat. 'Oh no, no, no,' she cried.

The sound of Winnie's cries broke Rachel's heart. 'Go and sit down. I'll close the pub,' she said, tenderly pushing her towards the back kitchen.

When she turned back to the bar, Felicity was standing beside Arnold. She looked down her nose at Rachel then said to her brother, 'Get me out of this horrid place. I warned you about associating with the working classes. This is exactly the sort of queer behaviour to expect. These people have no decorum.'

Arnold's eyes were on Rachel. 'Good evening,' he said to her solemnly, doffing his hat.

'Wait,' she called. 'Will I see you again?'

Arnold, now holding the door open for his sister, looked towards her and answered curtly, 'No, my dear, I doubt it very much.'

Rachel gasped and then Arnold was gone.

This was it. This was that bad feeling she'd had for weeks. But there was no time to think of herself now. Poor Winnie was in the back kitchen with her heart shattered. 'The show's over,' she yelled across the pub. 'Drink up, we're closed.'

Her announcement was followed by a few moans and groans from customers at having their evening cut short, but they finished their drinks and left. Only Terry remained and he was still holding Jan close to him.

'I'm sorry I didn't say something to Hilda,' he said, 'but Jan was so upset, I didn't want to start shouting me mouth off and upset Jan any further.'

'It's all right, thanks, Terry. There's nothing you could have said or done that would have made the outcome any different.'

'Is Winnie all right?'

'I'm not sure. I'd best go and see.'

'I'm fine, love,' Winnie said.

Rachel spun round to see the woman wiping her nose on a hankie as she waddled towards them. She stopped to take four glasses which she filled with brandy. 'I think we could all do with a stiff drink,' she said and handed the full glasses around. 'Cheers.'

Rachel sipped hers and looked over the rim of the glass at Jan. Her eyes were puffy and red and it was clear she didn't know what to say. Thankfully, Winnie took control of the situation, saying, 'Let's not dwell on what Hilda said. She's got a vicious tongue and tomorrow, when she's sober, she won't remember anything.'

Rachel saw Jan swallow hard and Terry held her a little tighter.

'We'll just carry on as normal. All right?' Winnie asked, looking at Jan.

'I'd like that.'

Rachel was pleased the tense situation between Winnie and Jan had diffused and Winnie seemed content to pretend that nothing had changed. But Hilda's vile outburst had done more than just damage the fledging relationship between the two women. Didn't they realise that Arnold had walked out on her? She suspected that Hilda's drunken outburst was one of the main reasons he'd decided to leave.

Anger coursed through her veins. The one good thing that had happened to her in years had been ruined by her sister, or mother, though she'd never accept Hilda as her mother – and wouldn't do so now that she'd broken her promise to stop drinking.

Rachel grabbed the brandy and poured herself another large drink. 'Anyone else?' she asked, holding the bottle aloft.

Jan shook her head and Terry showed her he still had a full glass.

'Erm, are you all right?' Winnie asked, frowning as Rachel filled her glass.

'No, not really,' Rachel answered and then promptly threw the drink down her neck.

'Rachel, that's not like you!'

She poured herself another and drank half of it. 'No, it's not. Arnold never wants to see me again, thanks to my moth— my sister. I can't bring myself to *ever* call her my mother. What sort of mother would set out to destroy her daughter's happiness?'

'Oh, love, she doesn't mean to. It's the drink that's to blame.'

'No, Win, it's not. It's her! She chooses to drink even though she knows what it does to her and how much it upsets me. Well, I'd like to know what's so bloody wonderful about being drunk. If you can't beat 'em, join 'em,' she said sourly before knocking back the rest of the glass.

Winnie spoke as Rachel poured another. 'You won't find your answers in that bottle, love.'

'Maybe not but at least it'll blot out the pain that that woman causes.'

Three more glasses later and against Winnie's advice, Rachel became aware of the room swimming. 'I shfink I's drunk,' she slurred.

'Yes, young lady, you most certainly are.'

'Who caresh about Arnold? I don't. Hilda done me a favour. He used me – used me to make his ex jealoush. Huh, I know, let'sh use the dumb blonde barmaid. She's so stupid, she won't know any better and she'll be grateful for the attention from someone like me – rich, posh, fabulous me – that's Arnold. And that's what he thought. Well, up Arnold Sanders! I hate him,' Rachel drunkenly ranted.

'Come on, love, you don't mean that.'

'I do, Win. He's 'orrible. He made me look stupid,' she answered, beginning to cry.

'Oh no, time I was off. I'll walk Rachel home, make sure she gets back OK,' Terry offered.

'One more for the road,' Rachel said, spilling the drink as she topped up her glass.

'I think you've had more than enough,' Winnie quipped, taking the almost empty bottle from her.

'If I wash my sishster, I'd tell you to bugger orf,' she replied, snatching the bottle back from Winnie. She staggered across the pub, tripped over a chair, then sat on the piano stool, swigging from the bottle of brandy.

'I'll put her to bed upstairs, Terry,' Winnie said quietly.

'She's going to have a stinker of a headache in the morning.'

'I feel sorry for her but copying what Hilda does isn't going to help. Good luck getting any sleep tonight. The amount of booze she's had, she'll be snoring like a navvy.'

'She can have my bed, Winnie, I'll sleep in with you,' Jan offered.

Rachel felt sick. She looked down at the floorboards. They came in and out of focus. 'I can hear you talking about me,' she said. 'I'm nuffink like my sishster.'

She drained the rest of the bottle and dropped it. It clunked to the floor and rolled towards the bar. That was the last thing Rachel remembered.

David heard his mother coming up the stairs and was sure he could hear Rachel groaning. He opened his bedroom door and peeked out. To his surprise, he saw his mother and Jan on each side of Rachel, almost dragging her up the stairs.

'What's going on?' he asked.

'She fell out with her chap and now she's drunk. Get back to bed, there's nothing you can do here and you're not supposed to be walking.'

'Jan knows I can walk,' he said, throwing her a hateful look.

'All right, get the door for us,' his mother said, indicating Jan's bedroom.

David opened it and stood back, bemused at the sight of Rachel being lowered onto Jan's bed in a rather undignified manner. 'It looks like she needs some strong black coffee.'

'I'll put a glass of water beside her in case she needs it in the night, but I think it's best to leave her to sleep it off. Jan will kip in my room with me. And it's too late for a cuppa for me. I'd be up half the night on the loo.'

'All right, good night,' David said before he returned to his bedroom. He lay in the dark listening to the sounds: his mother putting a glass of water beside Rachel, then she and Jan going to his mother's bedroom. The door closed and then all was quiet. His mind was tormented with images of Rachel in bed just feet away from his own. His groin stirred at the thought of slipping into the bed beside her and caressing her shapely body. He sat up and punched his pillow a couple of times in frustration, then lay back down. But he couldn't sleep. He couldn't relax and it was torturous knowing that she was so close by. Hadn't his mother said that Rachel had fallen out with her chap? Perhaps she'd need comforting?

An hour or so had passed and he was still wide awake, staring blankly at the ceiling. By now he'd convinced himself that his mother and Jan were in deep slumber and that Rachel, under the influence of drink, would be more welcoming of his advances. In fact, with her guard down, he hoped she'd finally admit that she fancied him as much as he did her. He threw the covers off and quietly crept next door. He opened the door, but couldn't see much in the darkness but he could hear Rachel gently snoring. He sat on the edge of her bed and gave her a soft shake.

'Rachel – Rachel, are you awake?' he whispered.

She moaned but her eyes remained closed.

He leaned down to her, his face just inches from hers. 'Rachel – wake up,' he said quietly, again gently shaking her.

'Urgh …' she groaned, 'I don't feel well.'

'Here.' David held the glass of water to her lips. 'Sip this, it'll help.'

Rachel pushed herself up and looked at him with bleary eyes. 'Where am I?' she asked.

'In Jan's bed. It's all right, you just had too much to drink.'

'Oh, blimey. What are you doing here?'

'My room is next door. I heard you making a noise. You sounded upset. I just wanted to make sure you're all right,' he lied.

'Upset? Am I?'

'I don't know, but drink the water.'

Rachel gulped down a few mouthfuls before handing the glass back to David. 'The room is going round and round,' she said and laid her head back on the pillow. 'I remember now. Hilda showed me up and Arnold left me. God, I hate her.'

As she closed her eyes again, he stroked her hair from her face. 'Don't worry about them, I'm here for you.'

'Thanks,' she mumbled and seemed to drift off to sleep again.

'Hey, Rachel, wake up.'

'Eh? What?' she said and slowly blinked.

'I'll stay with you to make sure you're all right. Would you like that?'

'Mmm,' she sighed.

He moved her over carefully and slid in beside her. 'I'm here, Rachel, there's no need to be upset.'

When she didn't protest, he roamed his hand over her clothed body and slipped it under her top then began to gently rub her breast. 'Do you like that?' he said huskily into her ear.

She didn't respond so he shook her again.

'Urgh – what?' she whined.

David pushed his body against hers and caressed her breast again. 'Do you like it, Rachel?' he repeated.

'Mmm,' she moaned in pleasure.

His hand then crept down and into her knickers. 'Is that nice?' he asked, fully aroused now.

Rachel made a grumbling sound which he took to be her excitement. He pulled down her underwear and climbed on top of her, easily parting her legs and entering her limp body. 'Is this nice?' he asked as he moved inside her.

She made a few faint noises which spurred him on and his pleasure mounted. He drove into her and then his back arched, a groan escaped his lips, and he was finished.

As he rolled off and lay beside her, Rachel didn't move. She remained on her back with her legs open.

'I'd better go back to my own bed before my mother catches me in here with you,' he whispered with a chuckle and he kissed her cheek. 'We'll keep this our secret.'

Rachel said nothing and he thought she'd fallen back to sleep again. 'Sleep tight,' he said. Satisfied, he returned to his own bed.

26

When Winnie woke up the next morning, she'd forgotten that Brian had left and was surprised to find Jan in her husband's bed. But then the events of the previous day came flooding back and she remembered that Rachel was in Jan's room. She recalled what Hilda had said: Jan wasn't her daughter and the realisation made her chest ache. As she gazed across at the girl, she wished with all her heart that Jan was the daughter she'd birthed. But Rachel had confirmed it; the facts couldn't be changed, though they could be forgotten.

'Good morning, Winnie,' Jan said, rubbing her eyes and smiling.

Winnie sat up and thought how nice it was to wake up to a smile with a pleasant greeting.

'Would you like a cuppa? I could bring it to you in here?' Jan asked.

'Yes, thanks, love, but I'll get up,' she answered, thinking she couldn't remember the last time anyone had brought her a cup of tea in bed. It was so much nicer to wake up to Jan rather than her grumbling husband.

In the kitchen, Jan filled the kettle and Winnie sliced some bread. 'I'll make some toast for Rachel. If she can keep it down, it'll settle her stomach.'

'How do you know she's poorly?' Jan asked.

'Oh, trust me, she will be.'

Winnie slathered thick butter onto the toasted bread and put it on a tray with a cup of tea. Though the atmosphere in the kitchen felt light, she knew there were many unspoken words between them and said delicately, 'Listen, love, all that business with Hilda yesterday about me not being your mum – are you happy just to forget about it and carry on as normal?'

Jan turned as white as a sheet and looked at her wide-eyed. 'I'm so sorry I didn't say anything sooner. I should have told you and I feel terrible that you found out through Hilda like that.'

'It doesn't matter, love. If it had been the other way round, I'm not sure I would have told you either. Look, I'm not suggesting that we live a lie, but kids get adopted all the time. All right, I realise you're a grown woman, but I could still adopt you – unofficially, I mean. We wouldn't have paperwork but my point is, I'd really like you to be my daughter.'

The colour came back into Jan's cheeks and her eyes welled. 'Thank you, Winnie. I'd love you to be my mother. Official or not, I'd be honoured to be your daughter.'

'Good, I'm glad that's sorted and there's no need for any soppiness. Now, I'd better get this toast to Rachel before it goes cold,' Winnie said, her eyes blurred with tears of happiness as she bustled out of the kitchen. Jan had agreed with her. Nothing was going to change and though Jan wasn't Alma, she would come to love her as her own. She'd come to realise that she'd probably never find Alma but Jan would fill the huge void in her heart.

Winnie opened the bedroom door to see Rachel was still asleep. As she carried the tray in, she thought it was odd that the girl's knickers were on the floor. They hadn't removed her underwear when they'd put her to bed. Rachel must have taken them off during the night. She placed the tray on the chest of drawers and gave Rachel a little shove. 'Oi, Miss Tipsy-tart, time to get up,' she said and pulled open the curtains.

Rachel began to stir and eventually opened her eyes. 'Eh? What?' she said, squinting against the morning light.

'Come on, it's nearly nine. Time to get out of bed.'

'What happened?' Rachel croaked.

'You drank yourself to oblivion, that's what happened. There's a cup of tea and some toast here. I've got aspirin, if you need it?'

'Thanks, Win, I think I might. Gawd, I feel rough.'

'I should think you do, young lady, but you won't be getting any sympathy from me cos it was self-inflicted. Let this be a lesson to you, my girl.'

Rachel nodded and smiled sheepishly at her. 'I'm never drinking again, not ever.'

'Good. Right, have your breakfast and sort yourself out. I'll see you downstairs.'

Winnie went back to the kitchen where Jan had made them a bacon sandwich. 'Thanks, love, this is a special treat. I reckon we'll get along just fine without Brian around,' she said, smacking her lips together. She pulled out a seat and sat at the table. As she bit into the sandwich, she thought how nice it was not to have to worry about her husband waking up and making his demands. Finally, Winnie could relax and enjoy having her daughter home. She didn't have to fear David being called up and now, without Brian to answer to, she could clear the debt with Errol. Perfect.

Rachel still felt ill and she drifted in and out of sleep. She was pretty sure that Winnie and Jan had put her to bed but something didn't feel right. Finally, she got up, got dressed and found a brush to tidy her hair. She sneaked past David's room but, to her dismay, the door opened and she saw him standing there with a smug grin on his face.

'Good morning. Did you sleep all right?' he asked.

Unable to bring herself to speak to him, she walked towards the kitchen but heard him sniggering behind her. Vague memories surfaced. She couldn't remember much about last night but she had dim recollections of him being in her room. To add to her suspicions, she'd found her underwear on the bedroom floor. She couldn't believe that Winnie or Jan had removed her knickers. She pushed the thoughts from her head and told herself she was being silly. It was probably just the hangover and the guilt she felt for behaving so badly. It was making her paranoid!

The kitchen was empty and when she looked at the clock on the wall, she knew Winnie would have gone downstairs to sort out the bar and open up. She poured herself a cup of tea from the pot and despite it being lukewarm, she gulped it down.

'You've been dead to the world. Jan is helping my mum downstairs.'

His voice made her jump and she spun round to see that David was walking towards her.

'I suspect you've got a bit of a headache?'

'Yes, pounding.'

'Go back to bed, my mum will understand.'

'No, David, I feel bad enough as it is. We're not all shirkers, unlike some I could mention.'

She saw a look of hurt in David's eyes but she didn't care. It was no more than he deserved.

'I'm only doing what my mum wants me to do.'

'Yeah, you keep telling yourself that,' she said and stamped past him, rushing downstairs to the pub.

'Ah, you're alive, then,' Winnie said.

'Sorry, Win, and thanks for putting me to bed.'

'You didn't leave us much choice, the bleedin' state of you. And you should thank Jan for giving up her bed. Have you had a cup of tea and something to eat?'

'I can't face food.'

'That doesn't surprise me, but do you feel up to doing some work?'

'Yes,' she answered, though she felt sick and tired.

'Right, then. Jan's in the cellar so go and give her a hand to bring up the crates.'

'Righto,' Rachel said, feigning enthusiasm.

Jan trudged up the narrow stairs, a crate in her hands.

'Let me take that,' Rachel said, relieving her of the weight.

'Thank you. I hadn't realised how heavy these are.'

'You get used to it. That's why I've got muscles like a bloke,' Rachel said, trying to keep her voice light-hearted.

'How are you feeling?' Jan asked.

'Fine. Why?' she answered defensively. Did Jan know something about what had happened last night?

'Winnie thought you'd be feeling poorly and would have a terrible hangover.'

'Oh, sorry, yes. I don't feel too clever but I'll survive. I hope you don't mind but I used your hairbrush and had a dab of your scent.'

'You're more than welcome to anything of mine.'

'Thank you. I don't suppose Hilda has been in with her tail between her legs?'

'No, not yet, but Winnie thinks it'll only be a matter of time.'

Rachel heaved the crate onto the bar. 'And Winnie's right. This has become a familiar pattern with Hilda. She'll walk in like nothing has happened, but I'm not letting her off the hook this time, and neither should you,' she said as she began removing the bottles and placing them on the shelf underneath.

'Let me guess, you're talking about Hilda?' Winnie asked.

'Yes. I was saying to Jan that we shouldn't let Hilda get away with it. She's ruined my chances with Arnold and shouldn't have blurted out what she did about you two.'

'Well, she did, but we've sorted things between us and Jan is now my unofficial adopted daughter.'

'Aw, that's nice.'

'As for you and Arnold, perhaps you could go and see him. Tell him that Hilda was spouting drunken rubbish and that you're not just after his money. You could say that you'd like him whether he was rich or not.'

'No,' Rachel answered, shaking her head emphatically. Even if Arnold walked into the pub now and declared his undying love for her, she could never be with him. It was clear that he'd never look at her as an equal.

'It's up to you, love, but it would be a shame to allow Hilda to spoil a good thing. As unlikely as it seems, you and Arnold got on ever so well and it was obvious for all to see that he thinks the world of you.'

'Maybe, but we're from different worlds. He'd never admit it, but he's ashamed of my class. And to be honest, I never felt good enough for him. I won't forgive Hilda but she's done me a favour.'

'I think that's nonsense but I can understand how you feel. And as for me and Jan, well, thankfully, there's no harm done. But like you, I'm not sure that I could bring myself to be nice to Hilda ever again. It's different for you, though; she's your mum.'

'I wish she wasn't! And if she really wanted to be my mum, she would have stuck to her promise and stayed off the booze.'

Winnie looked at her with such sympathy that Rachel could feel tears pricking her eyes. Winnie must have noticed because she was quick to say, 'Go and put the kettle on. I think we could all do with a cuppa before I open up.'

Rachel tapped her foot as she waited for the water on the stove to boil. Arnold filled her thoughts but she kept getting a niggling feeling that something else was amiss. Her knickers on the floor and a sense of David being in the room last night. It didn't add up. But she quickly reminded herself that for all of David's faults, she couldn't believe he'd take advantage of her, especially with his mother so close by.

Jan burst in. 'Someone was banging on the door, and when Winnie opened it, Hilda barged in,' she warned urgently, looking anxious.

'Oh, did she indeed,' Rachel said. She turned off the gas

and marched through to the pub and there, as bold as brass, Hilda stood, smiling at her.

'If you're here to apologise and expect my forgiveness, you can think again. I've had it with you, and if I never see you again, it'll be too soon.'

'Please, Rachel, I know I messed up but I promise it won't happen again.'

'Yes it will. It always does. I bet you ain't got a clue what you said last night, have you?'

Hilda lowered her eyes and shook her head.

'No, I thought as much. Well, you ruined any chance me and Arnold might have had and you nearly broke Winnie's heart.'

'Christ, I'm so sorry.'

'I'm sure you are, but it won't stop you doing it again. I want to love you, I really do, but you make it impossible. We're done. I can't do this anymore.'

She didn't wait to hear Hilda begging for her to change her mind. She dashed back to the kitchen where she held on to the sink to steady herself. Bile rose in her throat and she took several deep breaths in an attempt to stop herself from throwing up.

Minutes later, Jan followed her in and stood uneasily in the corner. 'Are you all right?'

'Yeah. That's that done,' Rachel said with finality.

'Are you sure you can't find it in your heart to try again? Maybe once you've calmed down, you'll feel differently?'

'No. Never. I know she's been good to you and you've only seen her drunk a couple of times, but I've had this my whole life. And if you get sucked in by her, she'll do the same to you, over and over until you snap. You're best off without Hilda Duff in your life. She's poison.'

'I realise she made a terrible mistake but she really regrets it.'

'Again,' Rachel replied cynically. 'I've told you what I think, but if you wish to remain friends with her, that's up to you. It won't make no difference to our friendship, but I don't want anything more to do with her. Is she still here?'

'Yes. Winnie is giving her a piece of her mind. Even Len arrived and chipped in, telling her it was about time she got her act together.'

'It'll make no odds. You can all talk to her until you're blue in the face but Hilda won't change. If being my mother isn't enough to keep her sober, what is?'

Jan didn't answer and Rachel could see she felt awkward.

'Look, I'm fine. Go with Hilda and make your dresses. Listen to her apologies and forgive her. You know that's what you're going to do. But please, don't ever mention her name in front of me. From now on, she's dead to me.'

Alone again, Rachel couldn't hold back any longer and she spewed into the sink. She turned on the tap and saw her tears fall into the running water. She despised the drunken Hilda but hadn't she been just as vile last night? She'd been so intoxicated that she couldn't remember anything. She wasn't even sure if David had been in bed with her! Oh, she was her mother's daughter all right, and had proven it, she thought in despair.

David lay on his bed thinking about Rachel. He'd been surprised at her offhand reaction to him this morning, but he put it down to her feeling rough. He hoped she didn't regret sleeping with him last night. Granted, she'd been drunk but she hadn't said no. And wasn't it true that people talk the truth when they're drunk?

'Yeah, she likes me really,' he said, placing his hands behind his head. She was just stubborn and wouldn't bloody admit it.

He closed his eyes and smiled, feeling aroused as he recalled how smooth her skin had felt and the way her nipples had responded to his touch. Now he just had to convince her that he could be a good man.

Throwing his legs over the bed, he wished he could go downstairs to see her. Perhaps he could get a message to her? Maybe get his mum to ask Rachel to come upstairs? Then he had second thoughts. It wasn't a good idea to involve his mother. She'd ask too many questions and wouldn't approve of what he'd done with Rachel last night. Perhaps he could write her a note? Slip it into her coat pocket? She always left it over the post at the bottom of the stairs. He could sneak it in without being seen.

Taking a pad from his drawer, David sat with his pen poised as he tried to think of the words. He had to get this right and didn't want to fluff it. After all, he'd been hankering after Rachel for years and now, finally, she'd shown him that he stood a chance. At last, she was going to be his girl.

He heard a light tap on his door and recognised it was his mother. Shoving the pad and pen under his pillow, he called, 'Come in.'

'Morning, Son. You all right?'

'Yep, couldn't be better.'

'Good, because I want a word with you.'

He could tell by her grave voice that it was something serious and he hoped she hadn't heard him with Rachel last night.

'It's about your sister.'

David sighed and rolled his eyes. '*Half*-sister,' he said scornfully.

'Drop the bleedin' attitude! Jan is here to stay. She's not going anywhere, so I suggest, no not suggest, I'm *telling* you, you'd better be more civil to her, or else.'

'Or else, what?'

'Or else you'll find yourself slung out, that's what. Don't get me wrong, David. I'm not favouring her over you but I've just got rid of one bully in this house and I won't tolerate another. Don't show yourself to be like your father. You're better than him.'

David looked down at his hands as it dawned on him that Jan had been telling tales. He should have known she would. And now he looked bad in his mother's eyes. 'Sorry,' he said feebly.

'I should think so too, but it's not me you should be apologising to. That young woman has done nothing wrong. She's had a rotten life. Not like you. You've never wanted for anything. It's not like I've asked you to give anything up for her, is it?'

David couldn't meet his mother's eyes and continued to stare at his hands.

'Well, is it?'

'No,' he answered finally.

'All I've asked is that you show her some kindness. That's all. But you couldn't even bring yourself to be nice to her. And do you know what makes it worse?'

'No.'

'It's the fact that you was sly about it. You went behind my back to threaten her. Christ, David, that's as low as a snake's belly. At least your father was up front!'

Her words cut him. He could see it looked bad and regretted being so dreadful. At least, he regretted being found out and perhaps that was the same thing.

'I mean it, David. I won't stand for anyone under my roof being bullied. Do you understand?' she asked harshly.

He nodded.

'Good. Now, there'll be no more said about it. I've got to get back downstairs.'

'Tell Jan I'm sorry,' he mumbled.

'Tell her yourself and make sure you sound like you mean it.'

'I will, Mum,' he said sincerely and looked up at her. 'And I'm sorry to you an' all.'

Her face softened. 'All right, Son. There's been a lot of upheaval this past few weeks and we've all had to make adjustments. And there's a war on, for Christ's sake. We need to stick together, eh?'

'Yeah. You're right, Mum. We do.'

She smiled, and as she turned to walk out, he called, 'Love you.'

'Love you an' all,' she said and left, closing the door behind her.

David pulled out his pad and pen again. There was no harm done, he supposed. If anything, he'd got off quite lightly with just a bit of an ear bashing. He decided to be nice to Jan from now on. After all, none of them were likely to get their hands on his father's money now. And if he stood any chance with Rachel, then it wouldn't hurt to have Rachel's friend on his side, hopefully singing his praises.

27

The next day, as Winnie served her regulars, she kept one eye on Rachel. The girl seemed out of sorts and it couldn't be her hangover now.

'Are you all right, love?' she asked quietly.

'Yes, Win, I'm fine, thanks,' Rachel answered, though her subdued tone was unconvincing.

'You must be upset about Hilda and Arnold but you haven't got to put a brave face on in front of me.'

'I know, thanks. But I'm all right, I swear. I know Arnold wasn't right for me. I always knew. I should have listened to my gut. But at least it shows there *is* life after Jim. And as for Hilda, well, I'm better off without her.'

Winnie was glad to hear that Rachel appeared to be taking recent events in her stride but she wondered if the girl was more hurt than she was letting on. Before she could give it any more thought, Terry breezed in with a broad smile.

'Sobered up, have we?' he asked Rachel.

She looked mortified as she answered, 'Yes. Never again, Terry. I'm never drinking again.'

'You did get yourself in a bit of a state, bless ya. Still, no harm done.'

'I hope I didn't show myself up too much?'

'Nah, course you didn't. You was quite funny really. But I'm glad I didn't have to get you home.'

Winnie placed Terry's glass on the counter. 'Cor, me and Jan had right fun and games trying to drag her up the stairs,' she told him. She turned to Rachel and said, 'For a small woman, you're a dead bleedin' weight when you're half-conscious.'

'Did David help you and Jan?' Rachel asked.

'No,' Winnie answered quickly. 'He couldn't, could he, cos of his back.'

'Oh, yeah, right,' Rachel said pensively.

'Jan's not in, Terry,' Winnie said, changing the subject from David.

'I know, but can you tell her I'm working late tonight? I'll see her tomorrow.'

'Sure, no problem. Tell you what, do you fancy having your tea with us tomorrow? I'm sure Jan would like that and now I ain't got to answer to Brian, I can invite whoever I like upstairs.'

'That would be smashing, thanks. I like your cooking,' Terry said, knocking back the rest of his half-pint. 'I've got to get back to the bakery but I'll see you tomorrow.'

'See ya, Terry,' Winnie said, and noticed that Rachel only offered him a half-hearted smile.

Whether the girl cared to admit it or not, she certainly wasn't herself.

'Tell you what, love,' Winnie said. 'It's pretty quiet this afternoon. Do you want to pop up to the butcher's on the high street and pick us up a nice bit of stewing beef? I'll do us a big pot of stew tomorrow and an apple pie for pudding. Do you fancy that?'

Winnie thought Rachel pulled a strange face at her suggestion and quickly added, 'Or we could have pork and roast spuds?'

'What – am I invited tomorrow too?'

'Of course.'

'Oh … I – erm …'

'Don't tell me you've got something else planned, cos I know full well that you haven't. It'll do you good to have a decent meal. And the fresh air will put a bit of colour in your cheeks. You look a bit pasty, if you ask me.'

'I – erm …'

'No excuses. I don't want to be sitting with Jan and Terry like piggy in the middle. David will have to have his tea in his room. It's a shame. He was in such a good mood this morning. Oh well. I'll take a few bob out the till and put it back later. And don't let old Mr Whitby fob you off with a gristly bit. Tell him it's for me; he'll make sure he gives you the best cut.'

Rachel pursed her lips and nodded. Winnie thought the girl would have been pleased about having her tea with them but instead she looked like she'd been invited to a funeral.

She watched as Rachel walked through to the back for her coat. Her shoulders were slumped, as though she had the weight of the world on them. Then she came back into the pub and Winnie handed her some coins.

'Come on, love, cheer up. I don't like seeing you like this,' she said.

Rachel attempted to smile as she put the coins in her coat

pocket. Then she pulled out a piece of paper. She unfolded it and as she read it, the colour drained from her face.

'What is it?' Winnie asked, noticing Rachel's hands were shaking.

'Nothing – nothing,' she answered as she shoved the paper back in her pocket before briskly walking off.

Maybe she'd found an old love letter from Arnold, or something like that, Winnie thought. Poor Rachel. But, knowing her, she'd soon bounce back to her usual bright self. Winnie just hoped it wouldn't take too long.

Rachel dashed around the corner out of sight from the pub and stopped to gather her thoughts. She held on to a small garden wall to steady herself and drew in several long breaths. She could hardly believe it and shook her head in shock. The doubts and the niggling feeling she'd had since yesterday – she'd been right all along and now she felt sick to her stomach.

She pulled the paper from her pocket and read the note from David again. The audacity of him, she seethed, furious at what he'd done and disgusted at herself for allowing it to happen. And now he seemed to be under the impression that they were in some sort of relationship. She thought the man was delusional and couldn't understand his twisted thinking. After suggesting that she sneak upstairs to his room, he'd even signed the note with a kiss. A kiss – the thought turned her stomach!

She leaned against the wall and squeezed her eyes shut, trying her hardest to recall what had happened that fateful night. Nothing came, only the vague image of him leaning over her. Did he ask her if she was all right? Offer her a sip of water? It was so unclear. But now she knew for sure that he'd had sex with her. The note said how much he'd enjoyed it. God, she felt so sick and ashamed.

Making her way to the butcher's, Rachel went over and over the bits she could remember. Sitting downstairs on the piano stool. An empty brandy bottle. Then darkness and David talking to her. Her fists clenched in frustration. Why, oh why couldn't she recollect what he'd done to her?

Heading back to the Battersea Tavern now with a cut of beef in hand, the journey had been done in a haze, her mind focused on David. As she approached the pub, she looked up at his bedroom window. And then it hit her. She cringed at a fleeting memory of him on top of her. She remembered wanting to tell him to stop. Had she told him? Had he forced himself on her or did she let him do it? No, she'd never allow him near her, never. But had the alcohol fuddled her judgement?

'You took your time,' Winnie said with a smile.

'Yes, sorry,' Rachel answered, still reeling.

'Take the meat upstairs for me, love. Thanks.'

Rachel stood and stared at Winnie for a moment. Her head felt as though it was spinning.

'Did you hear me?' Winnie asked.

'Yes, sorry, I was miles away,' she answered. She marched through the bar and up the stairs, determined to put David straight about whatever sickening notion he had about them.

After taking the beef to the kitchen, she sucked in a gulp of air before charging into his room.

David was lying on his bed but quickly sat up when he saw her.

'You got my note,' he drawled, his eyes looking her up and down.

'Yes, I got your note. You're not right in the head.'

'I thought you'd like a bit of danger – us, sneaking around,' he said, his eyes dark with lust.

'Stay away from me,' she snapped. 'I'm not interested in you and never will be.'

'Don't be like that, Rachel. That's not what you said the other night.'

'How could you?' she ground out furiously.

'Quite easily,' he said with a smirk. 'You didn't say no.'

'I was drunk! I don't know what happened, but I've got a pretty good idea. You took advantage of me and that – that's disgusting!'

'I gave you what you wanted and you loved it.'

'No, David, no I didn't! I would never have let you come near me if I'd been sober, and you know it,' she spat, her stomach churning. Gawd, she wished she could remember what he'd done to her.

'Just admit it, Rachel, you've always liked me.'

'No I haven't. I hate you,' she hissed. 'Don't you ever touch me again!'

'Suit yourself,' he said with a nonchalant shrug. 'If that's how you feel, you'd better leave.'

Rachel threw him one last look of contempt before stamping out. She hated herself as much as she hated David and couldn't believe she'd become so inebriated that she'd allowed him to have sex with her. Her cheeks burned with shame and she hoped no one would ever discover what had happened. She couldn't tell anyone. It was a secret she'd take to her grave. She could only pray that David wouldn't gloat about it.

28

Several weeks passed and it was now just a week before Christmas. Winnie jumped out of bed with a spring in her step. If she intended to throw the best Christmas party the Battersea Tavern had ever seen, she'd have to work through her list, which was as long as her arm. Hard work had never fazed her, but the thought of Brian walking in and claiming his pub did. She'd tried to push the worry of it to the back of her mind and kept herself busy with the Christmas preparations, but the fear kept encroaching on her days and was even more prevalent at night. She only had to be concerned for another week or two and then she'd seek legal advice.

In the kitchen, Jan had made a fresh pot of tea and had poured three cups. 'Is one of those for David?' she asked.

'Yes. He's awake, I heard him go to the bathroom and then back to his room.'

'I'll take it through, thanks, love. I assume he's been all right with you since I spoke to him?'

'Yes, Winnie; he's actually been quite friendly.'

'Good. You let me know if that changes,' she said as she picked up his cup and saucer.

After tapping on his door, she walked in to find him sitting up in bed and he greeted her with a wide smile.

'Morning, Son. Jan made you a cuppa,' she said, placing it on the side.

'Thanks.'

Winnie walked across the room and pulled open the curtains before lifting the sash window a little.

'What are you doing, Mum? It's freezing in here. Ain't you seen the snow outside?'

'Yes, but this room could do with a bit of fresh air. And it'll do you good an' all. By the way, you ain't helped yourself to the money in my tin, have you?'

'No, course I ain't. What good would money be to me? I ain't been outside for over a month.'

'Funny, that. I thought some had gone missing last month, but dismissed it, but I know this time I had some money put by. I could do with it now. I went to see the bank manager yesterday. He said that the bank account was in your father's name and I've no access to it. Not that it makes any difference now. The manager said your dad has cleared the account and closed it down.'

'Blimey, the sly old git. He'll be after the pub next. Do you think it's wise to wait till after Christmas to see the solicitor?'

'I don't know.' Winnie sighed. 'I can't lie, the worry of it keeps me awake at night but I've got so much to do before Christmas.'

'There's no point in making any plans if we ain't got a pub.'

'I suppose you're right, but to be honest, I don't think there's much a solicitor can do. The pub belongs to your father. He can do with it as he sees fit.'

333

'What if he sells it? Or what if he comes back and slings us out?'

'He won't come back, I'm sure of that, but I can't be sure that he won't sell the pub out from under me. I can't see your father walking away and leaving it all to me, can you?'

'No, I suppose not. Knowing him, he'd rather give it away than let you have it.'

'Exactly. But for now I'm going to try and focus on Christmas, which is why I could do with that money from my tin. Are you sure you ain't touched it?'

'Of course I'm sure! What about Jan? Have you asked her?'

'No, don't be daft; Jan would *never* go in my tin.'

'Oh, I see. So you accuse me but you ain't even asked her! That ain't on.'

'All right, calm down,' she said. In her heart she knew that David had helped himself to her savings, but it was clear he was never going to own up to it. 'I'll go and check with Jan now.'

Back in the kitchen, Winnie looked at her list. She'd placed a meat order with the butcher and could tick that off. Terry had said he would bring a Christmas tree in today. She'd get Rachel to decorate it as the girl had more of a flair for that sort of thing than she had. But she'd need to shop for a new angel for the top. The wings had fallen off her old one and were beyond 'make do and mend'. 'Would you mind doing a bit of shopping for me today?' she asked Jan. 'Only I need something for the top of the tree.'

'I don't mind at all. Me and Hilda are going up the market today to see Bill and Flo. It'll be no bother. Actually, I was wondering about Hilda and Christmas Day ...'

'No, love, she can't come here. I've softened a bit towards

her and I know you say she hasn't touched a drop of drink, but it wouldn't be fair on Rachel.'

'I understand. I just hate to think of her all alone at Christmas.'

'Bloody hell, you know how to pull on me old heart-strings. I don't like the thought of it either but I ain't sure how Rachel would react if Hilda turned up.'

'Perhaps you could ask her? Tell her Hilda really isn't drinking. Maybe she'd have a change of heart, seeing as it's Christmas.'

'I'll ask but don't hold your breath.'

Winnie looked back at her list. When Jan was out of the way, she would ask one of her regulars to go and pick up the second-hand sewing machine she'd bought for Jan's Christmas present. Oh, she couldn't wait to see the look on her face when she opened it on Christmas morning. She hoped it would keep Jan away from spending so much time with Hilda. Not that she resented the time they spent together, but Hilda could slip back into her old ways and she wouldn't want Jan around her when she was stinking with booze. Jan had led a sheltered life and was quite naïve, immature for her age. She needed a mother, thought Winnie, and smiled that she had filled that role.

She looked back at her list. It reminded her that there was an extra load of barrels being delivered today. She could have done with the money from her tin to give the draymen a little Christmas box. They were good blokes and rather than just using their heavy ropes to lower the casks through the drop and into the cellar, they'd help hammer in the large brass taps used to connect the casks to the pumps. Rachel liked it when they turned up because she enjoyed giving the horses a carrot or two. And one flutter of her eyelashes would have the draymen bringing up crates from the cellar and all sorts. Rachel certainly was an asset to the Battersea Tavern and Winnie wanted to find her a special Christmas gift too. The girl hadn't been herself since she'd split up with Arnold. Her joy seemed to have gone and she rarely smiled and joked these days. Winnie had hoped that Arnold would come to realise that he'd made a terrible mistake and turn up to see her again, but that hadn't happened and Rachel had been left miserable. She hoped Christmas would brighten Rachel's mood but with the prospect of Hilda joining them, she doubted it would.

David brought his empty cup and saucer into the kitchen and Winnie was pleased when she saw him smile at Jan. It was nice to see Jan more relaxed now. The strong words she'd had with her son had done the trick. Harmony was restored in the Battersea Tavern and now that Errol Hampton had been paid off, even the occasional times he popped in for a drink no longer caused an atmosphere.

'Is the doctor coming in to see me today?' David asked.

'No, love, tomorrow. Make sure you convince him that your back is still bad. I don't want him thinking you're fit enough for the army.'

'Don't worry, I will, but I'm so bored and fed up with being stuck indoors. I'm beginning to think that signing up ain't such a bad idea.'

'No, David! Don't you dare! You've seen the papers and heard the wireless. There's ships being sunk by U-boats and soldiers being shipped off abroad. It'll only be a matter of time before this war is on our doorsteps and I want you here, safe and sound.'

'What do you mean by that, Winnie?' Jan asked, frowning in consternation.

'I mean, they ain't billeting all the kids out to the country-side for the fun of it, are they? You've all seen the barrage balloon and the ack-ack guns, the bomb shelters and the blackouts. And what with no theatre shows except for the odd Christmas one they're allowing, I'm telling you, there's trouble afoot. But even so, I'd rather you were here and safe sheltering from bombs in our cellar, than shipped off to the front line.'

'Pack it in, Mum, you'll scare the life out of Jan. Anyway, if things are that bad, how come they're sending a load of our troops home from the Western front for Christmas?'

Winnie saw the colour had drained from Jan's face, and said, 'Sorry, I don't know why I've suddenly got all maudlin. Of course, you're right, David, there's nothing to be worried about, but I still don't want you signing up.'

'All right,' David agreed.

'Good,' she answered, though she knew it was the bother with Brian and the pub that was behind her fears. 'Now, I've got a lot to get through these next few days so I don't want you under my feet. While it's just us up here, you can go and sit in the front room, but keep away from the windows. And no more ridiculous talk of signing up.'

David wandered off and Winnie looked back down at her list. She hadn't been exaggerating; she did have a lot to get through, but she hoped she wasn't putting so much effort into Christmas for nothing. After all, her husband could snatch it all away from her, leaving her with nothing.

★

Rachel stood behind the bar and wondered how much worse things could become for her. She'd fallen out with Hilda, Arnold had left her and David, well, she shuddered at the thought of what he'd done to her. Yet this feeling that something awful was going to happen was still troubling her.

'Are you all right, love?' Winnie asked, breaking into her depressed thoughts.

'Yes, I was just thinking.'

'Well, stop thinking and get working. The draymen will be here any minute and you still ain't opened the drop.'

'Oh, sorry, I'll do it now,' she said and went outside. A thick blanket of snow covered the street so she took a stiff broom with her and swept the cellar's drop hatch before lifting the double wooden doors. The draymen's cart pulled up as she heaved the doors open.

'We would have done that,' Charlie said and doffed his flat cap.

'Thanks, but Winnie is on my back.'

'Cor, I wouldn't want to upset the old dear, she's a fierce one, her.'

'Winnie? You must be joking. She's got a heart of gold and wouldn't hurt a fly.'

'If you say so, but I've known her since before you was even thought of, young lady, and believe you me, Winnie can hold her own in a fight.'

'Winnie, fighting – surely not?' Rachel asked, bemused.

'Ain't she ever told you about the punch-up in here between Mr Higgins and his missus?'

'No, and I've never heard of Mr Higgins.'

'That's probably because he's kept his head down ever since Winnie gave him a shiner.'

'Really? Tell me more, and don't miss out a single detail.'

'Years ago, Mrs Higgins came in looking for her old man before he drank their rent money. Well, he didn't take too kindly to being shown up in front of his mates so he gave her a slap and told her to "p— orf". Next thing you know, Winnie's come flying round from the bar and punched Mr Higgins square in the face. And she didn't stop there. She picked up his pint and tipped it over his head before chasing him out of the pub, shouting that from now on he was barred. Tables went flying and folks said they'd never seen Mr Higgins run so fast. He was sporting a black eye for quite some time.'

Rachel couldn't help but chuckle at the image of Winnie punching the man.

'Then there was this young whippersnapper who pinched her backside. She chased him out with a broom just like that one.'

'Good on her. But she really is a kind woman.'

'I know, pet, I'm only pulling your leg, but them stories are true. How's she bearing up with Mr Berry gawn?'

'Fine. Have you seen or heard anything of him?'

'Just that he's over in Peckham. I hope he stays there an' all. He's always thought he was something special cos he owns this place but it's Winnie that does all the hard work. She's better orf without him, the arrogant so-and-so.'

'Yes, you ain't wrong,' Rachel replied, and hoped Mr Berry would stay in Peckham. If he didn't, she could end up without a job, and Winnie, Jan and David without a home.

The draymen began lowering the casks and Rachel went back inside to get carrots for the two magnificent shire horses. She remembered the first time she'd fed them and had been so nervous. But after advice from Charlie, she knew how to offer food to them on the flat of her hand so that they didn't accidently bite off her fingers.

When she came out of the kitchen, her heart sank at the sight of Errol Hampton and his girlfriend at the bar. Stephanie Reynolds eyed her with contempt. She'd never liked Rachel and Winnie said it was because she was jealous of her, as it was clear that Errol fancied her. Rachel wasn't happy to see them and hoped they wouldn't make it a regular thing. Winnie didn't seem pleased to see them either, but was quick to go over and serve them.

Rachel fed the horses the carrots and reluctantly returned inside.

'Dave still laid up?' Errol asked as she passed them.

'Yes, afraid so,' she answered. She hated lying to cover for him but had promised Winnie she would.

Then from behind, she heard a terrific scream coming from the cellar. She dashed to the door and peered down the narrow staircase to see Winnie at the bottom, lying on the floor and groaning. She gasped and ran down to the woman, asking frantically, 'Winnie, Winnie, are you all right?'

'No, love,' Winnie groaned in obvious pain. 'I took a fall and I think I've twisted me ankle.'

'Can you stand up? We'll get you back upstairs.'

With a bit of help, Winnie managed to get up, but she cried out when she tried to put her damaged foot to the floor. 'I don't think I can walk.'

Charlie appeared and said, 'I'll fetch a chair and we'll have to carry you up.'

'What was you doing? You know I see to the dray.'

'I don't know, love. I was checking how much longer they

were going to be so that I could pour them a drink. I missed the step, Gawd knows how.'

'Does anything else hurt apart from your ankle?' Rachel asked.

'Yeah, my shoulder, hip, wrist and elbow. But that's just bruising. I think I've done some proper damage to me ankle though. This is all I need right on top of Christmas.'

Charlie returned with Bob, the other drayman, and placed a chair on the floor. 'Now, then, what are we going to do with you?' he said and tutted.

'I don't know, love, but I don't think I can get back up the stairs.'

'If me and Bob hold you, do you think you can hop?'

'I doubt it, not that far,' Winnie replied and groaned in pain.

'We'll have to put our ropes around you and haul you out through the drop,' he said jokingly.

'Don't you dare, I'd never hear the end of it.'

'Well, we can't leave you down here.'

'I know I'm no lightweight, but perhaps you could carry me up on the chair?'

'We can give it a go,' Charlie answered.

'Rachel, I'm fine. Get yourself back to the pub, love. There's nothing you can do here to help and I need you up there keeping an eye on things.'

Rachel didn't like to leave Winnie stranded but the woman did have a point and so she went back upstairs.

Minutes later, Bob came up from the cellar. 'It's no good, I'll run down to the telephone box and call for an ambulance. Her leg is up like a balloon now.'

'Thanks, Bob. Please hurry,' Rachel said. She chewed on

341

her thumbnail. Despite Winnie's reassurance, she was worried about her. She thought about closing up, but she knew Winnie wouldn't be happy about that. Instead, when Len called out to her, she quickly served him another stout.

'Sounds like Winnie's got herself in a bit of bother,' he said.

'Yes, she's hurt her ankle,' Rachel told him and then went to serve Errol, who was asking for another round.

'Same again,' he said as he leaned over the bar to look at her legs. Stephanie gave him a sharp elbow and he glowered at her.

As she placed their drinks in front of them, Errol slapped the money down on the counter and said, 'I heard the commotion. What's going on?'

'Mrs Berry had a fall.'

'With her old man gone and Dave laid up, looks like you're by yourself and that could cause you problems.'

The way he said it sounded threatening and Rachel felt her pulse quicken. She was grateful when Bob came rushing back in and told her the ambulance would be here shortly.

'Can I get you a drink?' she asked, hoping he'd stay at the bar.

'Might as well. I'll only get in the way downstairs. I've shut the drop and the horses are tethered.'

Within minutes, the sound of the ambulance sirens neared and Bob went outside to direct them in.

'This way,' he said with authority as two ambulance drivers followed him. Rachel guessed the sound of the sirens would have most of the street come out to be nosy. And she knew Winnie wouldn't like to be a spectacle. With one eye on the bar and another on the cellar door, she heard Winnie grumbling in discomfort as they carried her up.

'Take her out the back door,' Rachel told the men, at least sparing Winnie from being dragged through the pub.

Bob dashed round and opened the door for them and Rachel reassured Winnie that she'd look after the place. As she was carried out, David appeared and looked genuinely concerned.

'I heard the racket. What's going on?' he asked.

'Your mum fell down the cellar stairs. She's not too badly injured but her ankle is twisted or maybe broken.'

'Bloody hell, you should have given me a shout.'

'You're supposed to be bedbound,' she reminded him, but it was too late to carry on the lie now as Errol was looking over the bar. Through the open door, he could see David standing in the passage.

'Oi, come here, Dave,' he called.

'Oh God. What shall I do?' he whispered to Rachel.

He sounded scared but it wasn't Rachel's problem. 'I don't know, go and see what he wants, I suppose,' she answered and went back into the pub leaving David looking afraid.

'He's out of bed, then,' Errol said.

'Yes, looks that way.'

'Tell him I want a word before he skives back upstairs.'

Rachel turned and called to David. 'Errol would like a word.'

Sheepishly, he skulked into the pub but Rachel had no sympathy for him. If David had got himself on the wrong side of Errol Hampton, the man could make mincemeat out of him for all she cared, just as long as he didn't do it in here on her watch.

★

343

David swallowed hard as he approached Errol and avoided eye contact with Stephanie. He couldn't imagine that she'd told him about them spending the night together because if she had, Errol would be hauling him over the bar by now.

'It's about time you crawled out from under your rock,' Errol said. 'We were only saying this morning that we wondered how much longer you was gonna hide your lazy arse, weren't we, sweetheart?'

Stephanie looked from Errol to David before replying, 'Yes, that's right, we were.'

'Well, Dave, it's good to see you up and about. I suppose you're the man of the place now, what with your father doing a runner. And now your poor old mum's had an accident.'

'Yeah, I suppose I am,' he answered, trying to hide his nerves, but he could feel sweat forming on his brow and his mouth felt dry.

'It'd be a shame if you let this place go. Your mother runs a tight ship. She's more of a man than you'll ever be.'

David didn't answer, for fear of provoking him. He got the impression that Errol was looking for trouble. There were only four other customers in the bar including Len and they were all quietly listening to the exchange. If Errol went for him, he knew none of them would jump in to help, which left him feeling very much alone and afraid.

Errol took a mouthful of his beer and glanced around, saying loudly, 'What sort of a bloke lets his dear, sweet mother work her fingers to the bone to pay off his debt?'

No one answered.

'A bloke like him, that's who,' Errol said, jabbing his finger in David's direction.

David glowered at the man but knew it would be foolhardy

to tell him to shut up. Instead, he pulled himself a half-pint and pleaded quietly, 'Leave it, Errol. You got your money, we're square now.'

'But we ain't square, Dave, are we?'

David didn't know what Errol meant and wished he would just drink up and leave.

'Your bad-back act don't fool me. I ain't stupid, Dave, I know your game. You've been playing ill so that you can avoid me and get out of doing your National Service.'

David could feel Len looking daggers at him now. The old man was patriotic and his son had been posted to Belgium. He could guess what was going through Len's mind. Filled with shame, he hung his head. He wanted to run and hide but that would just prove he was a coward.

'That's right,' Errol said, his voice loud. 'There's nothing wrong with the yellow-bellied shirker. He's been faking it cos he's too scared to fight for his country.'

At last David stood up for himself and spat accusingly, 'What about you, eh? You ain't any better. You're not signed up and in basic training – I suppose you've got out of it by using one of those fake medical exemption certificates that you're flogging.'

'It ain't none of your business but I ain't shirking. I've got good reason, unlike you, you little piece of shit.' Then Errol glanced at Rachel, 'Sorry about my language.'

Rachel stepped towards them. 'I think you should leave. If Mrs Berry was here, you'd be out on your ear by now.'

David held his breath, praying that Errol wouldn't turn on Rachel. He would have to defend her if he did. Thankfully, the man said, 'Come on, Steph. I ain't staying. The place is a dump and the beer's watered down. But before I go, Dave, you owe me two quid.'

'I don't owe you a penny,' David protested, confused.

'But you do, Dave. See, your mother paid back the money you borrowed from me but what about the two quid a week you're supposed to be giving to my Steph?'

David's heart began to pound so hard he thought it might leap out of his chest. If Errol was aware of Stephanie's blackmail, then it followed that the man knew he'd slept with her. How was his head even still on his shoulders, and would it be for much longer?

'Ha, you look like you're gonna piss yourself. Got anything to say for yourself?'

David's mouth opened and closed but no words came out. He stood, riveted to the spot, knowing that he didn't have a leg to stand on and any minute now Errol was going to batter the life out of him.

'Nah, I didn't think you'd have much to say. See ya around.'

With that, Errol spun on his heal and Stephanie followed as he walked out. David was left visibly shaking.

'You're a disgrace to your mother,' Len mumbled from the end of the bar.

Yes, he realised he probably was and felt humiliated. But, more than that, he was terrified of what Errol would do next. The man obviously knew about him sleeping with Stephanie and David knew it would only be a matter of time before Errol dished out his vengeance.

Another customer walked to the bar and banged his glass down. 'I fought in the trenches and saw my friends killed for our country in the Great War. Fellas like you make me sick,' he seethed and stormed out.

That was it. Everyone would know he was a shirker and now he had no way of avoiding conscription. Like it or not, and regardless of what his mum thought, he'd have to sign up. He reckoned he stood a better chance in battle with the enemy than he did on the streets of Battersea with Errol. And to top it all, Rachel hadn't minced her words when she'd told him she hated him. There was nothing left here for him anymore. Just a life living in fear without the girl he liked. Well, now was as good a time as any, so he shot upstairs, grabbed his coat and left by the back door, heading straight for the army recruitment office to enlist.

29

On Christmas morning, Winnie struggled to climb out of bed but Jan must have heard her moaning and came in to help.

'You should have called me.'

'It's all right. I'm getting better on these crutches. I thought I was going to fall flat on my face at first but I seem to be getting the hang of them now. Merry Christmas, by the way,' she said and chuckled.

'Merry Christmas to you too.'

'Is David up?'

'No, not yet.'

'I shall be dragging him out of his bed shortly. Now the cat's out the bag about his back, I won't have him hiding away in his room all day.' She'd been horrified when she'd returned from the hospital and had discovered that everyone now knew there was nothing wrong with David. Winnie had already decided that she'd tell everyone that he'd only just recovered. No one had to know he'd been swinging the lead all this time. She'd already thought of another way to get him out of National Service. She'd put her suggestion to him tomorrow, once Christmas Day was out of the way. She heaved herself up, saying, 'There's an awful lot to do today.'

'Please, Winnie, don't worry about any of it. Me and Rachel have got everything under control.'

'You're good girls. I don't know how I would have managed without you both,' Winnie said warmly, hitching a crutch under each armpit. 'Right, make way, I need the loo.'

After struggling in the bathroom, she hobbled into the kitchen to see Jan cooking eggs for breakfast and Rachel peeling vegetables at the sink. 'Blimey, you're keen,' she said.

'I got here first thing. There's a lot of spuds need peeling, carrots need slicing and peas need – peaing.'

'I think you mean, shelling, love,' Winnie corrected her and they all laughed.

She enjoyed the warm atmosphere in the kitchen but felt awful that there wasn't much she could do to help. Though she had to admit she was very pleased with how the young women were coping. They'd arranged the tables in the pub last night. Several were pulled together to make one large one and Rachel had decorated it with crackers that Jan had made, along with a centrepiece of pine, ivy and mistletoe. 'I would have worked myself up into a right old state by now. I'd be in a panic about the meat and fussing over the tables downstairs. You two have done me proud.'

'We couldn't have managed it without your supervision,' Rachel chirped. 'How's your foot this morning?'

'Sore, but the doctor said it would be for a few weeks. I wish I could take this bandage off, it's making me itch like mad.'

'Do you want a knitting needle?' Jan asked.

'Oh, yes, love, that would work a treat,' she answered.

349

Once Jan had gone in search of the needle, Winnie delicately asked Rachel, 'Are you sure you're happy with Hilda coming round later?'

Rachel placed the knife on the kitchen counter and pulled out a seat at the table. 'I can't say I'm happy about it, but I suppose I can put up with her – unless she's had a drink.'

'Well, she's not had one in a while now, so I don't see why she would today.'

'Have you forgiven her, Win?'

'I suppose so. I don't bear her no grudges but it was an awful way to find out that Jan isn't my Alma. Still, no harm done. I shall love and care for the girl like she's my own.'

Jan came back in carrying a knitting needle which she handed to her. Winnie slid it into the bandage and rubbed up and down. The relief was immediate and she sighed. 'That's better, thanks, love.'

'When are we opening our presents?' Rachel asked, her excitement showing.

'Soon enough,' Winnie answered. 'Let's get breakfast out the way first, and once I'm washed and dressed, we can sit down with a nice glass of sherry and open them.'

'Sherry, at this time of the morning?' Jan exclaimed.

'It's Christmas, love. I always have a glass of sherry on Christmas morning.'

'Oh, Win, do we have to wait until you're dressed? Can't you get dressed *after* we've opened the presents?' Rachel moaned.

'No, we can't. You'll just have to be patient.'

Rachel pulled a sulky face, but she returned to peeling the vegetables.

'Give us a knife and a bowl. I'll do some of that veg.'

'No you won't,' Rachel said firmly. 'You're not to lift a finger.'

Winnie smiled warmly at them both, grateful that they were there to carry the burden of preparing the biggest Christmas lunch that the Battersea Tavern had ever put on. Even if her ankle hadn't been twisted, she wasn't sure she would have managed alone. Neither Brian nor David would have helped; they would have left all the work to her to do single-handed.

'Jan, go and give David a knock. I need him up to shovel the snow outside. I don't want any of my customers ending up like me.'

'It's all right. Terry said he'd do it. He's going to carve the meat too and serve the drinks with Rachel.'

'Oh, he's a smashing fella. But that tree he brought takes up half the pub, the silly sod. I still want David out of bed, though. It's Christmas morning and we should all be together, especially as we have no idea what next year is going to bring, what with this blinkin' war an' all.'

Minutes later, David lumbered into the kitchen. Winnie noticed that there was no exchange of Christmas wishes between him and Rachel, and she assumed Rachel still had the hump with him over the episode in the pub with Errol. It had frightened the life out of the girl and Winnie was unhappy that she'd been left alone to deal with it. When Rachel had told her about the two pounds a week David was supposed to give Stephanie, she guessed that was the reason he'd stolen money from her tin. It was a mystery why he owed that slut money but she'd get to the bottom of it once Christmas was out of the way.

Winnie sighed. She'd been angry at first that he'd brought trouble to her doorstep but, despite it all, she still loved her son. Yes, he had made bad choices, but hadn't she done worse when she'd given up her daughter for adoption?

David kissed her cheek and then Jan's, wishing them both a merry Christmas. He poured himself a cup of tea and asked Rachel if she'd like one.

Rachel's back was rod straight and she very curtly told him, 'No thank you.'

Winnie could sense the tension between them and hoped it wouldn't mar the day. To make matters worse, they still had Hilda's company to look forward to.

Once breakfast was finished, they moved into the sitting room and Winnie went to get dressed. She checked her reflection in the bedroom mirror. She did look a sight with a thick bandage from her toes to almost her knee. Brian wouldn't have liked it. He'd have said it ruined the look of her new red dress. She'd bought it at his request and he'd been right, red did suit her, though the dress hugged her in all the wrong places, emphasising her wide hips and bulging stomach. Brian would probably have ordered her to take it off and change into something more flattering but, out of spite, she kept it on and limped through to the front room.

'Very festive,' Rachel commented, eyeing the dress.

'You look smashing, Mum.'

'Yes, Winnie, as pretty as a picture,' Jan added.

'Thank you. Now, let's get these gifts opened before Rachel bursts a blood vessel.'

One by one, they exchanged presents. Rachel was thrilled with the glow-in-the-dark flower broach from Jan.

'With these horrid blackouts, I thought it might be useful to wear on your coat when you're walking home at night; stop people bumping into you,' Jan explained.

'It's perfect, thank you,' Rachel gushed.

When Winnie opened her gift from Jan, she looked tenderly at the embroidered handkerchiefs and tears welled in her eyes. Stroking the words, 'Mother' with her fingertips, she said, 'This means the world to me.'

Jan seemed unable to speak and smiled lovingly back at her.

Next, David opened his gift and thanked Jan for the impressive cigarette lighter. 'This is much better than a box of matches,' he said, pleased, though Winnie thought something didn't seem right about him. She couldn't put her finger on it but he looked tense.

When Rachel handed her gifts out, saying, 'You've both got the same,' it didn't go unnoticed to Winnie that she hadn't given David one.

'Chocolates, lovely, thank you,' Jan said, beaming. 'This is the best Christmas I've ever had!'

'You've another present to open,' Winnie told her. She pointed to the dining table behind the sofa where something large had a cloth covering it.

Jan pulled the cloth off and gasped with delight when she saw the treadle sewing machine. 'Oh, Winnie, is this really for me?'

'Yes, love, of course it is. David has set the table up for you in the window, so you'll get plenty of light. We never eat at that table so it can be your sewing area.'

Then Winnie handed Rachel a small box, saying, 'It's not much but I hope you like it.'

Rachel looked inside, her eyes widening with delight.

'It was my gran's and I know you've always had your eye on it,' Winnie said.

'It – it's – beautiful.' Rachel smiled and pinned the small

blue-enamelled brooch to her dress. 'I don't know what to say. Thank you, Win.'

'Where's mine?' David asked.

'You'll be lucky to get anything more than a clip round the ear,' Winnie answered, before pointing to a package.

He undid the string, ripped off the newspaper and burst out laughing. 'Thanks, Mum, just what I need,' he said, holding the pyjamas up.

'Well, you spend most of your time in bed,' she answered, and though he laughed, his smile didn't reach his eyes.

'Not for much longer,' he replied and handed her an envelope. 'It's probably not the Christmas gift you wanted, but I hope you'll be proud of me.'

Winnie opened the envelope and pulled out a postcard. As she read it, the terrible realisation of what it was began to dawn on her. 'This is a National Service registration card,' she mumbled. 'Oh, Christ, David – please tell me this is a horrible joke. You haven't signed up, have you?'

'I had to, Mum, it was the right thing to do.'

If Winnie could have, she would have raced to her bedroom, thrown herself on her bed and sobbed her heart out. But she couldn't. She was stuck in the armchair with all eyes on her. 'Well,' she said, trying to hold herself together, 'As my boy is off to war, let's make this the best Christmas ever.'

Rachel tried not to giggle as she walked slowly down the stairs behind Winnie who was shuffling down on her bottom.

'You'd better not be laughing at me behind my back,' Winnie warned sternly.

'I wouldn't dream of it,' she fibbed.

Once in the pub, she helped Winnie take a seat at the top

of the table, telling her, 'Now, sit, relax and enjoy. Everything is under control and everyone is going to have a wonderful Christmas.'

'Thanks, love. I can't say I'm thrilled at David joining up but I suppose it was only ever going to be a matter of time. I shan't let it ruin the day.'

'Good, I'm glad to hear it.'

Jan emerged from the back kitchen, wiping her brow, and Rachel noticed she'd spilt something down the front of her apron.

'There's so much steam in there, I can't see what I'm doing,' she complained.

Rachel called across to Terry, who was stocking up the bar. 'Can you open the top window in the kitchen for Jan, please? I can't reach it. Give it a good shove, it's a bit sticky.'

Terry obliged and Jan followed him back into the kitchen. Winnie's guests would be arriving soon but they were ready for them. Piano Pete was the first to turn up, clutching a small bunch of wilted flowers for his hostess.

'I thought I'd get here a bit early and knock out a few Christmas tunes, get everyone in the spirit.'

'Smashing idea,' Rachel said and she took the flowers. She put them in a tall glass of water and placed it on the table next to Winnie.

Len and his wife, Renee, came in next. Renee Garwood brought the plum pudding. She brought one every year; it had a become a tradition. Rachel hadn't seen the woman for many months and was surprised at how frail-looking she'd become. Len and Renee were closely followed by Franky Elms and his son, Howard. His wife had died several years earlier and his daughters had gone to live with his sister. Howard was now sixteen and a strapping lad.

'I hope you don't mind, but I brought Karim with us. He's moved into a room next door and doesn't know anyone yet. He's never had a Christmas in England before and I told him your hospitality has no limits,' Franky said, pushing the Indian man forward.

Rachel stared wide-eyed at the dark-skinned man whose suit appeared to be three times too big for his skinny frame. She glanced over at Winnie to gauge her reaction. They'd never had such an exotic foreigner in the pub before.

'You're more than welcome, Karim,' Winnie said and told Rachel to set another place at the table for him. 'The more, the merrier, that's what I say. Now, come and sit beside me and tell me all about what you do for Christmas where you come from.'

' 'Ere, Win, my Howie has only gawn and joined up,' Franky said as Terry handed him a pint.

'But he's too young,' Winnie replied.

'I know, but they didn't ask too many questions. I reckon they'll take on just about anyone who's willing.'

'Didn't you try and talk him out of it?'

'Why would I do that? He left school two years ago and is man enough to make his own decisions. I think he's made the right one. If he can help, I say good on him. He's done me proud.'

'My David's joined up too,' Winnie said sadly.

Terry came back from the kitchen looking very flushed from the heat in the small room.

'How's Jan getting on?' she asked.

But before he could answer, Hilda came through the

door. Rachel felt her stomach flip but was pleased to see she appeared sober.

'Hello, darling, merry Christmas,' Hilda said awkwardly.

'And you.'

'I got you this,' Hilda said and handed her a small package.

Rachel hadn't bought anything for Hilda and she felt a stab of guilt. But, she reasoned, her mother didn't *deserve* anything. She unwrapped the gift to see a very old black-and-white photograph that had been coloured in with pencil. Looking at the image, she was sure it was Hilda as a young woman and she was holding a small child.

'That's me and you,' Hilda explained. 'Your Aunty Alice had this old camera and was always making the lot of us pose. We must have been the most photographed poor family in Battersea. Most of the pictures she took never came out but that one did. I've always treasured it.'

Rachel didn't know what to say, her feelings were mixed. She was grateful when Hilda spoke again.

'Looks like there's a lot going on. Anything I can do to help?'

'You can go and see if Jan needs a hand. I'm going upstairs to check on the meat.'

In the upstairs kitchen, Rachel bent over and opened the door to the stove. The smell of roasting turkey and pork wafted out but instead of making her mouth water, it left her with an overwhelming feeling of nausea. She slammed the door shut and her hand flew over her mouth as she heaved. Unable to make it to the bathroom, she leaned over the sink and vomited, her stomach lurching.

Hilda's voice came from behind. 'Blimey, Rachel, are you all right?'

She splashed some cold water onto her face and rinsed her mouth. Then she turned to Hilda, asking, 'What are you doing up here? I thought I asked you to check on Jan.'

'Yes, I did and she was getting on fine. So I thought I'd come up to see if you needed a hand. Good job I did; look at the state of you.'

'I'm fine,' Rachel said, feeling better. 'It must be all the excitement.'

'Or you're in the family way,' Hilda said and laughed.

But when Rachel's eyes filled with tears, Hilda said, 'Bloody hell, you're not, are you?'

'No. Don't be silly, of course I'm not.'

'Then why are you so upset?'

'I'm not,' she answered and marched towards the door. But Hilda's voice stopped her in her tracks.

'Did you and Arnold, you know – did you sleep with Arnold?'

Rachel, with her back to Hilda, shook her head. No, she hadn't slept with Arnold. She couldn't be pregnant with his child. If there was a baby growing in her stomach it would be David who had put it there. The thought repulsed her and she wished it wasn't true.

30

The next morning, David woke up but he hadn't been asleep for long. He'd spent most of the night with his mind turning over what he'd heard the previous day. When he'd seen Rachel go upstairs, he'd left it a few minutes, then followed. But then he'd heard Hilda's voice and had stood outside the kitchen, eavesdropping on their conversation. Hilda had suggested that Rachel was pregnant. She'd denied it and said she'd never given herself to Arnold. So if she was with child, David knew he was the father.

He'd lain in bed contemplating the idea and there wasn't a single part of him that relished it. He wasn't ready to be a dad. And once Rachel started showing, questions would be asked. It would come out that he'd taken advantage of her when she'd been drunk and, Christ, his mother would kill him if Errol didn't get to him first! He was still being ostracised for what had happened with Brenda, and to add to that, word would have spread about him shirking and lying about his back.

David ran a hand over his face. It was all too much. His father had done a runner and now he felt like doing the same.

Yet where could he go? Once the thought had come into his mind, he couldn't shake it. Scarpering seemed the best thing to do. He could start again, a new life where nobody knew him and he could avoid being sent off to training camp or having Errol beat him up.

When he heard movement, David knew that his mother and Jan were up and about. Unable to face them, he pulled the blankets up under his chin and rolled over. In the cold light of day, he mulled over the decision he'd come to. It still seemed like a good option. He'd have to rob the pub again. He would need money, so there was no other choice. He'd have to go soon, before he was due to start basic training, and before Rachel had to own up that she was pregnant and accusing fingers were pointed at him. He'd leave a note for his mother. She'd be upset but she had Jan to comfort her, he thought, salving his conscience. Though once his mother discovered what he'd done to Rachel, the upset would turn to raging anger directed at him.

He felt scared, thinking he'd be going somewhere he'd never been before and where he didn't know anyone, but the thought of staying and facing his responsibilities was far more terrifying. Errol, the Germans, father to Rachel's baby, the hostility towards him over the accident and Brenda's condition – he wanted to get away from them all. As soon as the opportunity arose, David planned on running far, far away.

As Rachel walked to work, she realised that the feeling of something awful going to happen had gone. And that was because it had transpired now. She was pregnant with David Berry's child. There couldn't be anything more awful than that!

She had missed her monthlies, but with all the preparation for Christmas, she hadn't given it a thought. Well, not until Hilda had caught her throwing up in the sink and had asked if she was in the family way. Unconsciously, she rested her hand on her stomach. It wasn't the baby's fault. But she didn't want it. How could she ever love the child? It would be a constant reminder of David and the way it was conceived. She hated him. When it came out that she was pregnant, she dreaded what people would say. She'd be labelled a slut. Women didn't sleep with men or have babies unless they were married. But she didn't think she could face the alternative; that was just too horrific. She'd heard of women seeking out back-street abortions who'd been left unable to have children – or, worse, who had died. But if she didn't, she'd have to live every day watching with disgust as her belly bulged.

When she reached the Battersea Tavern, Jan opened the door and told her the kettle was on. In the back kitchen, Winnie had her bad leg up on a chair and greeted her with laughter.

'Hello, love, I was just having a chuckle about that episode with Karim yesterday.'

'Yes, it was funny when you pulled that cracker with him and the noise made him duck under the table for cover,' she replied, forcing a smile.

'It must have frightened the life out of the man. He told me that, where he comes from, they don't celebrate Christmas. He said he's a Hindu, and they have this other celebration to some god who has an elephant's head. I've never heard the likes of it, but it was fascinating.'

'Sounds daft to me,' Rachel said.

'No dafter than a virgin having a baby.'

361

Rachel quickly lowered her eyes at the mention of a baby.

'Karim is a lovely chap and working hard to make enough money to bring his wife and three boys over. He said the dinner was delicious and he'd never had roast spuds before, though he wouldn't touch the meat. He only eats vegetables and is going to bring me some spices and show me how they cook spuds and spinach in India. I told him the spiciest thing I've ever had was a ginger biscuit. Talking of which, pass the tin down, Jan.'

'You was quite enamoured with Karim,' Jan said as she placed the biscuit tin on the table.

'I was. I've heard a lot of horrible things said about the darkies but Karim was such a polite young man. I'm going to make sure that any black or brown chaps are made to feel more than welcome in my pub.'

They heard a knock on the door and Jan said, 'That'll be Hilda. She said she'd get here early today to give us a hand with the clearing up.'

Jan went to the door and, once alone, Winnie asked Rachel, 'Is something bothering you, love? Only, you don't seem yourself. Hilda didn't upset you, did she? Cos if she has, I'll sling her out with a flea in her ear.'

'No, I'm just tired. I didn't sleep well; probably all that turkey I stuffed.'

'We're only opening for lunch today, so you can get an early night tonight.'

'Good morning,' Hilda greeted them, looking directly at Rachel.

'She's knackered, so don't expect to get much conversation out of her this morning,' Winnie said. 'Did you enjoy yourself yesterday?'

'Cor, I did, Winnie, thank you. You always do a smashing Christmas, but you outdid yourself yesterday.'

'Don't thank me. It's these girls who did all the hard work. I think with the war going on, we all needed that. And King George's speech, weren't it lovely?'

'Very moving. I reckon you could have heard a pin drop in all of Battersea. Everyone was listening to it. That was a good idea of yours to bring the wireless downstairs.'

'Is it all right if I take Hilda upstairs and show her my sewing machine?' Jan asked.

'Yes, love, of course. Give David a shout while you're up there.'

Rachel baulked at his name and she felt a wave of nausea again. No, please, she thought, not wanting to be sick in front of Winnie. The woman might guess she was pregnant and Rachel wasn't ready for anyone to know. She hadn't decided if she was going to go through with the pregnancy and if she wasn't, it was something she'd do alone.

Jan couldn't wait to excitedly show off her new sewing machine but, upstairs, she noticed that Hilda didn't seem as enthusiastic about it as she had thought she would be.

'I don't suppose I'll be seeing as much of you now that you can make your dresses here.'

'Oh, that hadn't occurred to me. Perhaps we could ask Winnie if you could bring your machine over and we could work together. It'd be much more fun than sitting here alone.'

'I don't know, Jan. I don't think that's such a good idea – you know, with the pub downstairs. All that booze under me nose; it'd be a right temptation.'

'Sorry, that was thoughtless of me,' Jan replied, cringing.

'It's all right, we can still go down the market together and you can come over to mine when you're sewing on your buttons and stuff.'

'Yes, but it won't be the same. I shall get bored up here by myself.'

'You could bring your machine to mine? There ain't a lot of room in my place but we'd manage.'

'Yes, I could, that's a great idea. I'll ask David to carry it over for me.'

'I'd prefer you to ask Terry. I know David is Winnie's son, but I don't want him seen on my doorstep. There's not a good word being said about him, so I'd rather keep me distance.'

'I understand. It was a bit awkward yesterday. You could see people were only being polite to him for Winnie's sake. He's not all bad though.'

'Huh, yes he is. Have you forgotten how he treated you when you first arrived?'

'I know, but he's nice to me now.'

'Don't be fooled. He's only being nice because Winnie told him to be. That's the problem with you, Jan. You always look for the good in people but believe you me, some people have only got bad in them.'

Jan didn't believe that. She thought everyone had redeeming qualities, even her mother.

Hilda changed the subject. 'Have you noticed Rachel behaving differently?'

'No, I can't say that I have. Though now you mention it, she was very quiet yesterday. Why, is something wrong?'

'No, darling, at least I hope not. But if you do notice anything, you'll tell me, won't you?'

Jan nodded and wondered what Hilda had seen in Rachel

that she'd missed. She'd keep a close eye on her friend from now on.

Back downstairs, Jan eagerly told Winnie of their plans to move the sewing machine to Hilda's. Winnie didn't seem too keen on the idea and offered a few objections, all of which either Jan or Hilda shot down. Eventually, the woman gave in and Jan said she'd speak to Terry later about moving it.

During the conversation and over a cup of tea, Jan covertly watched Rachel. Her friend sat in silence, mainly staring into her teacup. Hilda had been right to be concerned as it seemed there was definitely something bothering her.

Hilda slurped the last of her tea from the saucer then said, 'Right then, where shall we start, Winnie?'

'If Rachel stocks the bar, Jan can wash the glasses and you can make a start on the dishes. The pots and pans are all done and Terry put the tables back last night. I told you we should have done the cleaning up after dinner. I've never left it until the next day. You girls are a bad influence on me.'

'We was all having too much fun yesterday to worry about washing-up. Don't get your knickers in a twist, the place will be spick and span by opening time,' Hilda said, smiling.

'It had better be. And where's David? Did you knock on his door? I want him to sweep the pub through and close this window. It's bleedin' taters in here.'

'I knocked but there was no answer,' Jan answered.

'Oh well, I don't suppose he'll be getting much kip once he's in the army. We'll just have to manage without him.'

'Excuse me,' Rachel mumbled urgently and rushed out of the kitchen.

'What's up with her?' Winnie asked. 'She's gawn flying out of here like she's got the wind up her backside.'

'I'll go and check,' Jan said and shot Hilda a look before chasing after Rachel.

She looked in the pub but her friend was nowhere to be seen. Then she noticed the back door was ajar and she poked her head outside. She saw Rachel wipe her mouth with the back of her hand and noticed a yellow mark in the snow. Rachel looked shocked when she turned and saw her standing there. 'I came to see if you're all right. Have you been sick?'

'Erm, yes, but I'm all right now. I reckon I ate too much yesterday,' Rachel answered, smiling weakly. 'I think I made a pig of myself.'

Jan didn't believe her. She hadn't seen her overeating and Hilda's words rang in her head. 'Are you trying to hide something? If you're ill, please don't suffer in silence.'

'Jan, I'm not ill, I promise you. Let's get back inside, my feet are frozen.'

In the kitchen, Winnie and Hilda were laughing about Franky nearly breaking one of his few teeth on the sixpence in Renee's plum pudding. 'He shouldn't have called her a dozy cow,' chuckled Hilda. 'But you was quick to tell him off, Winnie.'

'I had to or else I reckon Len would have punched his lights out. He used to do a bit of boxing in his younger days.'

'You can tell. He's got cauliflower ears and a crooked nose. I bet the old fella can still hold his own,' Hilda said. She turned to Rachel. 'Are you all right?'

'She's been sick,' Jan said.

'It's cos I overate yesterday. I'm not used to so much rich food.'

Hilda looked past Rachel to Jan, her eyes narrowing. 'Can

you give me a hand, Jan? These pots need taking upstairs but I don't know where they go in the kitchen.'

Jan nodded and, once upstairs, Hilda asked, 'What was wrong with Rachel?'

'Like she said, she was sick because she overate.'

'Do you believe her?'

'I wasn't sure but she swears blind she's not ill.'

Hilda drew in a long breath and sighed loudly. 'Not ill, but maybe pregnant?'

'What? No, she can't be.'

'You're sure of that, are you?'

'Yes,' Jan answered. 'She never did anything like that with Arnold. In fact, she was always very impressed with him for not trying to push her.'

'And do you think she'd have told you if she *had* slept with him?'

Jan thought for a moment before answering, 'Yes, I think she would. We confide in each other, me about Terry and Jan about Arnold. No, I don't think she can be pregnant.'

'I hope you're right, Jan, because Gawd knows what will happen to her if she is.'

31

The next day, David awoke early, ready to put his plan into action. He'd stayed in his room for most of the day yesterday, saying he had a bad headache, and had only sneaked out to grab some food from the kitchen. Now that the Christmas break was over, public transport was running again. Having managed to avoid his mother and Rachel thus far, he hoped he'd be able to slip away without anyone noticing.

He climbed out of bed and threw his clothes on. Then he reached under the bed for a bag that he'd stuffed with his things. He pulled a letter from a drawer in the bedside table. He'd addressed it to his mother and would leave it on his pillow where he knew she'd find it. After putting his coat on, he took a moment to glance around the familiar room. It had been his bedroom since he'd been born and he'd seen it have several coats of paint over the years. He'd miss his bed, the sanctuary of the place, and he'd probably miss his mum too. But it wasn't enough to keep him there. The prospect of his mother discovering that Rachel was having his child and the way the baby had been conceived sent a shudder down his spine. He wished he hadn't been so careless but he'd never considered that she'd end up with a bun in the oven. To make matters worse, she'd spurned him and had made it more than clear that she despised him. He'd be flogging a dead horse if he wasted any more time trying to make Rachel fall in love with him. He could tell from the way that she looked at him, that even carrying his child, she'd always hate him. There was no time to waste thinking about that now. He had to leave before his mother or Jan woke up.

Creeping out of his room, he tiptoed down the stairs, carefully avoiding the third step from the top, which he knew creaked. Relieved when he reached the bottom, he hurried into the back kitchen and straight to the brown chipped teapot on the third shelf. Since his father had left, he knew that was where his mother hid the previous day's takings. It was clever, no one would ever think of stealing an old teapot. He delved inside and took all the cash, stuffing it into his pockets. There was a fair bit, enough to get him started in his new life, wherever that might be.

After quietly closing the back door behind him, he pulled his collar up against the cold weather, pulled his cap down and kept his head low. Thankfully, the streets were still quiet and dark, so he hoped he wouldn't be recognised. Walking at a brisk pace, it took him twenty minutes to reach Clapham Junction railway station and he wondered if his mother had realised yet that he'd gone. He pictured her crying as she read his letter.

Dismissing the image, he walked along the tunnel that ran under the railway lines and connected the many platforms. Several different stairways led up to where trains would pull in, carrying passengers off to various destinations. He paused and studied the sign on the wall at the bottom of the first flight of stairs. It listed the stations that the train on the above platform would stop at. They were too local, so he moved on through the tunnel to the next one. Black soot hung in the air and as he approached, the rumbling noise of an incoming train echoed through the tunnel and the screeching sound of the brakes pierced his ears. People got off the train and came down the stairs, the small crowd filing towards him. He looked at the sign on the wall. This train wouldn't be taking him far enough away either.

When he turned around, he was shocked to see Stephanie Reynolds blocking his way. He couldn't believe it and his pulse raced as he realised Errol could be close by. She stood with one hand on her hip and the other flicking the ash off a cigarette. Her eyes roamed from his bag to his face.

'Going somewhere, are you?' she asked accusingly.

'No, I − erm, well, yes.'

'Doing a runner?'

'No, course not. Just going to visit my aunt,' he lied, knowing his answer sounded weak and she'd probably see straight through him. 'I've got to dash or I'll miss my train,' he added and went to sidestep her.

Stephanie was quick to move in front of him.

'Yeah, and the rest. More like you're legging it from Errol.'

'Is he here?' David asked in panic.

'No, he ain't bothered about visiting me mum with me. Don't worry, you're safe − for now.'

'Why did you tell him, Steph?'

'Tell him what?'

'About us. I would have paid you. I was getting the money together.'

'Us,' Stephanie laughed mockingly. 'There was never any *us*.

Nothing happened, Dave. You was set up. You was so bleedin' plastered, I doubt you would have got it up.'

'But...'

'Errol put you in my bed. I weren't even there with you. I sneaked in early in the morning.'

David's mind raced.

'Look at your face,' she sneered. 'Did you really think I'd sleep with you? I wouldn't go near you if you was the last bloke on earth. We stitched you up like a kipper.'

'You bitch,' he spat.

'I'll tell my Errol you said that.'

David had heard enough. He shoved her roughly out of the way and moved on through the throng of busy commuters. How could he have been so stupid? But it made no difference. He still couldn't face his mother, Rachel or the army and decided it didn't matter where the train took him, just as long as it was out of Battersea. As he heard another locomotive pulling onto the next platform, he dashed up the stairs and through the steam, breaking into daylight as he reached the platform. The train came to a halt and he climbed on board without checking its destination. He didn't have a ticket, but he could probably buy one from the ticket inspector when he made his rounds. He'd go wherever the train took him. His life was now in the hands of fate.

'Give David a shout, love,' Winnie said as she shuffled down the stairs on her backside again. She'd become quite adept at tackling the stairs with her bandaged ankle and was pleased that the pain was beginning to subside.

Jan helped her climb to her feet and secure the crutches under her arms before running back up the stairs. She heard the girl knocking on his bedroom door and wasn't surprised when there was no response. Jan leaned over the bannisters and called down.

'He isn't awake.'

'Well, go in and wake him up, then. I'm not having him in bed all day again. He'll never pass muster as a soldier if he can't get up in the morning.' She hobbled through to the bar, pleased to see that Jan and Rachel had kept it clean and well stocked. Jan had even polished the brass. The pub was running smoothly but it was never far from her mind that Brian could walk in on them any day and sling her out.

Rachel came in through the back door using the key that Winnie had given her. 'Good morning, love, you're early again,' she said as she hobbled through to the back kitchen.

'The dray will be here today. I thought I'd have a bit of a sort out in the cellar.'

'Good idea, but don't you go lifting them casks. Leave it to Charlie and Bob. Put the kettle on for a cuppa. Jan's just giving David a shout.'

Rachel placed the kettle on the stove and then helped Winnie to lift her foot onto a seat. Jan appeared in the doorway looking anxious.

'I hope he didn't have a go at you for waking him up?' Winnie asked.

Jan slowly shook her head and edged towards her. 'He – he wasn't in his bed.'

'What do you mean? Where is he?'

'I don't know but this was on his pillow.'

Winnie took the piece of paper from Jan's hand and held it at arm's length as she began to read. 'No – no – oh my Gawd, he's gawn!' she cried, looking from Jan to Rachel, hoping one of them would tell her she'd got it wrong. She dropped the letter onto the table.

Rachel picked it up and gasped.

'Care to explain?' Winnie asked Rachel accusingly.

'I don't know what he's on about,' Rachel answered, turning away.

Winnie snatched the letter back from her and read it again. David had written how sorry he was but how he felt he had to leave. He wrote that he loved her and hoped she wouldn't be too upset. He didn't yet know where he was going, but she wasn't to worry about him, and at least he wouldn't be a soldier overseas. His next words asked her to tell Rachel that he was sorry. 'Sorry for what?' she demanded.

Rachel had moved to stand with both hands on the edge of the sink, staring into it.

'Look at me,' Winnie snapped.

'I can't,' Rachel croaked, her voice breaking and she began to cry.

They heard someone knocking on the door and Jan mumbled something about Hilda and went to let her in. Well, thought Winnie, if Rachel wasn't prepared to talk to her, perhaps she'd be more inclined to open up to her mother.

'What's going on?' Hilda asked, marching into the room. 'Jan said David's gone and it's got something to do with Rachel.'

'That's what I'd like to know,' Winnie said, handing Hilda the letter.

'I knew it,' Hilda sighed heavily.

'Knew what? Will someone please tell me what the hell is going on! My son has left. He's gone to Gawd only knows where and everyone seems to know why except for me!'

'Are you going to tell her or shall I?' Hilda asked Rachel who was still crying over the sink.

When the girl said nothing, Hilda looked at Winnie and blurted, 'She's pregnant.'

It took a moment for the announcement to sink in, and as it did, it left Winnie even more confused. 'Is this true, Rachel?' she asked.

Rachel nodded, sobbing harder now.

'And are you saying that my David is the father?'

Again, she nodded.

'So he's done a runner and left you to deal with it alone?'

Rachel was choking with tears and Hilda ran to her, gathering the girl in her arms, while Winnie sat shaking her head. She couldn't understand how this had happened. She'd seen with her own eyes that there'd been obvious animosity between David and Rachel and it hadn't been that long ago that she'd been smitten with Arnold. 'Are you sure it's David's baby?'

'Of course I'm bloody sure,' Rachel cried and pulled away from Hilda.

'But when did this happen?'

Rachel didn't answer and just hung her head.

'Have you got nothing to say, because the baby is Arnold's and you're trying to lay the blame at my David's door? If that's the case, no wonder he's done a runner.'

Rachel looked up, her face wet with tears. 'I never slept with Arnold,' she said quietly but adamantly.

'But you're saying you slept with David?'

'Not willingly,' she answered in barely more than a whisper.

'I hope you're not suggesting that he *raped* you?' Winnie

snapped, hardly believing she was asking such a ridiculous question.

'Not exactly. I mean, I don't know. I was drunk.'

Winnie thought back to that night when she and Jan had put Rachel to bed. There was no way her son would have taken advantage of Rachel in the state she was in. No, it couldn't have happened. Rachel was using it as a convenient excuse to cover up the fact that she'd had sex with Arnold and then he'd dumped her. She couldn't believe that the girl had stooped so low, probably hoping that David would take the blame and marry her. But she'd come unstuck, and David, fearing he wouldn't be believed, had run off. But she wasn't the first desperate girl to try and pin the blame on a man for an unwanted pregnancy. Winnie wasn't going to sit by and allow her to accuse her son of something so heinous. 'Get out,' she ground out through gritted teeth. 'Because of your lies, my son has gone and I have no idea where he is.'

Rachel looked desperately at Hilda.

'I said, get out. You lying cow, how dare you put this on my David. Go on, sling your bleedin' hook.'

'Come on,' Hilda said as she led Rachel out of the kitchen. She turned to Winnie. 'You know Rachel wouldn't lie to you about something as serious as this, Winnie. I'm surprised at you.'

Winnie said nothing until they had gone, but then turned to Jan, asking, 'Did you know that Rachel is up the duff?'

'I didn't have a clue.'

'Has she ever mentioned anything about David and the night she was drunk?'

'No, nothing,' Jan answered.

'I thought not.'

Winnie rested her elbow on the table and her head in her hand. Regardless of Rachel being pregnant and any accusations about David being the father, the fact of the matter remained — her son had left. It broke her heart to think she might never see him again. 'Do you mind, love? Can you leave me be for a while?' she asked as an overwhelming sadness washed over her.

Once alone, Winnie gave way to her sorrow and cried hard until her chest physically hurt. 'Oh dear God,' she cried, 'please keep him safe and bring him home to me.'

It was a cry that mothers across the land would be repeating as their sons were sent overseas, and at last Winnie wiped her tears and blew her nose. Somehow she had to find the strength to carry on because, one day, her son might need her. One day, he might come home.

32

'I'm not lying,' Rachel insisted as Hilda took the key from her and opened the front door.

'I know, darling, I believe you. Go and sit down and rest. I'll make you a cuppa.'

In her room, Rachel flopped onto her bed, shocked at Winnie's reaction. Why couldn't the woman see what David was really like? And Winnie didn't know the half of it! She bet Winnie wouldn't have stood up for him if she'd known he'd robbed her. Maybe she should have told her, but in the mood Winnie was in, she probably would have accused her of lying about that too.

'There you go, darling, nice and sweet,' Hilda said, returning from the scullery and handing her a cup of tea.

Rachel sipped the hot liquid. Things had just become a whole lot worse. Not only was she going to be an unmarried mother, but she was also going to be an unmarried mother without a job, and if she couldn't pay her rent, she'd be homeless too. The situation felt helpless and she felt tears welling in her eyes again.

'We'll get through this,' Hilda soothed.

'I can't believe Winnie. How could she take *his* side?'

'He's her son. It's only natural that she'd want to protect him. You look after your own.'

'I don't know how he found out I'm pregnant, but he obviously did and I hate him for running off.'

'Would you really have wanted to marry him?'

'No, but it would have been better than being an unmarried mother.'

'You are going to keep it, then?'

'I don't know. I've considered getting rid of it, but the thought of having an abortion scares the life out of me. I'm not sure I could do it. I know I don't want David's baby. Oh, Hilda, if it was anyone's but David's ...'

'You've got to do what's right for you and I'll be there with you, whatever you decide.'

'Did you think about getting rid of me?'

'No, darling, never. But it was different for me because I loved your father. Cor, what a pair we are, talk about mother and daughter, eh? But I never wanted you to make the same mistakes I made.' Quickly, she added, 'Not that you're a mistake.'

'I didn't make any mistakes though. I swear I never slept with Arnold and I was so drunk that I didn't know David had ...'

'It's all right, you don't have to explain it to me,' Hilda cut in. 'If I ever get my hands on that man, I'll rip him limb from limb.'

'I'll help you do it,' she said and smiled weakly.

'That's better. It's not the end of the world. You're having a baby, that's all. Worse things happen at sea.'

Maybe, thought Rachel, but at this moment in time, she

couldn't imagine anything worse than being pregnant with David's child. The thought made her skin crawl and she knew what she had to do. 'I can't keep it,' she said, resolute.

'Do you want to end the pregnancy or give the baby away?'

Rachel took a deep breath, then said sadly, 'End it.'

Winnie was aware that Jan was waiting just outside the door, listening to her heart breaking. She thought the sound of her sobs must have been harrowing and quickly tried to pull herself together. As she blew her nose, Jan quietly edged back in and pulled a seat out at the table.

'Are you all right now?' Jan asked.

Winnie looked at her through puffy eyes. She could tell what Jan was thinking. 'You believe Rachel, don't you?'

'I'm sorry, but yes, I do,' Jan answered uneasily.

'I suppose most people will believe her. I mean, my David's not done himself any favours with the way he dealt with Brenda or this Stephanie Reynolds situation. And who'd believe him now that everyone thinks he was lying about his bad back. But all that is a far cry from what Rachel is accusing him of.'

'Rachel didn't accuse David of rape, Winnie. She said she couldn't remember how it happened.'

'I don't believe *anything* happened. Maybe she told Arnold she was expecting, but he wouldn't accept that the baby is his. So she thought that if she blamed David, I'd make him marry her.'

'Winnie, I told you, I'm sure Rachel didn't sleep with Arnold, and I don't think she would want to marry David.'

Winnie shrugged. It was easier to believe Rachel was

falsely accusing her son than to accept the alternative. 'No, I don't suppose she does *want* to marry my David but a pregnant woman needs a husband and David was an easy target.' She ran a hand over her face as doubts niggled. 'Oh, I don't know, Jan. Am I being a fool? Blinded by love, as they say, and standing by the wrong person. After all, David said to tell Rachel he's sorry. If he's innocent, why is he apologising?'

Jan raised her eyebrows. 'I don't know, Winnie,' she answered.

Winnie sat deep in thought. Was she missing what was right under her nose? Finally, as the truth sank in, she uttered, 'Christ, it's true, isn't it? Rachel isn't lying. And now I think about it, the next morning, after we'd put her to bed, I remember seeing her underwear on the bedroom floor and thought it was odd. Bugger me, what have I done? Do me a favour, go and get Rachel. Tell her I'm sorry and drag her back here.'

Jan scraped her seat back. 'I'll be as quick as I can,' she said, hurrying out of the door. Winnie hoped it wasn't too late and Rachel would forgive her for not believing her in the first place. She couldn't fall out with Rachel. Not now. After all, the girl was carrying her grandchild.

Jan wanted to run but the snow and sludge on the ground made it impossible. She was so pleased that eventually Winnie had realised the truth. It had been awful when she'd thrown Rachel out and she'd felt uncomfortable listening to Winnie cry. Now she hoped the women could make amends.

There were only two places where Rachel was likely to be, at home or at Hilda's. Jan checked Rachel's home first and was pleased when Hilda answered the door. 'Winnie's had a change of heart,' she told her excitedly.

'And not before time. Fancy not believing Rachel in the first place. I hope you're here because Winnie wants to apologise to her?'

'Yes, I am.'

'You'd better come in, then.'

Rachel was sitting on her bed, her eyes swollen and red from crying and Jan hoped her news would bring her some comfort. 'Winnie believes you. She's sorry and wants you to come back to the pub so she can tell you herself.'

'Are you sure? She's not going to have another go at me?'

'No. She really is sorry. Will you come?'

'Yes, of course. It broke my heart to think she didn't believe me. I love Winnie; she's like a mother to me.'

Jan noticed that Hilda looked hurt by Rachel's remark, but she was pulling her coat on and told Rachel to do the same. A while later, after trudging through the snow, they were back at the Battersea Tavern and Jan couldn't wait for them to be one happy family again.

Winnie heard them coming and when Rachel walked into the kitchen followed by Hilda and Jan, she looked up at Rachel, her face full of remorse, and said sincerely, 'I'm so sorry.'

Rachel leaned forward and kissed her cheek. 'It's all right, Win, you had one shock after the other. I'm sorry I never said anything sooner.'

'Right, I'm glad that's all cleared up. I'll get the kettle on, shall I?' Hilda said, obviously trying to lighten the mood.

'Yes, love, and while you're there, pass me that brown teapot from the shelf. I had a thought when you was gone.'

Since Brian had left, the brown teapot was her hiding place for the pub takings and the thought crossed her mind that David might have stolen the money. When Hilda passed it to her and Winnie lifted the lid, she grimaced when she saw the pot was empty. 'As I suspected. My son, the thieving toe-rag, has pinched all my money.'

Rachel shifted uncomfortably in her seat. 'I need to get this off my chest so there's something else I should tell you,' she said, sounding anxious. 'When that money went missing from the till a while ago, it was David who took it.'

'How do you know?' Winnie asked, her brow furrowing.

'Because he came round to my place and begged me to cover for him. He said he owed Errol money and had to pay it back.'

'For Christ's sake, Rachel, why on earth didn't you tell me?'

'David said that if you found out, he'd run off, and I knew that would upset you. I didn't want to cover for him, but I felt he left me no choice.'

Winnie sighed heavily. She shouldn't be surprised but it still hurt to discover more shocking truths about her son. And once again, it was poor Rachel who was left carrying the burden. 'You were protecting me, and that was lovely of you. I can see now that David is a devious so-and-so. Him and his father are tarred with the same brush, both stealing off their own family. It makes them the lowest of the low, so good riddance to the pair of them.'

Hilda poured the tea and they all sat at the table while Winnie did a quick calculation in her head. 'Rachel, by my reckoning, you can't be that far gone. That means you'll be having the baby around July.'

She noticed Rachel and Hilda exchange a worried glance and it was Hilda who spoke. 'She's not keeping the baby.'

'What do you mean, she's not keeping it? Of course she is. She can't go to one of them back-street women. They're butchers. They could kill her.'

'It's her choice, Winnie,' Hilda said gravely.

'Oh, love, why would you do that?' Winnie asked Rachel, full of concern.

'I can't love this baby. I'm sorry, Win, I know you won't want to hear this, but the truth is I hate David and can't stand the thought of his baby growing inside me.'

Winnie could understand Rachel's feelings but she hoped she could persuade her to see it differently. 'You don't hate me though, do you?' she asked softly.

Rachel was quick to answer. 'No, Win, of course not. I love you.'

'Well, that baby in there is a part of me too. So isn't there a bit of you that could come to love the child?'

'Oh, Win, I wish it was that easy. But how would I cope as a mother without a husband? I'd have no money and nowhere to live. It's better I get rid of it.'

'But you don't *have* to. We'd all help out, tell her, Hilda.'

'Winnie's right. It's up to you, darling, but I'd help you. I'd be a much better grandmother than I ever was a mother. You could still work here and, between us, we can look after the baby.'

'And me, I'd help too,' Jan offered, and Winnie smiled warmly at her.

'And you could move in here,' she said. 'Let's face it, I

couldn't run the pub without you. There's plenty of room upstairs. You could move in too, Hilda.'

'Erm, no thanks. I don't think I'm ready to be living in a pub, not yet. It's hard enough just sitting here having a cuppa when I know there's a bottle of whisky almost within reach. No, I'll keep on at me own place, but I promise I'll show you all that I can be a good grandmother to that child.'

Rachel looked across to Jan who was quick to encourage her, saying, 'It would be wonderful, us three living together. Oh, please, Rachel, say you'll do it.'

'But what if I see the baby and can't love it?'

'You will. You won't be able to help yourself,' Hilda said with a knowing confidence.

'She's right, Rachel. Despite the despicable things that David has done, I still love him. He's my child. It's a mother's instinct. I can't explain it but the moment you push that baby into the world and hold him or her in your arms, you'll get a feeling like nothing else in the world.'

Then Jan added, 'I think you'll be a wonderful mother.'

Rachel's eyes passed over each one of them before, finally, she took a deep breath and said, 'I hadn't expected to get this sort of support from you all.' She looked down at her stomach and gently rubbed it. 'Christ almighty, I've got a baby in there.' She smiled, looking back at them with teary eyes. '*My* baby,' she whispered. Her face softened and Winnie could swear she was glowing.

'I want my child to have the best life I can give it ... Do you really believe I can do this?'

'I *know* you can,' Hilda said and she grabbed her hand across the table.

'*We* can,' Winnie added, placing her hand on top of theirs.

'Like the three musketeers,' Jan said.

Winnie wondered if Jan felt left out and said firmly, 'The four musketeers,' gesturing for Jan to put her hand over theirs too.

'Were there ever four musketeers?' Jan asked as she put her hand on the pile.

'There is now,' Winnie said, 'and soon there'll be five.'

They all laughed at this, even Rachel. 'I can't believe it,' she said. 'I'm going to be a mother. Mind you, we won't be able to stop the gossips and you know I'll have to take a lot of stick from folk, including the doctor.'

'You send 'em to me,' Hilda said and she growled jokingly. 'I'll deal with them in no uncertain terms. Anyway, who cares what anyone else thinks? It's none of their bleedin' business.'

'Let's face it, love. You won't be the first woman to have a child out of wedlock and you won't be the last,' said Winnie. 'I just don't want you making the same mistake that me and Hilda made. Giving up a baby wasn't the right decision for us and it brought us both a lifetime of unhappiness. I've no doubt that some people will gossip and give you a hard time, maybe calling you names, but they're just words. We all love you and that baby will be loved too. That's what matters.'

'I know, but it's still not a nice thought.'

'We could lie,' Hilda suggested.

'About what?' Rachel asked.

'No one knows David has run off, do they?'

Winnie shook her head. 'No, no yet.'

'If we say that you married him on the quiet before he was sent to training camp, who's to know any different?'

'I don't know, love, that's quite a big lie and then what do we say when he doesn't come home?' Winnie asked.

'That he was sent straight to the front, and, later on, we can say that he's missing in action,' Hilda answered.

Winnie baulked and Rachel interrupted. 'No. I won't have my child born into a lie and I can't pretend to be in love with David. No one needs to know what really happened and I'm not prepared to start making up fanciful stories of secret weddings and the like. As you said, it's none of anyone's business.'

'Will you still move in with me and Jan?'

'I'd love to.'

'And you'll let me be a grandmother to the baby?' Hilda asked. 'Not an aunt?'

'Yes, but you and Win will have to decide which one of you is going to be known as Grandma. The other one will be Nanna.'

'Oh, Rachel, I couldn't care less what I'm known as. I'm just over the moon that you're going to keep the baby and I'm going to be a nanna,' Hilda gushed.

'I think you'll find that's over the moon at being a *grandma*, Hilda. I'm the cuddly one, therefore I'm the nanna and Nanna Win has a nice ring to it, don't you think?'

They all laughed and agreed; it did indeed.

'Bugger it, let's have a sherry, 'cept you, *Grandma* Hilda,' Winnie said with a chuckle.

Jan fetched the bottle and four glasses. She poured tonic water into Hilda's and sherry into the others.

'A toast,' Winnie said.

'This ain't going to taste the same as a drop of whisky,' laughed Hilda, holding her glass aloft, adding, 'Sorry, Winnie, your toast.'

'Yes. I've had quite a Christmas, all in all. I've gained a

daughter and lost a husband, then gained a grandchild and lost a son. But that's good reason to celebrate. I've all the people in the world who mean the most to me right here under my roof. Cheers, everyone.'

'Cheers, Winnie,' they replied in unison.

Then she spoke again. 'No matter what happens, I shall fight till my dying breath to keep it this way. The Battersea Tavern is going to have *my* name above the door. It's our home and I shan't let anyone take it away from us.'

They all smiled at each other. With a war on, none of them knew what the future would bring. For now, they were content to be together, with a new life on the way to look forward to. The Battersea Tavern was going to be a house of women – unless Rachel had a son, Winnie thought. Grandson or granddaughter, she would love it. They all would.

Acknowledgements

Huge thanks to Deryl Easton for sharing her inspirational family stories with me. The best pen friend ever!

Thank you to Tracy Robinson, Beverley Ann Hopper, Sandra Blower and Jay Angel Griffin for their work in running the Kitty Neale fan group page on Facebook, especially to Tracy for setting it up.

Many thanks to my smashing readers. Your support is always appreciated.

And thank you to the wonderful team at Orion and my agent, Judith Murdoch.

Credits

Kitty Neale and Orion Fiction would like to thank everyone at Orion who worked on the publication of *A Mother's Secret* in the UK.

Editorial
Francesca Pathak
Victoria Oundjian
Olivia Barber

Copy editor
Marian Reid

Proof reader
Jane Howard

Audio
Paul Stark
Amber Bates

Contracts
Anne Goddard
Paul Bulos
Jake Alderson

Design
Debbie Holmes
Joanna Ridley
Nick May
Helen Ewing

Editorial Management
Charlie Panayiotou
Jane Hughes
Alice Davis

Finance
Jasdip Nandra
Afeera Ahmed
Elizabeth Beaumont
Sue Baker

Marketing
Brittany Sankey

Production
Ruth Sharvell

Publicity
Alainna Hadjigeorgiou

Sales
Jen Wilson
Esther Waters
Victoria Laws
Rachael Hum
Ellie Kyrke-Smith
Frances Doyle
Georgina Cutler

Rights
Susan Howe
Krystyna Kujawinska
Jessica Purdue
Richard King
Louise Henderson

Operations
Jo Jacobs
Sharon Willis
Lisa Pryde
Lucy Brem

If you loved *A Mother's Secret*, discover *Sunday Times* bestseller Kitty Neale's heartbreaking first novel...

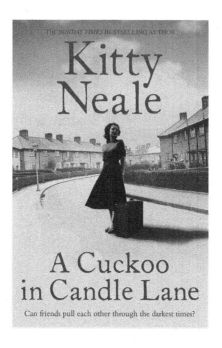

When Elsie and Bert Jones move with their children, Ann and Arthur, to Candle Lane, a modest street in Battersea, they miss their comfortable house in Wimbledon. But the move is the right thing to do, while Bert starts a new business.

They are a warm-hearted family and Elsie soon makes friends with her less fortunate neighbour, Ruth, and her daughter Sally.

But before long Elsie realises that all is not well in the house next door...

Can a fresh start bring her
true happiness at last?

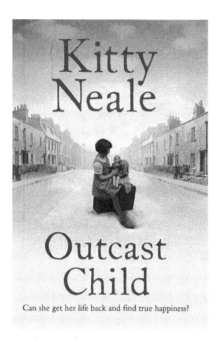

Daisy Bacon has an ordinary, happy life living with her family
in South London. Until tragedy strikes and her mother is
killed in a devastating accident. Blaming herself, Daisy retreats
into a world of silence, unable to utter a word.

When her father remarries, the family home becomes unbear-
able at the mercy of cruel stepmother Vera. Luckily, Daisy
can always count on her cousin Lizzie to bring sunshine to
her life. But when shocking truths about Vera come to light,
could it bring the possibility of a fresh start for Daisy after all?

Can she find hope in the darkest times?

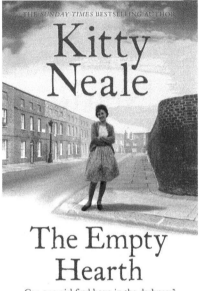

THE SUNDAY TIMES BESTSELLING AUTHOR

Kitty Neale

The Empty Hearth

Can one girl find hope in the darkness?

For the Pratchett children, home isn't a place of safety.

Their dad, coalman Alfie, is a bully, and his vicious temper dominates their small terraced house in Battersea. Handsome John and ugly-duckling Millie have learnt to dodge his moods, but Millie lives in fear for her mother, Eileen.

When Alfie's obsessive jealousy brings the family to breaking point, a crisis erupts. The Pratchetts' old life collapses around them and a new, shadowy future looms. But even in the darkest times, people can find hope. Could Millie turn out to be stronger than anyone could have imagined?